"MARSHAL!" SHE PROTESTED. "LET ME GO!"

Jesse sank down beside Tory, stretched his legs out on either side of hers, then slipped his hand around her waist and pulled her back against his chest.

"Hush," he scolded. "I just want to hold you a while. And why can't you remember not to call me Marshal? Jesse will do just fine."

"Let me go," she repeated. "We can talk without your being wrapped around me like a blanket."

But when Tory did not struggle to break free Jesse removed her hairpins, and released a flowing cascade of curls.

The warmth of his breath began to send tremors down her spine.

LOVE ME 'TIL DAWN

PHOEBE CONN

ZEBRA BOOKS
KENSINGTON PUBLISHING CORP.

This book is dedicated to my literary friend,

Julian J. Edney,

for his abundant help and inspiration during its creation.

ZEBRA BOOKS

are published by

Kensington Publishing Corp.
475 Park Avenue South
New York, NY 10016

First printing: March, 1992

Printed in the United States of America

Prologue

Arizona Territory, Summer 1881

Jesse wiped the blood off the marshal's badge and pinned it on his own worn leather vest. Next he helped himself to the slain lawman's hat, knife, and gunbelt. He withdrew the well-oiled Colt .45 from the holster with a reverent grasp. It had been four years since he had held a pistol, but this one slid into his palm with the easy familiarity of an old friend's handshake. He thought it a shame there was no time to conduct target practice that morning to make certain the Colt's aim was true. For the time being, he would just have to trust that it was.

Having already wasted more time than he had to spare, Jesse quickly searched through the fallen man's pockets, and transferred the twenty dollars he found into his own. He then rose with an easy stretch and scanned the barren landscape for the tenth time in as many minutes but the horizon was still free of the telltale clouds of dust that would have signaled a posse's approach.

As he swung the gunbelt around his slender hips, Jesse surveyed the dead man's buckskin horse and pack mule with an appreciative eye. Having fled Yuma with only the clothes on his back and a gentle pinto mare, he was in as desperate need of the marshal's gear as he was a spare mount. Unmindful of their owner's recent demise, the animals continued placidly grazing and showed no sign of skittishness as Jesse approached them.

A hurried inventory of the buckskin gelding's saddlebags turned up a wrinkled letter addressed to a Jonathan Kane, and Jesse assumed that was the deceased's name. He also found a curious document directing the sheriff of Cactus Springs to hand over a prisoner by the name of Victoria Crandell for transport to Prescott for execution.

"What the hell?" Jesse read the official paper again, but the wording was shockingly clear. Jonathan Kane had been on his way to escort Miss Crandell to her death, but instead had met his own.

Just the thought of a woman being hanged brought a wave of revulsion that left Jesse feeling thoroughly sickened. He had met plenty of men who deserved no better, but not a single woman who merited such a gruesome fate and he could not believe this one did, either. He raked his thumbnail across the dark stubble covering his chin and tried to imagine a hangman dropping a noose over a woman's head. Surely he would have to step close to adjust the fit to her slender neck. Would the hangman wear gloves, or would his calloused fingers brush his victim's nape and make her shiver with dread?

That grim vision brought a nearly overwhelming sensation of foreboding, and Jesse again surveyed the desolate horizon with an anxious glance. As he turned toward the west, a blinding ray of sunlight was reflected off the marshal's badge. Jesse shut his eyes to avoid the glare, but he could not escape the harsh mental image of a coarse rope biting into a woman's tender flesh.

Jonathan Kane's badge was as heavy as the responsibility it carried, but Jesse felt only its power, not its weight. Knowing his decision had been made the moment he had first read the marshal's orders, a sly grin tugged at the corner of his mouth. An audacious plan had come to mind, but he doubted either he or Miss Crandell had anything to lose by attempting it. Convinced it was worth a try, he refolded the directive and slipped it into his shirt pocket.

He had absolutely no respect for what passed for justice in the Arizona Territory, or for lawmen, either, but he figured

6

every human being deserved a decent burial. He saw to that chore, and marked the spot with the heap of stones he had scooped from the ground while forming a shallow grave. After repeating the few lines he could recall from a prayer he had learned as a child, he considered the funeral complete and plunked his new hat down on his sun-streaked curls.

Certain he was leaving behind no clues to link him to the lawman's murder, Jesse mounted the marshal's horse, and with the pinto mare Sam's wife had probably stolen and the pack mule trailing, he started out for Cactus Springs. He meant to carry out Marshal Kane's duties and he could not suppress a devilish chuckle as he hoped Miss Crandell would know exactly how he wished to be paid for his trouble.

Few men had the chance to escape from prison and arrange for a jailbreak in the same week, but Jesse Lambert was confident he was just the man to get away with both scot-free.

Chapter 1

Jesse reached Cactus Springs shortly after noon. Located on the Gila River, where its enterprising merchants took every advantage of travelers en route between Tucson and Yuma, the town was only one of many that had sprung up after silver had been discovered in the Arizona Territory in the 1870's. In the intense summer heat, Cactus Springs was nearly deserted, and the squat adobe buildings baking in the sun appeared as sleepy as the few residents who could be seen ambling up the main street.

Wanting to make damn certain his ruse would succeed, Jesse made his first stop at the barber shop. Shorn of the sun-bleached tips, his thick curls were a rich chestnut color that made the bright blue of his eyes all the more vivid. A shave, bath, and one of Jonathan Kane's clean shirts gave him as professional an appearance as any United States marshal was likely to have. After a final look in the barber's mirror convinced him of that, he left the shop whistling happily as though his conscience were as clear as the cloudless Arizona sky.

Five minutes later he strode into the jail and slapped the official order for Victoria Crandell's transfer on the sheriff's scarred desk. Thinking it likely Jonathan Kane might be known there, Jesse borrowed the name of a man who had owned a general store back home.

"Name's Howard Kessler. That paper explains why I'm here. I imagine you've been expecting me."

9

Jesse hooked his thumbs in his gunbelt and attempted to look real bored while the sheriff studied the document he had given him. The middle-aged man squinted slightly, then resorted to holding the directive at arm's length. A full minute passed before he looked up.

"What I was expecting was Marshal Kane," the sheriff confided before refolding the transfer order and slipping it into his already crowded top drawer.

"He's laid up," Jesse replied smoothly, "so I had to take his place."

"Nothing serious, I hope."

"Back trouble." That was the truth, but Jesse failed to explain that it was the bullets that had entered the marshal's back and exited through his chest that had really prevented Jonathan Kane's arrival.

Readily accepting Jesse's vague excuse for Kane's absence, the sheriff left his chair to come around to the front of his desk and shake hands. "Herb Ross. I've been sheriff here for nearly five years. Tory's our first female prisoner and I sure as hell hope we don't ever get another."

Jesse adopted what he hoped would be an appropriate smirk. "I'll bet she was nothing but trouble, but I'm ready to take her off your hands. I'd like to get started for Prescott this afternoon."

"You can't get her out of here too soon to suit me." Herb grabbed for the ring of keys suspended from a bent nail by the door and led Jesse down the narrow hallway to the jail's three small cells. Two were empty, and he called out as they reached the third.

"The marshal's here for you, sweetheart," the sheriff cooed sarcastically as he unlocked the door and swung it open.

Eager to get a good look at Miss Crandell, Jesse stepped into the open doorway and found it damn near impossible not to gawk. The prisoner was far younger than he had expected and dressed in a pale-green skirt and a sheer white blouse adorned with elaborate tucks and ruffles. She was seated on her bunk with her hands clasped tightly in her lap. She had honey-blond hair pulled into a bun atop her head, but several long strands had escaped the combs and fell in graceful tendrils at her nape. She was looking down, making it impossible to view her face clearly, but he could see enough to believe there was a good chance she was pretty.

Herb Ross took one look at Jesse's rapt stare and provided what he considered to be a valuable tip. "Don't let Tory's looks fool you. She shot Paul Stafford in cold blood in front of two dozen witnesses."

"That a fact?" Jesse asked as he silently willed the young woman to look up at him.

"Oh hell, yes. She just marched right into the High and Dry Saloon, called Paul a bastard, and blasted him clear to kingdom come with her daddy's shotgun."

"Son of a bitch," Tory corrected.

Her voice was low, yet appealingly feminine. "I beg your pardon, ma'am?" Jesse tried, hoping she would say more, but when she glanced up at him he had to grab the bars at his side for support. Miss Victoria Crandell was not merely pretty, but a stunning beauty whose sweet features and lovely complexion conveyed the unmistakable impression of innocence.

A perfect complement to her fair hair, her eyes were sparkling green and framed with a graceful sweep of long, dark lashes. Her well-shaped brows were arched slightly as she returned his curious stare. A flattering blush swiftly flooded her cheeks and Jesse wondered if she realized how easily he could imagine passion extending that delightful hint of color over the rest of her luscious feminine curves.

All he had wanted was a woman. Any woman would have suited him fine after four years of forced celibacy, but he had never dreamed the condemned prisoner he had set out to rescue would look so damn good. He had to swallow hard to keep from drooling.

Apparently unmindful of her dire circumstances, Tory rose with a ballerina's graceful elegance and came forward. She studied Jesse's openly appreciative expression for a long moment before responding to him. "I called Paul a son of a bitch," she repeated in a venomous hiss. "He held me prisoner in my own house for three days, raped me more

11

than a dozen times, and then bragged about it to half the town."

Shocked that any man would treat a gorgeous creature like Tory Crandell in such a brutal and shameful fashion, Jesse turned to Herb. "Is that true?" he asked.

Herb muttered a low curse and shook his head. "That's her story. All that Paul bragged about on the day he died was how he had finally convinced Tory to marry him. Everyone knew he was sweet on her and had proposed to her several times. Maybe his passions did get the better of him, but that was no reason to shoot him down like a mad dog. Besides, with Paul dead and unable to give his side of what happened, we'll never know the truth."

Tory fixed the sheriff with a defiant glare. "You wouldn't recognize the truth if it came from God's own lips."

Jesse's own bitter experience with the biased courts in the Arizona Territory made him instantly sympathetic to Tory's frustration. "I don't suppose there were any witnesses to the rapes?"

Surprised the marshal was showing an interest in her case, Tory took a deep breath, but still responded with obvious difficulty. "My housekeeper had been called home to Sonora for a family emergency. Her mother was ill. Within an hour of her departure, Paul arrived at my house. He stayed three days."

"You have no family?"

Tory straightened her shoulders proudly. "My mother died when I was three. My father was a respected botanist. We came here from Connecticut two years ago so he could do research on desert plants. When he died last April, I stayed on hoping to complete his work. Somehow Paul discovered that Dolores had left, and took advantage of the fact I'd be alone."

"Did your lawyer bring that out at your trial?" Jesse asked.

"What lawyer?" Tory scoffed. "The Staffords own this town. The only lawyer who lives here works for them."

"It must have been a brief trial," Jesse mused.

"It was a farce!" Tory insisted in a heated rush.

12

Herb feared things were getting out of hand and spoke before Jesse could ask any more questions. "Look here, Marshal, she shot the man in front of plenty of witnesses. Why she shot him doesn't matter. Paul's going to stay dead regardless of her reason. She had a fair trial. What she just can't accept is that she could have fifty trials and she'd still be found guilty at every damn one. Just take her and get going. I'm sick of the sight of her. After the hanging, her body's to be brought back here. The Staffords want her buried next to Paul. That don't make a lick of sense to me, but I'll give you the money to send her coffin back here."

At that remark, Jesse watched Tory's lovely blush instantly fade, leaving her fair skin deathly pale. When she moved away to gather her belongings, he could not help but wonder just how much of the insensitive sheriff's abuse she had had to take during her incarceration. He had a hard time stifling the impulse to break the man in two and kept his hands on the bars to keep from wrapping them around Herb's neck. He was amazed when Tory pulled a straw bonnet out from under her bunk and carefully tied the ribbons in an attractive bow beneath her chin. She then donned a pair of kid gloves and picked up a small carpetbag. She looked more like she was going to church than leaving for a difficult ride. When she started for the door, he noticed that while her skirt had an attractive drape, it wasn't nearly full enough to allow her to ride comfortably.

"Do you have any other clothes, ma'am?" Jesse asked. "I don't want to see such a nice outfit ruined by the ride."

Tory stared at the marshal. He was a tall man, and not what she would call handsome, although his deeply tanned features were pleasant enough, but he was the only one who had shown her any courtesy since she had been arrested for avenging her honor. She had to bite her lip to force back the tears his kindness inspired.

"I don't have anything else," she explained. "Our house burned down the day after, well, after Paul died. It just suddenly caught fire and burned to the ground. All my father's research, as well as all of our belongings, were lost. The sheriff hasn't a clue as to how it happened."

13

Jesse glanced toward Herb, who was regarding Tory with a threatening stare. From what he had just heard, the Staffords seemed the most likely suspects, but if they did indeed own the town as Tory claimed, then they would own the sheriff, too. It was no wonder a mysterious fire at the Crandell place hadn't been investigated.

"You know damn well it was renegade Apaches," Herb scolded. "They must have been after horses, and when they saw your house was unoccupied they put a torch to it. The Army's responsible for catching them, not me. I don't want to hear another word about it, either."

Too anxious to leave to encourage any further discussion on any subject, Jesse unsheathed Marshal Kane's knife. "If that's all you've got to wear, I better open the seam down the front of your skirt so you'll be able to ride. When we get to Prescott, you can just stitch it up again."

"I doubt there'll be time," Tory responded darkly, "but go ahead. The state of my clothes is of absolutely no importance to me."

She came to the doorway of her cell and Jesse bent down and took her hem in his hands. He knelt so close, the enticing fragrance of sweet perfume that clung to her garments assailed his senses and it was all he could do to concentrate on ripping out the tiny stitches when what he really wanted to do was start kissing her at the tips of her toes and gradually work his way up to her lips. He fumbled badly, even dropped the knife once, but finally managed to slit open the seam so that she would be able to ride a horse astride. He rose rather unsteadily and shoved his newly acquired knife back into its sheath.

"You do know how to ride, don't you?" he suddenly remembered to ask.

Again surprised by his thoughtfulness, Tory nodded. "Yes, I owned several horses when I was arrested, but, as the sheriff says," she added bitterly, "Apaches stole them."

"The marshal hasn't got any more time to waste listening to your complaints, missy," Herb interjected. "Now come on, Kessler, I'll get you that money."

When Herb turned away, Jesse could not suppress the

14

impulse to wink at Tory. She looked startled, but he raised his index finger to his lips to warn her to keep still. He then reached for her bag and gestured for her to precede him down the narrow hall to the outer office. When they reached it, the sheriff was already poking through the papers jammed into his top drawer and, after a lengthy search, unearthed an envelope he handed to Jesse.

"That ought to take care of it. See it gets to the right people."

"You can count on me," Jesse assured him. This time he reached for Tory's upper arm to direct her toward the door, but his grasp was as light as a caress rather than confining. She resisted his touch only a second, but he felt it as a surge of panic that he recognized all too easily. "We've got to get going, ma'am," he reminded her.

As the three of them stepped out onto the dusty street, Herb was immediately greeted by a hoarse shout from an approaching man. He was painfully thin, clad in black, and his skeletal appearance was made all the more pronounced as he strode toward them with a jerky, disjointed gait. Coal-black hair curled down over his collar and wild, bushy brows framed dark eyes that were afire with a blazing light.

"Sheriff!" he called again in a deep, booming voice. "What's this nonsense I hear about Miss Crandell being moved?"

"Is that the undertaker or the preacher?" Jesse whispered to Herb, for the man clearly appeared to be on a mission.

Herb shot Jesse a disapproving frown but then introduced him when the irate man drew near. "Mr. Stafford, this here's Marshal Kessler. He's come to take Tory up to Prescott. You knew someone would be coming for her this week."

Obviously shocked by that announcement, Eldrin Stafford's menacing glance first widened with surprise and then narrowed with suspicion. He noted Jesse's easy stance and, after a brief show of reluctance, grasped his outstretched hand though his expression remained a savage frown.

"How do you do, Marshal. I thought Jon Kane was coming for her."

Jesse shrugged. "He couldn't make it so they sent me." He

forced himself to smile, but he had taken an instant dislike to Stafford. The afternoon was uncomfortably hot, but the temperature surrounding the hostile man was several degrees below freezing. "I'm really sorry about your son," he added.

At that comment, Eldrin's expression grew all the more fierce. "You just get that bitch to Prescott. That's all I ask."

Again Jesse slumped his impressive height into a nonchalant pose. "Don't you worry about a thing, Mr. Stafford. I'll see that justice is done."

Clearly having a contemptuous disregard for that promise, Eldrin spit in the dirt. "The body's to be sent back here. Did Herb give you the money?"

"Now, Mr. Stafford, you know that I did," Herb Ross assured him in a childish whine.

Ignoring the sheriff, Eldrin continued to study Jesse with a malevolent gaze that swung in a lazy loop between his relaxed smile and highly polished badge. "I won't consider justice done until I see that slut buried next to Paul. If for any reason that doesn't happen, I'm coming after you, Kessler. You understand me?"

Displaying the icy reserve he had mastered in prison, Jesse nodded rather than ram his fist down the bully's throat. "Yes, sir, I do. Now if you don't mind my saying so, time's a wasting. The sooner we leave Cactus Springs, the sooner we'll arrive in Prescott." He turned to Tory who had been studiously avoiding looking at Eldrin Stafford. She was again deathly pale and he readily understood why.

"The pinto's your horse, ma'am," he told her. Again taking her arm, he led her to the sturdy mare and helped her mount before securing her bag behind the saddle.

"Aren't you going to tie her hands?" Eldrin challenged caustically.

Jesse paused as though he were actually giving that question serious consideration before he broke into a deep chuckle. "I've never lost a prisoner, Mr. Stafford, and I'm not going to lose this one, either."

A crowd was beginning to gather, and from the disparaging comments Jesse overheard, the bystanders

16

shared Stafford's harsh view of Victoria Crandell. Not wanting to risk a nasty scene that might delay their departure, he swung himself up into the buckskin's saddle and grabbed the pinto's reins. Attempting to look like a conscientious lawman, he saluted the sheriff and then, with the pack mule again trailing, led his attractive prisoner out of town.

He made straight for the Gila River as though he planned to follow it east and then the Hassayampa River north to reach Prescott. It was the route he would be expected to travel, but he went only far enough to make certain they were not being followed. He then paused to water the animals and fill their canteens before he veered away from the river and headed south toward the mountains.

Confused by the marshal's sudden change in direction, Tory started to call out, but then thought better of it since Prescott was the last place she wanted to go. She had not expected the marshal to be as friendly as this man appeared to be, and a faint hope began to flicker in her heart that she might be able to persuade him to let her escape.

He had impressed her as being too bright an individual to successfully elude by cunning or stealth. He was also too tall and muscular a man to escape by force, but Tory could not help but hope that he might show additional sympathy for her plight and let her go. She was more than willing to take her chances crossing the vast Arizona Territory alone rather than face certain death in Prescott. It was a horrible choice, and an extremely slim one, but the only one she felt she had.

Unmindful of his charge's dilemma Jesse kept up a steady pace until they reached the foothills. He drew his horse to a halt then and turned around to again make certain they were not being followed. They had a clear view all the way down to the river. There was no one in sight, but he wasn't satisfied that they would not be tracked even if no one was following their trail now. He pursed his lips thoughtfully as he considered their alternatives. For the time being, he decided the best one was simply to put as much distance as he could between themselves and Cactus Springs.

"I hope you're not tired," he told Tory as he removed his

new hat and used his sleeve to wipe the sweat from his brow. "Because we're not stopping any time soon. You get so tired you're in danger of falling off, let me know. Otherwise, just keep still."

Jesse was pleased when she did not immediately begin to pester him with questions. A pretty woman who could hold her tongue was rare indeed, and he began to consider himself even luckier than he had thought. He did not want to enter the mountains, but merely skirt the rocky slopes where their horses would leave no tracks. He planned to continue angling south while heading east and eventually follow the Santa Cruz River into Tucson. That had been his plan all along and he saw no reason to change it just because he had picked up a woman.

Jesse continued their journey until the night was so dark they could no longer make their way safely. He supposed he owed Tory some kind of an explanation but decided he would be wise to let her think she was his prisoner a while longer. He saw to their horses and mule, then made camp before handing her a piece of Marshal Kane's beef jerky and several dry biscuits.

"It's too dangerous to build a fire, so just wash that down with water. I imagine you got better meals in jail, but there's no use complaining because I've never been much of a cook."

At first Tory was confused by his remarks, but then she grew frightened. "Are you afraid Apaches might see a fire?"

Renegade Apaches were the least of Jesse's fears, but it was too convenient an excuse not to use. "Sure am, ma'am. But you let me worry about them. You just eat your supper."

Too upset by the terrifying prospect of being attacked by hostile Indians to be hungry, Tory had to clear a large lump from her throat before she could speak again. "I accompanied my father on most of his excursions to gather plant specimens. I know this isn't the way to Prescott, Marshal," she announced shakily. "Just where are you taking me?"

Jesse had been traveling since sunrise and had to cover a wide yawn before he replied. "Well now, that's a long story, and I'm really too tired to tell it tonight. You're right that

18

we're not bound for Prescott, but that's all you really need to know."

"I don't understand."

"We're not going to Prescott," Jesse repeated more emphatically. "Eat your supper and then go to sleep. I want to get an early start in the morning."

Thoroughly confused, Tory continued to hold her meager rations in a trembling grasp rather than eat them. "You kept looking over your shoulder," she reminded him. "Could renegades really be pursuing us?"

Jesse stretched lazily, but he was no more comfortable seated on the rocky ground than he had been in the saddle. He knew for certain that a posse would have been sent after him from Yuma, and once the citizens of Cactus Springs discovered he was no marshal, he could expect them to start tracking him, too. There was also Marshal Kane's murder to consider. Someone had shot the lawman. If it had been to prevent him from reaching Cactus Springs, the murderer would not be at all pleased to discover another marshal had taken his place.

Mr. Stafford had certainly looked shocked when they had first been introduced. Why? Jesse wondered. Had he known Jonathan Kane would not be arriving in Cactus Springs because he had had him ambushed? That possibility gave Jesse a bad start. Perhaps Stafford had had Kane killed so that he could hang Tory himself, or at the very least, volunteer to escort her to Prescott—which the pretty young woman would have been unlikely to reach alive. If that were the case, then Stafford would already have men out after them.

"What does Stafford do for a living?" he asked suddenly.

"He owns several mines, and a ranch," Tory told him.

"He'd have no trouble gathering men to follow us then?"

"Oh, no," Tory moaned. "Is that why you left the trail? Do you think Eldrin would send men after us? If they shot us and said Apaches did it, there would be no one to contradict them."

Her theory was too clever to discount and Jesse decided to just let Tory continue to think Eldrin might be tracking

19

them. He had never heard the name Eldrin before, but somehow it fit the belligerent man. "I think that's a likely possibility," he agreed. "Was Paul anything like his father?"

Tory could not help but shudder as she recalled the vile young man's lecherous touch. She had always despised them both. "The family resemblance was astonishing," she answered.

"Then it's no wonder you refused to marry Paul."

"It's a shame you weren't in Cactus Springs during my trial, Marshal. I sure could have used someone on my side." When he failed to respond, Tory wondered if she shouldn't deliberately press the issue and hope to win more of his sympathy. "Had my father still been alive, I know Paul would never have dared touch me."

Again Jesse had a sinking sensation that something just wasn't right. "What happened to your father?" he probed.

"No one really knows," Tory explained. "He was driving the buckboard into town. Apparently he lost control of the team and the wagon overturned. The doctor said he was killed instantly, so at least he didn't suffer. Still, it was a horrible shock to lose him in such a senseless accident. He was a brilliant scientist in addition to being a kind and loving father. I miss him terribly."

Jesse recalled the evil light in Eldrin Stafford's eyes. If Paul resembled his father as closely as Tory claimed, then he doubted her father's death had been accidental. Good Lord, he thought with a shiver of dread. Just what had he gotten himself into here? He was too tired to delve any deeper into the mysterious demise of Tory's father and Marshal Kane, but it took no great leap of logic to see how they might both be connected to the Stafford men's interest in her.

"What about your housekeeper?" he suddenly wondered aloud. "How did she find things at home?"

Tory sighed unhappily. "I don't know. Dolores didn't return to Cactus Springs."

"Had she intended to stay in—where did you say . . . So-nora?"

"No, she didn't," Tory replied, "but it's possible the situation was worse than she anticipated. Perhaps her

20

mother required her care or she died and Dolores was needed at home."

Jesse thought it more likely the woman had been sent home on a ruse, and then either paid or forced to remain there. If she had gotten there alive in the first place. Afraid he was letting his imagination run away with him, Jesse put a halt to that line of thinking.

"If you're not going to eat, then come here," he commanded sharply.

Instantly wary, Tory balked. "Why?"

"You're my prisoner, remember? Did you think I'd allow you to roam loose while I sleep?"

The possibility of being tied up was more than Tory could bear and she instantly rebelled. "You needn't worry about me," she argued. "Where could I go? It's so dark I'd probably fall and break my neck if I tried to escape."

"Come here, Tory," Jesse repeated.

There was something about the seductive timbre of his voice that drew Tory to him even as she grew increasingly frightened of what he might want. She had been so terrified of arriving in Prescott, she had not allowed herself to think of how he might mistreat her on the way.

"A marshal swears to conduct his duties in an ethical manner, doesn't he?" she asked apprehensively.

"He must," Jesse agreed, and he was inordinately pleased when she accepted that ambiguous answer and fell silent. "Are you coming here or do I have to come get you?"

Tory set aside the food he had given her, rose, and wiped her perspiring palms on her dusty skirt . . . but she did not move any closer. "Please don't tie me up," she pleaded softly.

Jesse didn't want to be shot with his own gun, or more correctly Jonathan Kane's gun, during the night, either. He licked his lips slowly. He was dead tired, but he still wanted her. The trouble was, she was a well-bred young lady rather than the dance-hall girl he had expected her to be and she would not be all that easy to talk into making love. Depressed by that thought, he sighed unhappily and slowly got to his feet.

"I'm going to spread out our bedrolls right here. I won't tie you up if you'll give me your promise that you won't try and run off. I don't know which would be worse, meeting up with Apaches or Eldrin Stafford, but I doubt you want to risk running into either of them. We probably ought to take turns standing watch, but I know I'd never be able to stay awake and I can't ask you to do something I know I can't do myself."

Her eyes had had time to adjust to the darkness, but all Tory could make out was the light color of the blankets he unrolled and little of the marshal himself. She heard rather than saw him remove his hat, boots, and gunbelt. She did not want to sleep in her clothes, but she did not want to remove them, either. Uncertain what to do, she remained motionless.

"It's late," Jesse scolded. "We've got to get up and out of here at first light, so you need your sleep. Come here and lie down. A saddle makes a poor pillow, but it's a whole lot better than a heap of stones."

Tory swallowed hard, then took the first step toward him. "I wish you'd tell me where we're going. It's impossible to have any interest in sleep when I don't know how many more days I have to live."

"I already told you that we aren't going to Prescott so there's no reason for you to feel you're in any imminent danger of being hanged." Jesse stretched out on one of the blankets and patted the other one. "Now come on over here."

Startled by the hint of anger that had entered his voice as well as what he had just said, Tory gathered her courage and approached him. "You truly mean we're not going to Prescott?" she asked as she knelt beside him. "Not ever?"

"Well, I sure as hell am not going up to the territorial capital, and as long as you stick with me you won't end up there, either."

"I don't understand," Tory mumbled, again thoroughly confused.

Jesse could see only one way to get any sleep that night and he sat up and pulled her into his arms. Even in the dark, and after four years without practice, he still found her lips.

Despite his best efforts to treat her in a gentlemanly fashion, he was overwhelmed with desire and covered her mouth with a bruising kiss. So stunned was she that several seconds elapsed before Tory began to struggle against him. He released her then, but only long enough to shift his position and pull her down beside him.

With her back firmly pressed against his chest and her wrists tightly clasped in one hand, he swung his left leg over both of hers to hold her still. He then whispered in her ear, "If you're ready to go to sleep I'll stop with that good-night kiss, but if you'd rather we stay up, then—"

"I'll go to sleep!" Tory quickly promised.

"Good girl," Jesse whispered against her cheek. He made himself more comfortable then, but maintained his hold on her and kept her snuggled close. For the time being, just holding a woman in his arms was enough, but he fully intended to make damn certain she repaid him for rescuing her from certain death. As he saw it, that was a debt it might take her months, or even years, of devoted affection to repay.

Terrified he might change his mind, Tory dared not move. She could feel the dull point at the top of his badge pressing into her shoulder blade and decided that while the marshal had appeared sympathetic, he was no better than Herb Ross, who had used every opportunity his authority provided to make her suffer. Even if Apaches and Eldrin Stafford were after her, she decided she could not be in any worse trouble than she was already in Marshal Kessler's custody.

Jesse could tell Tory wasn't relaxed enough to fall asleep and increased the pressure of his grasp slightly. "You didn't give me your word that you'd not try and run away," he reminded her.

How she could flee when he had her pinned to the ground Tory could not even imagine, so she readily complied. "You have my promise, Marshal," she lied smoothly, but she was determined to get away from him at her very first opportunity.

23

Chapter 2

By the time he arrived at his ranch, Eldrin Stafford's anger had reached the point of blind rage. He summoned his foreman and demanded an immediate explanation for Tory Crandell's transfer from Cactus Springs. "I told you," he threatened darkly, "to take care of the marshal long before he got to town. When he failed to appear, I'd planned to get people so stirred up they would have dragged the Crandell bitch from the jail and torn her to pieces with their bare hands. God, how I ached to see that! I wanted to hear her beg and plead the way Paul did when his lifeblood was running out of him."

Barely able to keep his own temper under control, Floyd Chaney gripped his hat in a frantic clutch as his boss berated him for botching a job he was certain his men had handled early in the day. "Tad and Nathan swore they saw Marshal Kane fall from his horse after they shot him. He couldn't have just gotten up, dusted himself off, and ridden on into town."

Eldrin let fly with a vile string of obscenities before he launched into a fiery criticism of Floyd's excuse. "Buzzards may have cleaned every ounce of flesh off whoever they shot, but it couldn't have been Kane's carcass, because it was another man, a Marshal Kessler, who was sent to take Tory into custody. I want every available man out after them. Shoot them in the back. Steal their mounts. Make it look like Apaches did it the way you were supposed to take care of the marshal!"

Floyd shifted his feet nervously. "Tad and Nathan swore they shot Jonathan Kane, but they forgot to bring in the marshal's horse. They said something about a pack mule being left behind, too."

Eldrin punched Floyd's shoulder with a powerful blow that staggered the foreman. "Must I handle everything myself? How many times must I repeat that they could not possibly have shot Kane because another man was sent to Cactus Springs in his place!"

Floyd was unconvinced. "If my men said they killed Kane, then they killed Kane," he repeated. When Eldrin responded to that claim with more scathing insults, he sent for the men in question and they quickly confirmed the foreman's account of what had happened. "You see," Floyd defended them, "they did what I told them. We can't help it if someone else showed up in Kane's place. That's not our fault."

Mystified, Eldrin leaned back against his desk. "Any of you ever hear of a Marshal Kessler? He rides a big buckskin and he had a pack mule."

After a hurried conference, Nathan responded. "We've never heard of Kessler, but Kane rode a buckskin and had a mule. You suppose it's just a coincidence?"

Eldrin straightened up abruptly before erupting into another fit of temper. "You fools left Kane's horse running loose and someone else rode him into town, leading his mule, pretending to be a marshal? Is that what you're telling me?"

Tad and Nathan exchanged innocent shrugs. "You were in town today, Mr. Stafford. You met him. We didn't," they muttered.

"Kessler was wearing a badge," Eldrin recalled through clenched teeth.

"Kane always wore his," Floyd pointed out. "You did say you wanted the body left on the trail rather than buried so it would look like Apaches killed him. I hate to say it, sir, but it sure sounds like an impostor made off with Tory."

Seizing upon the horrendous possibility that Tory Crandell had escaped judgment for her crime, Eldrin raked his bony fingers through his wild black mane and let out a piercing shriek. "My son screams for vengeance from his grave! Hanging is too good for the bitch! I want her roasted alive! I want her carved into tiny bits! Send men both north and south and I'll pay whoever returns with her bloody blond scalp a thousand dollars. Now go, leave me!"

Eager to avoid Eldrin's rage, Floyd got out the door ahead of Tad and Nathan. He jammed his hat on the back of his head and started planning as they left the house. "Hell, I don't see any sense in sending men north," he told them. "No impostor is going to escort Tory to Prescott. They must have headed south for Tucson."

"Or west to Yuma," Nathan suggested. "I'll take half a dozen men and go that way."

"I'll take an equal number south then," Tad volunteered. "But if we catch Tory, you can count on us all getting our fill of her before we finish her off."

"Be careful," Floyd warned. "You know what happened to Paul when he tried that."

Having been with the young man on the afternoon he had died, neither Tad nor Nathan felt like making a joke in reply.

Jesse awakened bathed in the first rays of a brilliant scarlet dawn. He was pleasantly surprised to discover he still held Tory clutched tightly in his embrace. His left hand cupped her right breast and he began teasing the nipple with his thumb. The sheer cotton of her blouse and the silk of her camisole offered such slight barriers to sensation that she might just as well have been nude. He enjoyed himself thoroughly. He had discovered the previous evening that she was not wearing a corset, but thought perhaps women's fashions had changed in the last four years. Whatever might be the current style, he already knew Tory's slender figure did not require stays and tight laces to achieve perfection.

She stirred only slightly but remained asleep, and that encouraged him to continue his affectionate explorations. He nibbled her earlobe lightly, and savored the delicate floral fragrance that clung to her hair. The blond curls had

27

fallen loose during the night and he buried his face in their silken folds and pulled her closer still. He had seldom spent the whole night with the women he bedded, but he now feared that he had been a fool not to remain with them when the female body was so seductively soft and sweet upon waking.

Despite the rocky hardness of the ground and the uncertainty of her fate, Tory had been so exhausted from their lengthy ride that she had slept soundly. She felt Jesse's lips caressing her throat and his hand fondling her breast, but the sensations were so wonderfully pleasant that they blended with her dreams and she remained completely relaxed in his arms. She sighed softly, but gave no other indication that she was aware of his attentions.

Fully aroused, Jesse longed to feel Tory's hands sliding over him and he had to force himself to remember that they had no time to waste getting to know each other better that morning. At best, he had only an eight-hour head start on the posse from the Yuma prison and no amount of lustful thoughts could suppress the peril they posed.

They wouldn't make the effort to take him back alive. Even if he surrendered they would just shoot him down and tote his body back to Yuma to demonstrate to the remaining prisoners just how futile escape attempts were. While he sure hoped Sam and his wife had disappeared into California, Jesse was determined that he was not going to be caught. Miss Tory Crandell might present a terrible distraction, but he was strong enough not to give in to it until it was safe to do so.

He sat up and gave her shoulder a savage shake. "Wake up," he ordered brusquely. "We've got to be on our way."

Rudely jarred awake, Tory was at first confused to find herself lying on the ground, but the instant she saw Jesse looming over her, she remembered exactly where she was and scrambled to her feet. Her whole body then complained, and there was not an inch of her supple form that failed to register a protest to either the ride from Cactus Springs or the night spent without benefit of a mattress. She placed her hands on the small of her back and flexed her shoulders, but that only intensified the pain and she failed to stifle a low moan.

"What's wrong?" Jesse asked as he began to roll up their blankets.

"I'm not used to sleeping on the ground," Tory replied, but then the subtle memory of his wandering hands as she had slept in his arms made such a complaint seem trivial and she fell silent. She was uncertain as to what had been the last of her dreams and what reality, but she feared he had taken liberties she would never have allowed while awake. The dark shadow of his beard gave him a far more sinister appearance than he had had the previous day and she dared not anger him for fear he would guess how eager she was to leave his company.

"I'll hurry," she assured him as she bent to open her bag. She took out her hairbrush, but as she began to draw it through her hair she again felt the peculiar sensation of his touch. Was it simply her imagination or had he been nuzzling her curls as she slept? she asked herself. He had turned away, but she did not need to observe his expression to recall the sound of his voice as he had ordered her to go to sleep. He had given her a choice she recalled all too vividly, and it frightened her to think he might soon begin to offer alternatives where neither option appealed to her.

Just as the previous evening, he did not object when she excused herself to seek privacy to attend to her physical needs, but she took care of that chore as quickly as possible. Breakfast was again beef jerky and dry biscuits washed down with water, and while that unappetizing fare did not appeal to her, she knew she would have to eat to maintain her strength for the day's ride. She also knew food was vital to keep her mind alert so that she would not miss an opportunity to escape when it presented itself. Because she did not want to suffer through another night in Marshal Kessler's arms, she prayed it would come before nightfall.

Luke Bernay had wavy gray hair and hazel eyes. He was only five feet three inches tall but so tough an individual that no one ever questioned his ability to do his job, and he was extremely good at it. He considered Jesse Lambert no challenge at all to track because he had known from the moment he had been hired just where the escaped convict was bound.

Lambert was from El Paso, Texas, and Luke knew without a shadow of a doubt, that was exactly where he would go. Convicts always hightailed it for home, and he had plucked more than one wanted man right off his family's front porch. Believing that finding Lambert was going to be almost *too* easy, Luke stopped off at the sheriff's office in Cactus Springs more as a courtesy to the lawman than in hopes of apprehending Jesse.

After introducing himself, Luke handed Herb Ross a prison photograph of the escaped convict. "This man come through here yesterday?" he asked.

Herb extended his arm to bring the photograph into focus. While Jesse's expression was one of utter disgust, he was still recognizable. "Yes, sir. This here's Marshal Howard Kessler. He was here in the afternoon to pick up a prisoner scheduled for transfer to Prescott."

That was the strangest damn story Luke had ever heard and he asked Herb to repeat it. When the sheriff had, Luke shook his head in disbelief. "Are you positive that's Marshal Kessler?"

Thinking his failing eyesight was being questioned, Herb grew defensive. "Well, I only met him yesterday, but that's Kessler, all right. Tall man, over six feet in height, muscular build, with reddish-brown hair and blue eyes. A lot of people saw him. You can show that photograph all over town if you like. Everyone will tell you the same thing."

Stumped for a response, Luke slammed his fist into his palm while he tried to imagine just what in the hell Jesse was up to. He took back the photograph and slipped it into his pocket. "His name isn't Kessler. It's Jesse Lambert and he's never been a marshal and never will be. He and another man escaped from the Territorial Prison in Yuma earlier this week. Near as we can figure, Sam Vincent fled into California, and Jesse is making his way to Texas. Maybe the prisoner he managed to free was one of his former partners. Just who was he?"

Again Luke listened in flabbergasted silence as Herb described Victoria Crandell as a young woman who had shot and killed the only son of the town's most influential citizen. "He just walked in here, said he was a U.S. marshal, and made off with a woman you had in custody?"

When put that, Herb Ross feared he looked like a stupid fool and he began to feel sick. "He was wearing a badge and had the transfer papers," he offered in his own defense.

"He was wearing a badge?" Luke was nearly beside himself now. "Where in the hell did he get that?"

Herb was shrugging helplessly when Eldrin Stafford walked through his door. Because Eldrin was the last man he wanted to discover what had happened, Herb felt completely defeated. He closed his eyes and rested his head on his desk.

"This town has a pitiful excuse for a sheriff!" Luke announced to Eldrin, but after he had introduced himself and explained why he held such a harsh opinion of Herb Ross, the gaunt man broke into an uncharacteristic smile.

"It's plain Lambert must have murdered Marshal Kane, stolen his badge as well as the transfer order, and come here to get Tory," Eldrin postulated confidently. "I'll send men out after them immediately. They can't have gotten far since yesterday, and there will be absolutely no reason for a posse to be lenient with two murderers. You needn't worry, Herb. This fiasco won't cost you the next election."

Astonished by that reassuring promise, Herb Ross opened one eye and peeked up at Eldrin. Finding the volatile man a model of composure, he gathered enough of his own to sit up. "That's very kind of you to volunteer your men, Mr. Stafford. You know I've only one deputy and it's all he and I can do to keep peace here in town."

"It's the very least I can do," Eldrin commented graciously.

Because he earned his living tracking down known felons and escaped convicts, Luke Bernay wasn't nearly so eager as the sheriff to have company. "You just tell your men to stay out of my way," he warned Stafford. "I was hired by the

31

authorities in Yuma to bring Jesse in and I intend to do just that."

Because of his diminutive size and feisty manner, Luke reminded Eldrin of a bantam rooster, and, amused by the comparison, he smiled again. "The more men out searching for an escaped convict and murderess the better. I'm sure you'll not be in each other's way."

Wanting to make certain of that, Luke tipped his hat and left the sheriff's office at a run. He leapt on his horse's back and headed toward the Gila River. He thought it likely that whatever tracks Jesse and Tory might have left on the trail would have been obliterated by now, but he was counting on being able to find the place where they had left the road and headed for the mountains.

Tucson was on the way to Texas, and Luke was confident Jesse would take the shortest possible route to reach it. Scanning the edges of the dusty trail for signs of riders heading south, he vowed as he had on more than one occasion that he was not going to allow amateurs to earn the reward money due him. That Jesse Lambert had picked up a murderess would surely slow the fleeing convict's pace. Luke chuckled with glee as he realized he would undoubtedly be getting double the reward for doing the exact same work it would have taken to catch Jesse. He had never tracked a woman, but Luke relished a challenge and knew he was going to enjoy catching this one.

After a couple of hours in the saddle, Tory's earlier aches and pains had blurred into one unrelenting agony. The marshal had continued to make frequent stops to observe the land over which they had just passed, and each time they paused she would also twist around in her saddle to study the stark terrain. Such a precaution proved unnecessary, however, for other than an occasional coyote or jackrabbit, they saw no other living creature.

At midday they stopped only briefly to rest the animals if not themselves. After another tasteless meal of jerky and dried biscuits they pushed on and reached the Santa Cruz

River before nightfall. Remaining wary, Jesse made camp a good distance away from the river rather than at a more convenient spot closer to its bank. Despite the gathering dusk, there was enough light to see their surroundings clearly. Jesse took care of their mounts and the pack mule before turning to Tory.

"Go down to the river, wash your clothes, and bathe," he instructed. "I've got an extra pair of pants and a shirt I'll lend you."

Not at all pleased to be ordered to bathe as though she were a naughty child who could not possibly appreciate the value of cleanliness on her own, Tory did not rush to follow his command. Instead, she eyed him with a suspicious glance. He had narrow hips and she had long legs, so she thought she might be able to wear his pants if she rolled them up, but he had such broad shoulders that she was certain any shirt that fit him would be far too large on her.

"I don't think we're close enough to the same size to share your wardrobe, Marshal," she argued.

Jesse was already going through Jonathan Kane's saddlebags searching for the garments he had offered to give her. He looked up and frowned. "It'll work to your advantage if we're mistaken for two men when we get to Tucson. You won't have to enter a contest for the best-dressed citizen. All you'll have to do is walk behind me and try not to attract any notice."

"I don't understand what it is we're doing," Tory complained with an anxious frown, but when Jesse started walking toward her, she began to back away.

Not having meant to frighten her, Jesse halted. "You're my prisoner and I don't have to explain anything to you, but I haven't forgotten Stafford may have sent men after us even if that possibility has slipped your mind. Now are you going to get yourself down to the river or am I going to have to carry you there and toss you in?"

While Tory was mortified that she had not realized he was merely trying to protect her by insisting upon a disguise, she still rebelled at the way he had done it. "If I wash these clothes, then I'll need others," she reminded him. She did have a couple of changes of lingerie, but she had no intention of sitting around the camp in no more than lace-trimmed silk while her clothing dried.

Realizing that was true, Jesse turned around and continued his search of Kane's belongings. Apparently interested in his appearance, the late marshal had packed several shirts, and Jesse chose a white one with a pale-blue stripe. "Here, take this," he called out to her, and when she came and took it from his hand, he rummaged around in the bottom of the roomy saddlebag for pants. Finding a dark-gray pair, he rose and gave them to her.

"I'll let you bathe first, but if you're not back here in fifteen minutes, *then* I'll come looking for you."

Insulted that he would accuse her of running off, even though that was precisely what she intended to do, Tory turned away without replying. She stopped to pluck fresh lingerie from her bag and left their camp.

Once at the river's edge, she chose a spot well screened by chaparral and hurriedly removed her once-beautiful clothes. Laying them aside, she waded out into the water and began washing her hair before scrubbing herself clean.

Tory had been gone only a few minutes when Jesse remembered he had not given her any soap and he dug it out of the marshal's bags and started off after her. He did not realize she had had enough time to disrobe, but when he saw she was already in the water he did not go any closer. He found that he could not turn away, either.

Completely fascinated by the alluring sight of her nude feminine form in profile, he watched in awed silence as she completed bathing. She moved in a graceful rhythm that mirrored the swiftly flowing river, but when she turned away from him he was shocked by the long red welts that criss-crossed her back.

Instantly certain that Paul Stafford was responsible for those lingering signs of abuse, he grew absolutely furious with the citizens of Cactus Springs who had condemned a beautiful young woman to death for meting out the only appropriate punishment to the man who had beaten and raped her. *They* were the criminals in his view, not the lovely blonde. Preoccupied with dark thoughts, he was unaware that Tory had seen him until she marched right up to him. She had pulled on the pants and shirt he had given her, but her hair was still wringing wet and fast dampening the shirt.

"You didn't bother to wait fifteen minutes, did you, Marshal?" she snapped angrily. "You just followed me and gawked, didn't you?"

Caught spying on her, Jesse made no excuses. He merely held out the soap. "At least you'll have it for your clothes."

Tory grabbed the bar from his hand, but as she turned away he reached out to catch her shoulder. "When did Paul whip you? Was it before or after he'd raped you?"

Horribly embarrassed by his question, Tory looked away. "Both."

"Did you show them your back at your trial?"

Tory's shoulders sagged dejectedly as she was forced to recall how badly Paul Stafford had made her suffer. When he had finally left her home after boasting that she would now have to take him as her husband, she had bathed in the hottest water she could stand. The soap had bitten into the cuts on her back like the sting of a thousand bees, but she had been too outraged to care. She could remember sitting in the steaming water until it finally cooled, but the remainder of the day was a hazy blur of nearly formless images.

"I've never denied that I shot Paul," she confessed in a choked whisper. "But my memory isn't clear. It's as though everything happened in a dream. I remember when I entered the saloon, the men standing at the bar turned and pointed at me. They were all laughing, but Paul's laugh was the loudest. It was an obscene giggle."

Jesse could imagine the scene she described all too vividly and he did not want to hear more. "I asked about the trial," he reminded her. "Did you show them your back?"

Tory shook her head. "I was too ashamed."

Moved to comfort her in his arms, Jesse reached out for her, but Tory twisted out of his embrace and strode back down to the water where she began washing her once-lovely blouse with such furious effort he thought she would probably rip it to shreds. Jesse waited where he stood, and when she had completed doing her laundry and returned the soap to his hand, he took his bath, but he could not get the memory of her scarred back from his mind.

When the marshal returned to their camp, Tory was sitting cross-legged on one of the bedrolls. She had taken care to spread them out several feet apart, but she doubted he would leave them that way. Because he had appeared to be genuinely concerned about her, she had decided to approach him directly on the subject of her fate. He had washed his shirt and she waited to speak until after he had spread it on the nearby mesquite thicket to dry.

"You seem like a reasonable man," she began.

"I like to think so," Jesse agreed. He had noted the wide separation between their bedrolls, but was amused rather than annoyed by their placement. It was still warm and he did not bother to don another shirt before he sat down opposite her on his bedroll. He was again too tired to follow up on the erotic impulses the first glimpse of her in the river had inspired, but he wasn't too tired to look—and she still looked awful good to him. She had combed out her hair, and while it was still damp, it framed her face with soft curls.

"Paul Stafford came very close to killing me," she confided. "If he had, I'm sure he would have just set fire to the house to cover the deed and blamed my death on Apaches." She hesitated a long moment, then met Jesse's gaze. "Do you think I deserve to die after what he did to me?"

The anguish that filled her lovely green eyes was unmistakable, and Jesse doubted he had ever been asked an easier question to answer. "No, ma'am, I sure don't."

Tory's hopes soared with that response. "Then you'll help me get away?" she asked eagerly.

Jesse was not quite ready to explain that he was already doing that. Recalling the way she had avoided his touch at the river, he pressed for the advantage he wanted. "That all depends on whether or not you'll make it worth my while."

That suggestive comment was accompanied by the first real smile Tory had seen from Jesse, and she did not know which was more disconcerting. A smile transformed his appearance so completely that he was no longer merely ordinary-looking, but actually quite handsome. In her haste to win his sympathy, she had simply ignored his state of undress, but now she could not help but notice that the thick mat of chestnut curls that covered his bare chest provided a stirring accent to his muscular build.

To suddenly find her traveling companion's appearance so unexpectedly appealing was not nearly as shocking as the bargain he seemed to be offering, however. Tory's disgust at his blatant attempt to take advantage of her easily outweighed the powerful surge of attraction his charming grin had created.

"Paul Stafford taught me all that I care to know about men," she promptly informed him. "If it's a whore you want, you'll have to look elsewhere, but I can offer you money. My father was not only on the faculty at Yale College for many years, he was wealthy in his own right. We had only a small amount to cover living expenses on deposit at the bank in Cactus Springs. There's still a fortune in New Haven."

The contempt that had filled Tory's expression when she had mentioned Paul was not lost on Jesse. There was no comparison between a brutal rape and what he had in mind, but it was plain she did not know that. What she needed was a man with the patience to make her understand the difference. After four years in prison, he doubted he had it. His smile vanished and he looked off toward the river as he tried to decide how to respond. Money did not interest him. Like her, he had considerable wealth of his own, or at least he *had* had it.

"It isn't your money I want," he finally revealed with the same sharpness of tone she had used with him. When Tory's pretty face filled with a red as bright as the sunset, he gave her the only reassurance he could. "Let's just drop the matter for the time being."

He got up to fetch the jerky and biscuits that were the only provisions Jonathan Kane had packed. He handed her her portion and resumed his place to eat his own. A casual glance revealed she had been right about the fit of the late marshal's shirts. Even with the sleeves rolled up, the shoulder seams nearly reached her elbows. If he wanted her

37

to pass as a young man in Tucson, he was going to have to find some clothes closer to her own size. And a hat, he remembered suddenly, as her beribboned straw bonnet certainly wouldn't do.

Tory saw the direction of Jesse's glance and looked down at her makeshift attire. The shirt was enormous, but she had only had to roll up the pant legs a time or two. Suddenly curious, she rose and pointed that out. "Just whose pants are these, Marshal? Clearly they aren't nearly long enough to be yours."

That was a point Jesse hadn't considered, but few men possessed his height, and obviously Jonathan Kane had not been one of them. He let his glance wander slowly from her bare feet up to her face, which was again filled with a charming blush. "Looks like I got the wrong pair from the laundry," he offered with a shrug. Unwilling to say more, he bit off another chunk of jerky and concentrated on chewing the tough square of dried beef. It had a good, spicy flavor, but was definitely a chore to eat.

While Tory found his excuse impossible to believe, she thought better of challenging him on it. She sat back down and crunched the biscuits he had given her, then, after several swallows of water from one of the canteens, she began nibbling on the jerky. She had never tasted the preserved meat before coming to Arizona, and she did not feel that she had missed anything, either.

"It'll take us a couple of days to reach Tucson," Jesse told her. "There's someone I've got to see there, but we won't be staying longer than overnight. I'll try and find you some better-fitting clothes, though."

There was just enough light left for Tory to make out his expression and she saw he wore the same determined frown she had grown to expect from him. "Where will we be going after Tucson?" she asked.

"That all depends," Jesse replied.

"Depends on what?" Tory asked hesitantly, afraid he might again demand the physical comfort she had no intention of giving him.

"On what I learn there." Jesse finished his meal before he

spoke again. "Right now we're going to sleep, and if you think I'll allow you to sleep way over there by yourself you're dead wrong."

"I hope that was merely a poor choice of words," Tory responded bravely.

Jesse had not realized what he had said, but it suddenly struck him as wildly funny and he could not help but laugh. "Yes, it was. Believe me, lady, I have every intention of seeing that you stay alive."

Tory was determined not to move an inch and, readily sensing that, Jesse got up and slid his bedroll over next to hers. The last faint traces of a golden sunset still lit the sky, but he saw no reason to wait for nightfall to go to sleep. "We're leaving again at dawn," he warned. "If Eldrin Stafford has figured out we aren't headed for Prescott, he or his men may be no more than a few hours behind us. I'm not going to let them catch us napping."

Chilled clear to the marrow by that awful possibility, Tory lacked any incentive to argue with him. She took a last sip of water and then stretched out on her blanket. That she was expected to sleep so close to the half-clothed marshal did not please her any more than it had the previous night, but she had had ample opportunity to learn it was futile to argue with him. Worn out after another difficult day, she let out a dejected sigh as she closed her eyes, but in the next instant Jesse reached for her, and her mood shifted instantly from weariness to blind fury.

"Let me go!" she cried. She placed her hands on his broad chest to shove him away, then pulled back as though she had been burned when the warmth of his bare skin sent a confusing mixture of desire and revulsion clear through her.

In that instant Jesse wove his fingers in her curls to force her head down on his shoulder. "Hush," he ordered gruffly. "I just want to hold you like I did last night. That's all."

His bare shoulder was the very last place Tory wished to lay her head, but when she attempted to turn away, his hold on her hair suddenly became an excruciating grasp. "You're hurting me," she complained as she covered his hand with hers.

"That's nothing compared with what you're doing to me," Jesse revealed with an amused chuckle. "Now calm down and I'll let go."

Tory did not trust the marshal to keep his word, but when she stopped struggling, he relaxed, let go of her hair, and patted her head like he would an obedient child. He had again made it obnoxiously plain that he was too strong a man to escape and Tory hated the helpless feeling of dread that realization created.

Lying trapped in his arms, she could not avoid resting her cheek against his bare shoulder, but she curled her hand up under her chin rather than place it on his heavily furred chest. The fragrance of the soap he had used to bathe still clung to his skin lending him an appealing innocence she was positive was not accurate. He seemed to resort to a show of strength whenever she defied him, but that was only when he got too close. Why couldn't he understand that she wanted to be left alone? she wondered.

"Now that's a lot better," Jesse complimented her. Actually she felt about as relaxed as a petrified log in his arms, but that was an improvement over the wild squirming of her initial protest to his embrace. He could not resist giving her a hug, but that spontaneous show of affection had no effect on the stubborn beauty. It wasn't until she finally fell asleep that he dared place a kiss on her cheek, but that wasn't nearly enough to satisfy his desires and he fell asleep determined that he was going to win the battle of wills with Miss Victoria Crandell, and soon.

Chapter 3

Keen eyesight combined with years of experience enabled Luke Bernay to follow Jesse and Tory's trail until it disappeared in the rocky slopes of the mountains. Certain the couple was making for Tucson, he was not discouraged, and at sundown made camp determined to overtake them before they reached the southern Arizona city.

He made good time the next morning, but was dismayed to discover that a small group of men riding ahead of him also appeared to be tracking someone. He knew Eldrin Stafford had intended to have men search for the escaped couple, but he did not understand how they could possibly have gotten ahead of him. He waited until they stopped to eat at noon and rode into their camp.

"Name's Luke Bernay," he greeted them cordially. "I'm trying to cut some time off the trip between Yuma and Tucson. Looks like you men are headed the same way."

Tad MacDonald noted only Luke's diminutive size rather than the bright glimmer of intelligence that sparkled in his hazel eyes and dismissed him as a threat to the successful completion of their mission. He was not inspired to tell the truth, however. "No, you're wrong," he replied. "We're just rounding up strays."

While the seven men did look like cowhands, the fact they had failed to locate a single steer that morning made them appear less than efficient. Certain they were up to something their leader had just refused to disclose, Luke tried a different ploy. "I ran into a man by the name of Stafford back in Cactus Springs. He told me if I saw any of his men, I should tell them to go on back home. Whatever they were looking for was found. You men happen to work for Stafford?"

Tad shook his head. "Sorry, but if we see Stafford's men, we'll tell them to head on home."

"I'm sure he'd appreciate it." Unwilling to waste another minute trading lies, Luke tipped his hat and continued his journey, but he was no less suspicious of the riders he had overtaken than when he had first seen them.

Tad waited until Luke had ridden a good distance from their camp before speaking to his companions. "What did you make of him?"

When his friends responded with indifferent shrugs, Manuel Ochoa, one of Eldrin Stafford's many Mexican hands, offered an opinion. "He was lying. I could see it in his eyes."

Tad tossed what was left of his coffee on the ground. "I didn't believe him, either, but only because it isn't like Mr. Stafford to trust a stranger with such an important message."

That opinion brought general agreement from the men, and discounting Luke's tale that they were to return to Cactus Springs, the seven rode on toward the Santa Cruz River, but darkness forced them to make camp before they reached its shores.

Hideous images of impending doom plagued Jesse's dreams and awakened him long before sunrise. Her fear of men forgotten in slumber, Tory was sprawled across him, her slender limbs tangled with his, but he again refused to take the time to enjoy her enticing charms. He could not shake the eerie sensation that whoever was tracking them was getting close and he dared not wait for the dawn to light their way.

"Wake up," he whispered insistently, and when Tory stirred against him, he shoved her aside as though he did not long to make love to her until noon and rose to his feet. "We've got to get going," he urged as he tugged on his boots.

42

"I'll saddle the horses. You clean up our camp."

Again startled out of her sleep, Tory needed a moment to collect her wits, but then she also got to her feet. "It's still dark," she complained. "How long did we sleep?"

Not having a watch, Jesse had no way of knowing, but he was certain it had been as long as they dared. "Someone's coming," he warned. "Eldrin's men . . . Apaches . . . someone. We've got to go."

Tory searched their surroundings for the clues she assumed he must have seen, but the darkness was so dense she could not even make out the mesquite bushes, let alone someone lurking behind them. "Did you hear something?" she asked.

Jesse pulled on the shirt he had washed and hurriedly buttoned it. "Let's just say I can feel someone coming and let it go at that." He had not been in prison long before the petty grudges between inmates, which had frequently erupted into brutal brawls, had taught him to sense trouble long before it actually occurred. It didn't matter whether it was men pursuing Tory or him—they were together and he did not intend for either of them to be caught.

Once he had the horses saddled and the mule ready, he stopped only briefly to speak to Tory. "Did you remember to pack the clothes you washed? We mustn't leave anything behind."

Tory had so few things to wear that gathering her scant belongings had been her first concern. "Yes, I got them all."

"Good, put your hat in your bag. There's no point in your wearing a man's clothes and a lady's hat." He then handed her a black silk handkerchief he had found among Kane's belongings. "Cover your head with this. From a distance it will look as though you have dark hair. Now here's some jerky. You'll have to eat it as we ride. We're going to head out into the river to cover our tracks for a while. When the sun comes up and it's warm enough for our clothes to dry quickly, we'll cross to the other side. Tucson is on the east bank so we'll have to cross the river to reach it eventually anyway."

"I'm not afraid of water," Tory assured him. "I know how

43

to swim."

"Let's just hope you don't have to," Jesse teased, but he hurried her into the saddle and got them underway before his premonition of imminent danger became too intense to bear.

As soon as it was light enough to observe the terrain, Tory began looking over her shoulder as often as Jesse. She had heard him promise Eldrin Stafford that he would see justice was done where she was concerned, but as soon as they had left Cactus Springs his every action had been contrary to that goal. While she was grateful they were on their way to Tucson rather than Prescott, she was confused why the marshal felt it necessary to speak with someone there.

Then what did he plan? she agonized. He had said he wasn't going to Prescott, but just where was he bound and did he plan to take her? When they stopped briefly at noon, she could no longer hold her tongue.

"I appreciate your sympathy for my situation," she said in hopes of winning his trust, "but I can't help but worry about what's going to happen to me after you've spoken with whomever you need to see in Tucson. Won't you please tell me what it is that you're trying to do?"

The anxiety which filled her expression was heart-wrenching, but their future was far too uncertain for Jesse to confide his plans. Nor could he take the risk of her becoming hysterical if he told her the truth about himself. Whatever trust she had in him was because of the badge he wore, so he dared not remove it as yet.

"Miss Crandell," he stated, trying his best to sound like a well-seasoned lawman, "you're just going to have to believe me when I say that you're in no danger from anyone as long as you're with me. Now we got such an early start that we'll reach Tucson by nightfall, but I plan to circle the town and head in from the east. We'll get you some clothes even if we have to steal them off a clothesline. I'd thought of a hat, but you'll need sturdier boots as well. You'll never pass for a young man wearing a woman's shoes."

"How long will I have to masquerade as a man?" Tory asked in hopes of gaining some insight into his plans.

"I'm not sure," Jesse replied truthfully. Without a hat

44

to shade her fair complexion, her face was already sunburned, and Jesse knew that was his fault. "Here, you wear my hat for the rest of the day," he insisted, but when he plunked it on her head, it promptly slid down over her ears and obscured her vision. He couldn't help but laugh as she struggled to raise it above her brows.

"Fix your hair so the bun will keep the hat in place," he suggested, but he couldn't resist leaning over to give her cheek a kiss. Just as he had expected, she jumped back to avoid any further show of affection though he had not intended to try for anything more.

"Don't worry," he teased, "I'm not going to have you dress like a boy and then let anyone catch me kissing you. No, sir, I've got my reputation to consider."

He was still chuckling to himself as he walked toward his horse, but Tory was not amused. He had been smiling at her again, which she certainly wished he wouldn't do because it was becoming increasingly difficult to ignore how nice-looking a man he truly was. Not that it mattered, since she was definitely through with men.

She yanked her combs out of her hair and, after following his instructions, secured her bun at precisely the right spot on the back of her head to make his hat fit properly. It did shade her eyes, but the fact she still did not understand what his business was in Tucson made the afternoon's ride no more pleasant than the morning's.

When Tucson came into sight in the distance, Jesse drew his small caravan to a halt. "I hate to ask you to bathe in the river again, but I want both of us to look as good as we possibly can when we get into town. You can put on those same clothes because I'll soon get you some new ones, but you ought to be clean to try them on." This time he remembered to give her the soap, but he made no promises about the length of time he would allow her to bathe. He stayed away from the riverbank while she was in the water so she would not feel as though she were being closely observed, but he nevertheless stayed near enough to keep her in sight.

Jesse brought their horses down to the river while he bathed, which was a good thing since Tory would have been seriously tempted to try to escape him. She did not know a soul in Tucson, but the marshal had been so uncommunicative about his plans that she was still afraid her life could be numbered in days rather than years. She watched him shave as she dried her hair in the sun. When he finished and turned toward her, her lips trembled as she tried to return his smile. He was certainly a confident individual, but she doubted she would ever trust another man regardless of how charming his smile might be.

Jesse soon had them back on the trail, but true to his word, after circling the city he stopped at a general store on the east side of Tucson to purchase better fitting clothing for Tory. He took the precaution of removing the badge from his vest before they entered the one-story adobe building in case anyone should come around later asking about a United States marshal. He then referred to Tory as his kid brother and took care to keep her shielded from the owner's view while she made her selections and tried on hats and boots.

When she was dressed in new garments and had picked out what he considered a sufficient amount of extra clothing, he paid for her purchases out of the money Sheriff Ross had given him to cover her burial. He was especially tickled by the fact Eldrin Stafford was paying for the clothes that would help Tory elude him, but he wisely did not point that out to her.

As they remounted their horses, Jesse handed Tory her mare's reins. "It'll attract too much attention if I lead your horse any farther, but you've got to promise me that you'll stay close. You can't outrun me on that little pinto anyway, but don't be so stupid as to try. I'm the only one standing between you and the hangman and you ought to consider me your best friend."

Tory did not need that piece of insulting advice and lifted her chin proudly. "I won't get lost," she assured him sarcastically.

"Good girl—or rather, good *boy*," Jesse replied with a wink, and he laughed when it made her cringe.

He knew his way around Tucson and led them on into town at a leisurely pace. Most of the saloons were located near the intersection of Meyer and Congress Streets. Because it wasn't liquor that he wanted, they continued one block north of Congress to the red-light district on Maiden Lane. Jesse was looking for a particular woman, not just an obliging one, and he hoped she would still be working where he had last seen her. They rode on past a sporting house known as the Silver Spur, but cautiously left their mounts and mule tethered behind another such establishment two doors away before approaching it from the rear. Sounds of piano music and laughter coming from the first floor carried easily to their ears.

"Is this what I think it is?" Tory asked.

"Yes, ma'am, but don't worry. I just asked you to dress like a boy, I don't expect you to prove your manhood."

Tory shied away from him. "That isn't in the least bit funny, Marshal."

Jonathan Kane's badge was still in his pocket, and Jesse lowered his voice to deliver a stern warning. "Don't refer to me by my title while we're inside. I just need to ask some questions and then we'll find ourselves a bed for the night."

"A bed?" Tory inquired skeptically.

"You've already slept with me twice, so don't bother to object tonight because I'm just going to tell you to stop wasting your breath. Now come on, both our lives may hinge on what we learn here and we'll not find out anything as long as we're standing out here arguing."

Tory shook her head sadly. First she had been condemned to death for putting one of the most despicable bastards ever born out of his misery and now she was walking into a whorehouse dressed as a young man. What degrading ordeal could possibly be next? she wondered fretfully. "Are you sure information is all you want here?" she asked.

Despite his best intentions to pass her off as a young man, Jesse couldn't resist giving her a teasing hug, though he stepped back quickly. "Pull your hat down a little lower," he directed. "It already covers your hair, but I don't want anyone to notice how pretty you are."

Too angry to care how she looked, Tory's sweet features formed a taunting frown. "Let's just get this over with and be on our way."

"Yes, ma'am, or excuse me, yes, *sir,*" Jesse replied, and after clapping her on the shoulder, he yanked open the back door of the Silver Spur and and ushered her inside ahead of him. They were at the end of a long, dark hall, and before anyone appeared to stop them, Jesse took hold of Tory's arm and urged her up the back stairs. When they reached the second floor, he pulled his hat down low to shade his face and opened the door of the first room on the right.

Ignoring the surprised glances of the couple in the bed, he spoke as though he expected to have his question answered, and promptly. "Is Mayleen Tyler still in the corner room?"

A heavily madeup redhead peered over her customer's shoulder and nodded. "She sure is, but wouldn't you rather wait for me?"

"Thanks, another time," Jesse assured her and, keeping his hold on Tory, he continued on down the hall. When they arrived at Mayleen's room, he did not bother to knock there, either. He simply opened the door and strode in with Tory by his side.

Mayleen Tyler was the product of a beautiful Mexican mother and a Texan who had left her with no more than his last name. Olive-skinned with long, curly black hair and luminous brown eyes, at twenty-four she was the prettiest girl at the Silver Spur and knew it. Clad in a pale-pink robe, she was kneeling in front of a slender, dark-haired young man who was seated on the side of her bed, too drunk to put on his own boots. When she saw Jesse, she leapt to her feet and ran toward him.

"Jesse!" she greeted him in an excited rush. "I thought you got twenty years!"

Jesse caught Mayleen before she smacked into his chest and held her at arm's length. He nodded to Tory to shut the door, and then gave the pretty prostitute a curt order. "Get rid of your friend."

"That's exactly what I'm trying to do," Mayleen insisted, "but the professor's too drunk to go. I got him dressed, but he can't even stand up, let alone walk down the stairs. He's one of my favorites so I'll not have him thrown out. He'll just have to pay for the rest of the night is all."

Jesse studied the inebriated man for a few seconds and came to the swift conclusion that he was as incapable of leaving as Mayleen had described. That also rendered him incapable of causing any trouble, so Jesse just chose to ignore him and got to the real reason for his visit. "You knew I didn't have anything to do with robbing the stage. Why then were you so quick to lie and provide an alibi for Gerry instead of telling the truth to save me?"

Crushed by the burden of her own guilt, Mayleen didn't even attempt to break free of his confining grasp. She simply hung her head and wept. "It was all Gerry's fault," she sobbed. "He swore there was no way that I could clear your name without sullying his. He told me that even if he confessed, no jury would believe that you weren't involved when most of the stolen money was found in your room."

"And just how did that money get there?" Jesse drew the trembling girl close and continued in a threatening whisper. "Gerry framed me for a robbery he pulled with some crazy friend and you helped him do it. The selfish coward was always jealous of me, so I can understand what drove him to such unconscionable meanness, but not you. I treated you well, Mayleen. You knew I was innocent. I didn't deserve to go to prison for a crime I didn't commit."

"I told him that," Mayleen agreed with an emphatic nod that jostled her thick curls this way and that. "Over and over again I begged him to tell the truth, but he wouldn't do it. He swore that because you were caught with the money, you'd never be set free and there was no point in your both going to prison." She paused to sniff loudly. "He claimed to love me as much as I loved him. He promised to marry me and take me home to Texas. I believed him, too."

"How could you have thought he was telling you the truth when he told nothing but lies about me?"

Tory was thoroughly confused by the marshal's conversation with the sultry brunette. She glanced over at the young man seated on Mayleen's bed. He appeared to be equally perplexed by the mention of robbery and prison. He had donned a pair of glasses, but still obviously saw things no

49

more clearly than she did. He was dressed in a tweed suit, but his shirt buttons were misaligned and he looked as utterly forlorn as Mayleen.

"Will you please tell me what's going on here?" Tory had to ask.

Jesse shot her a disapproving glance. "I thought I told you to keep quiet."

"No, you didn't," Tory argued.

"Later," Jesse promised before turning his attentions back to Mayleen. "Where's Gerry?" he asked.

"He's gone. He left Tucson a few weeks after you were sent to Yuma and he's never come back."

"And in four years you didn't tell the authorities the truth?" Jesse scolded harshly.

Mayleen looked up at him, her expression filled with remorse. "I expected Gerry to come back for me. By the time I realized that he wasn't going to, I didn't think anyone would believe me. I didn't have any proof."

Jesse released her with a rude shove. "Well, Gerry sure as hell did, didn't he? How much of the ten thousand dollars he kept did he give you to ensure your silence?"

Badly shaken by his hostile accusations, Mayleen walked slowly back to the bed and sank down next to her befuddled customer. He gave her a lopsided smile and laced her fingers in his. "I never saw a penny of the stolen money," she swore dejectedly.

Jesse pondered her answer for a long moment before deciding it was the truth. "Who was the second man, Mayleen? I'm sure you know who he was."

"Conrad Werner."

"Conrad? Good Lord, I didn't think he had it in him. He was tall, though, and I have a hunch that was all Gerry needed, just a man tall enough to be mistaken for me. Where can I find Conrad?"

Mayleen wiped her nose on the back of her hand. "He's dead. He was killed in a cave-in at one of the mines soon after your trial."

Disgusted that he could not force Gerry's accomplice to tell the truth and clear his name, Jesse cursed his luck. Too tired to plan his next move, he was anxious to find lodgings. "We need a place to spend the night," he explained. "You certainly owe me that much."

Before Mayleen could respond, the drunken man spoke. "Why don't you stay with me?"

When Jesse and Tory's attention shifted toward him, he flashed a sheepish grin. "Allow me to introduce myself," he offered in a silken slur. "I'm Professor Ivan J. Carrows, a geologist by trade. I have a house I used to share with an attorney, but he's gone back East, so there's plenty of room. I would be happy to take you there if only my legs would cooperate. Unfortunately, they have refused."

With an intense gaze Jesse studied the slightly built man as he debated the wisdom of taking him up on his offer, but Tory was intrigued by his title and immediately began to question him. "Where were you a professor?" she inquired.

Ivan gestured with a shaky wave. "Here, there, at several universities too small to attract your notice, young man."

Tory looked up at Jesse, who seemed to be pleased that her disguise had proven so effective in hiding her gender. Then Mayleen spoke and his smile vanished instantly.

"You pick up a taste for boys in prison, Jesse?" she cooed seductively. "I'm sure that I can make you remember what it is you used to like so much about women."

Insulted as well as appalled by her erroneous assumption about his relationship with Tory, Jesse did not dignify Mayleen's offer with a reply. Instead, he walked over to the tipsy professor and hauled him to his feet. "Just tell us where you live, Ivan, and we'll take you home."

"Oh good," Ivan responded with a high-pitched giggle. "I love having houseguests. It provides such a wonderful excuse for a party."

"The party is over for the night," Jesse assured him. "We're just looking for a place to sleep."

Had Jesse not been holding him so tightly, Ivan would have slid to the floor. As it was, he was too dizzy to think clearly. "I live a few blocks from here. It's on the right—no, the left. You tell them, Mayleen."

"I think I better go with you," the prostitute proposed.

51

"You'll never find the house in the condition you're in. Just give me a few minutes to dress." She darted behind a screen in the corner and, as promised, soon emerged in a simple blouse and skirt. She yanked on a pair of boots and then rushed to the door.

"I have to tell Rose that I'm going out," she suddenly remembered.

"No you don't," Jesse contradicted sharply. "You can tell her tomorrow that you spent the night with the professor. I don't want anyone nosing around his place tonight."

Mayleen looked distressed by that order, but after a brief hesitation she nodded her consent. She opened her door slowly, checked to make certain no one was in the hall, and then gestured for the others to follow her. Jesse motioned for Tory to precede him, and then got a firm hold on Ivan and brought up the rear. Once outside, they had to make their way to where they had left their mounts and Jesse shoved Ivan up into his buckskin's saddle. Unable to sit upright, the professor leaned forward at a precarious angle, but Jesse grabbed the back of his belt and succeeded in adjusting his balance.

"You lead the way," he told Mayleen. "And you ride and bring the mule," he directed Tory.

It was now dark, and with Jesse distracted with keeping Ivan on the buckskin, Tory recognized a chance to flee, but unfamiliar with the layout of Tucson, she feared she could not go far without getting herself into even worse trouble than she was in already. Uncertain what to do, she cursed the fact she had so little courage and reluctantly rode the mare beside the drunken professor. She continually glanced to her right and left to make certain no one was watching their peculiar procession. When they arrived at Ivan's house, he directed them around to the rear to the small corral where he kept his own horse.

Jesse helped Ivan dismount, and then propped him against the corral while he removed the saddles and bridles from their horses and the pack from the mule. After making certain the weary animals had sufficient water and hay for the night, he shut the corral gate behind them and took another firm hold on their host. Ivan stumbled along toward the frame dwelling, had to be carried up the steps, but swung open the door and welcomed them all inside.

"It's too early to retire," Ivan complained. "I have plenty of whiskey. Let's all have a drink."

"No thanks. Where's your bedroom?" Jesse asked. Mayleen lit a lamp, and when Ivan flailed his arm to indicate the direction, Jesse carried him into his room. He sat him down on the bed, and then stepped back. "Mayleen, I want you to see that Ivan stays put. The kid and I will be leaving in the morning just as soon as we can get fresh mounts, but I don't want any trouble from the professor before we go."

Still carrying the lamp, Mayleen came to the bed, and offered another suggestion. "Why don't you have your young friend stay in here with Ivan? Then you and I can take the other bedroom. Isn't that a much better idea? I'll bet you've missed me as much as I've missed you."

Jesse regarded the impetuous young woman with an incredulous glance. "If you'd cared anything for me, you'd not have repeated Gerry's lies. You just keep an eye on Ivan. That's all I want from you tonight."

Hurt by his cold rejection, Mayleen's dark eyes again filled with tears, but Jesse was unmoved by that tardy show of emotion. He lit the lamp on the nightstand, and taking it with him, led Tory from Ivan's bedroom into the one next door. He was so grateful to see a real bed, he began to peel off his clothes as soon as he had closed the door, and then set the lamp on the dresser.

Too curious to follow his example, Tory remained where she stood. "You can't just go to sleep without telling me what's going on. Even if you were framed by some man named Gerry, how can you be a United States marshal if you've served time in prison?"

Jesse sat down on the side of the bed to yank off his boots and socks. "That's far too complicated a story to begin tonight. What we need now is sleep. I'll tell you whatever you want to know once we leave Tucson."

Disappointed by his stubborn refusal to confide in her, Tory pursed her lips thoughtfully. "Where are we going?"

53

Now barefoot, Jesse stood up and shook out the pillows. Despite the departure of Ivan's previous tenant, the bed was still made and he could not wait to get into it. He pulled back the covers and then reached for the buckle on his gunbelt. "Mexico," he revealed softly.

"Mexico!" Tory took a step toward him and then drew back when he laid his gunbelt on the nightstand and unbuckled his belt. "You don't have any authority in Mexico," she reminded him.

Hell, Jesse knew he didn't have any authority anywhere, and he started to smile. "I've got all the authority I need where you're concerned, Miss Crandell, and don't you forget it. Now stop pestering me with questions and come to bed."

Tory's eyes widened as he dropped his pants, but she was relieved somewhat when he climbed into bed without removing his long underwear. She was still not inspired to join him, however. Having to sleep beside him partially clothed on the trail was one thing. Getting into the same bed when he was half naked was quite another. She looked around for another place to lie down, but the room's only other possibility was a large wardrobe, and she couldn't very well curl up in the bottom of that. Exasperated, she approached the bed.

"All right, I'll share the bed, but I'm sleeping on top of the covers."

Jesse pounded his pillow to get it to conform to the shape he wanted. "Suit yourself," he replied.

Tory watched as he closed his eyes and, apparently exhausted, let out a lengthy sigh. The bed did look wonderfully comfortable, but even sleeping on top of the covers would force her to sleep much too close to him. After several minutes when Jesse didn't stir, Tory realized that if he had wanted to force himself upon her he could have done it anytime in the last three days. He certainly would not have waited until they had a bed to do it.

Forced to see her reluctance to join him as foolish, she pulled off her boots, removed her hat and scarf, and stretched out beside him. The pillowslip felt cool beneath her cheek and she would have been asleep in a few seconds had

54

someone not suddenly begun pounding on the professor's front door.

Jesse was out of bed in an instant. He grabbed up his gun and hurried to the bedroom door, but he opened it only a crack. When he heard the sound of wood splintering as the front door was kicked in, he turned back toward Tory.

"Get under the bed and stay there," he ordered sharply. "No matter what happens, just remember that I tried to save you and don't think too badly of me."

Fearing the absolute worst, Tory was terrified that Eldrin Stafford and his men must be forcing their way into the professor's house. She did not need to be told twice to hide. She scrambled off the bed and grabbed her boots, hat, and scarf to remove all evidence of her presence. She dove under the bed where she covered her head and prayed that whoever had followed them to Tucson would show enough mercy to kill them quickly.

Chapter 4

Calvin Lawrence and Arnold Fritsch came crashing through Ivan's front door with such unexpected ease they very nearly plunged headlong into the far wall of the parlor before they could catch themselves. Avoiding that mishap by the narrowest of margins, they shook off the splinters and sawdust they had picked up on their rude entry and began shouting for Ivan.

"Get out here, you miserable excuse for a geologist. We know you're home so there's no point in hiding like the pitiful coward you are!" Calvin bellowed. To give emphasis to his words, he kicked over a bookcase and then sent its contents flying into the walls with the brutal force he was ready to unleash on their hapless owner.

To Ivan's credit, rather than stumbling out the back door and hiding beneath the steps, he staggered down the hall and into the parlor. He had his arm around Mayleen's waist for support, but he had covered the distance from his room on his own power. "What's gotten into you two?" he asked as he surveyed the damage Calvin was gleefully inflicting on his parlor.

Arnold was closest to the geologist and started for him, but Calvin quickly overtook his partner and shoved him aside. "We're sick of digging and coming up with none of the high-grade ore you said we'd find. That would put any reasonable man in a foul mood, and neither of us has ever been accused of being reasonable!"

Frightened by the men's show of bad temper, Mayleen shrank back, but rather than following her example, Ivan stood his ground, although, deprived of her steadying hands, he swayed dangerously. While his speech was still slightly slurred from the effects of the whiskey he had consumed earlier that night, his mind was clear enough to grasp the severity of his situation. "I didn't guarantee that you'd find silver, Cal. No geologist can do that. All I said was that it was likely your claim would be a rich one."

Calvin responded to that calmly voiced explanation with a derisive snort. "Is that what he told us, Arnold?"

"No, sir." Arnold stepped to his partner's side with an arrogant swagger. He was the taller of the two, but also the younger, and was used to taking orders rather than giving them. "He swore that we'd take so much silver out of our mine that our great-grandchildren would still be rich off it."

Ivan could not recall exactly what he had said, so he did not dare call Arnold a liar, but he sincerely doubted that he had ever made such an extravagant prediction. "There are numerous veins of silver in the area," he managed to argue in a heroic attempt to remain coherent, "and plenty of prosperous claims. Be more patient. You haven't been working the mine long."

"Two months is too damn long when we're not any closer to getting rich than we were when we started!" Calvin yelled right back at the trembling professor. "You must have been as drunk when you did our survey as you are tonight." He raked Ivan with a contemptuous gaze and then grabbed the geologist's lapels and yanked him close.

"The pile of rock we own ain't good for nothing but ballast, and, as we see it, the fault is yours. We could have staked other claims, but no, you told us to dig where all we'd ever have to show for our efforts is a blasted hole!"

Already dizzy, the last thing Ivan needed was to be jerked this way and that like a child's rag doll. He tried to keep his balance and failed, but each time his feet slipped out from under him, Calvin hauled him upright.

"A geologist makes predictions," he mumbled again, "not guarantees."

"No," Calvin rasped mere inches from Ivan's face, "a conscientious geologist can tell a man where to dig and find riches, but you're a drunken fool who ought not to lay claim to any profession, let alone one that will cause a miner the misery you've given us. You couldn't find silver even if you passed out on the richest vein in all of Arizona."

Thoroughly disgusted with the geologist, who was fast growing limp from the constant shaking, Calvin slammed his fist squarely into Ivan's chin. The inebriated man's head snapped back, sending his eyeglasses flying. Mayleen screamed, but Arnold quickly caught her around the waist and pulled her away so that she could not interfere with the just punishment his partner was meting out.

Jesse had seen enough. He stepped away from the bedroom door and cautiously eased it shut. His bare feet made no sound as he moved across the room. Laying his Colt aside for a moment, he hurriedly adjusted the covers so the bed would not appear to have been hastily vacated should the irate miners glance into the room. He then quickly pulled on his clothes. Tory had not extinguished the lamp on the dresser, but Jesse did so now. Shrouded in darkness, he was no less sickened by the sounds of the savage beating Ivan was taking, but there was no way he could stop the abuse without jeopardizing Tory's life as well as his own.

Rationalizing that he did not even know the geologist who had inspired such violent complaints helped somewhat. The fact Ivan was a friend of Mayleen's and that the foolish young woman had failed to help Jesse when he had desperately needed it also made it easier to remain in hiding. He bent down beside the bed.

"Just stay as quiet as the dust under there for a little while longer," he whispered. "They're sure to get bored with beating Ivan in a minute or two." *Or kill the poor drunken bastard,* he thought but did not add. Tory did not respond, but certain she had heard him, Jesse tiptoed back to the door. This time he stood behind it where he would be hidden should anyone enter the room. He could still hear the miners cussing, but their insults were being delivered in a much slower rhythm and he was certain they were tiring of making sport of Ivan.

Rose Flannery, the madam at the Silver Spur, employed two burly men whose job it was to keep the patrons in line, so Mayleen had had ample opportunity to see men take a beating. She had never cared about any of those unfortunate souls though, and Ivan truly was one of her favorites. He was a gentleman who had often had so much to drink by the time he came to her bed that he just fell asleep in her arms. She was positive he had never hurt anyone in his life and she struggled with all her strength to escape Arnold's hold in her efforts to rush to her friend's defense.

"Stop it!" she screamed again and again. "You'll kill him!"

Calvin gave the now slack-limbed geologist another shake. "Naw," he denied. "We don't want him dead." He made certain Ivan was still conscious before he continued. "We want you to prepare another survey for us," Calvin told him. "You're going to confirm the discovery of high-grade ore in our mine so that we can sell it to easterners who don't know any better than to buy a worthless hole in the ground." Satisfied he had convinced Ivan just how painful it would be to refuse that demand, he released him and laughed as he slid to the floor.

"You understand me, Carrows?" he threatened. "We'll be back tomorrow to escort you out to our claim. You're going to draw more of your pretty diagrams and swear the new owners will have the riches you tricked us into believing we'd find."

Ivan gazed up at Calvin through the red haze of blood dripping into his eyes. It took him a long moment to digest the stocky man's demand, but he refused to agree to it. "I won't lie," he vowed harshly.

Infuriated by that ridiculous comment, Calvin quickly responded with a vicious kick to Ivan's ribs. "Oh, you'll lie all right. You'll do the survey exactly as we tell you to or I'll give

Arnold a chance to work you over until what's left of you will beg to follow any order we give."

Mayleen was still trying to twist free of Arnold's grasp and he lifted her clear off her feet to keep her from getting any leverage. "Why don't I teach his girl some respect right now?" he offered with a lecherous grin.

"That's not his girl," Calvin corrected harshly. "She's just a whore from the Silver Spur and can't mean anything to Carrows. Leave her be. He's going to need someone to clean him up so he'll be fit to ride in the morning. You hear me, Carrows? Tomorrow you're going to call me *sir* and do exactly what I say."

This time Ivan was hurting too badly to argue, but he would never agree to fabricating surveys to further Calvin and Arnold's schemes. He might not have much, but if he compromised his integrity he would have nothing at all. The instant Arnold released Mayleen, she knelt beside him. A heady wave of her enticing perfume nearly made Ivan vomit, but as she drew his head into her lap he fainted before he suffered that final humiliation.

Her bruised arms still aching from the fierceness of Arnold's grip, Mayleen looked up at the disgruntled miners and made a silent vow to see they suffered for what they had done to Ivan. While she was relieved they had dismissed her as a whore of no consequence, she knew that could not possibly be the truth. All of her regulars cared about her. Some had even proposed marriage. She did not have to take Calvin's insults, but fearing he and Arnold would continue to abuse Ivan should she speak her mind, she settled for no more than a hostile frown as they swung open what was left of the front door and strode out of the unconscious geologist's house.

Jesse waited until he had heard the miners' horses galloping away before he opened the door. Glancing into the parlor, he discovered that Ivan looked even worse than he had anticipated, but Mayleen appeared to be taking good care of him. Dismissing them, he walked back to the bed and lit the lamp. "Come on out," he coaxed Tory.

"They've gone."

Despite Jesse's reassurance, Tory was still too badly frightened to move. She stayed right where she was, clutching her boots, hat, and scarf with frantic fervor. She had been able to overhear enough of the miners' shouted insults to understand why they thought they had a right to beat Ivan, but just because they had left did not mean someone even more dangerous was not about to arrive. That horrible thought kept her pressed tightly against the floor.

"Tory?" Jesse called a little more loudly. "Come out of there. I'll not take a chance on those two coming back before we've left in the morning. We're heading out now." He waited a few seconds more, and when Tory still did not respond or appear, he knelt at the end of the bed, reached under it to grab her arm, and gently eased her out. He pried her fingers from her scarf, slipped it over her hair, and then covered it with her hat.

"Good boy," he greeted her with a happy grin. "Just don't forget to keep your pretty curls hidden so Ivan and Mayleen don't realize you're a beautiful woman rather than a handsome kid." He rose then, hauled Tory to her feet, and waited for her to pull on her boots. "Come on, let's tell them good-bye and be on our way."

As soon as Jesse and Tory entered the parlor, Mayleen began to berate them in a shrill screech. "Why did you hide? Would you have let them beat Ivan to death?"

Jesse stared at her coldly. "Why not? You had no qualms about letting an innocent man go to prison. Why should my morals be any higher than yours?"

Mayleen knew she deserved that rebuke, but Ivan was a sweet man who did not and she began to sob. "Hate me all you like," she moaned. "But please don't let Ivan die."

"Oh, hell, Mayleen, he's not going to die." Jesse bent down, scooped the disheveled scientist from her arms, and carried him back to his bedroom. He laid him on the bed, and then dipped the end of a towel into the pitcher on the washstand. He wrung it out slightly and tossed it to Mayleen. "Just clean off the blood. His nose is probably

62

broken, but I doubt anything else is."

Eager to help her friend, Mayleen perched on the side of the bed and began to wipe Ivan's face with tender pats. Jesse turned back toward the doorway and found Tory had followed them. She was observing them with an alarmingly vacant stare. Her gaze shifted briefly to the injured man on the bed, but quickly swung back to him. If she were moved by Ivan's plight, it certainly was not apparent in her expression. Jesse wondered if, like him, she simply did not care what happened to the drunken man, or if she had suffered far too much herself to care about anyone else ever again. That was a surprisingly painful thought.

Afraid she might bolt, Jesse approached her slowly and placed his hands lightly on her shoulders. She was on the verge of hysterics, and he dared not hang around Ivan's house a minute longer than necessary for fear she might become too distraught to travel. "Did you understand me?" he probed gently. "We're leaving now. Those miners got in here too easily and the next bunch of visitors won't even have to bother breaking in the door. We've got to get out of Tucson tonight."

Mayleen's efforts to clean Ivan's face had revived him sufficiently to overhear Jesse's remark. While he would have welcomed the oblivion of a drunken stupor, his mind was gradually beginning to clear. He did not know what had happened to his eyeglasses, but he did not need to see clearly to argue. "Wait!" he blurted out. "Please wait."

Annoyed, Jesse glanced over his shoulder. "We appreciate your hospitality, Carrows, but we've got to be on our way."

Ivan struggled to sit up, found the resulting pain overwhelming, and slid back down among the pillows. It took him several seconds to catch his breath, but then he promptly began to plead his case. "I'm a scientist," he reminded Jesse. "I search for the truth. I don't invent it. I won't prepare false surveys for Calvin and Arnold. It would violate all my principles."

Unwilling to release Tory, Jesse dropped one hand to her upper arm and guided her over to Ivan's bedside. The poor

63

man's bloodshot eyes were nearly swollen shut, but still they shone with a defiant glimmer. "Were they right?" Jesse asked. "Were you drunk when you did their original survey?"

"No," Ivan swore convincingly. "I never drink while I work. Everyone will tell you I'm the best geologist in Tucson."

"Calvin and Arnold wouldn't," Jesse pointed out snidely.

Ivan was in no mood for humor. Rather than laugh, he started to cough, and then could not stop until after Mayleen had brought him a glass of water. His ribs ached so badly he was afraid every single one was crushed, but he raised his hand to plead for patience. "Please," he begged. "I want to go with you."

"You want to *what?*" Jesse gasped incredulously.

"I want to go with you," Ivan repeated weakly. "I won't falsify surveys. That would be professional suicide. I can't take another beating tomorrow, either. I'm already hurt so badly Arnold would kill me for sure."

"Look, Professor, you're in no shape to ride, and you don't even know where we're going," Jesse reminded him.

Ivan closed his eyes for a long moment while he gathered the strength to speak. "I can ride if I have to, and it doesn't matter where you're going. I just have to get out of town."

"All right," Jesse challenged. "Get up and pack your things. If you can do that much, you can come with us."

Knowing that was completely beyond his capabilities for the present, Ivan had to fight back tears. "At least give me an hour to pull myself together," he begged.

"Sorry, but we don't have an hour to spare." Anxious to leave, Jesse turned away and pulled Tory along with him.

As terrified for Jesse's safety as for Ivan's, Mayleen leapt off the bed and ran after Jesse. She grabbed his arm and held on. "You said you needed fresh horses. I can help you get them. What about supplies? You must want those, too. By the time you get everything you require, Ivan will be feeling well enough to leave, too."

A quick glance at the battered professor only served to

confirm Jesse's original opinion that he would not be going anywhere soon. "The man's too weak to get off the bed, let alone ride, Mayleen. Can't you see that?"

"Then I'll come along, too!" the vivacious young woman volunteered. "I can take care of him so he won't slow you down any. Oh please, let us come along. You're going back to El Paso, aren't you?" Without waiting for Jesse to confirm her guess, she plunged ahead. "I want to see Gerry again just as badly as you do. He promised to come back for me, so he betrayed my trust just as badly as he did yours!"

Jesse's eyes narrowed menacingly. "You haven't even come close to suffering what I have these last four years, Mayleen. Don't try that argument on me ever again."

Mayleen recoiled from the hostility of his gaze, but did not back down. "I loved Gerry," she whispered insistently, "and he used me, too. That gives me every bit as much right as you have to confront him with his lies."

"Not even close," Jesse replied.

He made another attempt to leave the room then, but Mayleen continued to cling to his arm and forced him to stay. "Let me help you with the horses," she begged. "At least let me do that. Then if Ivan feels up to traveling when we get back, we'll go with you. That's a fair exchange, isn't it? If I get you the best mounts in Tucson, won't you please let us come along?"

Thoroughly exasperated with her, Jesse succeeded in peeling her hands off his arm. He was about to refuse her offer in terms she could not mistake, but then he realized he would be a fool to do so when they did need fine mounts and there was such little chance Ivan would be ready to travel before dawn. Viewed that way, he decided he had nothing to lose.

"All right," he announced with feigned reluctance. "I'll take you up on the offer to find us horses, but if Ivan isn't well enough to travel when we get back, then Tory and I will leave you both behind."

Delighted to have won at least a partial concession from him, Mayleen broke into a radiant smile. "Ivan will be fine," she promised optimistically.

When Tory swayed slightly as she covered a wide yawn, Jesse suddenly realized she was not much better off than Ivan. They had ridden hard all day and then been frightened half out of their wits before they had gotten even five minutes' rest. He might be able to tough it out without sleep, but she probably could not last much longer. After a slight nod to Mayleen silently requesting a moment of privacy, he drew Tory out into the hall. Taking the same stern tone he had repeatedly used with her, he gave her a firm order.

"I want you to stay here with Ivan while Mayleen and I go for the horses and supplies. It's far too dangerous to take the time to give you the answers I promised now, but I will once we're on the trail. I don't want to provide Stafford or any of his men with a chance to catch up to us, do you?"

Tory had not drawn a deep breath since Calvin and Arnold had first begun to pound on Ivan's door. The mere mention of Eldrin Stafford conjured up such hideous visions of what he would do to her that she had not the slightest desire to argue with Jesse. She was also far too tired and frightened to attempt to find somewhere to hide on her own in Tucson. Then she recalled something Mayleen had said.

"Are we really going to El Paso?" she asked.

Her fright-filled gaze prompted Jesse to tell the truth. "Yes, that's where we're bound. No one will ever find you there."

Tory hardly dared hope that she could escape a date with a hangman indefinitely, but she leapt at the chance to try. "I'll stay with Ivan," she quickly agreed. "Just don't forget to come back for me."

Even looking scared to death and dressed like a boy Tory Crandell was so incredibly appealing that Jesse had to smile as he gave her his word. "I'm the best friend you'll ever have, Tory. I won't desert you."

When Jesse and Mayleen left a few minutes later, Tory found herself staring down at Ivan's badly bruised face and wondering what she could possibly do to help him. He was simply collapsed upon the bed, but she feared any attempt to ease his limbs into a more comfortable pose would only cause him additional pain. Finally she decided she would just remove his boots and and then try to get some rest herself.

Ivan tensed as the kid pried off his right boot, but the skinny lad had a surprisingly gentle touch and he felt little discomfort. "Thanks," he mumbled as his left boot fell to the floor. "There's a bottle of whiskey in the cupboard in the kitchen. Get it for me. That's all I need."

Ignoring his request, Tory moved the bedroom's only chair so that when she sat down she could prop her feet on the edge of the bed. She crossed her ankles, and folded her arms under her bosom to get comfortable. She wanted to close her eyes and try to sleep but that was impossible with Ivan staring at her so intently.

"I thought you wanted to leave with us," she reminded him.

"That I do," Ivan agreed.

"Then you'll have to be sober."

Ivan moaned as though she had struck him. "You let me worry about that. Just go get the bottle and hurry up about it."

Tory remained seated. "If you're well enough to travel, then you ought to be well enough to get it yourself."

Ivan struggled to sit up and propped himself against a pillow. He had never felt so thoroughly wretched, and he needed a drink badly. "How does ten dollars sound?" he asked.

Tory shook her head. "How does waking up in the morning and finding one of your miner friends sitting here sound?" she countered.

Ivan failed to suppress a shudder, but the threat of having to face Calvin and Arnold again did not dim his desire for a shot of whiskey. "All I'm asking for is a drink to take the edge off the pain. I'll not pass out on you."

Tory covered a wide yawn. "I don't care whether you pass out or not," she informed him coldly.

Badly disappointed, Ivan peered at his companion, but his

vision was too poor to make out the insolent boy's expression clearly. "Would you please go and look for my eyeglasses? If Cal broke them I have an extra pair, but I'm not sure where I put them."

Deciding that was a reasonable request, Tory forced herself to rise, go into the parlor, and conduct a search. She did not see the missing eyeglasses at first and so returned the bookcase to an upright position and began replacing the books Calvin had scattered about the room. She soon discovered that Ivan had not only geology texts, but novels and poetry as well.

Thinking that he must enjoy reading as much as she did, she searched diligently until she located his eyeglasses under a chair. The wire frames were bent slightly, and she straightened them as she walked back to his bedroom. After polishing the lenses on her shirttail, she handed them to him.

"Thank you." Ivan took care as he slipped them on, and was grateful to discover that the bridge of his nose was not too tender for him to wear them. He then took the opportunity to study Tory more closely than he had been able to previously. Because his own features were too finely sculpted to be considered the masculine ideal, he felt an instant kinship for the surprisingly attractive boy. He had always liked women himself, but he could readily understand why, if Jesse preferred young men, he would have picked this one.

"Does Jesse treat you right?" he asked.

Tory had not heard Marshal Kessler's first name until Mayleen had addressed him by it. Jesse fit him, though, and she mouthed the name silently to herself as she returned to her chair. "Yes," she finally responded. Although she still did not understand why, he had not escorted her to Prescott and she would always be grateful to him for that.

There was something about the graceful way the boy resumed his seat that made Ivan surprisingly uncomfortable. He had never been attracted to a member of his own sex, but damn it all, this lad was positively alluring! His hands were delicate, and his creamy complexion was unshadowed by even the hint of a beard. As though able to read his thoughts, Tory glanced toward him, and Ivan quickly looked away for fear his gaze had become openly admiring.

"Damn it all! I need a drink!" he insisted with growing frustration.

Tory was unmoved by his complaint and settled a bit lower in her chair. "Like I said, get it yourself." She closed her eyes, but instantly saw Eldrin Stafford's evil visage and was jolted wide-awake. Believing the least Jesse could have done to protect her was barricade the shattered front door before he and Mayleen left, Tory was instantly inspired to attend to that chore herself. As she got up, Ivan called out to her.

"Are you going for the whiskey?"

"No, sir, I've got better things to do."

A quick survey of the parlor convinced her the bookcase would provide the best barrier, but she then discovered she would have to remove the books to be able to shove it in front of the door. With a weary sigh she stacked the leather-bound volumes on the floor, moved the bookcase into place, and reshelved the books. She placed two chairs against the bookcase for additional weight and then checked every window in the house to make certain it was closed and locked. Jesse had carelessly left the back door unlocked, but she quickly turned the key and pocketed it.

She was as sure as Jesse that Eldrin would begin a search for her the instant he learned she had not reached Prescott. But when would that be? Were he and his men only hours behind them as Jesse seemed to believe, or was the vicious man still in Cactus Springs as yet unaware of her whereabouts? Shivering with dread, she rubbed her arms as she returned to Ivan's bedroom. He greeted her with no more than a disgusted frown, but she was too worried about her own chances for leaving Tucson safely to be concerned about what he thought of her.

"How long have they been gone?" she asked the bedridden man.

"Not nearly long enough for me to feel up to riding," Ivan

admitted. "What if I offered you twenty dollars for fetching the whiskey?"

Tory returned to the chair and resumed her casual pose. "Save your breath," she scolded. "You're in enough trouble without getting drunk again."

Ivan knew he was still more drunk than sober, but that did not prevent him from craving another drink in the worst way. "Say, I didn't mean to be inhospitable," he apologized. "Bring the bottle and a couple of glasses and have a drink with me."

"No thanks, I don't drink," Tory replied.

Disgusted that ploy hadn't worked, Ivan cleverly attempted another. "You know what Jesse and Mayleen are probably doing right now, don't you?"

"Looking at horses, I suppose."

"They would have bought the horses first," Ivan agreed. "Then I'll bet Mayleen talked Jesse into stopping by her room at the Silver Spur. They seemed to have been real friendly at one time, even if he's mad at her now. She gets him back up in her room and I'll bet he can't stay angry with her longer than it takes her to step out of her clothes."

When Tory greeted that opinion with the coldest expression Ivan had ever seen, he knew he was on the right track. Jealousy drove plenty of men to drink, and it sure looked like his comments had made Tory jealous. "You ever had a woman?" he asked, but continued without waiting for the boy's response. "Mayleen is all soft and warm and cuddly. I've never met a man who could get his fill of her. I'll bet your Jesse is no exception. He might like a boy now and again, but if he's had Mayleen before, he'll want her again."

Rather than prompting Tory to fetch his whiskey and share it, Ivan found himself staring up into a pair of long-lashed green eyes that smoldered with fury. The kid had stood and come so close Ivan could see the inviting fullness of his lips and pearly whiteness of his teeth. Again shocked to find himself drawn to the attractive boy, Ivan almost wished Tory would hit him, but after stirring emotions the bewildered geologist considered forbidden, the lad turned

70

and left the room with no more than a disgusted sneer.

Filled with a craving for whiskey he found impossible to overcome as well as a newfound self-loathing for a weakness he had previously never suspected he possessed, Ivan lay awash in both physical and mental pain. Only one thought saved his sanity, and that was that Calvin and Arnold would make short work of him in the morning if he were not able to leave Tucson before they returned. Determined not to suffer another painful and humiliating minute at their hands, he struggled to pull himself together as he had sworn he could, but he found it to be the most difficult challenge of his life.

Chapter 5

Casting frequent appreciative glances in Jesse's direction, Mayleen rode the pinto mare to the Dubois Livery Stable. The owner's residence was next door, which made doing business a simple matter even at night. That Wayne Dubois was one of Mayleen's regulars was also an extremely helpful factor.

At Jesse's insistence, Mayleen introduced the Texan simply as George, whom she described as an excellent judge of horseflesh. Then, determined to provide a mount for herself, in addition to one for Jesse and Tory, she asked Wayne for three of his finest horses in exchange for the buckskin, pinto, and mule Jesse had brought to Tucson. Hoping to ensure Wayne's cooperation, she wrapped her slender arms around one of his bulging biceps and batted her eyelashes coyly.

"I told George you have the finest horses in all of Arizona."

While Wayne was flattered by Mayleen's praise for his stock, he was not so distracted that he failed to notice her companion. He knew better than to ask for a last name when none had been given, but something about the tall man struck him as familiar. "Don't I know you from somewhere?" he asked.

Thinking it possible Wayne might recall his face from the photographs the *Citizen* had run during his trial, Jesse had pulled his hat low, and he now took the precaution of turning away as he responded. "I doubt it, and while I'd like to stay and chat, I need three horses more than entertaining conversation."

Equally anxious to complete their business, Wayne gave Mayleen an enthusiastic hug and whispered a promise to visit her soon. He then escorted Jesse on a tour of his barn. "The buckskin I'll trade even, but I want to see some cash before I replace the pinto and mule."

Jesse still had the better part of Jonathan Kane's twenty dollars plus most of Eldrin Stafford's burial fund, and readily agreed. "I need three sound mounts and I don't object to paying what they're worth."

Pleased to find Mayleen's friend so agreeable, Wayne extolled the merits of each of his horses and was not surprised when the taciturn stranger selected the three finest mounts in his stable. All young geldings, two were bays, whose sleek reddish-brown coats were accented with glossy black manes and tails, and the third was a handsome dappled-gray.

After an astute bit of bargaining, Jesse not only completed the transaction to his satisfaction but persuaded Wayne to throw in a saddle at no extra charge. In spite of her enthusiasm for the trip, Jesse doubted Mayleen would be traveling with him, but on the slim chance that she might, he wanted to have a horse and saddle for her. What he actually expected to happen, however, was that he and Tory would simply leave the extra saddle at Ivan's and use the third horse to pack their gear. He was sorry to have to part with Marshal Kane's buckskin as the horse had proved his worth, but he had always had a fondness for dappled-grays and considered it a piece of luck to now own such a fine one.

Mayleen lingered longer than Jesse would have liked to thank Wayne for his help, but he forgave her when they finally reached the dry goods store and the sultry beauty again used her wiles to entice the owner into opening his store despite the lateness of the hour. Sick of beef jerky and dry biscuits, Jesse bought enough bacon, flour, beans, and coffee to keep four people fed for a week. Confident they could replenish their supplies en route, he hurried Mayleen out of the store before the owner, who had also remarked on how familiar he looked, had the chance to recall just where he had seen him.

"I'll need my clothes," Mayleen protested as Jesse turned back toward Ivan's house.

"Have you got anything else fit for riding?"

Jesse had been none too gracious all evening, so Mayleen wasn't surprised by his belligerent attitude. "Yes I do, but I'll need you to come upstairs with me and tell me how much to pack."

"Pack the absolute minimum," Jesse ordered. "I'll wait in back with the horses."

Mayleen did not argue until they reached the Silver Spur. She dismounted, and then stepped close to Jesse and ran her hand up his well-muscled thigh. "I want you to come inside with me. If Rose sees me alone, she'll just send someone up to my room and then I might not get away for hours."

Jesse regarded the flirtatious young woman with a skeptical stare. "If what you really want is the opportunity to get me alone, forget it, Mayleen. My only interest is in leaving Tucson as fast as I can. I've got no time to spend with you." *Nor the slightest bit of interest in doing so.* He did not bother to add that sentiment, but it was plain in his disgusted expression as he batted her hand away.

"You really are sweet on that skinny kid, aren't you?" Mayleen asked in an incredulous whisper.

"Hell, no!" Jesse denied without thinking, but the resulting wave of guilt was surprisingly sharp. He had been taken with Tory Crandell from the moment he had first seen her seated on her cot in the Cactus Springs jail, but he was not about to reveal that the lanky lad Mayleen found so easy to ridicule was really a beautiful woman. Guarding Tory's identity was an essential part of protecting her life, but he had not meant to give Mayleen the mistaken impression that he did not care for his youthful companion.

"You just leave Tory out of this," he cautioned.

Mayleen was frightened by his icy glare. She could easily imagine how lonely a man might become in prison. She was also sophisticated enough to understand how men might assuage that loneliness with handsome boys. Jesse was out of prison now, though, so she did not see why he would not prefer her to Tory. Thinking it silly to argue about it behind the Silver Spur when it would be so much easier to convince him she was the better choice once they reached her room, Mayleen again invited him to accompany her.

"Forgive me, I didn't mean to insult your friend," she offered with an engaging smile. "We won't be upstairs more than a few minutes, but I do need you to come with me so Rose will think I'm working. I found you the good horses I promised. Now you have to keep your part of the bargain."

"I don't recall anything about helping you pack," Jesse grumbled as he swung down from the gray horse. "Well, come on," he ordered as he strode past her. "Let's get your things and be on our way."

He held the back door open for her, and Mayleen brushed against him as she stepped through it, purposely pressing the fullness of her breasts along his chest. Unlike Ivan, who was built like a gangly teenager, Jesse's physique was superb, and she sighed seductively as she allowed her imagination to strip him nude.

Jesse grabbed her arm and pushed her ahead of him to put a stop to her foolishness. "All we are going to do in your room is pack, Mayleen. Is that clear?"

"Of course, Jesse," she giggled, but she was still hoping for a great deal more as they climbed the back stairs. She was so anxious to reach her room that she was nearly skipping as they traversed the long hall, but her carefree stride came to an abrupt halt when Rose Flannery suddenly appeared to block their way.

"Were you looking for me, Rose?" Mayleen greeted the madam brightly before the petite woman had the opportunity to demand to know exactly where she had been. "I had to help the professor get home safely. With him passed out on the floor, I couldn't have invited anyone else into my bed." She looped her arm through Jesse's and attempted to pull him on past Rose to her room. "I'll be busy the rest of the night with George."

Jesse raised his hand as though he meant to tip his hat,

then kept his head ducked low so Rose could not get a clear look at him in the dimly lit hall. He saw more than he wanted to of her, however. He had never been a regular patron of the Silver Spur himself, but when he had last been in Tucson he had often toted Gerry back to their boardinghouse after the young man had overindulged himself with both liquor and women at the popular brothel. On none of those occasions had Rose treated either of them politely. Just the opposite had been true. She had been downright nasty and had admitted no responsibility for causing Gerry's disgraceful state, nor had she shown the slightest bit of gratitude toward Jesse for carting his stepbrother away.

Coldly forbidding rather than charming like the prostitutes she employed, Rose Flannery was a tiny woman whose weight had never exceeded eighty-five pounds in her entire life. Her severely tailored garments were always as black as her hair, while her skin was the translucent ivory of a woman who never allowed the sun's punishing rays to touch her pale flesh. It was impossible to guess her age. She might have been thirty-five or fifty, but Jesse didn't really care. It was her dark eyes that bothered him. They were always filled with a suspicious gleam, and tonight was no exception.

Displeased with Mayleen, Rose reached out and grabbed her by the arm. "Jack and Ross are paid to handle the men who can't hold their liquor. You are never to leave here in the middle of an evening. Never. Do you understand? You've been gone over an hour and give me no choice but to keep every penny of what you earn tonight as a reminder not to make the same careless mistake twice."

With Rose's nails cruelly digging into her upper arm, Mayleen found it easy to hang her head and appear contrite. "Yes, Mrs. Flannery. I won't disappoint you ever again."

"No, you most certainly won't," Rose replied in a threatening whisper, and without glancing up at Jesse, she released Mayleen and continued on down the hall.

Relieved to have escaped Rose for the moment, Mayleen hurried Jesse on into her room. "I'm not going to miss that witch!" she assured him the instant she had closed her door.

"She never runs out of excuses for docking our pay, but I've still managed to save quite a bit." Hoping to impress Jesse with her thrift, she struggled to move the marble-topped nightstand away from her bed. She then knelt and quickly pried up a loose floorboard. After removing a small metal strongbox, she stood and proudly displayed its contents.

"It's nearly five hundred dollars, and I know for a fact the professor has plenty more at his place. You can't have much money if you just got out of prison. If you take us with you, you'll not have to worry about running short of cash before you reach home."

Getting their hands on ready cash was an insignificant problem compared to the others Jesse and Tory faced and he was not even tempted to let Mayleen buy her way into their journey. "This isn't like purchasing a ticket for the stage," he warned. "I already know that Tory can match whatever pace I set, but I doubt your professor will be able to sit a horse for a week. You needn't get involved in his problems, nor pay Gerry a visit. If you're sick of Tucson, leave. You've got the money right there to go, and you don't need a man to escort you."

Discouraged by his lack of enthusiasm for the fine sum it had taken her years to save, Mayleen set the metal box on the bed and replaced the floorboard to conceal the hiding place. She then shoved the nightstand back against the wall.

"You don't understand anything," she complained. "I knew better than to fall for the men who paid for my favors, but Gerry wasn't like any of the others. He was always so sweet to me. He brought me little presents and teased me constantly to make me laugh. I thought we were really in love," she confessed shyly.

"What he did to you was unforgivable, Jesse, and I'm so ashamed of my part in it, but what Gerry did to *me* was even worse." Mayleen's eyes filled with tears as she summarized her pain. "All of his pretty promises were lies. He gave me such beautiful dreams and then stole them," she described sadly. "Stealing a person's dreams is worse than stealing their money. Lots worse."

Unmoved by the tears Jesse felt certain Mayleen could

summon on cue, he was not in the least bit sympathetic. "It still doesn't compare to framing an honest man and sending him to prison. That I was his stepbrother—family!—meant nothing to him. You'll only be in my way, Mayleen, and if you think you can convince me to go easy on Gerry, you're wrong. I intend to see he spends the rest of his life in prison for what he did to me. Now why don't we save ourselves any further trouble and say good-bye right now. Ivan's not going to be able to travel tonight, or any time soon."

Horrified by that demand, Mayleen quickly offered another suggestion, "I'll go without him then!" She crossed to her wardrobe and began searching through her silk and lace gowns for practical riding apparel. "You're absolutely right. Ivan's problems don't concern me. Seeing Gerry again is what I really want. I'm as eager as you are to make him suffer, and if Ivan can't come along, then that's just too bad."

"You'd abandon poor Ivan just like that?" Somehow Jesse wasn't at all surprised that she would.

Mayleen had a brightly colored carpetbag into which she hurriedly began stuffing her travel wardrobe. Garments went flying this way and that in her haste to choose between those that were essential and those she could do without. When she glanced up, she found Jesse's hostile frown unsettling. "Don't look at me like that. I care about Ivan, I really do, but I *loved* Gerry." After scooping up her toilet articles and the small strongbox, her packing was complete and she eased the bulging bag to the floor. "You needn't tell me how stupid I was. I already know." She came toward him then, her walk a slow, seductive sway.

"I picked the wrong brother four years ago," she admitted boldly. "I liked you best right from the start, but it was Gerry who cared about me. He didn't mind what I was, while I never felt I was good enough to please you. It's been four years. We've both changed," she cooed as she raised her arms to encircle his neck. "Maybe I look better to you now."

Jesse watched her expression become enticingly affectionate without feeling the slightest twinge of desire. She was undeniably pretty, but even as she snuggled close to caress his chest with the tips of her ample breasts, he was completely unmoved. When he had escaped from prison, all he had wanted was a woman, and Mayleen would have suited him just fine. He might even have gotten a perverse thrill out of sleeping with Gerry's former mistress but one glimpse of Tory Crandell had put a halt to those thoughts. The prospect of making love with the dark-eyed vixen who was so eager to bed him was no more inviting than sleeping with the coldly aloof Rose Flannery would have been.

Jesse put his hands around Mayleen's tiny waist and pushed her away. "Save that act for Ivan and the other men who are willing to pay for it. I'm not."

"I'd not ask you for money!" Mayleen exclaimed, highly insulted. "I just want to be with you. I can't believe you don't want me."

Jesse shook his head. "I'm not that stupid, Mayleen. All you want is to see Gerry again and you don't need to sleep with me to do it. You could have gone to El Paso any time you pleased. I've wasted enough time here. Let's go. If Ivan feels up to traveling, then the both of you may come with us. If he's too weak to leave his bed, then neither of you will. That's the bargain we made and I'll not change it."

"You're not being fair!" Mayleen protested dramatically.

"You're right," Jesse readily agreed. "I quit being fair four years ago when my stepbrother and his girl told enough lies to get me sent to prison!" He yanked open her door, and not caring whether or not she followed, he started down the hall with a brisk stride. Mayleen caught up with him, though, and, dragging her carpetbag, she chased him to the bottom of the back stairs where they found Rose Flannery waiting with Jack and Ross as though the cynical madam had known all along that Mayleen had planned to leave the Silver Spur that night.

"Just where do you think you're going now," Rose asked with a truly venomous stare that swept Mayleen with a blood-chilling intensity.

"Why Mrs. Flannery, I wasn't going anywhere!" Mayleen protested innocently. Her success as a prostitute was due not only to her remarkable beauty but also to her extraordinary ability to tell men exactly what they wished to hear. She had long ago discovered that her talent for inventive lies worked equally well on women.

"I was just giving George some of my old clothes to give to his little sister." A clever lass, Mayleen quickly set her bag on the floor and pulled out a cotton blouse. "See? I'm just giving him some of my old things I don't wear anymore." Next she displayed a faded skirt and a petticoat that had seen better days. "These aren't much more than rags to me, but his sister will be thrilled to get them."

Not wanting to take the chance Rose might suddenly decide to search the bag herself and discover her money, Mayleen slammed the satchel shut and handed it to Jesse. "There are you, George. You just take those things on home and tell that sister of yours to enjoy them. You can return my bag next time I see you." Desperate to escape Rose, Mayleen gave Jesse a nudge toward the door and prayed he would understand that she would meet him at Ivan's as soon as she possibly could.

Jesse was as well aware as Mayleen that her carpetbag held her money, and he was not at all pleased with the way she had handed it over to him. While he thought it likely she was counting on the fact he would not leave town with her life savings, he had no qualms about leaving the cash with Ivan. Certain she had outsmarted herself rather than him, he broke into a wide grin.

"This was real sweet of you, Mayleen. See you soon." He nodded to Rose as he eased his way past her and her two assistants. "'Night, Mrs. Flannery, boys," he said.

Using both his impressive size and the weight of the carpetbag to clear a path, Jesse edged his way out the back door. Wasting no time, he hurried on out to the hitching post where they had left the horses. He could feel Rose Flannery's eyes boring into his back, but if she had not recognized him just now, he doubted that she ever would. Hell, he thought, the madam met so many men each day that she would never be able to recall the name of a man she had not seen in four years. He lashed Mayleen's carpetbag behind her bay's saddle, and then mounted his dappled-gray and leading the bays, started down the narrow lane toward Ivan's house.

Mayleen had just breathed a sigh of relief when Rose stepped away from the open door and smacked her across the face with the back of her hand. "That was Gerry Chambers' brother, wasn't it? What's he doing out of prison so soon, and, more importantly, what did he want from you? Certainly not old clothes," she scoffed.

Mayleen raised her hand to her badly bruised cheek. "You're mistaken, Rose," she pleaded. "That man's name is George, and when he mentioned his kid sister didn't have much to wear, I was happy to give him what I could spare."

No more impressed by Mayleen's lies than she had been the first time, Rose struck her again. Then she turned to the men. "Follow him," she ordered. "Find out where he's going and what he does when he gets there."

"Yes, ma'am," Ross quickly agreed, and he and Jack hurried away to saddle their horses.

Not trusting anything Mayleen Tyler said, Rose marched her right back up the stairs to her room. "I've got better things to do than keep an eye on you," she announced from the doorway. "We'll talk again tomorrow, but I know you're smart enough to understand that I'd send Jack and Ross after you if you ever left me. By the time they finished with you, no man would ever want you again. Not even for free." Certain that dire threat would keep Mayleen obedient, she closed her door, locked it, and pocketed the key.

Mayleen mumbled a sorrowful good night, but the instant she heard Rose step away from her door, she ran to the corner window and raised it. A bougainvillea-covered trellis adorned that side of the Silver Spur and, ignoring the sharpness of the vine's thorns, Mayleen scrambled down it and, without a backward glance toward the brothel that had been her home for the last six years, she raced toward Ivan's.

When Tory heard horses being herded into the small corral behind the house, she went to the kitchen window and peered out to make certain it was Jesse before she unlocked the back door. She did not see Mayleen at first, but felt certain the young woman was there. Had Ivan not offered such a provocative reason for the delay in their return, she would have gone outside to greet them, but she felt no such impulse now.

She knew precisely how long it took for a man to satisfy himself with a woman, and enough time had certainly elapsed for that to happen. Not that it was any business of hers how Jesse and Mayleen chose to amuse themselves, but the mere thought of the act now sickened Tory so badly that she had to sit down at the kitchen table to avoid growing too dizzy to stand.

The marshal had been kind to her, so even if he had served time in prison she was inclined to believe he was as innocent as he had claimed he was to Mayleen. Tory certainly wasn't innocent, though. On the contrary, she was as guilty as sin of the crime of murder. She rested her head in her hands and tried to force away the horrid image of Paul's insolent smirk, but it refused to fade.

It was Paul's abuse she had recalled the instant Ivan had begun to speculate on the nature of Jesse and Mayleen's activities, and those were memories she would have given anything to erase. When, a few minutes later, Jesse came through the back door followed by a breathless Mayleen, she found it impossible to glance their way.

"Rose never forgets anyone," Mayleen swore. "She recognized you and sent Jack and Ross out to find you, but they'll just search the saloons. They'll never think of coming here. Just to be on the safe side, we ought to wait until dawn to leave. They will have given up by then and we can ride out of town without worrying about them being on our trail." Still short of breath from the dash to Ivan's house, she hurriedly slid into the chair opposite Tory's before she glanced over at the stove.

"Do you want me to make some coffee?" she asked, but Jesse shook his head.

Jesse had expected at least a smile from Tory, and her downcast expression and averted gaze disappointed him. "How did you and the professor get along?" he asked her.

"Poorly," Tory replied honestly. "He's well enough to complain. Maybe that's a good sign."

"I better go check on him," Mayleen volunteered. She covered a wide yawn as she rose to her feet. "Let's stay here a couple of hours, Jesse. We could all use the rest, and it will give Jack and Ross time to get bored with looking for you."

Jesse had not liked the looks of Rose's men. Powerfully built, if not his equal in height, they had looked like the type who enjoyed meting out beatings, and he had absolutely no desire to ever cross their paths again. He was also concerned about the fact Rose had recognized him. How long would it take for Wayne Dubois, or the man at the dry goods store, to place his face? Was it possible they already had? Would they go straight to the sheriff to ask why he had served less than half of his sentence, or would they shrug it off as none of their business?

He was exhausted, but remaining in Tucson a moment longer than necessary struck him as positively suicidal when he had already been recognized. He sank into the chair Mayleen had just left and laid his cheek on his outstretched arms. "We'll rest when we're well out of town," he told her. "Go see if the professor is ready to go. If not, it will just be too damn bad. Tory and I are leaving."

Once Mayleen had left the room, Jesse peeked up at Tory. "We're alone. Tell me what really happened with the professor."

The richness of his deep voice encouraged Tory to confide in him, but she had to swallow hard before she replied. She dared not reveal any of Ivan's erotic speculation, but she could report his insistent request for whiskey, and did.

Jesse sat up and shook his head sadly. "I'm sorry. I should have just told you to ignore the poor fool rather than to look after him."

Unable to reveal just how badly Ivan had upset her, Tory simply shrugged. "He reminds me of one of my father's colleagues at Yale. I didn't realize he was a heavy drinker until just before we came out to Arizona. I had always thought he was just an unusually charming man until then." Tory suddenly grew embarrassed. "I must sound very naive."

"Not at all," Jesse assured her. "I know the type you mean.

84

He's always filled with good cheer, but it comes straight out of a bottle. Ivan will have to promise to stay sober if he comes along with us."

"Is that even possible?" Tory inquired thoughtfully.

"I won't take him along if he won't give me his word on it. There's too much at risk, but maybe he's not up to traveling and it won't even be a question."

As if on cue, Mayleen returned to the kitchen. "Ivan wants to see you. He's determined to go, but he needs another hour or two. I didn't tell you this before, Jesse, but Rose said if she finds out I'm gone, she'll send Jack and Ross out after me. She threatened that they would leave me too ugly to attract a man. She might have already discovered that I'm not in my room so I can't go back to the Silver Spur. I have to come with you regardless of whether or not the professor does, but with another hour or two, he'll be fine. I know that he will."

It was the stricken look on Tory's face that convinced Jesse to be lenient. It was clear the pretty blonde believed Mayleen was in real danger, so he could not just shrug off Rose's threats as he would have liked. "I doubt Mrs. Flannery would harm you," he said thoughtfully. "You're far too valuable to her."

"You saw the way she treated me," Mayleen reminded him. "Like dirt! I'm nothing to her, and the instant she discovers I'm gone, she'll send Jack and Ross out after me, too."

"Well, they'll certainly be busy tonight, won't they?" Jesse joked as he rose to his feet. "I want to see Ivan. If he can convince me he'll be able to travel with another hour's rest, I'll give it to him, but if there's the slightest bit of doubt about it, this is where we part company."

When Mayleen followed him down the hall, Tory was too curious to miss the coming conversation to remain behind. She stayed by the door, though, and listened attentively as Ivan pled his case. He did look better. Apparently Mayleen had helped him change his shirt and comb his hair, and the resulting improvement in his appearance went a long way toward making him look fit to travel.

"I'm just a little shaky is all," he explained. To illustrate his

85

point, he eased himself off the bed and stood on his own. "See, I won't collapse. My ribs hurt like hell, and my face will probably never look the same, but I can make it. Just give me another hour to rest and I won't slow you down. In fact, I'll be an asset. I'm sure I know my way around the Arizona Territory better than you do, so I can serve as a guide. I'll not be a burden."

Impressed by the geologist's courage, as well as his professed knowledge of the terrain they'd have to cross, Jesse was about to agree, but first he glanced back toward Tory. "What do you think, kid? Shall we take them along or not?"

While she did not even like Ivan, Tory was too kind-hearted to doom him to another brutal beating from the miners who had promised to return. As for Mayleen, despite the fact the dark-haired girl had made fun of her, Tory didn't want to see her come to any harm, either. "It looks like we all have our reasons for leaving Tucson. We might as well travel together."

Jesse nodded. "I agree. Now we're going to sleep. You two can do whatever you please, but be ready to leave in an hour." He captured Tory in a bear hug as he went out the door and hustled her next door to the room they had previously shared.

"Just what do you think you're doing?" Tory demanded as she struggled to break free of his grasp.

Releasing her immediately, Jesse closed the door and raised his hands to plead for mercy. "I'm just feeding their imaginations a little bit, that's all. You and I know nothing's going to happen between us, and that's all that really matters. Now I intend to sleep for an hour. You can either watch me or make good use of your side of the bed to rest. I can't say when we'll next have a chance to sleep so I'd advise you not to waste this one."

Tory watched him discard his hat and boots before stretching out on the bed, but this time he kept on his gunbelt and clothes. Convinced sleep was all he had in mind, she followed his example and lay down, too, but it took a long while before she was able to relax.

"You've still got a lot to explain," she reminded him.

Rather than argue with her, Jesse slipped his arm around her slender waist and drew her close. "Later, kid," he promised smoothly. "I'm too tired now to talk."

Dreading his embrace, Tory held her breath as she waited for his hands to begin to wander and the wet feel of the kisses she would never accept. When Jesse didn't move, she realized he really had fallen asleep and felt very foolish for being frightened. She reminded herself again that he could have forced himself upon her long before this had that been all he wanted. That whatever he did want was still a mystery was deeply troubling, but for the moment she lay cuddled in his arms and wondered what their chances were of escaping the Jack and Ross Mayleen had mentioned. She felt as though the entire territory was out looking for them, and that encouraged nightmares rather than peaceful dreams for the few brief minutes she finally managed to sleep.

Chapter 6

As promised, Jesse slept exactly one hour before awakening. He sat up, meaning to wake Tory, but found her troubled expression so poignant that he hesitated to disturb her. Clearly her dreams weren't sweet, and he could easily imagine the gruesome images that must haunt her. Sighing sadly, he put his hand on her shoulder and gave her a gentle squeeze rather than his usual rude shake.

"It's time to get going," he whispered.

Tory stirred slightly, unconsciously snuggling against him, and Jesse was embarrassed by how easily he became aroused. Sound asleep and totally unaware of him, Tory heated his blood as the blatantly sexual Mayleen never would. Unable to resist an overwhelming temptation, he placed an adoring kiss on her cheek before turning away and rolling off his side of the bed.

"It's time to go," Jesse urged in a louder tone as he yanked on his boots. "We've got to put as much distance between ourselves and Tucson as we possibly can before sunrise," he reminded her. "Does our host have anything worth eating in his kitchen?"

Tory sat up slowly and covered a wide yawn. Feeling more tired than when she had lain down, she eased herself off the bed before replying. "I don't know. I didn't look."

"Well, go and look now," Jesse ordered. "I'm going to see if Ivan feels fit enough to ride." He paused at the door and turned back toward her. "I intend to get his word about the liquor, too. Staying sober has to be his responsibility, not ours."

Tory struggled to pull on her boots and did not comment as Jesse left the room, but she was puzzled. The marshal had just spoken as though they were partners rather than a lawman and prisoner. While he was undoubtedly a most unconventional marshal, having served time in prison and also totally disregarding his orders where she was concerned, he had impressed her as an extremely determined individual whom she doubted ever changed his course of action, or an opinion, once he had decided on it. His change of tone was therefore most unusual and she was anxious to discover why. She was in as great a hurry as he was not only to be on their way, but also to hear the story he had promised to tell.

She retied her scarf, donned her hat, and wondered how long her flimsy disguise could possibly continue to fool Ivan and Mayleen. When she and Jesse had arrived in Tucson she had hoped to find an opportunity to break away from him, but now such a rash action seemed foolhardy in the extreme. Eldrin's men could find her too easily in Tucson, but she would be impossible to locate once she left the city for the desert trails. At least she certainly hoped so, and leaving the bedroom mimicking Jesse's confident stride, she hurried into the kitchen to make breakfast.

Jesse knocked lightly at Ivan's door, but the badly beaten man and Mayleen had merely been talking rather than sleeping, and she quickly let him in. "Are you ready to go?" he asked.

Mayleen had already packed Ivan's clothes and helped him on with his boots, and this time when he left his bed he did not intend to return to it. "Yes," he announced proudly. "Everything's packed. I come and go so frequently, it will take several weeks before the neighbors realize I'm gone for good."

"There's just one thing before we go," Jesse cautioned. "You'll have to stay as sober as you are right now. Don't even think about bringing any liquor along. If you can't give me your promise that you won't drink while the four of us are traveling together, then we'll have to part company right now."

Mayleen shot Ivan an anxious glance, but he returned it with a relaxed smile. "I'll be fine," he swore convincingly. "Last night was the exception rather than the rule. I told you I never drink when I'm working, and I consider this trip far more serious than a job. My life's at stake, and I'll not gamble with it by drinking."

Jesse walked over to him and extended his hand. "As long as you understand I won't gamble with anyone's life by allowing irresponsible behavior, we'll get along just fine. I'm the boss, and what I say goes. I want that understood from the beginning."

Ivan gripped Jesse's hand as he agreed to his terms. "It is. You needn't worry about me. I might not be able to defend myself with my fists, but I can shoot, and my knowledge of the territory will be an asset," he assured Jesse.

Convinced the geologist meant what he said, Jesse allowed the enticing aroma of freshly brewed coffee to lure him away. The instant he had left the room, Mayleen reached for Ivan's saddlebags. "You may have planned to take that bottle of whiskey I brought from the kitchen, but I'm unpacking it right now."

Ivan leaned down to wrench the saddlebags from her grasp. "I need that to keep my ribs from hurting so much I can't ride," he argued. "You needn't worry about me getting drunk. It won't happen. I'll just take a sip every once in a while to keep the pain bearable. Jesse will never know if you don't tell him, and you know he's not going to let you go with him if he refuses to take me."

Jesse had made that fact too plain for Mayleen to dispute Ivan's contention, but she was not at all pleased to be forced to go along with his deception. "I've never seen you when you weren't drinking, Ivan. You won't be able to fool Jesse, and then I'm the one who'll suffer."

"No you won't, sweetheart." Sincerely fond of the raven-haired girl, Ivan placed a light kiss on her forehead. The bruise where Rose had struck her cheek was faint but noticeable, and he ran his fingertip over it lightly. "Nobody is going to hurt you ever again. Just trust me, I won't let you down."

Mayleen frowned pensively as she studied his battered features for some sign that, like too many men, he was just telling her what she wanted to hear, but she saw only the sweetness he had always shown her. She stepped forward to hug him, but he dodged away. "Oh, I'm sorry, I'd forgotten about your ribs."

"I sure wish that I could," Ivan sighed sadly. "Come on, let's have some coffee and be on our way before Jesse can change his mind about traveling with us."

When he put his arm around her shoulders, Mayleen walked with him out to the kitchen, but she was still worried about the fact Ivan was disobeying Jesse's orders before they had even left the house. Would he keep right on lying? That prospect really frightened her because Gerry had told her enough lies to last a lifetime. She did not want to risk another broken heart by believing in Ivan Carrows if he made promises he wouldn't, or couldn't, keep.

Luke Bernay rode into Tucson shortly after sunrise, but Jesse and his party had ridden out long before dawn. The talented tracker knew Jesse had to have stopped there and figured that a man traveling with an attractive blonde was bound to have garnered considerable notice. Again following his standard practice of checking in with the law, he stopped by the sheriff's office as soon as he had eaten breakfast.

Like a bulldog, Craig Toland was powerfully built, but in addition to his obvious strength, he was also blessed with a keen mind. He had heard of Luke Bernay's remarkable prowess as a tracker, and felt honored to have finally met him, but by the time Luke had explained his mission, Craig's expression was grim. He took his time studying the photograph the diminutive man had handed him.

"I remember Lambert," he revealed in a low, rumbling voice. "Have you met him?"

Luke shook his head. "Not yet, but I intend to real soon."

Toland fixed Luke with a darkly determined stare. While he admired the man's skill in hunting down wanted men, he felt torn by what he remembered of Jesse. "If you ask me, and unfortunately my opinion carried no weight in court, you're after the wrong man. Jesse Lambert is no thief, and even if he were, he wouldn't be so stupid as to rob a stage and then hide the loot in his own room. He swore he was framed, and I believed him. It's a damn shame the jury didn't."

While intrigued, Luke was far from dismayed. "It isn't my job to worry about the man's guilt or innocence. I was hired to find him and return him to the custody of the prison authorities in Yuma. That's my only concern."

"Well, as I see it," Toland mused aloud, "once a man separates law from justice in his mind, he's in a heap o' trouble."

Offended, Luke's expression grew as hostile as he feared the opinionated sheriff was about to become. "I'm no philosopher," he complained, "but it seems to me that if people don't respect a jury's decision to sentence a man to prison, then we'll have neither law nor justice, and that will be a real sorry state of affairs."

When Craig Toland nodded to acknowledge that point, Luke brought him up to date on Jesse Lambert's crimes, which included not only an escape from prison, but the murder of a United States marshal and the abduction of an attractive female prisoner awaiting execution.

Stunned, Toland asked for more details, and felt badly frustrated when Luke had only the few he had already imparted. "That doesn't make a lick of sense to me," the sheriff complained. "If Lambert was innocent of the robbery, which I still believe he was, he would have escaped from prison to clear his name, not to go on the wild rampage you describe."

"Oh there was nothing wild about it," Luke corrected. "He was as cool as you please. He shot the marshal, stole his orders, made a fool of the sheriff in Cactus Springs, and took off with Victoria Crandell in broad daylight."

"Jesus!"

"Exactly," Luke agreed. "If I catch them here in Tucson, I reckon I could just hand Miss Crandell over to you to get her off my hands. I imagine she can be hanged as easily here as in Prescott."

Craig Toland did not want any part of that. "I sure don't relish the thought of hanging a woman," he announced with a shudder. "And you say this one is pretty?"

"That's what I was told."

The sheriff tapped the photograph of Jesse against his desk and then passed it back to Luke Bernay. "I don't know what to think of Lambert now. Maybe serving four years in prison turned him into an outlaw, if he wasn't one when he arrived. There's still ten thousand dollars of the hold-up money missing. I'd sure like to get my hands on that but I doubt it's still here in Tucson. Lambert had a brother. No, make that a stepbrother, Gerry Chambers, who always struck me as knowing one hell of a lot more than he let on. He used to be sweet on a little brunette by the name of Mayleen Tyler who works over at the Silver Spur. She's still around even if Gerry's long gone. She might know something."

Luke nodded as he made a mental note of the name. Luke had heard of the Silver Spur and knew precisely what kind of establishment it was. "It's a mite early to be paying calls at a whorehouse. Did Lambert have any friends he could still count on to help him?"

"That I don't know," Toland replied with a shrug. "I wasn't the only one who believed his story, but I've forgotten just who the others were."

While Luke doubted that the sheriff had ever forgotten anything, it was obvious the man was on Jesse's side rather than his. Not inclined to waste any more time in idle talk, he replaced the photograph in his shirt pocket and rose to his feet. "Thanks for your help," he offered as he prepared to leave. "With any luck, I'll catch up with Jesse and Miss Crandell before they reach El Paso. I'll be sure and let you know if they have any of the missing money with them. I imagine there would still be a substantial reward."

"Of course there would." Craig Toland walked Luke to

the door. "There's one other thing that's still missing," he suddenly remembered to add. "It's a real fancy pearl-and-cameo necklace that was taken from one of the passengers when the stage was robbed. A Mrs. Tribett was her name, and I thought I'd never hear the end of it. She came in here every day for months demanding that I find her precious necklace, but it never turned up. Or at least, it hasn't yet. If you see Mayleen Tyler wearing it, come right back here and get me."

"I'll do that," Luke promised, and thinking he would not find anyone awake at the Silver Spur before noon, he began making the rounds of the stables where Jesse might have switched mounts and the dry-goods stores where he could have stocked up on provisions.

Wayne Dubois' livery stable was Luke's third stop. Wayne appeared to pay scant attention as Luke showed him Jesse's photograph, but he was amazed to learn Mayleen's friend was an escaped convict. As soon as Luke mentioned the robbery that had sent Jesse to prison, Wayne remembered the trial and understood why he had looked familiar. It gave him a real bad feeling to think how easily he had been duped into helping Jesse flee the law. Wayne prided himself on being an honest man, and he did not enjoy the role of unwilling accomplice one bit.

He thought of Mayleen Tyler, though, and knowing he did not want to jeopardize the warmth of their friendship over some escaped felon who was probably halfway to Mexico, he shook his head when Luke finally asked if he had seen Jesse either alone or with a comely blonde.

"No, sir," he swore as he turned away. "You're the only stranger I've met this week, and I sure as hell haven't seen no good-looking blondes."

Wayne had looked Luke straight in the eye when he had introduced himself, but not when he had replied to his questions, and that made Luke real suspicious. He then began to curse the fact that he had not thought to ask Sheriff Ross in Cactus Springs to describe the horses Jesse and Miss Crandell had ridden out of town. He did know they had been leading a third horse, however, or perhaps a mule.

"Say," he called out. "I'm looking for a pack mule. You got one?"

Wayne called over his shoulder, "Yeah, I got several. They're in the first corral if you want to have a look."

"I'll just do that," Luke replied with a jaunty wave. He circled the barn and attempted to look like he was sincerely interested in buying a mule while he tried to think what to do. A red-haired lad was pitching hay to the mules, and Luke strolled over to him.

"I'm looking for a mule, but I don't want one that's been used too hard. Any of these had an easy life?"

Always willing to pause for a rest, the boy set his pitchfork aside, wiped his perspiring brow on his sleeve, and pointed to one of the mules he was tending. "That one came in last night so I don't know nothing about him, but the others are all good. You'll need to ask Mr. Dubois. He's the only one who can talk prices."

"Thank you, son," Luke said, and appeared to be on his way to do just that, but then suddenly returned to the corral. "You get any horses in last night? A friend of mine was going to sell a roan I liked, but I forgot to ask him where."

"Along with that mule, Mr. Dubois took in a big buckskin and a pinto but no roans," the young man replied as he resumed hefting hay into the corral.

Luke was far too clever a man to walk away now. "Looks like I got here too late. I bet the stable's best mounts were sold last night, too, weren't they?"

Astonished by the accuracy of that question, the lad broke into a wide grin. "How did you know?"

"Lucky guess, but I'd never be able to describe them."

"Two bays and a dappled-gray," the lad answered with a ready laugh. "Whoever bought them knew horses. I'll say that for him."

"You didn't see him, though?"

"No, it was after I'd gone home. Mr. Dubois handled it alone."

Luke thanked the boy and sauntered off as though he had not a care in the world. He knew there was no point in confronting Dubois as the stable owner would undoubtedly lie again about who had brought in two horses and a mule and left with three fresh mounts. Perhaps Dubois was a friend of Jesse's. Perhaps he was just averse to answering questions, but whatever, Luke was pleased with what he had learned.

At ten past noon, Luke knocked on the front door of the Silver Spur. It was opened by a heavily madeup young woman in a scandalously low-cut red gown. When he asked for Mayleen Tyler, her welcoming smile vanished and she hurriedly ushered him back out onto the porch.

"Mayleen's gone," she explained in a frantic whisper, "and Mrs. Flannery doesn't want to hear her name ever again."

Luke feigned deep disappointment. "Oh, no, I had my heart set on seeing Mayleen. When did she leave?"

"Last night, I guess, or early this morning. Nobody knows for sure. She just disappeared."

Before Luke could pose another question, Rose Flannery came to the door. "Is there a problem here, Charlotte?"

"Why, no, Mrs. Flannery, there's no trouble."

Luke removed his hat and bowed politely. "Good afternoon, Mrs. Flannery." He was delighted to find her as tiny a person as he himself was and his grin was genuinely warm. "I'm just looking for this man," he explained as he handed her Jesse's photograph. "Have you seen him?"

Rose was not nearly so impressed with Luke as he was with her. After a cursory glance, she returned the photograph to him. "No, we have only women living here, no men."

"Well, now, I didn't mean for you to think I expected him to be living here. I just thought you might have seen him. I believe he's a friend of Mayleen's."

"Who?" Rose asked with a puzzled frown.

"Mayleen Tyler," Luke repeated. "I understand she used to work here."

"You've been misinformed," Rose insisted and, brushing Charlotte aside, she closed the door in Luke's face.

Luke had not seen even a flicker of recognition in Rose's

dark eyes as she had glanced at Jesse's photograph, but he thought it likely she not only knew Jesse but knew that Mayleen was with him. "How curious," he mumbled to himself. If Jesse had planned to fetch Mayleen from the Silver Spur, why had he stopped off in Cactus Springs to help Victoria Crandell escape from jail? Luke could readily understand a man's wanting female company after four years in prison, but two of them? In Luke's view, that was downright suicidal!

"Mayleen must have been holding the missing ten thousand dollars," he deduced, but he could not for the life of him discover the connection between Victoria Crandell and Jesse. That stumped him completely. Certain the threesome must have already left Tucson, he treated himself to a thick steak before leaving town. He believed that it would take little effort to overtake a man traveling with two women, and he began whistling happily to himself as he headed out after them.

The sun was high overhead before Jesse called a halt for a rest. They had been angling south and east, heading toward the San Pedro River, which he intended to follow down into Mexico. They had been riding hard all morning, and he was not surprised to see Ivan Carrows slide from his horse, rather than dismount, and collapse not two feet from his side.

"You should have told me you needed to stop before this," Jesse scolded as he approached the geologist, who lay sprawled in his mount's shadow.

Ivan was in excruciating pain. He ached from head to toe, but he had not even been tempted to beg Jesse to stop as long as he was still plagued with vivid visions of what Calvin and Arnold would do to him should they catch up with him. "I'm all right," he lied.

Jesse doubted it. Mayleen joined them then, and knowing she would pamper her battered friend until it was time to move on, he excused himself and went to sit beside Tory. She had splashed her face with cool water from her canteen to rinse away the layer of dust they had all picked up from the trail. The damage the sun had done to her fair skin the previous day had softened to a golden glow he found most attractive. It was difficult to ignore the urge to hug her, and he leaned back on his elbows in an effort to stifle that impulse.

They had seen a few miners and a freight wagon or two along the road, but had ridden on without exchanging more than a wave. "Anyone tracking us will be looking for the two of us and a mule. They'll not follow up on reports of three men and a woman traveling together. Even if they are curious about the woman, she'll be described as a brunette and can't be mistaken for you."

Recalling how he had awakened her the day before with fears for their safety, Tory's apprehension returned. "Can you still feel them coming?" she asked.

Unlike the eerie sensation to which Tory referred, Jesse was now simply filled with the certain knowledge someone was dogging their every step. A posse of several men or a lone tracker might be following him from Yuma, but he was equally convinced Eldrin Stafford would not allow Tory to slip through his clutches without a vigorous effort to find her.

"I can feel them," he finally admitted. "They're not as close as they were the other night by the river, but they're still coming. We'll hit the San Pedro River late tonight and turn toward Mexico. If Ivan isn't strong enough to ride as hard as we have to, I'll leave him and Mayleen in Tombstone, but I'm getting us out of the Arizona Territory as fast as I can."

As he spoke, Tory studied Jesse's profile. He had a well-defined jawline which she thought reflected the strength of his character handsomely. Embarrassed to be observing him so closely, she quickly looked away. "Something's changed, Marshal," she pointed out softly. "You've begun treating me more as a partner than a prisoner. Is it merely to fool Ivan and Mayleen or is there another reason?"

Jesse was equally fascinated with the lovely young woman at his side, but he still wasn't ready to take her into his confidence. "I warned you not to call me Marshal in front of them," he reminded her.

Tory looked past him to make certain the other couple could not possibly overhear her words. They appeared to be engaged in an argument of some sort. They were whispering to conceal the fact, but she could tell by Mayleen's expression that something was wrong between the two. "They're paying no attention to us," she informed Jesse. "Won't you please answer my question? Am I still your prisoner, or have you set me free?"

For a shattering instant that filled him with a glimpse of eternity, Jesse saw the future reflected in Tory's cool green eyes. "You'll never be free of me," he responded with an intensity that alarmed her, but he did not care. He might have avoided telling her the truth about himself, but his attachment to her was one thing he did not mind declaring. One way or another, Tory Crandell would remain his prisoner until staying with him was the only choice she truly wished to make.

He rose to his feet and offered her his hand to help her up. "Come on," he announced gruffly. "It's time to go." He saw the panic fill Ivan's face as he started toward him, but the wiry geologist made it to his feet, and with a boost from Mayleen, he returned to his saddle without complaint.

"Next time we stop, we'll have something to eat," Jesse promised his already weary companions, but it wasn't the prospect of food that teased his senses as they continued their ride. It was the thought of escaping anyone tracking them so that Tory could again dress as the woman he longed to call his own.

Tad MacDonald and his six men arrived in Tucson shortly after noon and began making the rounds of the saloons to assuage their thirst. Tad was careful to sound real nonchalant when he asked if anyone had seen a United States marshal by the name of Kessler traveling with a pretty blonde, but all he received for his trouble were confused stares and not a scrap of useful information.

After an hour's rest and a hot meal, Tad sent his men to

make inquiries at all the hotels and boardinghouses. While none had seen Victoria Crandell's male companion, they could describe the willowy blonde in such minute detail, they even included the extraordinary length of her eyelashes. Once again, there were no reports of the recent arrival of such a stunning young woman and they were all discouraged when they returned to the Congress Hall Saloon where they had agreed to meet.

"Damn it all!" Tad swore before downing another beer. "They've got to be here somewhere."

At thirty-eight, José Gonzales was not only the oldest of the Stafford men, but also the most serious. He rolled the brim of his cream-colored hat between his palms as he tried to decide where he would hide a beauty like Tory Crandell. "The man must have friends here," he mused aloud. "People he trusts to open their homes to him. He and Tory might not venture out for weeks."

"Someone will see her . . ." George Flood insisted in the soft drawl of his native North Carolina. "A neighbor, a delivery boy—someone. All it will take is for one man to get a good look at her and the news will be all over town in less than an hour." George was in his mid-twenties. He had given up mining as far too strenuous an occupation to pursue, but he had a flair for cruelty that made working for a man with Eldrin Stafford's meanness downright enjoyable.

Hank Short was the clown of the group and offered his suggestion as a teasing jest. "What we need is some wanted posters that show how pretty Tory is. That will start every man in Tucson looking for her."

Impressed with that idea, Tad leaned forward to speak to the man seated opposite him. "You can draw, Manuel. Get some paper and start making some sketches. I'm going over to the sheriff's office to get his cooperation."

"The sheriff?" Juan Lopez gasped in surprise. "¡Madre de Dios!"

"Tory's the fugitive, you fool. We don't have to be scared of the law," Tad scoffed.

"Perhaps not, but still—" Juan persisted.

Carl Olson was the most taciturn of the ranchhands, but

101

he was prompted to offer an opinion now. "Tad's right. Tory's the criminal, not us," he stated with a deep chuckle that soon had all the men laughing along with him. There was not a man among them who had not had his share of brushes with the law, but they wisely kept the details to themselves and never pried into another man's background for fear he might be prompted to look too closely at their own.

After giving his men the order to simply sit and wait for him, Tad left the Congress Hall and made his way to Craig Toland's office. He had no sooner introduced himself as heading up a posse from Cactus Springs than the sheriff waved him down into a chair.

"Yes, Mr. MacDonald, I know all about Victoria Crandell escaping from your jail. Luke Bernay was in here this morning with the very same tale. You probably know of him, even if you haven't met him. Other than some Indians I know, he's the best tracker in the Territory."

Tad was astonished by that piece of news until he recalled the friendly stranger who had passed them on the trail. "I should have known Luke would beat us here," he remarked with a cocky grin. "He may be no bigger than a minute, but he's fast."

"That's the man," Craig agreed. "Now I'll tell you the same thing I told him. I don't know anything about this Crandell woman, but I did know Jesse Lambert, and I can't believe he'd kill a marshal any more than I believe he robbed a stage four years ago. I won't argue with the fact he's escaped from the Yuma prison, 'cause that's obviously a fact, but I just can't believe he's turned murderer."

Tad MacDonald knew damn well who had shot Marshal Kane because he and Nathan had done it, but he was an accomplished liar and smiled innocently, as though he had absolutely no knowledge of the crime. He and his men had left Cactus Springs before Luke Bernay had arrived, so they had not known Jesse Lambert's name or desperate circumstance, but Tad chose not to share that fact with the sheriff.

"Lambert doesn't concern us," Tad assured him. "Our only job is to recapture Victoria Crandell and make certain

102

she keeps her date with the executioner in Prescott."

Craig Toland sat back in his chair and tented his fingers across his chest. "My deputies and I will keep an eye out for Jesse and your Miss Crandell, but I doubt that they're in Tucson. Jesse's from El Paso, and Bernay seemed to think all he'd have to do is track them there. You might follow his example."

"El Paso?" Tad murmured to himself. He was amazed to have found the sheriff had so much helpful information, but was careful not to admit just how ignorant he had been when he had arrived at his office. Instead he rose to his feet and shook the lawman's hand.

"Thanks for your help, Sheriff. I think it would be worth our while to ask a few more questions around Tucson, but if we don't get any answers, then we'll likely as not head out for El Paso, too."

Craig wished Tad good luck and watched him go, but he could not shake his original impression of Jesse Lambert as an honest man. "Well, whatever he is," the sheriff muttered under his breath, "he'll never get out of this mess alive."

Tad dashed back to the Congress Hall, and for nearly half an hour regaled his men with what he had learned about Tory's companion. "Tory's got herself an escaped convict," he revealed with a hearty chuckle. "Can you imagine that elegant bitch sleeping with a criminal? It's a damn good thing Paul is dead or he'd kill her for this!"

Eldrin Stafford's men howled at that joke and, inspired to learn they were tracking two people with prices on their heads, they threw out their chests as though they were a legitimate posse and left Tucson intent on letting Luke Bernay lead them straight to Tory Crandell and her outlaw lover.

Chapter 7

Rose Flannery frequently interrupted with derogatory comments as Jack and Ross reviewed their futile attempts to locate Mayleen Tyler. Mistakenly believing the silly chit would behave herself after the scolding she had received, Rose had tended to business the previous night and had not checked on Mayleen again until late that morning. It was impossible to pinpoint the exact time the popular prostitute had fled the Silver Spur, but Rose was exasperated that the men she had sent after her had returned empty-handed.

"If only you'd not let Gerry Chambers' brother escape you last night, then I'm positive we'd know right where she is." She was positively livid over Jack and Ross's bungling. "You've checked with all her regulars? She's not hiding with one of them?" the irate madam probed.

Jack knew they had done their best to locate Chambers' brother, but the man had simply vanished by the time they had saddled their horses and, embarrassed by a similar lack of success with Mayleen that morning, he shrugged helplessly. "No, they were all shocked when we said she was missing."

"And real upset by the thought she might not be coming back," Ross added. "They weren't just trying to fool us, either. Nobody's seen her since yesterday."

"What about Professor Carrows?" Rose suggested. "Mayleen saw him home last night. Did you try his place?"

"Sure did." Jack went on to describe the damaged

condition of the front door. "There were a couple of miners there looking for him. They were mad as hell because he wasn't there to meet them."

Rose leaned forward to drum her beautifully manicured nails on her desk in a staccato rhythm. "Carrows frequently traveled through the mines. Mayleen might have gone along with him this time. Take a day or two and see if you can locate Carrows. If Mayleen's with him, persuade her to return to us by whatever means necessary. If you don't find her in that amount of time, give up the search and come home. She's been here six years and it's high time I replaced her with a younger girl anyway."

"Yes, ma'am," the men replied before leaving her office with the exaggerated show of respect she demanded. Neither enjoyed working for a woman, but Rose Flannery paid them more than enough to soothe their damaged pride. But as for finding Mayleen, they would not put much effort into the task.

"I knew we shouldn't have left here last night," Calvin swore in a disgusted snarl. Pulling Arnold along with him, he gave up their brief vigil in front of Ivan Carrows's rented home. "He's gone and he ain't coming back. Now either we find him, or we'll have no chance of selling that worthless mine!"

"We hurt him real bad. He was too beat up to go far," Arnold reminded him. "I bet we can find him in no time."

"Well, come on then, let's go!"

Believing a bruised and limping Ivan Carrows would be hiding out there in Tucson, the two miners began combing the town, but by sundown they had failed to find a trace of the geologist they had abused with such vigor. Not wanting to start back to their mine after dark, they proceeded to alleviate their frustrations with whiskey, but rather than toasting each other, they cursed Professor Ivan J. Carrows with every last drop.

*   *   *

Relying on dogged determination, Jesse kept his weary companions moving toward San Pedro Creek until it became obvious that goal had been far too ambitious for the day. He and Tory could have made it, but Mayleen and the professor clearly could not. Not wanting to attract any notice, or uninvited company, once Jesse had decided to stop, he led them south, well away from the trail to Benson, before making camp.

While they had failed to reach the river, they had covered more than thirty miles, and Jesse hoped to keep up the same brisk pace for as long as it took them to reach El Paso. He had the trip laid out in his mind, and after the foursome had shared supper, he knelt at the edge of their campfire and traced it in the sandy soil.

"We're about fifty miles north of the Mexican border," he explained first. "We'll bypass Benson, and try to make Tombstone tomorrow afternoon. We'll camp outside of Bisbee the next day and cross into Mexico the following morning, head east, and gradually angle north until we reach El Paso. It will take us perhaps nine days to cross Mexico and reach Texas. That will make this trip twelve days in all. What do you say, Professor? Will you be able to make it?"

"I have little choice," Ivan replied with a lopsided grin that quickly became a grimace. "If Calvin and Arnold catch up with me, I'll be a dead man. That's most inspiring."

"What about you, Mayleen?" Jesse inquired. "Can you take nearly two weeks of riding as hard as we did today?"

Mayleen brushed an ebony curl off her forehead with an impatient swipe. "Of course I can," she exclaimed. "It would be worth a journey twice as long to see Gerry again. Besides, now that I've left Tucson, I can't risk going back with Rose Flannery so angry with me."

Jesse sent a significant glance Tory's way, and she nodded. "I can keep up."

"Good. Now let's turn in so we can get an early start again tomorrow."

"Just what do you mean by early?" the professor asked.

Jesse noted his fearful glance but just laughed. "You're free to go your own way, Carrows, but if you're traveling with us, you'll be moving out before dawn."

Mayleen began to question Jesse then, and Ivan's interest strayed to Tory. The smoldering remains of their fire cast the boy's delicate features in high relief and he was again startled by how appealing the young man was. Tory was sitting cross-legged with his hands dropped in his lap. It was scarcely a feminine pose, and yet the grace of the lad's gesture stirred feelings of forbidden desire that caused the geologist a horrible cringe of mental anguish.

Disgusted with himself, he rose carefully and made his way over to the spot where Mayleen had unfurled his bedroll. He then faced the considerable challenge of stretching out without creating any new stress on his badly battered body. He had succeeded in medicating himself with whiskey during the day, and he was relieved to think he would not have to be nearly so cautious about sneaking a drink now that night had fallen.

It took her several minutes of cajoling, but Mayleen finally persuaded Jesse to take a brief walk with her. "I'm worried about Ivan," she confided as they started away from the camp. She pretended to stumble on the uneven ground and then linked her arm through his as though such a move was merely a practical necessity to prevent a fall rather than a thinly disguised excuse to touch him.

"There were tears rolling down his cheeks this afternoon. He's really hurting. Couldn't we stop to rest more often tomorrow?"

Jesse came to an abrupt halt and turned to face her. "No, we couldn't. If he can't keep up, then he'll be left behind. That's all there is to it. Did he ask you to beg me to go easy on him?"

"No, of course not. He'd be mortified if he knew why I asked to speak to you privately." Not one to miss such an opportunity to further her own cause, she snuggled close and spoke in a soft, seductive purr. "We don't have to go back to the camp just yet, do we? I don't really feel like going to sleep."

Jesse grabbed her wrists as she began to unbutton his shirt. "I warned you before not to treat me like one of your paying customers."

Mayleen drew back, but only slightly. "This isn't business. I really like you. We'll be together nearly two weeks. Why don't we use the time to get to know each other better?"

Jesse did not even dignify that question with a response. Instead, he twisted the forward young woman's right arm behind her back and, over her loudly screeched protests, marched her into their camp. "Good night," he uttered between clenched teeth. Too restless now to go to sleep, he walked away intent upon enjoying the solitude of his own company for a while.

Thinking the marshal was answering a call of nature, Tory did not begin to worry about him until he had been gone more than ten minutes. She was seated on her bedroll on the opposite side of the fire from Mayleen and Ivan. The pair was talking in hushed voices, and it again seemed to Tory as though they were arguing, but after paying closer attention, she realized that wasn't the case. The professor was suggesting something—coaxing, wheedling, enticing Mayleen with honeyed whispers while she was repeatedly refusing his request.

Fearing that despite his cuts and bruises Ivan wanted to be intimate with the dark-eyed beauty, Tory got up and started after Jesse. She had readily understood why she had to disguise herself as a young man, but that didn't mean she would look the other way while Ivan and Mayleen carried on. That was too much to ask of any woman, and most especially too much to ask of her!

Jesse heard Tory tramping toward the spot he had chosen to rest. It took no great leap of intuition to tell by the dirt she was kicking up that she was angry about something. He was too tired to deal with her that night and rose so quickly from the comfortable mound where he had been sitting that he frightened her badly. She recognized his silhouette against

109

the moon and caught herself before her scream left her throat, but he felt certain she was still shaken.

"I'm sorry," he whispered. "I heard you coming and I should have called out to you. What's wrong? Do they need me back at the camp?"

"No, they seem to be entertaining themselves," Tory explained with an exasperated sigh. "But I didn't have to sit there and watch."

"Just what do you mean by 'entertaining themselves'?"

"Use your imagination," Tory snapped.

"Really?" Jesse found it difficult to believe Ivan felt up to what Tory seemed to be describing. "I thought the professor was too sore to have any amorous thoughts."

"Apparently not."

Jesse did not know which was more amusing—Ivan's interest in romancing Mayleen or Tory's disgust. "Let's just give them a little privacy then and by the time we go back, they'll have gotten it out of their systems." He took her hand and guided her back to the comfortable spot he had found. "Just sit here with me a while. I'll speak to Ivan and Mayleen tomorrow about being more discreet."

Anxious for a chance to talk with him, Tory made herself comfortable. Rather than taking a place at her side as she had expected, however, Jesse sank down behind her, stretched his legs out on either side of hers, then slipped his hands around her waist and pulled her back against his chest.

"Marshal!" she protested vehemently, but his motions had been too swift for her to leap to her feet and escape his grasp. "Let me go!"

"Hush," Jesse scolded. "I just want to hold you a while. And why can't you remember not to call me Marshal? Jesse will do just fine."

Certain he was about to begin pawing her, Tory held her breath, but the marshal simply kept her pressed snugly against him and left his hands on her waist. She hated being held so tightly, for it was too strong a reminder of the way Paul Stafford had prevented her from escaping his loathsome touch.

110

"I can't breathe," she finally whispered.

"Sorry." Jesse relaxed his hold her on slightly. "Is that better?"

"Much, but I'd rather you let me go completely. We can talk without your being wrapped around me like a blanket."

"No, we can't," Jesse argued. "This is too nice." He gave her a fond squeeze, but relaxed again so as not to press his luck. When she did not struggle to break free, Jesse removed her hat and pulled off her scarf. He found her hairpins, and released a flowing cascade of curls. He rubbed his cheek against the silken strands and gave a contented sigh that was dangerously close to a moan.

"God, but you feel good."

"Damn it, Marshal! I may be your prisoner, but I'm not your whore. Why don't you go back to camp and take turns enjoying Mayleen's favors? She seems eager to accommodate you."

"That she is, but I happen to like long-legged blondes rather than petite brunettes. Now try and remember not to call me Marshal."

Tory tilted her head and combed her hair with her fingers in a futile attempt to keep him from nuzzling her nape, but Jesse just chuckled, hugged her more tightly, and began to kiss her earlobe. "Mr. Kessler, please!"

That name confused Jesse sufficiently to make him draw back a minute, but then he realized the sheriff had introduced him as Marshal Kessler and Mayleen had called him Jesse, so those were the only two names she knew him by. He weighed the advisability of revealing the truth, but decided he would save himself a lot of grief if he waited until they were in Mexico rather than within a few hours' ride of a town where she could hide from him as well as Eldrin Stafford indefinitely.

"Jesse," he whispered against her ear. "Please call me Jesse."

The warmth of his breath sent tremors down Tory's spine, but they were caused by fear, not desire. Rather than his affectionate warmth, she felt only the strength of his well-muscled frame and was terrified by how easily he could crush the life from her, or worse, steal her very soul and leave her among the living.

"When are you going to tell Mayleen and Ivan the truth about me?" she asked in an attempt to distract him.

Jesse had longed to hear her speak his name with something approaching affection and he was badly disappointed by her response. "Never, if it's possible. It's none of their business."

"You can't be serious!" Tory argued. "They think they're escaping their problems by going with you to El Paso. They don't have any idea how much trouble I'm in. Would they be so eager to travel with us if they knew you were supposed to have taken me to Prescott and why? What if while you're sitting here hugging me, Eldrin and his men are just over the last rise? What if they walk into our camp in the morning? They'll shoot everyone, not just me. That's too important a secret to keep. Ivan and Mayleen ought to know the risk they're taking traveling with us. They're in far more danger than they realize."

And so are you, Jesse thought but did not admit aloud. It disturbed him to think she was as much in the dark about his circumstance as Mayleen and Ivan, but it did not prompt him to confide in her. "Hey, aren't you the one who suggested that since we all had good reasons for leaving Tucson, we ought to go together?"

Embarrassed by that reminder, Tory made no attempt to deny it. "Yes, I did, but that was before I had a whole day to think about it. There might be two angry miners after Ivan, and maybe someone from the Silver Spur looking for Mayleen, but they scarcely compare to Eldrin Stafford. He'll be out for more than blood and it isn't fair not to warn Ivan and Mayleen what they can expect if he finds us."

"He won't," Jesse vowed.

"But you could feel him coming before. If he was close outside Tucson, he can't be far behind now."

Unwilling to explain that what he had felt might very well have been whoever was tracking *him* rather than *her,* Jesse drew in a deep breath and let it out slowly. That night he felt only the peaceful calm of the desert and he did not want to

112

think about being relentlessly pursued until he was cornered and killed. His hold on the slender blonde tightened once more and he closed his eyes and let his mind fill with a magical vision of what it would be like to make love to her right there in the moonlight.

"Kiss me," he ordered gruffly.

Fearing that was but the first of a series of requests for more than she would ever give, Tory made a desperate attempt to elude him, but again failed. He was too strong and had her caught not only in his arms, but also used his legs to prevent her from getting away.

"Go to hell!" she cursed.

"If I end up in hell, my darling, you'll be there with me," Jesse predicted darkly, and forcing her to turn so her back was wedged against his bent knee, he captured her in a confining embrace. "Kiss me," he insisted again, "and I'll let you go."

"I'd rather kiss a gila monster!"

"That's no way to treat me after all I've done for you," Jesse reminded her. "I could still take a detour through Prescott. In fact, I just may do it if you don't give me a kiss."

With that gruesome threat, Tory could actually feel the hangman's noose tightening around her neck. Feeling as though she was truly being strangled, a painful gasp escaped her throat as she shrank away from Jesse. Stunned that he would say such a dreadful thing, she realized he was no better than Paul Stafford. Rather than violently raping her, he was going to use hideous threats and intimidation to force her to submit to him. That would really be no different from rape, she agonized. It would be the very same horrible humiliation all over again. Unable to bear the anguish of that possibility, she began to sob, and her shoulders shook like a brokenhearted child.

"Tory?" Jesse had not meant to frighten her, but it was obvious now that his tactless request for a kiss had completely unnerved her. He brushed her hair away from her face and tried to kiss away her tears, but his affection only served to upset her all the more. He began to rock her then, and tried to take back his insensitive threat with sweet

113

promises to guard her life with his own. A full five minutes passed before she seemed to be listening to him and, encouraged, he repeated his effusive apology.

"I don't know what got into me," he said. "I just wanted you to kiss me so badly, I tried something I felt sure would work. It was a stupid thing to say, though, because I didn't mean it. I won't ever let anyone hurt you. Not ever, and you've nothing to fear from me."

Tory gradually relaxed in his arms. This time when Jesse began to kiss away her tears she did not object, but she did not respond, either. She just sat stiff in his arms and waited for him to stop. When his lips brushed hers, she turned away to avoid his kiss and he did not try again. He did not release her, either. He kept her cuddled against his chest and rested his cheek against her temple. It was a loving pose, but she was still too frightened to draw comfort from it.

"I want to go back to the camp," she finally found the courage to demand.

"I'm not ready to let you go." Jesse doubted he would ever want to release her. He longed to just go right on sitting there until dawn. It had never felt so completely natural to embrace any other woman and he knew he would be overcome with loneliness the instant he released her. He had mistakenly believed he had learned all there was to know about being lonely in prison, but he ached for Tory's acceptance with a far more powerful need. He might have lied to her about his name and about being a marshal, but he had been telling the truth about protecting her.

"You needn't be afraid of me, Tory," he promised again, but when she still did not seem to be reassured, he gave up the effort as lost for the time being. Reluctantly he got to his feet and helped her up, but she immediately broke free and, after grabbing up her scarf and hat, ran back toward their camp.

Jesse returned far more slowly. With every step he cursed the four years he had wasted in prison. They had made him so anxious for a feminine touch, he had terrified the most appealing young woman he had ever met. She would not even speak his first name let alone return his kiss, but he could not bear to think that she never would.

"Patience!" he scolded under his breath, but where Tory Crandell was concerned, he just did not have any.

Ivan was asleep by the time Tory returned to camp, but Mayleen was too upset to rest as peacefully. Her bedroll was next to Ivan's and she lay inches from his side, but there was no comfort to be drawn from his nearness. He wanted her to go into Benson for him. He had begged her to make up any excuse that would allow her to go into town and buy whiskey, but she had refused. Despite her best efforts to endear herself to Jesse, the tall Texan barely tolerated her, and she knew that if he caught Ivan with whiskey he would leave them both stranded with neither destination nor home to which to return. That was not a risk she would take for Ivan, or anyone else for that matter.

Mayleen rose up slightly as Jesse approached the camp. He and Tory had certainly taken their time coming back, and she struggled to repress the crude images of what they had been doing. When Jesse stretched out closer to Tory than she thought two men ought to sleep, she lay back down and looked away. It was plain why Jesse was immune to her feminine charms when other men found them so appealing but, sadly, Mayleen knew she had no other resources.

In spite of the lack of affinity between Jesse and her, she was determined to go to El Paso and see Gerry. Maybe Jesse was wrong about his stepbrother. Maybe something beyond Gerry's control had prevented him from coming back to her. Perhaps he had been badly injured in a mishap at his ranch or had become seriously ill. Had he been too proud to send for her? Jesse had never seen the warm glow in Gerry's eyes when he had professed his love for her. He had not heard any of Gerry's beautifully worded promises of the life they would share. Despite what she had told Jesse, she had never really lost hope that Gerry would return for her.

The huge tears that filled her eyes whenever she remembered Gerry came once again and she hurriedly wiped them away. It would do no more good to cry over her lost love that night than on any other, but she knew she would miss him as long as she lived. She had to get to El Paso, she just had to, and she was not going to let Ivan's incessant cravings for whiskey get in her way. He was going to have to get sober and stay that way just as he had promised. That was all there was to it.

Luke Bernay stopped in Benson, but found no one who had seen anyone matching Jesse or Tory's description or recalled any strangers riding a dappled-gray horse, and bays were too common to cause notice. Giving up the attempt to find someone with information on the fugitives, he treated himself to another fine meal and debated his next move.

There was more than one way to reach El Paso. He could swing north and follow the Butterfield Stage route through New Mexico, or head south and approach El Paso through Mexico. Knowing that escaped convicts weren't fond of company, Luke tended to think Jesse would prefer the Mexican route through vast stretches of unoccupied territory. It would be a more difficult journey, but that would not deter a wanted man.

Luke also had another reason for heading south. There had been talk lately of trouble on the White Mountain Apache reservation at San Carlos. Luke would just as soon stay as far away as possible from any Indians who might be tempted to leave their reservation and cause grief to travelers. The mere possibility of an Apache uprising was enough to send a wise man into hiding, and Luke prided himself on being clever.

As he lingered over a second piece of apple pie, he began to plan his trip south through Tombstone and Bisbee. Even if he did not overtake Jesse Lambert before he reached the Mexican border, he was reasonably certain of reaching El Paso without having to shoot his way out of an Apache ambush. He had been in the Arizona Territory for nearly twenty years. The Apaches had had ample opportunity to kill him long before this and he sure as hell was not going to provide them with another.

116

Tad MacDonald and his men also reached Benson that day. As ordered, Manuel Ochoa had made some sketches of Tory Crandell, and he and his companions showed them around town. They gathered a great many appreciative whistles, hoots, and obscene comments, but the informal posse had nothing tangible to show for their trouble.

The seven men had made themselves at home at a table near the window of the mining town's rowdiest saloon when Tad saw Luke Bernay enter the dry-goods store across the street. He choked on his beer, but managed to sit up in his chair and pound on the table to get his men's attention.

"That little tracker from Yuma just strolled into the store across the way. What a piece of luck. This is going to work just as I'd planned. The great Luke Bernay can wear himself out tracking Tory and her convict, while all we have to do is follow him. Come on, let's be ready to go when he leaves town."

Tad's suggestion was greeted with the enthusiasm he had expected and half an hour later when Luke Bernay rode out of Benson, Tad MacDonald and his men were not far behind.

The second day of their journey, Jesse rode beside Tory in a conscious effort to make her more comfortable around him. If she enjoyed his company, she gave no indication of it, but he took every opportunity to admire the elegance of her profile and easy grace in the saddle. She rode her new mount with the same casual aplomb she had ridden the pinto. He was prompted to compliment her poise, and not simply for something to say.

"You're an excellent rider. I wish Mayleen had your skill. It doesn't look like she's been on a horse in years. As for Ivan, well, he's in too much pain to be able to tell if he's much of a horseman or not."

Disconcerted by Jesse's charming smile, Tory gave no more than a nod to acknowledge his compliment before focusing her attention on the trail. "I mentioned that I used to accompany my father when he gathered specimens. Riding comes easily to me and I've always enjoyed it."

Recalling her comments about her parents, Jesse encouraged her to say more about him. "It's a shame your father's work was lost."

"It was a small tragedy compared to his death."

"Well, yes, of course, but you said that you had hoped to complete his work and—"

This time Tory turned so that she could look Jesse straight in the eye. "It really isn't necessary for you to keep me entertained, Marshal. I'm certain we'll make better time if we pay closer attention to where we're going anyway."

While that was undoubtedly true, Jesse was sick of being addressed by a title he had not earned. He reached over and grabbed Tory's wrist to be certain she understood how deeply he meant what he said. "Don't ever refer to me as 'Marshal' again. Call me Jesse, or don't speak to me at all!" With that emphatically voiced order, the Texan gave up the effort to keep her amused and urged his dappled-gray gelding to a faster pace to again station himself ahead of his party. He did not glance over his shoulder at her once, but he hoped Tory found his back more interesting to view than the sparse vegetation of the desert terrain ahead.

Then he reminded himself that she undoubtedly knew the names of every plant they passed. Whether it was a yucca blooming with delicate flowers, a magestic saguaro with its prickly arms outstretched toward the heavens, a graceful ocotillo whose wandlike branches were covered with thorns, or the prickly pear with its abundant fruit, she would know them all.

There were probably a thousand other desert plants he had never bothered to notice, let alone seek to name. He was briefly tempted to ask her to teach him those he did not know when it occurred to him that she would see right through his ploy and repeat her demand to be left alone. How he wished that he could! But he was not fool enough to think that he could ever ignore a woman he wanted so badly.

* * *

By carefully measuring his swallows, Ivan made the bottle of whiskey last until the afternoon. Certain that Jesse's attention was focused on the trail ahead, the aching geologist then hurled away the empty container. Even that easy gesture caused him nearly unbearable agony.

"You've got to help me," he implored Mayleen. "We'll be stopping near Tombstone soon. You've got to go into town and buy me some more whiskey. I won't be able to stand the pain if you don't."

Ivan's features were still so badly bruised that she could readily appreciate how the rest of his slender body must look, but she still wanted no part of his scheme. "Absolutely not. If you're hurting so bad, then go into Tombstone and see a doctor. That would do you far more good than continuing to drink when you promised Jesse you'd quit."

"A doctor?" Ivan whispered softly, and then seizing upon the idea, he quickly agreed. He would be happy to go see a doctor. It was a reasonable excuse to get into town and that was all he needed, just the opportunity to replenish his supply of liquor.

"You're right, Mayleen honey, what I need is a doctor. Help me convince Jesse to let me go into Tombstone. Will you do that much, please? A doctor will wrap my ribs and then I'm sure I wouldn't feel nearly so bad as I do right now."

Not totally unsympathetic to his plight, Mayleen agreed after a brief pause. "All right, Ivan, I'll do my best to talk Jesse into letting you go into Tombstone, but I can't guarantee that he'll allow it."

"You just try, honey, that's all I ask." Ivan hung his head as though the misery that filled his body was about to kill him. He did not dare look up and let Mayleen see his smile, but the thought of getting a drink in his hands made him so happy that for a long while he did not feel any pain.

Chapter 8

Carrying out his original plan to stop for the night near Tombstone, Jesse kept his companions riding until they were within sight of the rowdy silver boomtown on Goose Flat Mesa. Again he took the precaution of setting up camp well away from the road, but he did not relax his guard even then. There were still a couple of hours of daylight left, which meant they could all be recognized if another traveler strayed near. He kept a watchful eye to see that none did as he unsaddled the handsome dappled-gray gelding he had yet to name.

Ivan spared himself the torture of dismounting as he approached Jesse. "I need to go into Tombstone," he begged in an agonized whisper. "There's a doctor there who's had plenty of experience tending men who've been in fights. I want him to wrap my ribs. It's not that I can't take the pain, but they'll heal a lot faster if I get the proper care."

The professor had been so thoroughly miserable the last two days that Jesse had no reason to doubt that his desire to seek medical attention was sincere. "Where's the mine that your disgruntled clients own?" he asked.

"It's just outside Benson," Ivan explained, "so there's no danger I'll run into them. I don't plan to wander around and sightsee. I'll just have Dr. Goodfellow do whatever he can for my ribs and come right back."

While Jesse hated to refuse the clearly suffering professor's request, he was not about to let Ivan take advantage

121

of him. "I'm sure you haven't forgotten what I said about liquor. If you stop to have a drink, don't bother coming back. I won't allow you to stay."

Because Jesse had yet to catch him drinking, Ivan was confident he could get away with it indefinitely. The Texan was certainly strict, but too preoccupied with his attractive young friend to keep close track of his other companions. Ivan did his best to smile despite the pain it caused his swollen lips. "I've already agreed to your conditions, Jesse. You don't have to keep repeating them."

Unable to trust Ivan to stay out of trouble if he went into Tombstone alone, Mayleen hurriedly rushed to his side. "I'll go along with you, Professor. We ought to have some spices to give our meals more flavor. Maybe I can get a few eggs for breakfast, and some fresh fruit would be good if there is any. Is there anything you and Tory need, Jesse?"

Jesse was tempted to forbid the talkative young woman a trip into town, but the prospect of spending some time alone with Tory was so inviting he sent the attractive fugitive a questioning glance. "If there's something you need, Tory, I'll give Mayleen the money to buy it," he offered.

Tory shook her head, then changed her mind. "Peppermint candy?"

Jesse laughed, but, as promised, he supplied Mayleen with several coins to buy some. He busied himself setting up camp as the two left, but his mind was focused squarely on how to impress Tory more favorably than he had in the past. He knew she had been through one of the worst experiences a woman could ever face, but he did not want her to spend the rest of her life dwelling on that tragedy.

Then a truly awful possibility occurred to him and he completely lost interest in making camp. In a valiant attempt to be tactful, he cleared his throat and concentrated on speaking without stammering. "How long ago did Paul die?"

Tory had been gathering stones to encircle a fire. Astonished by the unexpectedly painful question, she lost her hold on the rock in her grasp. As it fell, the fingertips of her right hand were crushed between it and the stone she had

122

just put in place. Tears flooded her eyes and she shook her hand in a vain attempt to defuse the sudden burst of pain. She rose, clumsily opened her canteen, and poured cool water over her hand.

"It was six weeks ago," she called out in a choked sob.

Certain that he had inadvertently caused her unfortunate mishap, Jesse sprinted across the short distance that separated them. He reached for Tory's injured hand and examined it with a sure yet gentle touch. The skin of her knuckles was scraped and bruised, but no bones were broken. Grateful she had escaped serious harm, he raised her throbbing fingers to his lips.

"This was my fault," he apologized. "I shouldn't have startled you."

To her absolute horror, Jesse did not simply apply light kisses the way a mother would to reassure an injured child. Instead, he looked her straight in the eye and caressed her aching fingertips with his tongue and lips as though her flesh were positively delicious. She tried to yank her hand free, but he responded by tightening his hold on her wrist, and sucked her index finger into his mouth.

Although alarmed by the fact he would take such a shocking liberty, Tory felt her face flood with the heat of a bright blush which rapidly spread clear to her toes. Jesse's mouth was warm, his lavish kiss adoring, and she could not tear her gaze from his when he was looking at her with an intensity meant to touch her very soul. She could scarcely draw a breath, and when she began to weave slightly, Jesse brought his seductive gesture to an end and grabbed for her shoulders.

"Are you all right?" he asked in an anxious rush.

Tory shook her head and he guided her over to her bedroll and eased her to the ground. In the next instant he seated himself beside her and pulled her across his lap. He tossed her hat aside and untied her scarf to free her sun-streaked curls. He started to rub her back, then remembered the still-healing scars and hugged her instead.

"I'm so worried about you," he revealed in a husky

whisper. "You don't deserve all the awful things that have happened to you."

It was the clear ring of sincerity in his deep voice that kept Tory from struggling to break free. She had lost track of how many times he had pulled her into his arms, but he had never done more than simply hold her snuggled against him. He had not shaved since they had left Tucson, but the roughness of his beard against her cheek wasn't unpleasant. She closed her eyes and tried to be reassured rather than frightened by his nearness and strength. She was not altogether successful, but at least the horrible panic that had seized her the first time he had gathered her into his arms was gone.

"What suddenly made you curious about Paul?" she asked when she grew calm enough to speak.

Jesse coughed, cleared his throat, coughed a couple more times, and then tried to find the courage to ask what he really wanted to know. "I know this is a real personal question, and I apologize for that. I wouldn't ask it if it weren't important. I just wondered if enough time had passed for you to know whether or not, well . . ." He paused then, certain he was going about this all wrong. "I just wondered if you knew whether or not you were carrying his child."

Sickened that he could even imagine such a devastating possibility, Tory looked off toward the limestone-covered hills. "They don't sentence pregnant women to hang here, Marshal. Didn't you know that?"

"*Jesse*," he reminded her, but knowing he had handled his question very poorly he could not be cross about her repeated failure to use his first name. "No, I didn't. I guess the subject just never came up. Anyway, I'm glad to hear it. I was just worried about you is all."

"You certainly take your responsibilities seriously, don't you?"

"You're not a responsibility, Tory," he objected immediately. "You never have been."

"How can you say that?"

Part of Jesse longed to tell Tory the truth, but he dared not take the risk while it was still so likely that she would choose

124

to go her own way without him. She had been privy to enough conversations about Gerry to merit hearing the truth about his stepbrother, though, so he decided to begin with him. It might enable him to win her sympathy, if not the respect he hoped to receive.

"I was glad Ivan and Mayleen needed to go into Tombstone because I wanted a chance to talk with you. Maybe then you'll see why I'm so anxious to get to El Paso, even if you don't understand why I'm taking you along."

Intrigued, Tory turned toward him slightly, prompting Jesse to adjust both their poses for comfort's sake. She had not expected to be able to tolerate a man's touch ever again, but she was gradually becoming accustomed to Jesse's. That was a surprising realization, but she doubted she would ever want to accept his boisterous brand of affection.

Paul Stafford had put a violent end to her romantic illusions. He had not only stolen her innocence, but dashed her hopes for a happy life with a husband and children as well. Even if she were to be hanged, Paul had already killed her. Her hand hurt, but that discomfort did not compare to the painful ache that never left her heart.

She looked up at Jesse. "I've heard enough to know you're going after your stepbrother. If he robbed a stage and framed you for the crime, then I don't blame you."

"Thanks. It's nice to have you on my side." When Tory glanced away as though she were embarrassed by his praise, he could not help but be amused. Distracted only a moment, he quickly gathered his thoughts and began his story. "My mother died in 1861. I was eleven. I think my father would have joined the Confederacy and thrown his life away in the war if he hadn't had me to raise. He was too fine a man to abandon me, though. After the war he married Zina Chambers, a young widow, whose husband had been killed defending the southern cause. Her son, Gerry, was ten and I was fifteen.

"I wasn't all that pleased about my father getting married again, but I was polite to Zina and I tried to be a proper older brother to Gerry. Trouble was, he wouldn't meet me

125

halfway. He was always jealous and demanding. Finally I gave up trying to be his friend and avoided him whenever I could. That tactic worked fairly well until my father died. I was twenty-two then and able to take over the running of our ranch, but at seventeen, Gerry was an arrogant hothead who was only old enough to cause trouble.

"We barely tolerated each other until five years ago when Gerry decided he wanted to come to Arizona. My father had left half the ranch to me and half to Zina and Gerry, so money was never his problem. He always had plenty, and if he wanted to invest in a silver mine, then there was no talking him out of it. Zina begged me to go with him, and because Gerry's thoughtless behavior had caused her so much needless anguish, I agreed.

"Once we got to Tucson, Gerry quickly learned that prospecting entailed much harder work than he was willing to do so he just invested in other men's attempts to strike it rich. Unfortunately, none of his partners was any more ambitious than he was and none of their claims proved profitable. Gerry didn't really seem to care, though. He was too busy spending his time gambling, drinking and, well . . . amusing Mayleen to worry about business."

"And what were you doing?" Tory asked without thinking. Then, certain she should have kept her curiosity to herself rather than ask such an impertinent question, she grew flustered. "No, you needn't tell me. It's none of my business."

Even knowing how badly she would cringe, Jesse could not resist the temptation to brush her cheek with a kiss and did so. He then gave her a teasing squeeze. "I was doing the same thing I'd done in Texas—establishing markets for our beef. The mining towns were growing so fast that beef was in short supply and I arranged for several cattle drives which proved to be extremely profitable. Then one day I was arrested for robbing a stage . . ."

Jesse paused then, and Tory shrank back as the sparkling blue of his eyes began to burn with a fierce light. "Apparently Gerry was unwilling to return to Texas without having made the fortune in silver he had boasted he'd find. He had always fared poorly when compared to me and fixed it so he would be the only one going home. He and Conrad Werner robbed the stage, hid most of the money in my room, and then left an anonymous note suggesting the sheriff search it. The man did, and nothing I said after that mattered.

"Gerry's timing was perfect. I'd been returning from Benson when the robbery occurred. I'd just been riding along minding my own business on the very same road the stage used, and I had no one to vouch for my innocence. Gerry, as you've heard, had Mayleen. I didn't want to believe he had done it, but when I was sentenced to prison, he broke into the widest grin I've ever seen. That's when I realized just how much he'd always hated me. I would have killed him had I been able to get to him, but I was hustled right off out of the courtroom and off to prison before I could even call his name."

"You spent four years in prison before becoming a marshal?"

Jesse nodded rather than elaborate on that question. "You know what being in jail is like. Prison is a thousand times worse and four years is an eternity."

"Especially to an innocent man," Tory pointed out.

Inordinately pleased by that bit of sympathy, Jesse rested his head against hers. He knew he ought to confess he was a fugitive, but he simply could not bring himself to do so, not when she felt so incredibly good in his arms. All he really wanted to do was make love to her, and knowing she would never allow that, he eased her off his lap and rose to his feet.

"Why don't you just rest," he suggested. "I'll see to the camp and get dinner started."

"Thank you," Tory murmured softly.

"For what?"

"For being so nice to me."

Jesse continued to back away. "I just treat you the way a gentleman ought to treat a lady."

Sorry to have embarrassed him, Tory stretched out on her stomach and rested her cheek on her arm. She pretended to be napping, but she watched him through the veil of her lashes, unobserved, for a very long while.

Mayleen was more than merely apprehensive about visiting Tombstone. As they entered the prosperous mining town, she could not help but recall the day she had ridden into Tucson with Tom Pankow, a man she ought to have known would plunge her neck-deep in trouble.

She had been all of seventeen that summer, and so eager to leave Nogales that she had fled home with the first handsome stranger who had paid any attention to her. She had been too skinny and awkward to arouse any interest in the young men she had grown up with, but Tom had considered himself a man of vision and had praised her as a budding beauty.

He had stood her in front of the hazy mirror in his rented room and called her untamed curls a magnificent ebony mane, her eyes so delicious a brown they rivaled luscious chocolates, and her smile more radiant than a summer sunrise. Now she was ashamed of how eagerly she had lapped up his effusive praise. When he had begun to unbutton her faded dress, she had leaned into his caress the way a contented cat rubs against her master. She had not really understood what making love was all about, but Tom had initiated her into that ageless rite so smoothly that she had yielded up her virginity without a moment's thought to the consequences.

They had proven to be excruciatingly painful consequences, too. She had learned that fast when Tom had been caught cheating at cards and had fled Tucson even faster than he had left Nogales. Only this time he had gone alone, without even telling her good-bye. She had had far too much pride to go back home where her mother would have beaten her senseless for her stupidity and no respectable man would ever have offered marriage. Instead, she had applied what Tom had taught her about pleasing men, gone to work at the Silver Spur, and had taken care of herself ever since.

While this was her first visit to Tombstone, she knew Allen

Street by its reputation. The south side of the mining town's main thoroughfare was the site of respectable stores and businesses. Already tired of the meager meals they had shared along the trail, she cast a longing glance toward the restaurants, but she knew they dared not remain in town long enough to sample their fare. The north side of Allen Street was home to saloons and bawdy houses of every description. Mayleen would have shied away from that side of the street, but Ivan headed straight for the Crystal Palace Saloon.

"Now don't get all excited," he cajoled. "Dr. Goodfellow's office is on the second floor. Come on, we'll ride around to the rear where the entrance is."

Mayleen had already had her mouth open to object, but fell silent when she glanced up and saw Dr. Goodfellow's name painted on the window. A piano player with more muscle than talent was pounding out a tune she recognized from the Silver Spur, but rather than hum along, she tried not to listen as they circled the Crystal Palace. She helped Ivan dismount, and then slowly climbed the stairs by his side. That late in the afternoon, it was not unusual that they found the doctor free, and Mayleen sat down in the waiting room while he examined Ivan.

She had never gotten into the habit of reading the *Citizen* in Tucson, but the *Epitaph* was laying on a table by her chair and she picked it up rather than stare at the wall. The headline blared out the news of trouble among the Apaches, and after overcoming a wave of terror, her lips moved in a silent recitation as she read the article describing the widening influence of a young medicine man.

Noch-ay-del-klinne, who was also called The Dreamer, was reportedly preaching the resurrection of the dead to the Coyotero, or White Mountain Apaches. Inspired by his impassioned promises to raise the great chiefs Diablo and Eskiole, his disciples were eagerly carrying out his instructions and performing a series of ghost dances which were drawing increasingly large numbers of participants.

Mayleen had heard tales of the Apache all her life and

believed them to be a violent and cruel people who had once tortured their captives before putting them to a hideous death. That a medicine man would attempt to raise the dead did not surprise her, but the possibility that he might actually be able to accomplish such a gruesome feat was terrifying. She studied the map accompanying the article, and noting the White Mountain reservation at San Carlos was well north of Tombstone, she began to breathe easier. Still, renegades respected no borders, and some of The Dreamer's more ardent followers might have left their strictly regulated reservation and be traveling south at that very moment.

"That's all we need," she murmured to herself, "Apaches bent on raising the dead." When Dr. Goodfellow and Ivan stepped out of his office she jumped in fright, then caught herself and rose to her feet with ladylike grace.

Dr. George Goodfellow had short dark hair neatly parted in the middle and a bushy mustache. While not a particularly handsome man, he was widely respected for his medical talent. He favored Mayleen with a friendly smile as he explained he had done what he could for Ivan.

"You ought to just take him home and put him to bed, ma'am, but the professor tells me that's not possible."

Anxious to be on their way, Mayleen started edging toward the door. "No, I'm afraid it isn't." She was dressed in a simple white blouse and dark-blue split skirt. With her hair tied at her nape and tucked up under her hat, she hoped she resembled a respectable woman rather than one of the heavily painted girls who worked downstairs at the Crystal Palace. The doctor's smile seemed genuine, and she relaxed slightly.

"We appreciate your seeing Ivan. He's been in a lot of pain."

"Please, don't even mention the word pain around me," Ivan scolded. He had already paid the physician, and after bidding him good-bye, he slipped his arm around Mayleen's waist and escorted her down the stairs. "There's a drygoods store right across the way. I saw it out the window. We might as well leave our horses here while we take care of

130

our shopping."

Mayleen studied Ivan's expression closely. The pain of his injuries was still plainly etched on his features, and she did not want to tire him needlessly. "Why don't you just sit down here on the steps and rest while I go into the store?"

"Will you buy me some whiskey?"

Mayleen shook her head emphatically. "Of course not."

"Then I'll have to do my own shopping. Don't give me any more arguments, Mayleen. If Jesse hasn't caught me drinking yet, then he won't tonight, tomorrow, or ever. I promised you I'd not get drunk, but I need some spirits to keep myself going. You can't begrudge me that. You can see how pitiful I look, but you can't even come close to imagining how ghastly I feel. I've got to have the whiskey, Mayleen, or I won't be able to go any farther. Are you willing to give up your hopes of seeing Gerry again to stay here in Tombstone with me?"

"You're threatening me again, Ivan Carrows, and I don't like that one bit." Mayleen rested her hands on her hips as she tried to decide what to do. "In the first place, you can't stay here because Calvin and Arnold are sure to hear about it. Getting out of the Arizona Territory is as important to you as it is to me. Don't try and pretend that it isn't.

"Now from what I just read in the *Epitaph*, there's likely to be trouble with the Apaches on the White Mountain Reservation. If there is, they'll head straight for the Sierra Madre Mountains in Mexico because that's always been their favorite place to hide. Now you might think you can continue to fool Jesse, and maybe you can, but do you want to take on a band of Apaches without a clear head?"

The mention of Indian trouble frightened Ivan as badly as it had Mayleen. He had thought all the Apaches had been peaceably settled on reservations, but if they were about to start raising hell, as they had in years past, he wanted no part of it, drunk or sober.

"I can't take on anyone feeling the way I do," he reminded her. Pretending to give in, he settled himself down on the bottom step. "You go on and do the shopping. I'll just sit

131

here and moan."

"Promise me you won't go into the Crystal Palace and start drinking," Mayleen insisted.

"Sure, I promise," Ivan mumbled as he attempted to find a comfortable position and failed. No matter how he positioned his arms and legs, something hurt, and badly.

Feeling sorry for the badly bruised man, Mayleen bent down and placed a kiss on his cheek. "I'll hurry. We have to get back to camp before dark or I'll never find it."

"Don't worry," Ivan assured her. "I know exactly where it is." To avoid causing himself any additional pain, he sat very still until she had had enough time to cross Allen Street and enter the store, then he struggled to pull himself upright. He went back upstairs to Dr. Goodfellow's office and talked him out of some empty medicine bottles. He then bought some whiskey from the Crystal Palace, filled the innocent-looking bottles and shoved them into the bottom of his saddlebags.

It sorely tested his resolve not to sample the liquor right there, but despite the success he had had fooling Jesse for the last two days, he did not want to risk being caught drinking now. He prided himself on his self-control. He was no drunkard. He might imbibe more than he should, but that did not mean he was a drunkard. When Mayleen returned with her purchases, she found him seated exactly where she had left him. He tried to greet her with a smile, and she came to help him to his feet.

"See," he bragged proudly. "I'm still sober." He would stay that way until after dark when the "medicine" he had obtained would help him ease the pain and get to sleep. That was all he wanted, just to get ahead of the pain and sleep.

Araña was tall and well-built, but he worshiped the short, slender Noch-ay-del-klinne. After being among those corraled on the reservation like cattle awaiting slaughter, Araña, like most of the Apache, was sick of the white man's abuse and did not question the mystical Dreamer's promises.

132

With the return of the great Coyotero chiefs, the Apache would again rule the land they had been free to roam for centuries before the white man had arrogantly announced that what they called the vast Arizona Territory was theirs to rule.

Among the first braves to join in the dances, Araña had swayed for countless hours as the beat of drums had echoed the pounding rhythm of his heart. He believed in the power of the Ghost Dance as deeply as he believed in Noch-ay-del-klinne, but after several weeks Diablo and Eskiole had yet to reappear. The Dreamer now said the departed chiefs would not come as long as the white man existed on their lands. He called for all of their accursed kind to be put to death before the corn was ripe.

Knowing the Army would soon learn of the severity of the threat posed by The Dreamer, Araña was sure the military would use the mystic's fiery words as an excuse to arrest him. The Ghost Dances fueled the fury in the Apaches' hearts, but Araña was capable of coldly logical thought as well. If The Dreamer wanted the white men swept from the land, then he was eager to take up that challenge. Rather than dancing, he would do what an Apache warrior was born to do: he would make war.

That very night he spoke to his friends. A slow smile lit the face of each one. Sick of having no work, of being cheated by corrupt Indian Bureau officials, of having meager rations that too often failed to fill their bellies, they instantly rallied to his cry for vengeance. The Dreamer had said now was the time, and Araña and more than a dozen other young braves fled the reservation eager to bring the medicine man's magical visions into reality no matter how harsh the method.

Jesse was surprised, but very pleasantly so when Ivan returned to camp in the same feeble, but sober condition in which he had left. The spices and herbs Mayleen had purchased gave the pot of beans Jesse had had simmering a greatly enhanced taste, and he complimented her cooking more than once as he ate. She had found a few oranges, and they peeled them and ate them with childlike delight. Their journey had barely begun and already they were acting like an orange was a rare treat. After the monotony of prison food, Jesse could readily appreciate something so sweet, but he chuckled at his companions as though he was used to far finer meals than the one they had just shared.

Mayleen had been so worried about getting Ivan back to camp that she did not remember the newspaper article about the Apaches until they were preparing to go to sleep. She then summarized it quickly. "I feel like a fool now," she apologized. "I should have stocked up on ammunition while I had the chance."

"You can go into Bisbee tomorrow," Jesse reminded her, "but I don't think you need to worry. The White Mountain Reservation must be a hundred miles north of here, and if all the Indians are doing is dancing, I doubt we'll be attacked on the trail."

Ivan was as badly troubled by Mayleen's report as he had been the first time he had heard it, and felt he had something valuable to contribute to the discussion. "There was an Apache chief named Nana, who was raiding in New Mexico until he was caught recently. I heard he and his band could travel seventy miles in a single day. That means the White Mountain Reservation isn't nearly as far away as it sounds."

Disgusted that Ivan would frighten the women, or the one woman he knew to be among them, Jesse drew himself up to his full height. "Haven't you got enough on your mind without worrying about renegade Indians? Come on, let's get some sleep, then tomorrow we can try to come close to covering seventy miles ourselves. That way we'll be far ahead of any Indians out looking for mischief."

Tory kept still until she and Jesse had stretched out on their bedrolls. Then she spoke in an anxious whisper. "You were worried about renegades when we left Cactus Springs. Are you just trying to keep Mayleen and Ivan from getting scared?"

Jesse reached for her hand in the darkness and brought it

to his lips. "I've gotten us this far, Tory. An Indian or two won't prevent us from reaching El Paso. Now either give me a kiss or go to sleep. Which is it to be?"

"You already know the answer to that one." She had almost called him Marshal again, but caught herself at the last minute. "Good night, Jesse," she said instead. He laughed as she withdrew her hand and turned her back to him, but she was in no mood for his teasing. Ever since her father's death bad luck had dogged her steps and she was desperately afraid if the Apaches were about to go on the warpath, she was going to find herself right in their way.

Chapter 9

Despite his teasing reassurances to Tory, Jesse had awakened before dawn filled with the very same skin-crawling apprehension that had plagued him on the banks of the Santa Cruz River outside of Tucson. Stopping in the old Spanish town had not confused or slowed those giving pursuit. They were coming still, tracking him with the relentless, brutal vigor of bloodhounds.

He had awakened the others and gotten them on the road to Bisbee while the stars still lit the desert sky with a million dazzling lights. He had pushed and prodded, been down-right rude, but only Tory had understood the reason for his haste and had followed his orders without complaints. Midmorning they stopped briefly for breakfast, then continued south. Frequently Mayleen and Ivan would struggle far behind, but Jesse did not slow his pace to allow them to catch up. He and Tory kept right on traveling as though they could actually feel the hot breath of their invisible pursuers on their necks.

With no real enthusiasm for their task, Jack and Ross made a cursory search for Mayleen Tyler and Ivan J. Carrows. When their efforts went unrewarded they returned to the Silver Spur, and with hats in hand, convinced Rose Flannery that whether or not the missing pair were together, they were in any case impossible to find.

"You were right to come back without wasting another day. I've already replaced Mayleen, but that doesn't mean I've forgotten or forgiven her. Just keep your eyes open," Rose directed. "If you ever see her again, and I don't care where it is, bring her straight to me. My girls must know if they run off in the dead of night, they'll be caught and punished for it. It might take months or even years for it to happen, but they can't escape me forever."

"Yes, Mrs. Flannery," the men agreed as she dismissed them with a wave of her tiny hand. They shook their heads in wonder as they strode out the back door, for they were both positive Mayleen Tyler was far too smart to ever come back to Tucson now that she had found the courage to leave the Silver Spur.

"I'm going to miss Mayleen," Jack admitted. "She was such a pretty little thing and always laughing and singing."

"Christ Almighty," Ross swore. "I'd no idea you were sweet on her."

"I didn't say I was," Jack argued sullenly. "I just said she was real pretty."

"Jack's in love with Mayleen," Ross joked in a childish singsong cadence.

Jack did not miss a step. He just turned and punched Ross square in the face so hard he dropped the burly man in the dirt. "You keep your opinions to yourself from now on!" he ordered, and sorry he had ever praised Mayleen in front of such an ignorant dolt, he went off to find more intelligent company until it was time to report back to the Silver Spur for work.

Calvin Lawrence and Arnold Fritsch spent the morning seated outside the entrance to their mine. More than a little drunk and still cursing Ivan, they were plotting how best to convince easterners their mine would yield a bonanza. When Araña and his howling band swept over the rise with the sudden chilling harshness of an evil wind, they lost several precious seconds simply staring at them with mouths agape before scrambling to their feet. Neither had been wearing a pistol, so their only recourse was to turn and make a wild dash for the safety of the mine entrance.

Skilled at hunting, the braves had no difficulty hitting a moving target. Each of their arrows found its mark. The miners were dead before their faces slammed into the rocky soil.

Araña remained seated astride his pinto as the mine and the adjoining shack were searched for food, weapons, and ammunition. He urged his men to hurry, and was elated when not only Colt pistols were found, but two Sharp's rifles as well. He had the miners' bodies hidden deep inside their mine, then confiscated their mule and horses. With a loud whoop, he wheeled his horse toward the south, toward Mexico where they would establish a *ranchería* from which to make war. If all the white men died as swiftly as the clumsy miners, then they could easily rid their land of the white scourge before the corn harvest and make The Dreamer's thrilling prophecies come true.

Luke Bernay was a skilled tracker because he was keenly atuned to his surroundings. He could scan a vast desert landscape and see the telltale signs marking his quarry's passage where others saw only rock and sand. He took advantage of every rise to study the road ahead, but had yet to catch sight of Jesse and his two female companions. He felt certain they were following the well-traveled road between mining towns to lose themselves in the constant flow of freight wagons and miners, and yet no one he had passed could recall seeing a man traveling with two women.

One miner did remember a dappled-gray horse, however, if not its rider. Another recalled seeing a woman, possibly Spanish, in the company of three men, but Luke discounted that report as unimportant to him. He just kept riding toward Bisbee certain that once Jesse headed into Mexico he would be far easier to locate and apprehend. His mind preoccupied with how best to capture Jesse without endangering his women in the process, Luke failed to note the riders who never fell far enough behind to lose him from sight. His attention focused on the man he was tracking, he did not realize Tad MacDonald and his men were pursuing him with a matching lethal determination.

Jesse stopped on the outskirts of Bisbee, but rather than make camp for the night, he simply called a brief rest while Mayleen went into town to replenish their provisions and purchase the shells she feared they might need. While he doubted they would even see an Apache, let alone have reason to fire at one, he thought the extra ammunition might come in handy for other targets. While they waited for Mayleen to return, Ivan napped on the ground and Jesse sat talking quietly with Tory.

"I'm sorry we didn't think to bring a few of the professor's books. Having something to read would make the time pass more quickly."

"I haven't been able to read," Tory admitted softly. "I've too much on my mind, I guess, but I can't concentrate on a story anymore."

"Well, I guess I could have read the book and then told you about it."

"Yes, that might have worked," Tory responded with only a slight smile. She waited a moment, and when Jesse did not speak again she voiced one of her main concerns. "You changed the subject the last time I brought this up, but I want you to tell Mayleen and Ivan that I'm your prisoner and that it's likely Eldrin Stafford has sent his men to find me. They ought to have the choice of staying here in Bisbee where they'll have no more trouble than what they've brought on themselves."

Uncomfortable under her insightful gaze, Jesse looked off toward town rather than at his attractive companion. "No, the fewer people who know who you are, the safer you'll be. I know we've increased the risk to them, but it can't be helped. Besides, Mayleen and Ivan are used to taking care of themselves. They'll be able to do it no matter what happens."

"Not if Eldrin's men ride up and start shooting they won't!" Tory implored. "Besides, I'm tired of the way they

140

look at us as though they don't approve of our traveling together."

Jesse had not imagined that he would be so anxious to have Mayleen return, but he did not like the turn the conversation had taken and could think of no way out of it. Tory might look sweet, but her fair beauty hid a stubborn streak he had not even suspected she possessed when they had first met. Fortunately, he was equally determined to get his own way.

"The less they know about you the better. Now don't bring this subject up again because it's getting real tiresome."

Jesse's menacing scowl intimidated Tory into silence. He had vowed that she would be safe with him, but would he keep that promise if she told Mayleen and Ivan about herself without Jesse's permission? Her brow was furrowed with a deep crease as she carried on a silent debate within her mind. She knew Jesse was eager to confront his stepbrother, much too eager to take what would now be a lengthy detour through Prescott, but what if he were so disgusted he just rode into Bisbee and left her with the sheriff there?

Hoping that ghastly possibility had not occurred to him, Tory decided to keep still until they were well into Mexico where leaving her would not be such an easy alternative. Then she would pull off her hat and scarf, introduce herself as Victoria Crandell, and explain how she had come to be condemned to death. Her confession would provide a dramatic interlude if nothing else, but Tory felt certain Mayleen and Ivan had every right to know the truth and that it was wrong of Jesse to conceal it.

Mayleen had just tied her purchases behind her saddle when a man walked up to her. Startled, she turned and found a grinning stranger standing much too close. He was tall, lean, and in desperate need of a bath and shave. Caught between him and her horse, she first tried to elude him politely. "Excuse me," she offered with a smile as she attempted to inch past him.

"There's no need for you to rush off," the man insisted.

141

"Didn't I see you at the Silver Spur in Tucson last month? I was visiting with Charlotte then, but I've got plenty of time now for us to get acquainted."

He leaned even closer and winked at her as though she was privy to some private joke. She looked around quickly, hoping there might be someone nearby who would come to her rescue, but other than three men, who from their leering stares appeared to be with the overly friendly man, no one was giving their conversation the slightest notice.

"I'm from Nogales rather than Tucson," she replied. "Now I'm in a hurry, so please move out of my way."

Rather than comply with her request, the stranger rested his left hand on her saddle to prevent her from leaving and raised his right to caress her cheek. "I'm sure you've got enough time to be nice to me, little lady, and maybe even a few of my friends. Let's just go on across the street to the hotel." He lowered his hand to her breast as though he actually believed the boldness of his touch would convince her to agree.

Mayleen shuddered slightly and swallowed hard. She dared not start screaming and risk attracting a crowd that might include Jack and Ross. She knew that she and Ivan had kept Jesse from making as good time as he would have liked, so it was possible the two men from the Silver Spur had traveled a lot faster. They could not only be in Bisbee but be seated at a table in the nearby saloon.

They would come running if they heard her screams, but they would swiftly provide a reason for her to shriek even louder. All it would take was a well-placed slash or two to ruin her looks. They might even lop off an ear! Her hair would cover that, but the prospect of enduring such horrible pain was more than she could bear.

She did not have much of a choice, she realized. She could take the risk of hideous consequences if she created a commotion there in the street or she could give the man what he wanted, after she had made him take a bath, of course. He was no worse than the other men she had entertained over the years. She glanced up at the hotel, and was sickened by the thought of having to check into a room with the demanding stranger. When she realized how disgusted Jesse would be if he found out what she had done, she was filled with a sudden inspiration.

She drew herself up to her full height. "Do you make it a habit to accost virtuous women on the street? I am la Doña Maria Elena Sepulveda and my husband is so insanely jealous he would shoot you dead without a moment's thought for insulting me as you have. Look behind you—he is just up the street." She waved then. "See, here he comes."

The string of Spanish names and mention of a jealous husband was enough to make the amorous man whip around to see just who might be coming his way. He saw a couple of miners he recognized, a gambler he had never liked, and several Mexican vaqueros who were indeed walking toward him. Fearing one might be the pretty young woman's husband, he started backing away even as he turned to apologize.

Mayleen had needed only a few seconds' inattention on the man's part to draw herself up into her saddle. By the time he opened his mouth to apologize, all he got for his trouble was a mouthful of dust as she rode away. She raced her weary mount all the way back to where the others were waiting and burst into tears when she tried to explain why she was late.

While Ivan knew he was too weak to defend her, he apologized for not having ridden into Bisbee with her. "Men don't bother women who have an escort, so this never would have happened if I'd gone into town, too. I'm getting better every day. You won't have to run any errands alone after this."

Ivan sounded sincerely distressed, and Mayleen knew that he was, but she was hurt that Jesse did not make a similar promise. His only reaction was a slight frown, as though what she had described was a trivial mishap rather than an instance of how quickly her past could catch up with her. It was obvious that serving time in prison had not softened his heart. He still thought of her as a whore and would not sully his name by associating with her.

"He's the one who ought to have gone into town,"

Mayleen snapped accusingly as she pointed to Tory. "The kid ought to be running errands, not me." When Tory looked away as though her comment was absurd, Mayleen's temper flared anew. She first gave Tory a brutal shove and would have punched her in the face had Jesse not stopped her.

"Just what do you think you're doing?" he demanded. "Tory's not to blame for what happened in Bisbee, and if you can't treat him right you'll go no farther with us. Is that understood? Either you act like a lady or you tell us good-bye. Now which is it to be?"

Tory took hold of Jesse's arm. "Wait, it's all right. She didn't hurt me."

"That doesn't mean she won't the next time she's mad!" Jesse quickly pointed out.

Mayleen was beside herself now. "Will you just listen to what you're saying? You're worried that I'll hurt your precious kid! He's real pretty, I'll give him that, but he ought to be able to take care of himself!"

"Mayleen, really . . ." Ivan began in a soothing tone.

"You stay out of this, Professor," Jesse ordered harshly. "Now which is it to be? Can you behave like a lady or not? I've got no more time to waste on you. There's still plenty of daylight left, and I plan to use it." He nodded toward Tory's horse and she turned away reluctantly and swung herself up into the saddle.

"Just like that you'd leave me here?" Mayleen cried out incredulously.

Jesse did not reply. His mount was packing most of the supplies so Tory and he had everything they needed. He walked over to the dappled-gray, mounted in one fluid motion, and turned south.

Mayleen stood with her hands on her hips. "How dare he treat me like this?" she asked Ivan. "How dare he?"

"He didn't want us along in the first place, Mayleen. You know that. Now come on, let's just go and catch up with them. He'll probably have forgotten the whole thing by sundown." Ivan walked over to his horse, a gentle sorrel gelding who stood quietly as he rummaged through his saddlebags for one of his hidden bottles. While Mayleen stood staring off after Jesse and Tory, he took a long swig. Fortified for the time being, he returned his "medicine" to its hiding place and led his horse over to Mayleen.

"Come on, let's go."

"I just don't understand why that skinny kid is more important to him than I am," Mayleen complained in a choked sob.

"Although my memory of your conversation with him at the Silver Spur isn't all that clear, wasn't there something about you helping his stepbrother send him to prison?"

Mayleen raised her hand, and she would have smacked Ivan a good one had the fear in his eyes not appalled her. She dropped her hand to her side. "I'm sorry. You're right. Jesse has a damn good reason to despise me and I ought to give up on him because he's never going to like me."

Ivan needed a moment to recover from the fact Mayleen had almost struck him, and then he attempted a smile. "*I* like you."

Mayleen had always regarded the bespectacled geologist as kind of cute, if not outright handsome, and she was embarrassed by how much she had revealed. "You just forget I said anything about Jesse, you hear." She found an unbruised spot on his cheek to kiss and went toward her own horse. "Come on, we don't dare let them get too far ahead or we'll never find them."

"We'll find them, Mayleen, don't you worry. I said I know my way around here and I do."

Even without looking over his shoulder Jesse could tell that Mayleen and Ivan had resumed following them. He laughed to himself until he glanced over at Tory and saw her downcast expression. "Hey, don't let what Mayleen said bother you. She's not worth it."

"Oh really? And just how much is a convicted murderess worth?"

"Oh Christ," Jesse sighed, but then he thought of the perfect retort. "Probably a lot more than a convicted felon."

"But you're innocent," Tory reminded him.

"If you'd had a fair trial and an impartial jury, *you* would have been found innocent."

"Paul would still be dead," Tory mused darkly, "so there would always be people who would call me a murderess."

"Well, they'd be wrong," Jesse insisted.

While Tory thought that was a wonderfully generous point of view, she knew few would share it, but it did encourage her to believe the marshal meant what he said about protecting her. The pair rode for a long way, the silence between them strained until finally Tory could no longer hold her tongue.

"If Mayleen knew the truth, she wouldn't be so insulted about the attention you give me. We'd all get along better and this trip wouldn't be half so difficult."

Jesse failed to agree. "If Mayleen knew you were an attractive woman, she'd be so jealous none of us would have a moment's peace. I just wish Ivan would hurry up and get well so that he can keep her occupied."

Certain she knew exactly how Jesse expected Ivan to accomplish that, Tory did not reply. She knew men and women were supposed to enjoy making love, but she could no longer understand how any woman would willingly submit to such abuse. Perhaps all men weren't as brutal as Paul Stafford, but wouldn't the act still be the same? Paul had covered her face with a pillow to smother her screams, but even now, she could still hear them echoing in her mind.

Toward sundown, Luke Bernay decided to try getting ahead of Jesse and his female companions. Fairly certain a man traveling with two women would make camp early, he pushed on. Swinging to the east, he got positively excited by the prospect of lying in wait for the escaped convict. This was definitely the time to do it, now, when he could almost smell the fugitives, he was so close to apprehending them. He pushed his horse hard, but by the time he finally stopped to make camp, he was confident he had not only overtaken Jesse Lambert, but would take him into custody the following day. Delighted by that possibility he fell into a contented sleep.

Tad MacDonald and his men did not understand why Luke had veered off the main road, but beliving in his reputation, they continued their discreet pursuit. Unwilling to draw the tracker's attention by building a fire, they sat huddled together chewing beef jerky and making rude jokes about what they intended to do with Victoria Crandell. It was such a fascinating pastime, they did not miss their hot meal at all.

Outside of Bisbee, Jesse chose the shortest route, which took them straight south into Mexico, rather than the southeastern trail which continued at an angle for another twenty miles before crossing the border. He knew he had driven his party to the limit that day. They were all as exhausted as their mounts, but he kept everyone moving until he was certain they were on Mexican soil before he called a halt.

Thanks to his secret stash of liquor, Ivan did not feel nearly as poorly as could have been expected. Having Dr. Goodfellow wrap his ribs had helped immeasurably, and although he made his way round their camp with the same slow shuffle he had used the previous evening, he was still on his feet. He kept well away from Jesse to make certain the Texan did not detect the odor of whiskey on his breath, and made himself useful gathering what firewood he could.

No one seemed to be in the mood to chat that night, and as soon as they had cleaned up after supper, the travelers wrapped themselves in their bedrolls. As usual, Jesse had made camp well away from the trail, and again, certain none of them could stay awake, he did not suggest they take turns standing guard. Relying on the sixth sense which had served to warn him of danger in the past, Jesse was asleep moments after bidding Tory good night. When he awakened at dawn and found the camp surrounded by Apache braves, his first thought was that he was still dreaming. Then he realized the reality was worse than any nightmare.

Drawn by the light of their campfire, Araña and his men spent the night camped within a short distance of Jesse and his group. Arising before dawn, they had planned to shoot whomever they found, steal what they owned, and continue riding toward the Sierra Madre Mountains. In the first pale light of dawn they had surrounded their prey, but finding a black-haired woman and fair-skinned youth among them, Araña had delayed their executions while he pondered what to do. He had left the reservation bent on driving out the white man, but he could take no pride in killing their women or boys.

When Jesse opened his eyes, Araña pointed Arnold Fritsch's rifle at his heart. "Wake them," he ordered.

Jesse could have reached for the gunbelt he had placed under his saddle, but he doubted he could have gotten off a single shot before the Indian killed him. Even if he did succeed in shooting one or two of the Apaches, there was too great a risk his companions would die in the crossfire. He raised his hands slowly, shoved his blanket aside, and rose to his feet.

"You can take whatever you want. You needn't hurt us," he offered with far more confidence than he felt.

Again, the Indian gestured with his rifle. "Wake them."

As he had done so often recently, Jesse gave Tory's shoulder a shake to wake her. She slept with the scarf tied over her hair, and the instant she opened her eyes he flopped her hat on her head. "We have company," he informed her in an anguished whisper, for he blamed himself for the danger they faced. "Just let me do all the talking." He moved on then to wake Mayleen and Ivan, who were as badly startled as he had been by their uninvited and unwanted visitors.

"Stand up," Araña commanded. He swung the rifle toward Ivan, and then lowered it when he discovered the trembling man was putting on spectacles rather than reaching for a pistol. The little woman was clearly terrified, while the boy was looking at him with a curious expression that betrayed no fear. The lad's eyes were a cool green rather than brown, but Araña had seen that same unshakable calm in only one other person: The Dreamer.

Intrigued, Araña urged his pony closer. The boy did not even flinch. "You are brave," he complimented. "Can you shoot?"

"No," Tory replied, thinking Eldrin Stafford would certainly give her a fiery argument over that claim. While she knew they were in dire straits, she felt the same leaden detachment she had experienced ever since Paul's death. It was not confidence that she projected, but simply the emotionless acceptance of what she knew to be the worst of fates. The Indian did not know that, however.

He seemed to have sufficient command of the English language to carry on a conversation and she strove to make the most of it. "I'm interested only in plants." She gestured toward the slim, graceful branches of an adjacent vermilion-blossomed ocotillo. "The people in the East have never seen your marvelous plants."

Araña was taken aback by that remark. *"Our* plants?"

"This is the land of the Apache, is it not?" She gestured with both hands. "These are then *your* plants."

Araña laughed, as did several of the other braves. When he translated Tory's words, the ones who had not understood her laughed as well. "You are the only white man who says this land belongs to us."

Tory risked a smile. "Then you must take very good care of me and my friends."

"I will decide what I must do." The Indian studied her for a long moment, and then gave a slight nod. "I will spare you and two others. Pick the one to die."

Certain Tory had to despise her as much as she disliked him, Mayleen let out a hoarse cry. "No! You can't let him choose. He hates me!"

Araña glanced toward the distraught woman. Despite her tears, she was a beauty, but he was unmoved. "Will you beg for your life after all my men have had you?"

Mayleen had not thought that far ahead, but she nodded enthusiastically.

"Go with him," Araña called out to one of his men. "If you please him, I will give you the chance to please another."

As the brave he had selected dismounted and came

149

forward, Ivan grabbed Mayleen's arm and pulled her back. "Have you savages no respect for women? You can't ask her to bargain for her life with her honor!"

"She has agreed," Araña reminded him. "Shall I shoot you? Then there will be no need for her to please any of us."

Ivan was no coward, but he could not find the words to volunteer for his own execution. He sent Tory a pleading gaze, hoping she would try to change the bloodthirsty Indian's mind. "Please," he whispered.

Jesse was certain he knew exactly what the wily Apache was doing and that it was a despicable trick. "He means to kill us one at a time," he warned. "After he shoots the first one, he'll tell Tory to pick another to die." He took a step forward. "If all you want is to drive the whites out of the Arizona Territory, you've already succeeded with us. We're on our way to Texas. You've no reason to make war on us."

Araña spoke to Tory again. "Is he telling the truth?"

"Only you know what you plan," she pointed out smoothly, "but yes, we're bound for Texas."

Araña surveyed his four captives with a malevolent gaze. "I will keep the woman," he announced, "but only two of the men." Again he nodded toward Tory. "Choose one to live and one to die."

Out of the corner of her eye, Tory saw Ivan began to sway as though he were about to faint, and Mayleen quickly shifted her weight to provide the necessary balance to keep him on his feet.

Remembering Mayleen's report of the article about the unrest on the White Mountain Reservation, Tory tried a desperate tack. "I will not have the blood of my friends on my hands. If you must shoot someone, it will have to be me, but I must warn you that The Dreamer is not the only one who can raise the dead. If you kill any of us, we will come back to see that you die as well. That is a power we have even beyond the grave."

Jesse did not believe his ears. He was grateful Tory had not claimed to have the ability to raise the dead herself, because he was certain the Apache would have promptly shot him or Ivan and told her to resurrect him. Impressed by her cleverly worded bluff, he joined in.

"Doesn't The Dreamer need all his power to bring your chiefs back to life? Can he do it if the strength of his braves is drained away battling our ghosts? Take whatever it is you need and let us part in peace."

"You are not fit to speak The Dreamer's name!" Bursting into a fit of rage, Araña dug his heels into his mount's flanks and, lunging forward, swung the butt of the rifle into Jesse's temple, instantly knocking him unconscious. When Tory bent over the fallen Texan, he reached down to yank her away.

"Come," he ordered gruffly, and drew her up behind him. "Tie the man to his horse," he called to his braves. "Bring the other man and the woman, too. They will make fine hostages, if nothing else." He laughed then, and skillfully maneuvered his pinto out of his men's way as they helped themselves to everything the four travelers had owned.

Tory had to hang on to the Apache's waist to remain astride his horse. To accomplish that feat without pressing close enough for him to feel the softness of her breasts took all that remained of her concentration. "I have a horse," she pointed out.

Araña did not listen. He had sensed the green-eyed boy's power when he had first awakened, and he wanted him close. "Hush!" he scolded harshly. "I am your master now!"

Intending to stay alive long enough to escape, Tory did not argue with his command, but remained silent as though she were docilely accepting it. Falling into the hands of renegades was every bit as terrifying as she had feared until she remembered that, as an escaped prisoner, she was a renegade herself.

Chapter 10

When Jesse came to, the sun was high overhead and flies were buzzing around the bloody gash in his temple with an incessant whine. The Apache might have given him the worst headache of his life, but he congratulated himself on having survived the Indian's brutal blow. At least he thought he was still alive. He was lying in an uncomfortable, contorted pose, his arms and legs jutting out at weird angles he was positive they would not have assumed on their own. He guessed that unconscious, he had simply been tossed aside and left to lie exactly as he had fallen.

Gradually his awareness progressed from his own pain to the voices of the Apaches who had taken him prisoner. He was facing the wrong way to see them, but he could hear them plain enough. The problem was, he could not understand a word they said. He concentrated on the tone of their voices, the rhythm of their speech as they conversed, hoping to at least detect whether or not they sounded hostile, but he soon gave up the effort as fruitless. He simply did not know enough about the Apache language to make accurate judgments about their mood.

Face down in the dirt, he could only see out of his right eye, but from what he was able to view of the terrain, they were no longer near the border but closer to the foothills of the Sierra Madre Mountains. He fought to get past the throbbing agony that reverberated within his skull, failed miserably, sank down into unconsciousness for a moment, and then was rudely jarred awake by a steady stream of water cascading onto his face.

He struggled to move, and made the painful discovery that his abdomen hurt nearly as much as his head. Finally he managed to push himself up into a sitting position. He looked up to find the Apache who had hit him holding his canteen and grinning as though he found drenching the white man highly amusing, but Jesse was not prompted to smile in return.

"I want your horse," the brave said.

Jesse was not foolish enough to believe that was a request rather than a demand, but he nodded agreeably. "Consider him a gift."

"What is his name?" Araña asked.

Jesse squinted to block out the sun's bright glare as he studied the brave's cocky grin. The Indian was a handsome brute, he had to give him that. His glossy black hair was long rather than cropped at the shoulders as many of his men wore theirs. His blue cotton shirt was open to the waist revealing a powerfully muscled chest. His trousers fit close, encasing legs both long and lean. As was the Apache custom, he wore moccasins that extended to the knee like a boot. Obviously a proud individual, Jesse had had no reason to change his original impression of the brave as both clever and mean.

"I neglected to ask when I bought him."

Doubting that, Araña's eyes narrowed slightly, but he did not make an issue of it and call the seated man a liar. "In the sun his mane and tail ripple with light like a river of silver," he remarked instead. *"Un río de plata,"* he repeated in Spanish. "I will call him Río."

Astonished to find the abusive Indian had such a poetic nature, Jesse nodded again. "That's a fine name."

On a sudden impulse, Araña knelt beside Jesse. "The green-eyed boy wants you alive. I don't. Do not cross me again."

Jesse doubted he could stand without becoming violently ill, but stubbornly returned the brave's threatening glance. "I've no quarrel with the Apache."

"You are white!" Araña reminded him. "That alone makes us enemies."

Araña rose and walked away before Jesse had time to reply, but he was not at all pleased by their conversation. The Apache's dark gaze had bored right through him while they had talked, and Jesse did not think it would take such an observant man long to realize Tory was no boy. Would he be so impressed with her then, or simply call her a white witch and promptly slit her throat?

Appalled at his own helplessness, Jesse began searching for his companions. He finally spotted Mayleen and Ivan huddled together, but Tory was nowhere to be seen. Several pinto ponies blocked his view, and he hoped she was just on the other side. "God help us," he whispered. He had mistakenly believed that being sent to prison was the worst thing that could ever happen to him. Now he knew he had been wrong. He had discounted Mayleen's warnings of unrest among the Apaches and led them straight into the Indian's path. How he could have been such an arrogant fool he did not know, but he prayed none of them would have to pay for his mistake with their lives.

By noon, Luke knew his plan to circle ahead of Jesse Lambert and lie in wait had failed. There had been no sign of the escaped convict and his women friends on the sparsely trafficked trail into Mexico, and he was thoroughly disgusted with himself for not being able to overtake a felon and two undoubtedly silly females. It was positively humiliating not to be able to outride such a farcical group and, thinking perhaps that his basic premise on Jesse's destination had been wrong, he returned to Bisbee. After a hearty meal he began to search each side of the trail for some trace of Jesse's camp.

He found the remains of several recent campfires, but one in particular captured his interest because the surrounding sandy soil was trampled with the prints of more than a dozen unshod horses. "Apaches," he murmured thoughtfully as he scanned the site for anything, no matter how insignificant it might appear to others, that might reveal what had happened there. Leaving his horse to graze on the sparse grass, he walked along slowly examining the ground more closely. There were footprints aplenty, a few boots, many moccasins, but no proof the camp had been Jesse's until the edge of a metallic object partially buried in the soil suddenly reflected a bright ray of sunshine.

Hurrying over to it, Luke discovered Marshal Kane's badge. "Hallelujah!" he shouted excitedly. He had thought Jesse would have gotten rid of such incriminating evidence long before this, but then he began to wonder why the escaped convict had not done a better job of hiding it once he had decided to part with it. Puzzled, he dropped the palm-size shield several times. Each time it fell, it did not land flat, but instead sliced into the earth at the same angle he had found it.

That consistency made the methodical man all the more curious. Had it simply fallen out of Jesse's pocket as he mounted his horse? To test that theory, Luke shoved the badge in his back pocket and swung himself up into his own saddle. He then dismounted and remounted several times, but the badge remained firmly tucked in his hip pocket. He then theorized that for it to have fallen out of Jesse's pocket, the man would have had to be standing on his head.

Since that was ridiculous, he progressed to the next possibility: Jesse might have been slung over his saddle rather than seated in it. He was tall. The Apaches would have had to jostle him this way and that to get him over the back of a horse, while the animal might have been dancing about in an uncooperative fashion. Concentrating on their task, the Indians could easily have missed seeing the badge fall.

Luke began to swear then, for it seemed obvious the man he had been tracking so diligently had gotten himself captured by Apaches. "If that don't beat all," he grumbled to himself, not relishing the thought that his perfect record might now be broken. A couple of years earlier, an escaped convict had drowned before he had caught up with him, but Luke had at least recovered the waterlogged body and collected the reward. Apaches weren't nearly so kind as a river, however. He doubted there would be enough left of Jesse Lambert after they finished with him to prove he had ever existed.

Disgusted by such a miserable piece of luck, he was about to start back toward Bisbee when the same seven men he had overtaken outside of Cactus Springs rode up. He had not believed their story then, and now he was positive they were Eldrin Stafford's men.

"Good afternoon," he greeted them cordially. "I must say I'm surprised to see you boys looking for strays way out here."

Tad MacDonald chose to ignore Luke's jest. He had thought allowing the tiny tracker to do all the work while they followed him the perfect plan until Luke Bernay had started riding in circles. One morning of watching the man chase his tail had been enough for Tad.

"You know damn well we're looking for Victoria Crandell and not cattle. Since she's with the man you're hunting, we ought to work together. Now just what in the hell are you doing?"

Luke was an excellent shot, as many an escaped convict had discovered too late. He was no fool, however, and never drew when he was so badly outnumbered. In this situation, he thought the truth the perfect choice. He flashed the marshal's badge and pointed out the evidence that supported his contention that Jesse and his female companions had been captured.

Tad was elated to discover Jesse Lambert had carried Marshal Kane's badge so far, as it sure made the convict look like the lawman's killer. He dismounted to study the tracks Luke claimed belonged to unshod Apache ponies and did not dispute his interpretation. "We heard there was trouble up at the White Mountain Reservation," he remarked.

"It looks as though it didn't stay there," Bernay replied. "Now I don't know what you boys want to do, but I'm not going up against renegades on my own. I'll wait for the Army to handle this and scrape up whatever I can of Jesse Lambert later." Taking advantage of the fact Tad and his men appeared to be completely dismayed by the strange turn of events, Luke mounted his horse and started back to Bisbee without bothering to bid them farewell.

"You want me to stop him?" José Gonzales asked.

Tad took off his hat and wiped his forehead on his sleeve. "Hell, no. The man's got the right idea. Let's just go on back to Bisbee and wait for the Army to deal with the Apache. Then we'll take whatever is left of Tory back home. Mr. Stafford wanted her hacked to pieces and I'm sure he doesn't care if the Apaches do it rather than us. He just wants her dead."

"But we wanted her alive," George reminded him, "for a little while at least."

"Fine, then you just follow them tracks," Tad challenged with a harsh laugh, "and see if you can rescue her. I'd rather just buy a woman in Bisbee than pay for that slut with my life."

Taking his advice, George turned his horse north. "Don't get all riled up. I agree with you. One woman is as good as another."

"I don't know," Manuel remarked sadly. "I think Tory Crandell might be better than most."

"*Deadlier* than most is what you mean," Tad scolded. "Now come on, let's get back to town before any more Apaches show up and start taking prisoners." Thinking that a wise move, his men ceased to talk about the woman they could not have, and instead began to speculate on those they could.

Jesse was able to sit astride one of the Apaches' pinto ponies that afternoon, but his head ached so badly that he quickly gained a grudging admiration for how bravely Ivan Carrows had endured the hardships of travel. After four years in Yuma, Jesse was used to the oppressive heat, but he was a stranger to pain this sharp and constant and it took all his courage not to beg to be allowed to just stop and lie down.

He thought there was a damn good chance the Apache would grant that request with a bullet, so he did not utter so much as a tiny moan let alone a plea for sympathy. He just kept on riding, sick to hs stomach and nearly blinded by pain. Tory was just ahead of him, next to the brave who had caused his misery. The handsome devil was now riding Río. Jesse struggled to keep his attention focused on Tory. At times her image swam before his eyes, but he stayed in the saddle until the Apache stopped for the night. Ivan hurriedly came to his side to help him dismount, and Jesse was ashamed to think he had not once shown the geologist the same concern.

"Thanks," he mumbled. Unable to stay upright on his own, he grabbed for Ivan's shoulder to keep him from moving away.

Araña had seen that touching display of friendship, and approached them. "Care for the horses," he ordered the two men.

Ivan was too worn out to think clearly and began to argue. "I'll do it," he volunteered. "You can't beat a man the way you did Jesse and expect him to work."

Araña was tall for an Apache, and looked down his nose at Ivan. "Be quiet or I will do worse to you. Now see to the horses."

With a valiant show of willpower, Jesse managed to draw himself upright and, reluctantly, Ivan moved away to do Araña's bidding. Jesse turned back to the pony he had ridden and began to remove the saddle, but before he had loosened the cinch, he was ovecome with a wave of dizziness and could do no more than slump against his mount. He felt a small hand on his back, patting him in gentle encouragement and, expecting Mayleen, he turned to send her away only to find Tory at his side.

"I'll do his work," she promised Araña.

"No, you will cook," the brave insisted.

"I'll take care of the horses and then cook," Tory replied. "I can do both."

Araña had been swift to threaten Ivan, but he did not scold Tory. He was fascinated by the boy's green eyes, for he saw not only sorrow in their depths but wisdom as well. "I mean to kill as many white men as I can. If he cannot work, then he will be next."

"Next, rather than first?" Tory forced herself to inquire.

Araña smiled slightly. "No, he will not be the first, nor the last, but he can be the next."

Jesse was aware of the morbid tone of their conversation, but he could not quite grasp the fact that they were talking about him. The cursed Apache had already taken his horse. He would not give up his woman as well. He opened his mouth to state that fact, but at the last instant he recalled that he dared not let on that Tory was female rather than male.

"I can work," he offered without conviction.

Tory slipped her arm around Jesse's waist. "You see, he'll be fine," she assured Araña. "You've no need to threaten him—or any of us." She lifted her chin proudly, silently daring the belligerent brave to object. His dark glance locked with hers, but she refused to be the first to look away. They might have stood there several hours before one gave in had the Apache searching Ivan's saddlebags not found the bottles of whiskey. His loud whoop demanded Araña's attention, and he turned and walked off as though Jesse's imminent death had not been the subject under discussion.

"How badly are you hurt?" Tory asked her friend.

Jesse swallowed hard. "Let's just say I wouldn't feel it if he shot me."

"Hush," Tory scolded. "If he's kept us alive this long, we have a chance. That's all we need."

From all the noise, it appeared the Apaches were excited about something, and Jesse looked over Tory's head to see just what it was. He had a clear view of the braves, but was too dizzy to make out what they were doing. "What's causing all the commotion?" he asked.

After first making certain he would not fall, Tory moved around his pinto and immediately saw exactly what was going on. "It looks as though Ivan had some whiskey stashed in his saddlebags. The brave who helped himself to Ivan's belongings this morning didn't have time to search them then. No wonder Ivan was so quick to help you just now. All day he must have been terrified that they'd find the whiskey and you'd kill him if the Apaches didn't."

"Jesus," Jesse murmured softly. "Indians don't think the way we do sober. Drunk there will be no reasoning with them." Then he had an even worse thought. "Oh, dear God, what about your blouse and skirt? Have they found them yet?"

"No," Tory replied, but there was much more than those two pieces of clothing. All her underwear was silk and of decidedly female design. "They left my things alone. For some reason, their leader seems to like me."

"Just in case he changes his mind, try and bury your blouse and skirt when nobody's looking—the lady's shoes, too. What did you do with the hat with all the ribbons?"

"I left it in the trash behind the store where we bought these clothes."

"Good, that's one less thing to worry about." Jesse tried to smile confidently, but he could hear the braves' voices getting louder as they shared the whiskey, and he was afraid they had a long and wretched night ahead.

Araña did not prevent his men from drinking the whiskey, but he did not take so much as a single sip himself. All his life he had observed the white man's attempts to dominate the Apache by providing them with liquor. In a drunken stupor his people were no threat to the whites, and of no value to themselves, either. Fortunately, the braves had not found enough whiskey to get beyond giddy foolishness to the staggering drunkenness he found offensive. He did not interfere with their fun, for he had more serious matters on his mind. The Apaches did not take prisoners. Not only were their raids swift, but the ease with which they escaped pursuit legendary. Prisoners had no value whatsoever to such a highly mobile fighting force. None of the braves who had rallied to his call had a wife so there were no women and children among them to slow them down. Each carried all he owned on his pony.

Araña knew the four prisoners he had taken that day endangered them all, and yet he did not regret his original decision to bring them along. They were a nuisance, but should his mission end in failure, he intended to bargain for

161

his own life with theirs. He watched Tory and Ivan moving among the horses. They kept glancing over their shoulders at his men. Their obvious fright strengthened his resolve. By the time he was finished, that very same stricken expression would have settled over every white face in the Arizona Territory.

He strolled over to Tory. "You have enough food for us all. Cook it."

"All of it?"

"Yes." Araña's smile was menacing. "We have been hungry too long. Now cook for us. If there is anything left, I will give it to you."

Tory did not thank him for that small consideration. They had carried sufficient supplies for four people for several days, but with the sixteen braves she had just counted, there were twenty in the camp. Lord, she sighed to herself. They were outnumbered four to one. It was pointless to argue over who ate their rations.

"I'll need Mayleen to help cook for so many people," she informed him.

"Is that the woman?"

"Yes."

Araña took a moment to study the braves who were now sprawled about the campsite. Some were still giggling among themselves. Others had fallen asleep. The woman had already said she would sleep with them. He would continue to let her worry about how long it would take them to remember her offer and begin taking her aside. He would enjoy watching the dread mount within her, but they were committed to fulfilling The Dreamer's goals and had no time to waste raping white women, or sleeping with willing ones.

"She can cook as long as she is not wanted," he finally agreed.

The brave cocked a brow in an insolent arch, silently asking if she understood him, and Tory nodded. She knew full well what he meant and, disgusted by it, turned away. She could scarcely stand by and allow Mayleen to be repeatedly raped by savages, but if she interfered, then her sex might swiftly be discovered. She knew precisely what would happen then: she would be raped as well. Ivan had already started a fire, and as she walked toward the flames, she vowed she would send every Indian in the camp to hell before she would become their whore.

"If they eat everything tonight, what will we eat tomorrow?" Mayleen whispered anxiously.

Ivan was quick to respond. "Let's just try and live through tonight and let tomorrow take care of itself." They had already fried up all the bacon and added some of the drippings to the beans. Mayleen was patting out biscuits, but that night they were misshapen blobs rather than the light pillows of dough she usually produced.

Jesse was seated, leaning back against a tree, perhaps ten feet away. His eyes were closed, but Ivan doubted the Texan was sleeping. He knew he would really be in for it when Jesse recovered his strength, but at least things were not as bad as they might have been. He had sampled his hidden whiskey liberally the previous night while he was feeling better, and would have run out in another day or two. The Indians had not gotten as much as they would have had they captured them outside Tombstone. That was a scant consolation, but Ivan was nevertheless grateful that the braves had merely gotten sleepy rather than violent.

Small, and skinny as a child, Ivan had taken plenty of abuse from bullies while growing up, but he knew that long-remembered humiliation would never compare to the pain the Apaches might inflict. They were fully capable of practicing the most hideous tortures. Ivan had long agreed with the stridently vocal residents of the Arizona Territory who called for the Army to solve the lingering problems with the Apaches by wiping out every last one of them. These Apaches could not possibly know his feelings about them, of course, but every time he looked away from the pot of beans he was stirring, he was certain he saw the loathing in their eyes.

They were all going to die, and Ivan was certain he would be first. Bullies could smell cowardice and he was positive he reeked of it. "Jesse was right," he mumbled. "They're just playing with us. We'll never get out of this alive."

Tory set the coffeepot over the flames and stepped back in time to see Ivan wipe a tear from his eye. "The very least you can do is die like a man, Ivan. Stop sniveling like an addlepated schoolgirl. You don't see Mayleen crying, do you?"

The usually talkative Mayleen hadn't said more than two words in thirty minutes and Ivan knew she had to be scared as witless as he. She glanced up at him now, but quickly looked away, confirming that belief. "What makes you and Jesse so brave?" he asked accusingly. "Are you just too stupid to see how much trouble we're in?"

They had camped near a river, and, unwilling to listen to insults from Ivan, Tory picked up their canteens and headed toward the water. She did not ask for permission to go. She just went, as if she had to get the water to boil the beans. Her father had possessed an extensive collection of maps, and she now regretted the fact she had not studied them more carefully. There were several rivers in northern Sonora, but she had no idea which one this might be. Not that it mattered much, but knowing where they were would have provided *some* comfort.

Araña had seen the argument at the campfire and, amused, followed Tory down to the river. "Your friends do not seem to be happy," he teased.

Tory rinsed her face and hands before turning to reply. "They have no reason to be happy." She would have called him by name, but until that instant, she had not cared what it was. "What is your name?" she asked now as she straightened up.

The Apache reached for one of the canteens and took a long drink before answering. "Araña. Do you know what it means?"

"Spider," Tory responded. "I know some Spanish."

"But no Apache?"

"You could teach me some."

Araña gave a derisive snort. "No, our language is all we have. I'll not share it."

164

He was standing at a respectful distance, and even with the river at her back Tory did not feel threatened. He had ridden beside her all day, and while his comments had been few, they had not been hostile. She had caught him casting many a sidelong glance in her direction, and hoping he had not guessed her secret, she struck a more masculine pose and slid her hands into her back pockets as Jesse frequently did.

"You speak English very well," she complimented sincerely.

"I was sent to school in Santa Fe. The Dreamer went there, too. Neither of us stayed long," Araña confessed with a hearty chuckle.

It suddenly struck Tory as unbelievably strange that she had to hide her hair under a hat to look like a boy while Araña wore his flowing black mane halfway to his waist. His teeth were very white, making his smile all the more handsome against his golden-brown skin. Appalled that she could find a savage appealing, she reached out for the canteen. When he handed it to her, she bent down to refill it.

"Do you like to swim?" Araña asked.

"Yes," Tory answered, and then terrified that he might insist she go for a swim with him, she changed her reply. "No, not really, I don't."

Araña knelt beside Tory and dipped his hands into the swiftly flowing current. Its coolness refreshed him and he used both hands to wash his face. Then, turning playful, he hit the water with the heel of his hand to splash Tory. When she scrambled to escape being splattered, he laughed.

"After supper, you will come swimming with me," he ordered.

"No, really," Tory hung on to the canteens as she backed away. "I don't swim." She did, in fact, swim quite well, but certain he would expect her to strip off her clothes, she dared not agree to join him.

"I will teach you."

"Why?" Tory gasped. "Why would you want to do that?"

Araña stood and dried his hands by running them through his hair. "Must I threaten to kill one of your friends to make you mind me?"

"What a ghastly thing to say."

Araña took a step toward her. "Do not fight what I say then."

While only a moment before she had thought his smile charming, Tory now saw only an arrogant desire to demean her and backed away. "I don't understand what it is you want."

"I want to go swimming," Araña reminded her.

"*I* don't."

"But you will anyway or I will hurt your friends."

"Spider is a good name for you."

"*Gracias.*"

Apparently bored with their conversation, he waved toward the camp and Tory started back ahead of him. Supper was ready and Tory was surprised there was some food left after the Apaches had eaten, but she had never had less of an appetite.

"Has he bothered you?" Jesse asked when Tory handed him a plate and sat down beside him.

Tory shook her head. Jesse had threatened her himself on several occasions, and that fact coupled with his injury kept her from revealing Araña's intention to take her swimming. She put a piece of bacon between two halves of biscuit and forced herself to eat, but the dreadful possibilities that might soon occur at the river kept her from tasting the bites she swallowed.

"I'll be stronger tomorrow," Jesse promised. "Just stay beside me."

"I'll try."

"No, promise me you'll do better than that."

Tory set her plate aside as she saw Araña approaching. "None of us is in any position to make promises," she whispered before the brave came close enough to overhear.

"Come," Araña said as he walked by.

Jesse leaned forward. "Where is he going?"

Reluctantly, Tory rose to her feet. "His name is Araña. He wants me to go swimming with him."

Readily understanding the peril in that request, which he

166

assumed had been stated as a demand, Jesse also set his plate aside. "Give me a hand, please."

Astonished that he would even attempt to get up, Tory nevertheless labored to help him up, then reached out to steady him when he began to sway. "What do you think you're doing?"

"You think I'll let you have all that fun alone? Come on, I won't fall down in the water. Just get me there."

"Are you crazy? You're so dizzy you'll surely drown."

"That's not all that bad a way to die," Jesse remarked philosophically. "Now come on, let's hurry before our Indian friend comes back for us."

Tory slid her arm around Jesse's waist so that he could lean against her and they started off toward the river in a lurching, stumbling gait.

"You'll be fine if you just stay behind me," Jesse stressed.

"He'll expect me to get naked!" Tory said with some embarrassment.

"I'll have my back to you, and he won't be able to see through me. We'll be all right. You'll see."

"Oh, sure!" Tory scoffed. Jesse was having such a difficult time just staying upright that she doubted he would be any help at all. No, she was going to have to get into the water without allowing Araña a clear look at her and stay submerged far away from him until it was so dark he could not observe her figure as she got out. Considering all the trouble they were in, that did not seem like all that great a challenge until she got to the river and saw Araña had already begun swimming.

"Help me off with my clothes before he has a chance to send me away," Jesse ordered in an urgent whisper. "If he wants to play tag, just stay behind me and he'll never know you aren't my kid brother."

"Is that what you intend to tell him? That we're brothers?"

"Sure, why not?"

Araña started swimming toward them, and horrified that he was going to come out of the river and expect her to converse with him while he wore nothing but water droplets, Tory tried to find where to begin to help Jesse off with his

167

clothes. Sensing her nervousness, the Texan began to laugh, then eased himself down onto the muddy riverbank so she could remove his boots.

"Hey, Araña," he called out. "It's a fine night for a swim." He got his shirt unbuttoned and had tossed it aside by the time Tory had removed his boots and socks. He then scooted out of his pants and underwear and managed to enter the water, if rather awkwardly. A strong swimmer, he noted that Araña had an equally powerful stroke.

"Sorry I'm not up to challenging you to a race," Jesse called out. "Tonight it will be all I can do to stay afloat."

Tory had glanced away rather than watch Jesse disrobe. Paul Stafford was the only man she had ever seen naked and she had not admired the sight. The prospect of cavorting naked with two equally aggressive males instantly sparked the desire to flee, but she knew exactly what Araña would do if she did: He would start shooting her friends to make her come back, and she could not do that to them.

The twilight was not nearly as deep as Tory would have liked, and she looked up and down the riverbank hoping for a large mesquite bush, if nothing else, to shield her from the Apache's view, but there wasn't so much as a sprig of grass close enough to the shore to provide a screen. Knowing how painful Jesse's effort must be to help her, she forced herself to follow his example and sat down to remove her clothes.

She laid her hat aside, but left her scarf in place to hide her hair. Surely no man ever swam with his head covered, but she had absolutely no choice in the matter and she prayed Araña would mistake the dark scarf for her hair. After taking a fortifying breath, she hurriedly entered the water while Jesse was waving his arms wildly at the Apache brave who held both their lives in his hands.

"Let's drown the bastard," she suggested as she swam up behind Jesse, and his answering chuckle did not discourage the idea.

Chapter 11

Araña found it difficult to decide if he had hit the man called Jesse too hard, or not nearly hard enough. It was the green-eyed boy's company he had sought, not the tall man's. Although the boy was peeking around Jesse's shoulder, it certainly looked as though he could swim. That meant he had lied. If he had lied about one thing, then he had lied about others.

A slow smile brightened the brave's expression, for it now seemed the boy's promise that he and his friends could return from the grave had been no more than a valiant boast. If he chose, Araña now believed he could kill all four of his captives and not be haunted by their ghosts, but fear of that unlikely consequence had never been his reason for keeping them alive. He turned and swam against the current for several strokes and then turned back toward the white man and boy.

"I will race him," he challenged.

"He's a poor swimmer," Jesse revealed with an expansive shrug that again shielded Tory from Araña's view. "It wouldn't be much of a contest."

Araña did not argue. Instead he gestured for Tory to come out from behind Jesse, and, after a long pause, the lad did. His white shoulders made it plain he never went without a shirt, but few white men did, and Araña dismissed the paleness of his skin as unimportant.

"I will give you a head start," he called out. "Start

169

swimming toward the bend. I will count to ten before I come after you."

Tory shot a quick glance over her shoulder and found the bend was so far away that Araña would have plenty of time to beat her no matter how generous a head start she had. What if he reached out to touch her as he swam by? Or worst yet, pulled her under in an enthusiastic hug? His first reaction would undoubtedly be shock, but she feared his next move would be to haul her out of the water and make what he would consider fine use of her feminine form.

That possibility made her shiver with dread. She looked up at the stars that at dusk were only faintly visible. She and her father had frequently marveled at the spectacular beauty of the desert sunset, but that night the vivid streaks of orange, fuschia, and purple that lit the sky were keeping the river well illuminated long past the time she needed night to fall.

"You just start swimming," Jesse whispered. "I'll handle him."

"How?"

"Swim!" Jesse ordered.

When he started splashing her, Tory backed away, then, too anxious to swim with the smooth easy strokes her father had taught her, she started toward the bend with awkward, flailing motions. She was tired, and fearing Araña would somehow slip by Jesse and overtake her, she actually thought she felt the brave's fingertips gliding over her bare hip. That frightening sensation caused a sharp break in what was at best an ungainly rhythm. Gulping for air, she got a mouthful of water and began to choke. She had to stop to catch her breath, found she could no longer touch the river's rocky bottom, and for a panic-filled instant thought she might be the one to drown.

Admiring Tory's initiative for what he mistakenly believed was an imaginative portrayal of distress, Jesse dismissed her loud sputterings and concentrated on stopping Araña. "You can't want to race Tory," he shouted. "You could float by him. There would be no honor in beating such a poor swimmer. You would just look foolish racing him now."

Not one to take taunts of any kind from a white man, Araña swam toward Jesse rather than Tory. He stopped just out of the Texan's reach and flipped the hair out of his eyes. The man's wild splashing had reopened the gash in his temple, and a thin stream of blood was trickling down the side of his face and pooling at his shoulder. Knowing the wound must be painful, the Apache had to respect Jesse's courage in loudly begging for more abuse. That meant he was very brave, and therefore dangerous.

"I warned you not to cross me."

"Hell, I'm not crossing you," Jesse contradicted. "I just don't want to see you making a fool of yourself racing a kid who can't swim more than a dozen strokes without having to stop for a rest."

Still trying to clear the water from her lungs, Tory had made no progress at all toward the bend and Araña came to the sorry conclusion that Jesse was right. The boy was as poor a swimmer as he had claimed. All the wily brave had wanted was a quiet place to talk, to see if the thoughts reflected in Tory's green eyes were wise ones. He was now too annoyed with Jesse to ask good questions, however, and he started toward the shore.

"See that he does not drown," Araña called over his shoulder. Once out of the water, he dried himself off with his shirt, and then pulled on his pants. When he noticed Jesse had not moved, he scolded him again. "Go on! Pull him out of the water before he drowns or I will drown you, too!"

The brave was out of the water, and that was all Jesse had wanted. Tory had actually begun swimming again, and he took his time catching up with her to put enough distance between them and Araña to keep the brave from observing them closely. He started to reach out for her, and then, at the last possible second, realized how badly she would react to that. He drew back his hand and called out her name instead.

Recognizing his voice, Tory turned and began treading water. It was finally getting dark, but she was all too aware of

171

the fact neither she nor Jesse had on a shred of clothing. The river's refreshing coolness had apparently enlivened Jesse considerably. While she was glad to see he was feeling well enough to pursue her, it made her horribly uncomfortable that he had caught up to her so easily.

"Where's Araña?" she asked.

"I convinced him a race was a stupid idea," Jesse bragged. "Come on, let's go back and get dressed before the rest of the tribe comes swimming." Tory's lashes were spiked with tears, but he assumed the moisture was a natural result of her time in the water and flashed a wide grin. "I told you I'd take care of things," he said. "But flopping around like you were drowning was a big help."

While she was tempted to tell him it had not been an act, he was close enough for Tory to see the blood oozing from his temple. She knew Araña might permanently disable him the next time Jesse interfered in something he wanted to do. "You've got to be careful of Araña," she advised rather than complain about his failure to realize she had not been clowning but in serious trouble.

Jesse could stand easily and, insulted, he reached out to take her arm and draw her close. He had meant only to make certain she did not misunderstand his meaning, but his thumb brushed the smooth swell of her left breast. He felt a shudder of fear jolt clear through her, but a powerful sensation of a far different nature shot through him, and not even the chill of the river dimmed its fiery heat. He released her as abruptly as he had touched her and swam away, confident she would follow soon enough. When he left the water, he also used his shirt as a towel before yanking on his pants.

Tory was relieved to find the Apache had not taken their clothes, but she waited until Jesse had dressed and turned his back to leave the water. It was now dark enough to hide her figure from anyone wandering near the river, but she dressed so quickly no one would have caught more than a glimpse of her slender figure had it been high noon.

Jesse did not speak to her as they walked back into camp, and as they approached the fire she discovered his expression was as forbidding as Araña's usually was. She touched his elbow. "Did I do something wrong?" she asked.

Jesse shook his head rather than attempt to answer that question. She had not done a damn thing except be a desirable woman, and he knew that was the very last thing he ought to say or that she wanted to hear. The Indians were huddled around Araña, and having no desire to intrude on them, Jesse led Tory over to where Ivan and Mayleen had unrolled their four bedrolls. He eased himself down on his blanket; having spent what little energy he had swimming, he felt completely drained. His head still ached badly, but now with a dull throb rather than soul-shattering intensity.

Following Jesse's example, Tory sat down on her blanket but focused her attention on the circle of Apache braves rather than her fellow captives. The Indians had ridden like demons that day, traveling many more miles than Jesse had been able to cover when he had been in charge. That made any hope of escaping on horseback foolish in the extreme. Perhaps when they entered the mountains, they could slip away on foot, but then how would they survive without weapons to hunt for food?

Ivan observed Tory's preoccupied frown and could not stifle his curiosity. "What happened at the river? Did the Indian tell you his plans?"

Ivan's terror over their situation was painful to observe, and Tory was sorry she had nothing encouraging to report. "No. He just wanted to swim."

"Swim!" Ivan hissed. "The man constantly threatens to kill us, and you two went swimming with him?"

"That's enough," Jesse cautioned sharply. He did not feel up to dealing with the scientist now for having brought the whiskey along, but he sure as hell would not forget to do so later. "Let's go to sleep before they think of more work for us to do."

"It's not having to work that bothers me," Mayleen murmured softly. Gathering firewood or cooking was no trouble at all in her opinion. She sat hugging her knees, watching the Indians, wondering what they were discussing with such fervor, and fearful at any second that one might

173

look up and notice her. All it would take would be for one man to walk over to her and she knew the others would follow. She would not fight them, but she feared they would be so brutal that she would never survive being assaulted by them all. For a whore to die of repeated rapes struck her as the cruelest of fates. Hadn't she suffered enough for foolishly giving herself to the wrong man when she had been little more than a child?

Jesse and Ivan were lost in their own thoughts, and it was Tory who noticed the tears rolling down Mayleen's cheeks. "You've been very brave," she told her. "Don't lose heart now."

Embarrassed by Tory's compliment, Mayleen wiped away her tears on the back of her hand. "I'm sorry for what I said this morning. I shouldn't have made fun of you, but I know you don't hate me for it."

"Of course I don't," Tory assured her.

The Apaches suddenly ended their conference, but as they rose, they stepped back to form a circle. One produced a small drum, and as he struck a slow, rhythmic cadence, the others began to dance. Their moccasins slapped against the dusty earth in time to the drummer's beat while their bodies swayed with an easy masculine grace.

"Why are they dancing?" Ivan asked in a fear-choked whisper.

Jesse shook his head sadly at the geologist's ignorance. "It's got to be the Ghost Dance. They're still trying to raise the dead."

With the flickering flames of the campfire casting long shadows on the dancers, the scene held the magical fascination of a long-forgotten dream. Against her will, Tory found herself studying Araña, for the pride of his bearing made him easy to recognize even in the dim light. She had never met anyone even remotely like him, but his attractive appearance scarcely made up for his deadly goals. He was clearly a born leader, but had he been born in time to save his people?

"Where do they get the strength to dance after riding all day?" she asked Jesse.

"They *are* tough, aren't they? Come on, this might go on for hours and I've got to get some sleep." He struggled to rise, and then pulled his blanket more than a dozen feet away from its original position.

Tory followed him with her bedroll. "Did you tell Araña that we're brothers?" she suddenly remembered to ask.

"No, I didn't have the chance." Jesse stretched out on his blanket and said a silent prayer that they would all live to see the dawn. "I will, though."

Tory made a point of placing her blanket at what she hoped would be considered a brotherly distance from Jesse's rather than right next to his, which was the close proximity he had always insisted on. As she lay down beside him, she had another thought. "We should have cut my hair when we had the chance," she said.

Jesse raised up slightly. "No, your hair is far too beautiful to crop short."

"Thank you, but the only thing that's keeping Araña from seeing I'm a woman is a thin scarf, and how long will that fool him?"

"What are the braves doing?"

"Dancing," Tory replied with a befuddled frown. "You know that."

"Yes, I do, and I think they're far too involved in their efforts to raise their dead chiefs to care about women. Think of it as a religious quest. Women don't interest them or they would have been taking turns with Mayleen since the minute we made camp. We'll get through this, Tory. You didn't escape a death sentence just to die at the Apaches' hands. I'm sure of it."

Jesse longed to lean over and kiss her, but dared not. The braves might appear to be engrossed in their dance, but what if one saw him? "I'm going to do my best to make friends with Araña. He's bright. It's certainly worth a try to convince him killing isn't the answer."

Tory could not argue with that sentiment. She propped her head on her arm and watched the braves dance in a slow, swaying circle until the beat of their drum lulled her to sleep. Longing to again hold her cuddled in his arms, Jesse felt as though they were separated by a wide chasm rather than inches. He was exhausted, but even as sleep overtook him, he wanted Tory more than rest.

Too frightened to fall asleep as readily as Tory and Jesse, Ivan and Mayleen watched the braves dance until they could no longer keep their eyes open. Mayleen pushed Ivan away when he attempted to hold her close. She was too grateful that the Indians had ignored her to risk giving them any ideas they had not already had on their own.

Araña felt invigorated rather than fatigued by the lengthy dance, and when it drew to a close he was uninterested in sleep. Meaning to wake Tory and talk with him while his obnoxious male companion slept, he knelt beside him. He reached out for the lad's shoulder, and then drew back when he noticed a wisp of long blond hair had escaped his scarf and lay curled across his cheek.

The inquisitive brave paused to consider Tory's effeminate manner, white shoulders, pitiful attempts to swim, and came to an abrupt conclusion. Tory had tried to make a fool of him, and he could not abide that. He grasped the knot that kept the scarf in place and removed it with a sharp tug that instantly awakened the young woman. She sat up, badly startled. No longer confined, her fair curls spilled down over her shoulders.

Araña handed her the scarf. "I should cut out your lying tongue," he threatened in a hoarse whisper.

Clutching the silk square in a frantic grasp, Tory felt more naked now than she had in the river. The Indians had built up the fire and, although heavily veiled in shadow, the fierceness of Araña's expression was impossible to mistake. She turned to look at Jesse and found him sound asleep. She spoke softly so as not to wake him.

"Please, you must understand. I killed a man. If the law catches up with me, they will shoot me just as quickly as the Army would you. My disguise was to protect me from them, not you."

That was too wild an excuse to be a lie and Araña pulled her to her feet as he rose. He then took her arm and led her toward the river. When he was within a few feet of the shore, he shoved her down into the sandy soil. Standing in front of her, he demanded an explanation. "How did you kill the man?"

The subject was so distasteful that Tory had to swallow hard before confessing that she had shot him. "He treated me very badly," she added haltingly. "I couldn't let him come back and do it again."

"He raped you?"

That question brought back a torrent of hideous images that Tory had to overcome before nodding. She had not expected any sympathy from the brave and was startled when he reached out and patted her head gently. Looking up, she thought it a shame she could not see his face clearly. As it was, she had felt his caress, but feared his thoughts were not nearly so comforting.

"And if you're caught?" Araña asked.

"I'll be hanged," Tory admitted, "if they don't shoot me on sight."

"What about Jesse? Does he know all this?"

"Yes."

Araña now knelt in front of her. "You are his woman?"

Tory shook her head emphatically. "No. He is, well, he is no more than a friend."

"Why?"

"Why?" Tory repeated, stalling for time to come up with a coherent response. "I won't belong to any man," she finally blurted out.

"Because of the man you shot?"

Huge tears welled up in Tory's eyes but she managed to reply. "Yes, because of him."

Araña slid his hand around her neck and eased her head down on his left shoulder. The sweetness of the moment convinced him he had made the right choice in taking her and her friends hostage rather than dealing with them as harshly as he and his men had the others they had ambushed along the trail. From the first instant he had seen her there had been something about her that set her apart, and now he could finally appreciate what it was. He caressed her cheek with his fingertips and then tilted her chin to bring her lips

177

within reach. His kiss was very quick and light, but it was a kiss.

"Cover your hair again. Do not tell the others that I know what I do. Do you understand? They are not to know."

"Yes, I understand," Tory assured him. "But only Jesse knows I'm a woman. Ivan and Mayleen don't."

That she had fooled her own traveling companions surprised Araña, but he considered her reason a good one. "What is your real name?"

"Victoria, but I've always been called Tory."

Araña straightened up and drew her to her feet. He waited while she retied her scarf around her head and then escorted her back to her bedroll and walked away as though his discovery would not change both their lives.

When she awakened the next morning, Tory first reached for her scarf and was relieved to find it in place. The midnight conversation with Araña tugged at her memory and now she did not know which made her more ashamed, that she had confided in an Apache or that she had promised not to tell Jesse about it. He was still asleep and she again got up without awakening him. She thought the gash in his head should probably have had stitches, but then again, when it was healed his curls would cover most of it so his looks would not be badly harmed.

Unable to shake the uncomfortable feeling that she had betrayed Jesse, Tory hurried away to help Ivan saddle the horses and then added what she could to Mayleen's efforts to prepare breakfast from the previous night's leftovers. Once up, Jesse was in good spirits, but unable to share his mood, Tory simply avoided him.

Anxious to leave, Araña wasted no time breaking camp. The sun had barely cleared the horizon before they were underway. Again Tory rode by his side, but his frequent smiles told her this day would be very different from their first.

They continued to follow the river as they progressed farther into the Sierra Madre Mountains. The Apaches followed ancient trails that led through wide canyons and over sharp ridges. They paused briefly in a rocky gorge at midday, and the Indians shared generously of the beef jerky they had taken from their victims. Tory still found it unappetizing fare, but made an effort to eat while Mayleen and Ivan sat silently staring at the braves as though they feared each bite they took might be their last.

Jesse was bored with the morose couple's company and sat down beside Tory. "We can't be going much farther if Araña wants to conduct frequent raids. Has he told you his plans?"

"No," Tory swore too quickly. "He hasn't said much at all."

"Hey, what's wrong?" Jesse asked.

"Nothing," Tory lied. "It's just that I'm tired of running."

A mask of sorrow had been etched on her delicate features for most of the time Jesse had known her and he gave her hand an encouraging squeeze. "I'm going to give you the same advice you gave Mayleen: Don't lose heart now."

Tory's faint smile swiftly faltered. "Could this be what hell is like, Jesse, a difficult journey that never ends?"

"This one will end in El Paso. I've already promised you that."

His bright blue eyes were still slightly clouded with pain, and Tory knew he ought to save his energy for the trip rather than for talking with her. "Yes, I know you have. Thank you."

Jesse could readily see from her hastily averted glance that she was not interested in further conversation. His head felt better, but not nearly good enough to suit him. He needed to be able to think clearly to plan an escape. That thought brought him an unexpectedly hearty chuckle. He had managed to escape from the heavily guarded Yuma prison and to free Tory from the jail at Cactus Springs. Somehow he was going to have to draw on the method of those successes to elude Araña and his men.

They made slow progress that afternoon. In places the

trail was so steep and narrow Tory could not bear to look down. She just held her breath and prayed her horse did not lose his footing and send them both plummeting to the rocks below. When at last they crossed a particularly difficult ridge to traverse and entered a valley fed by a cool stream she was elated when Araña called a halt. Huge trees of pine, oak, and cedar shaded the grassy meadow and she doubted Eden could have been a more inviting spot.

Seeing her delighted expression, Araña broke into a smile. "This is where we will stay. Tomorrow we will build *wickiups,* and you will have a proper place to live."

Tory had seen the circular Apache dwellings outside one of the forts she had visited with her father. The portable houses were constructed of a frame of wooden ribs covered with branches. Like the *tipis* of the plains Indians they were devised for easy transport by nomadic tribes. She had never expected to live in one, nor have it described as a proper home. She knew better than to refuse such a gracious offer from the Apache, but she certainly hoped he did not expect her to share his *wickiup* as a wife. Her cheeks flooded with a bright blush as she recalled the tenderness of his kiss, but she did not want any more in the way of affection from him.

Araña correctly read the confusion in her glance, but did nothing to dispel it. Instead he raised his finger to his lips to ensure her silence and turned his pony away to begin organizing his *ranchería.*

Tory dismounted and led her horse over to the stream. He had certainly proven his worth on the mountain trails and she patted his neck with real affection as he took a drink. They had managed to survive another day, but Tory feared she might not live to see another dawn. Her only hope was that Araña would again dance with the others, and be too lost in The Dreamer's quest to seek her out. His touch might be gentle, but she knew if he demanded more than a kiss, she would surely lose what she knew to be a tenuous grip on her sanity.

Jesse walked over to her then and she could not hide her tears. "He means to stay here," she informed him. "Whatever our fate, this is where it will overtake us."

Jesse disagreed. "No, the only thing that will happen here is that we'll be able to hunt and have better food and a more comfortable place to sleep. Don't let the bastard see you crying. He can't leave more than one or two men to guard us when he goes out on a raid. I can handle them and by the time he returns and finds us gone, we'll have covered too many miles for him to ever catch up with us."

"How can you possibly believe that?"

Jesse was pleased by that flash of spirit. "We'll not retrace his trail, but cut our own over the mountains. He's too busy saving the Apaches from extinction to follow us. Mark my words, the sooner he leaves on a raid, the sooner we'll be free." He winked at her then and patted her gelding on the rump before sauntering off to care for his own horse and all the others.

Araña brought Mayleen a bag of beans, and a ham they had taken from Calvin and Arnold's shack and told her to again prepare supper. She had not realized the Indians had any food to share and wondered what else they might produce. She dared not appear demanding and inquire, however. "Thank you," she responded instead, but she quickly turned away to hide the terror that still filled her eyes.

In a more generous mood that evening, Araña permitted his captives to eat when his men did. He ate quickly and then walked over to where they sat. Making himself comfortable on the grass in front of them, he studied each of them silently before speaking. "The tale of the Apache is a sad one. For years we have been given promises of food in exchange for peace, but whenever we have laid down our arms we have been left to starve. The Indian agents who are supposed to provide for us cheat us instead. They sell the goods meant for us and get rich while we go hungry. The Army is no better. They sell supplies meant for us and pocket the money. Your people do not want to live in peace with us. You wish us dead."

When Araña paused, Jesse spoke up. "I'll agree you've

181

been treated badly, but you mustn't blame everyone with white skin for what's happened to you. You have been given reservation lands. Your people could be content there."

Deeply insulted, Araña's expression filled with fury. "You know nothing about my people! We are not farmers, and yet we have tried to farm the land given to us only to be moved time and again before we can harvest our crops. White men take the water that should belong to us and are not punished. No, we are told we have no right to the water! An Indian cannot have so much as a bucket of water for his crops if a white man wants it!"

Disgusted they had not understood his rage had good cause, Araña rose to his feet, turned his back on them and walked away.

"Was that your idea of making friends with him?" Tory asked. Embarrassed that she had been so devoted to her father's research that she knew little about the Apaches' problems, she leapt to her feet and ran after Araña.

"You're absolutely right," she said as she caught up to him. "Jesse doesn't know what he's talking about. If the situation is as dreadful as you describe, then surely something can be done."

Araña halted abruptly. "The Dreamer is doing something."

"Yes, yes, of course he is," Tory agreed, "but even if he can raise some of your chiefs from the dead—"

"He will!" Araña interrupted.

Clearly the man believed in The Dreamer's cause, but Tory did not. "When these chiefs return, will they create a better life for your people?"

"Yes! It is only through war that whites will learn we can not be penned up and left to starve!" Too angry to want to debate the issue, he kept on walking, and when Tory followed, he did not tell her to go away. He went down to the stream and followed it to the end of the small canyon. The rocky crevices in the mountainside would make a good place to fight, and he climbed from one to the next until he had a clear view of the valley. He then watched Tory make her way up to him with an agility he had to admire.

"Do not argue with me," he scolded. "I would rather die fighting for my people than starve with the cowards on the reservation."

The small sandy ledge where he sat was wide enough for the two of them, and Tory considered his comment an invitation to join him. She had heard tales about Indians all her life, but Araña was the first one she had ever met face-to-face. Being his prisoner was the worst of situations, but she could not help but believe the man's commitment to his people was sincere.

"If your people are not farmers, how did they live before the white men came?"

Surprised by her interest, Araña answered, "We spent our tme hunting and making war. The Apaches are born warriors."

Tory pursed her lips thoughtfully. "Living in peace does not come naturally to you?"

Araña shook his head. "Nor to the white man. He will use any excuse to kill an Indian."

"But there is so much land in the Arizona Territory, isn't there enough for us all?"

Araña laughed at her innocence. "The white man never has enough. Besides, there's gold, silver, copper, coal—who knows what other riches lie beneath the ground. The white man cannot bear the thought the Apaches might get any of it."

Tory grasped that argument instantly, for she knew greed would prompt men to go to any lengths to achieve their goals. Still, she was positive war between the Apaches and whites was not the answer. "You mustn't kill anyone else, Araña. You just mustn't," she implored.

Thinking her impossibly foolish for making such a ridiculous request, Araña did not reply, but instead leaned over to kiss her. His lips brushed hers very lightly at first, but then he wanted more and cupped her cheeks with both hands. He felt her lips tremble, and leaned back.

"Forget the man you shot," he suggested convincingly. "Think only of me."

Tory could not seem to draw a breath. She stared in rapt

fascination while Araña's dark eyes closed as he drew her near for another kiss. He was being so gentle with her, but his kindness failed to overcome her fears. She tried to choke back a sob, but failed.

Sorry he had not pleased her, Araña ended his kiss, but kept Tory clasped in his arms. "You killed a white man who wronged you. I want the same privilege, but I want them all dead."

Sick and tired by his preoccupation with death, Tory sat back slightly. "Please don't hurt Jesse and Ivan. Let them go if they annoy you, but please don't hurt them."

"Ivan is a coward," Araña offered with a disgusted sneer.

"Yes, he is that, but he means you no harm."

"And Jesse?" the brave inquired.

"He's certainly no coward," Tory explained, "but all he wants is our freedom."

"No it isn't," Araña reminded her, and he could tell by the blush that filled her cheeks that he was right. "Go on back to him, but do not tell him what we have said, or," he added with a teasing grin, "have done."

Eager to go, Tory got up and started back down the mountain, but she knew he need not worry she would say too much. That she had kissed an Indian brave was a secret she would take to her grave. Appalled by that grisly thought, she feared she was becoming as morbid an individual as Araña.

When she reached level ground she turned to look back up at him. He was standing now, and the gentle evening breeze had caught the ends of his long hair. He was a handsome sight, and yet at the same time, a very disturbing one. She heard the drummer begin the slow beat of the Ghost Dance and hurried on ahead of Araña to be the first to reach camp. His tale of his people's plight had touched her, and she prayed that somehow her words of reason would soon touch him.

Chapter 12

The birds awakened Tory in the morning. She had not realized how quiet the desert had been until the birds that lived in the valley began to greet the new day long before dawn. Their exuberance echoed all around her in high-pitched songs that not only filled the trees where the feathered revelers nested but spilled out over the meadow as well. At another time, their musical calls would have delighted her, but not today.

Thinking she would never get used to sleeping on the ground, Tory shifted her position restlessly. She glanced toward Jesse, found him also awake and watching her with an expression that was not at all friendly. She had again been vague in her report of her conversation with Araña. She had known even as she had spoken that Jesse had suspected there was far more to the exchange than she would admit. It was clear that even after several hours of sleep he held the same opinion.

"Should we get up?" she asked.

"No, not until Araña starts shouting for us to get to work. Prisoners never show a bit of initiative."

He looked so distressed at the memory that Tory wished she could think of some way to restore his usually high spirits. "It can't take more than a day to build *wickiups*. The Indians will leave to conduct raids then. Maybe we'll be able to escape tomorrow."

"Are you sure that you still want to go?"

"What do you mean?"

His meaning crystal clear in his view, Jesse could not believe she did not see it, too. "Araña is handsome in his own way. His interest in you would undoubtedly double if he realized you were a woman. Perhaps you'd enjoy that."

That Jesse could imagine that she would welcome any man's attentions shocked Tory so deeply that it took her a moment to respond. She finally got up and went down to the stream rather than tell him what she thought of him to his face. That he could be jealous of Araña, when all she had done was attempt to make the Apache seek a peaceful solution to his grievances, made her absolutely livid. Perhaps the brave had kissed her, but she had not responded to his affection any more warmly than she had to Jesse's.

She splashed water on her face and sat back on her heels. How had she ever gotten herself into such a horrible situation? Her father had scoffed when his colleagues at Yale had described the Arizona Territory as too uncivilized a place to visit. Earl Crandell had simply laughed at their warnings and promised they would have a fine adventure. Well, it had been an adventure all right, Tory agreed, but certainly not a fine one.

She did not hear Araña approaching and jumped when he laid his hand on her shoulder. "Good morning," she greeted him shyly.

He knelt by her side before speaking. "Today you will help me build a *wickiup* and tonight you will share it with me. If Jesse objects, I will kill him. Tell him what I intend to do so he will have the whole day to accept it. I would kill him now, but he is strong enough to work and it would be a waste not to use him."

Araña's expression was stern. His mind was made up and he clearly would not change it. "I don't think a man who despises whites ought to be sharing his *wickiup* with a white woman," Tory pointed out. "What if I gave you a son? Would you love only the half that is Apache?"

"Would you love only the half that is white?" he taunted.

They were so different in all respects that Tory could not truly believe they might produce a child together. "I don't

186

want us to be enemies, Araña, but if you kill my people, that's all we'll ever be."

"I do not care if you despise me," he scoffed. "That will only make you more exciting." He rose and walked away, the matter settled in his mind.

Tory stared after him, unable to think of anything more to say or do. She was an escaped murderess. Could having an Apache husband make things any worse? Yes, she decided, it definitely could. The stream was wide but shallow. She could not drown herself here. Araña had taken their knives, and when he loaned Mayleen one to cook, one of the braves always stood by to make certain she was the only one who used it. There was the rocky mountainside she and Araña had climbed the previous day. Perhaps she could make her way up higher and throw herself off it.

She sat quietly observing the bubbles in the swiftly flowing stream and attempted to gather the courage to end her life until she realized what Araña would do to her friends if he found her lifeless body at the base of the cliff. He might keep Mayleen alive to prepare meals, but he had made his dislike for Jesse and Ivan more than plain. He would kill them both, and she doubted it would be quickly, either. No, he would be so angry with her that he would torture them for hours until they begged to be shot rather than suffer another minute of the agony he would undoubtedly inflict.

Her body felt as though it were made of lead as she rose to her feet. Araña was a cold-blooded killer, but so was she. Perhaps they were a perfect match after all.

Jesse observed Araña's determined frown as he returned from the stream, and knew whatever had transpired between the brave and Tory this time had not been pleasant. When Tory reentered the camp after a long delay, her expression was one of such heart-wrenching despair he could not bear to see it and immediately confronted her.

He had hidden an important secret about himself, but he demanded the truth from her. "Something has happened between you and Araña," he insisted. "Whatever it is, it's too important for you to keep to yourself. I won't be mad at you, only at him. Tell me what it is."

Even with several days' growth of beard, Jesse looked concerned rather than menacing, but Tory just shook her head. "Paul destroyed whatever love I could have given a man. Don't throw away your life for me. It would be a waste. I'm not worth it." She walked past him to where Araña had begun cutting a circular outline of perhaps twelve feet in diameter into the turf to mark the place where he would build his *wickiup*.

"What do you want me to do?" she asked him.

If Araña was surprised by her willingness to help, he did not let it show. "First we will make this circle six or seven inches deep. Then I will cut some poles to make the frame and you can gather branches to cover them. I'm sorry I have no shovels. We will have to use sticks to dig. It's the way we were forced to plant our crops."

Tory had too much on her mind to worry over their lack of tools. She took the pointed stick he had fashioned and began to excavate the interior of the large circle while he sharpened the end of another stick for himself. The grass-covered earth was soft, and easy to remove. She worked beside Araña, helping him construct his home, but she let her mind go blank as she had so often in the Cactus Springs jail. Her past was too painful to recall, her future nonexistent, and the present merely to be survived.

Araña would not trust either Jesse or Ivan with an ax, so he put them to work excavating the circular bases for other *wickiups* while he and his men cut the long lower boughs from pine trees. After stripping off the branches, they placed the bare limbs at regular intervals around the circle he and Tory had created and then secured them at the top. They covered the poles with the severed branches as well as those Tory had gathered and then packed the earth removed from the inner circle around the exterior to reinforce the base.

Pleased with his efforts, Araña stepped back to admire his new dwelling. Several other *wickiups* were in various stages of completion, and he was satisfied his *ranchería* would be established by the end of the day. He did not have the patience to await sundown before announcing his intentions where Tory was concerned, however. He reached for her hand, drew her close, removed first her hat and then her scarf to display her flowing curls to everyone's view.

He said nothing, but glared at Jesse with a mocking stare that demanded either meek submission or a vigorous protest. As for Tory, she shook her head to warn Jesse not to interfere.

Mayleen dropped the branches she had gathered and stood gawking alongside Ivan. "Why didn't you tell us Tory was a girl?" she gasped. Not pleased to have been duped, she demanded an explanation from Jesse. "Well?" she continued. "Why didn't you tell us?"

Jesse paid absolutely no attention to the irate prostitute. "How long have you known?" he shouted at Araña as he walked toward him.

"Long enough," the brave replied smugly. He then broke into peals of deep laughter his men readily echoed.

Jesse did not need to ask Tory if she wanted the Apache because he knew damn well that she did not. All she wanted was to be left alone, and he could not allow her to pretend otherwise. "Tory is a woman," he announced boldly. "She is not a horse that you can steal. Let her go."

"No," Araña refused just as adamantly. "She is mine."

"You will have to kill me first," Jesse swore.

"It will be a pleasure," Araña replied before speaking in his own tongue to several of his men who came forward, clearly eager to make short work of Jesse.

"Stop it!" Tory screamed. "I told you to stay out of this, Jesse. I'm not worth fighting over and you know it."

"Well, I say that you are!" Jesse shot right back at her. He dodged to avoid the approaching braves, but kept on talking to Araña. "This is just between you and me. You want my woman, so you are going to have to fight me for her. Aren't you man enough to fight me yourself? Does it take half a dozen Apaches to kill one white man?"

"Jesse, let her go!" Mayleen shrieked, but Ivan quickly clamped one hand around her waist and the other over her mouth to silence her.

Stung by Jesse's last taunt, Araña called off his men. Jesse was taller than he was, heavier, too, but that would also mean that he would be slower and far easier to kill. Certain he could beat him, Araña drew his knife and ordered one of his men to pass a knife to Jesse. He brought Tory's hand to his lips before releasing her.

"She was never your woman," he murmured in a low, menacing growl. He gestured for Jesse to come forward, daring him to come within range of his well-honed blade.

Jesse tossed his hat aside, and while he appeared to be watching only Araña, he also took careful note of the positions of the other braves. After three days, he recognized each as a distinct individual. Several were nearly as handsome as Araña, others had faces which could only be described as bland. A couple had such sharp features that they looked downright mean, and Jesse wanted to make certain he knew exactly where those two stood.

He began to circle slowly, close enough to lure Araña into striking out, and yet far enough away so that he could easily avoid him. He knew he was at a disadvantage because he dared not kill the brave. He had to simply disarm him, leaving him vulnerable and in a mood to bargain.

"I've crushed many a spider beneath the heel of my boot," he boasted. "I can do the same to you."

Araña laughed at Jesse's efforts to unnerve him and tossed his knife from his right hand to his left and back again. "This is one spider you'll never touch," he responded.

Tory had retrieved her hat and scarf and, feeling sick to her stomach, kept them clasped over her heart as she moved back out of the men's way. She might have kept right on going had she not bumped into a brave who refused to let her by him. Forced to stand and watch a brutal fight she felt certain would surely end in Jesse's death, her vision was soon obscured by tears. The man was being a complete and utter fool and that he was doing it for her was tragic.

She remembered his arrival in Cactus Springs and how he had listened to her side of the story of the events leading to Paul's death and had actually been sympathetic. He had saved her from a hangman's noose and, while he had never explained why, he had made her feel safe and protected while she was in his care. Now he was risking his life for a reason she could not begin to understand. He had more courage than sense, it seemed, but she could not bear to see him suffer even the slightest injury on her account.

Araña was closest to her now. The sun cast blue highlights on his long ebony mane and, despite the wildness of his appearance, she thought they were very much alike. As they had worked on the *wickiup,* he had continued to describe the despicable way his people had been treated with a conviction she had had to admire. According to him, the Apaches had been lied to, cheated, and murdered with a terrifying frequency.

His people had every reason to hate the white men who had abused them so badly, but Jesse had not been one of them, and she wanted desperately to end this senseless fight. She took a step, meaning to throw herself between the two men, but the brave behind her quickly grabbed her arms and jerked her back out of the way. She already knew neither man would listen to reason, but she struggled to find some way to prevent them from killing each other.

Araña was as agile as the insect for which he was named, and leapt out of Jesse's reach each time the Texan lunged for him. He would dart close and then escape Jesse's thrusts with a playful ease. Moving suddenly to his left, he watched Jesse slip and instantly took advantage of the taller man's momentary lapse of attention while he fought to regain his balance. Wanting the fight to last as long as possible, Araña did not slash his throat, but jabbed his forearm instead and gave a gleeful laugh as he drew blood.

Jesse's headache had returned with near blinding intensity shortly after the fight had begun, so he had already known he was in serious trouble long before he felt the searing pain in his arm. It was all he could do just to see the constantly leaping and lunging Apache, let alone parry his fiendish, slashing blows. Araña fought with the devil's own cunning, but Jesse stubbornly refused to let him win.

The proud fugitive's thoughts were too full of Tory for him to give in. He wanted to live to see her smile, to hear her laugh, to watch her be the joyful woman she had every right to be. Attracted first by her stunning blond beauty, he had soon fallen in love with her courageous spirit. She was a woman well worth fighting for, worth dying for, but he knew she deserved a champion who would survive any test to defend her.

His sleeve now soaked with blood, Jesse had no choice but to attack while he still had the strength left to do so. He threw his whole body at Araña this time, and catching the brave's right wrist, forced his knife away. He pushed the Indian down into the dirt and used every ounce of determination he possessed to keep him there. Breathing hard, he was unable to make any demand before a volley of shots rang out from the far end of the valley.

Jesse was as horrified by the sight of the rapidly approaching cavalry troops as Araña and his men, and he scrambled off the startled brave and yanked him to his feet. "Come on," he yelled. "We've got to take cover!" He reached for Tory, caught her hand, and pulled her along as he joined the braves in running for the rocky mountainside beyond the stream. He saw Ivan and Mayleen staring like witless children and made a grab for them, too.

"Come on," he screamed, "or you'll be caught in the crossfire!"

The obvious truth in that warning jolted Ivan out of his stupor, and he and Mayleen joined the others in dashing for the safety offered by the cliffs. They all clawed their way up the mountainside, seeking cover wherever it could be found. Higher and higher they scrambled, sending loose rocks raining down on those below.

Dizzy from his head wound and loss of blood, Jesse nonetheless kept pushing and pulling his friends up the face of the cliff. The Indians had paused long enough to pick up their weapons and ammunition so he knew they would put up a fierce fight, and all he wanted was a safe place to hide. At last they reached a protected ledge and he stopped as soon as he realized they would all be safe behind the outcropping of rock surrounding it. With shaking hands, he began to unbutton his shirt.

"Here," he ordered as he passed it to Tory. "Wrap up my arm before I bleed to death."

In a welcome flash of foresight, Ivan had grabbed up a canteen as they had dashed through camp, and he handed it to Tory. "Rinse the wound, and then give him a drink," he suggested.

Jesse took a refreshing gulp, but then refused more. "We better save all we can. The Apaches will never surrender and we could be stuck up here for days."

Agreeing with that prediction, Ivan sat down and pulled Mayleen into his arms. "Just keep your head down," he ordered.

Tory used the knife Jesse had kept to slash his shirt into wide strips. She then covered the deep gash in his arm with a thick wad of material and wrapped it firmly to keep it in place. "I'm sorry, I'm not very good at this."

Jesse tilted his head back against the cliff and tried not to laugh. The soldiers had reached the base of the mountain and were returning the Apaches' fire. "A neat bandage is the least of our problems, my dear."

"I'm not your 'dear.' How could you have risked your life over me?"

"You're welcome," Jesse sighed, but in the next instant a bullet ricocheted off the rocks behind him and he shoved Tory down across his lap in an attempt to keep her safe. "If Araña's so damn clever, why didn't he think to post a sentry?" he complained.

"You sound like you're on the Apaches' side," Ivan swore in astonishment.

Tory struggled to sit up, but Jesse refused to release her and kept her pressed to his bare chest as he replied, "I am. It's possible the Army is looking for Tory and me as well as for Araña and his men. We'll have to pretend she's a boy again and give them false names. I'll say she's my kid brother Sean, and that I'm Patrick O'Shaughnessy. Those are good names."

"I don't think I can spell O'Shaughnessy," Tory confessed.

Jesse had to laugh then. "Christ, woman, when did you start worrying about such silly things?"

Tory was too frightened to reply, or to care about how close he was holding her. She clung to him for a long while before replying, "This is all my fault," she apologized. "I've brought you nothing but bad luck."

Jesse stroked her hair lightly. "Hush, you've done nothing of the kind, little brother."

Still wrapped firmly in Ivan's arms, Mayleen was fascinated by their conversation. "I still don't understand why you didn't tell us Tory was a girl!"

Another of the soldiers' bullets cut through the air so close they heard an audible whine, and Jesse scoffed at her question. "That's our business, Mayleen, so just shut up about it. Maybe you two ought to think up some new names, too. Someone might have figured out that the four of us are together and that wouldn't be good for any of us."

"We'll be damn lucky if we aren't killed," Ivan reminded him. "Names won't matter then."

"Well, on the chance you don't die," Jesse scolded, "you better have some new names ready. How about Matilda and Mortimer Murphy?"

"Why have we become Irish all of a sudden?" Mayleen asked.

"Carlos and Consuelo Gonzales?" Jesse suggested instead.

Ivan needed a drink, and badly. They were sitting amidst a hail of bullets, and Jesse expected them to come up with new names. All he cared about was getting a drink. He wondered if the soldiers had a bottle or two with them. Hoping they did, he began to pray the battle would soon be over. Climbing up the mountain had bruised every inch of him that had not been bruised before and he was thoroughly miserable. He held on to Mayleen knowing she would think he was being protective of her, but, in truth, he was just too scared to let go.

After another bullet came uncomfortably close, Jesse urged Tory to move farther along the ledge. Ivan and Mayleen felt secure where they were and did not follow, but that suited the Texan just fine. Once he was certain they were safely concealed, he again pulled Tory into his arms. "I doubt the Army will have heard of us, but just in case they have, I'm going to say the O'Shaughnessys were coming from Las Cruces and have now decided to go on back home."

"What makes you so sure the Army is going to win?"

"Now there's a thought," Jesse admitted with a grimace. "If the Apaches manage to shoot every last one of the soldiers, then I guess I'll have to fight Araña all over again."

"No, you mustn't!" Tory argued. She tried to sit up to make conversation easier but Jesse refused to let her go and she was forced to remain huddled against him. She had set her hat and scarf aside and the fingers of her right hand were spread across Jesse's stomach with her thumb resting in the small indentation created by his navel. She had not noticed until that very instant how natural the gesture seemed when surely it was not.

Jesse had forced her to sleep with her head on his shoulder on more than one occasion, but she had avoided touching him as best she could then. Now the smooth warmth of his bare skin seemed as familiar as her own flesh and she did not understand how such a remarkable transformation could have occurred. He was the same man. Why was she no longer frightened by his touch? she wondered.

The coarse curls covering his chest matched the dark hue of his beard rather than the lighter reddish-brown hair on his head. Thoroughly distracted, she toyed with the crisp hairs that narrowed to a thin line above his navel until he started to laugh and covered her hand with his.

"This is an odd time to want to tickle me," he teased.

While she was deeply embarrassed that she had actually been fondling him, Tory left her hand in Jesse's. "Sorry," she murmured, not realizing she was so close her lips would graze his chest. With rifle fire splattering into the rocks just below them, she knew she ought to be helping Jesse plan their next move, but she was all too aware of him to be logical.

She closed her eyes for a moment, but he was much too near to shut him out that easily. It had been the knife fight, she now knew, for the danger Jesse had willingly faced on her behalf had stirred feelings she had thought she no longer

195

possessed. She had not wanted to see him hurt not only because he had rescued her from certain death, but because she had gradually come to care for him without even realizing it. She bit her lower lip to force back the tears that threatened to overwhelm her. Fighting for control, she looked up at him.

"Don't fight Araña again," she implored him. "I'd make a far better wife for a renegade than for you."

Jesse knew precisely what she was doing: sacrificing herself to save him. But he would never allow it. "I'll fight the bastard as often as it takes to convince him you're my woman rather than his," he stated with unmistakable conviction. He again wound his fingers in her silken curls and forced her head against his chest. "Stay down," he ordered gruffly, despite the tenderness of his gesture. They were in far worse trouble than she realized and he sure as hell did not want to see her get shot.

While it was impossible to see how the lively battle was going, from the amount of fire coming from the mountain it certainly sounded as though the Apaches had plenty of ammunition for the fight. They would not have weapons on the reservation, so Tory knew they must have taken them from the whites who Araña had admitted killing. She wondered how many there had been. Apparently the Army had been in close pursuit, but, like Jesse, she hoped they did not realize one of the Apaches' hostages was a woman already condemned to death. Yes, it would be better to introduce herself as Sean O'Shaughnessy. She just hoped she had the chance.

After a violent beginning, the hostilities soon developed a rhythm, a recognizable ebb and flow of rifle fire that continued throughout the day. At times there were brief periods of calm, but each was shattered by additional gunshots. Once Tory thought she heard the soldiers calling Araña's name, but the only answer came from a rifle. Neither Tory nor Jesse felt hungry, but they did slide the canteen back and forth between themselves and Mayleen and Ivan at regular intervals until it was empty.

As dusk neared, Jesse began to stretch. "Once it gets dark, I'll make my way down to the stream and fill the canteen," he promised.

"No, it's not worth the risk," Tory warned him. She was positive she was as uncomfortable as he, having spent the day on the same narrow ledge that left their limbs cramped no matter how frequently they had adjusted their positions.

Jesse took a deep breath and held it a long moment before letting it out. "I've heard the Apaches don't fight at night. I doubt the Army will waste ammunition when they can't see where they're firing. I won't be in any worse danger than I've been in all day."

"No," Tory argued. "You might fall. Even worse, either side may mistake you for the enemy and shoot."

"If I didn't know you better," Jesse mused aloud, "I'd think you're actually growing fond of me."

Tory wasn't up to taking his teasing and refused to admit that he had guessed the truth. Instead, she stuck with the previous subject. "It would make more sense for all of us to try and move higher, to go over the mountain, rather than for you to climb down just to fill a canteen."

Jesse flexed the fingers of his right hand as he considered her suggestion. Her bandage, crude as it was, had stemmed the flow of blood from the deep cut, but his whole arm felt sore and weak. There was also the fact he had felt dizzy coming up the mountain. That sensation might swiftly return if he exerted himself. He thought he could make it down to the stream and back, but that was as ambitious a plan as he dared concoct. He did not want to admit that to Tory, however.

"No," he countered. "We'll have to stay here. You and I might be able to climb the mountain in the dark, but Ivan and Mayleen wouldn't even try and I'll not leave them."

"I didn't ask you to."

"I know you didn't," Jesse assured her. The temperatures were far cooler in the mountains than out in the desert and all they had to look forward to was a cold and miserable night unless the Apaches decided to surrender, which he doubted Araña would ever do. As both sides took advantage of the waning light to fire off several last rounds, he again pulled Tory close. She had not once complained that he was holding her too tight, and as for him, he did not think he would ever tire of hugging her.

"Just go to sleep," he suggested. "That will make the night pass faster."

"I'm not tired." Tory found it impossible to want to sleep in the middle of an armed battle. "Will the soldiers advance?" she asked. "They might be able to get into better position during the night and then open fire as soon as it gets light."

"I've never served in the military so I've no idea what they might do, but that certainly sounds like a good strategy to me." After a moment's thought, he continued. "It's also possible the Apache might shift positions. If I were Araña, I'd move my men off the mountain, circle the Army, and ride out of the valley taking their horses with me. Stranded here, they would no longer be a threat."

"Do you suppose Araña's thought of that?"

"He's very clever," Jesse complimented sincerely. *Too damn clever to leave the woman he had chosen behind,* he thought but did not add. He could easily imagine Araña scaling the mountainside, finding Tory, and then finishing him off with one shot. It was not a pleasant thought, but the more Jesse considered it, the more likely it seemed that Araña would come for Tory and then disappear with his men leaving the Army left guarding a deserted mountain. It would not be completely deserted, of course, for Mayleen and Ivan would still be there to greet them at dawn.

What a remarkable welcoming committee, Jesse thought to himself with a hearty chuckle. Tory attempted to muffle the sound of his laughter with her hand, but he simply grabbed her wrist and kissed her palm. The next thing he knew, her fingertips had slid over his temple and into his hair with a gesture that struck him as being deliciously affectionate. Perhaps it was only that it was what he wanted so badly, but he wasted no time in debating her intentions.

He pulled her down across his lap and kissed her with a

passionate enthusiasm that left her too stunned to draw away. "I love you," he whispered before covering her mouth with another devouring kiss. For all he knew, that might well be the last night of his life and he wanted to spend it making love to the woman he adored. That he had damn little room, and that Tory might not be all that eager to consummate their love did not faze him one bit.

Chapter 13

Tory merely had been withdrawing her hand when her fingers inadvertently strayed into Jesse's thick chestnut curls, and his passionate response was completely unexpected. His fevered kisses were seductively sweet, but the fright that surged within her was paralyzing. She wanted only to escape him by whatever means possible, but the fact they were in such a confined space, combined with his possessive embrace, prevented her from gaining even the smallest bit of leverage to push him away.

Wherever she placed her hands she found the heat of his bare back or chest so inviting that she did not want to scratch him with her nails. In desperation she reached again for his hair but that only served to inspire further adoring kisses from the eager young man. His ardor presented a sharp contrast to the sweetness of Araña's affection and she suddenly recalled the brave's admonition that she think only of him.

Could she now think only of Jesse rather than the horror his demanding affection recalled? It was what she sincerely wished to do, but in the next instant she scraped her elbow against the rocky face of the cliff and, startled, cried out in pain.

Jesse leaned back to see what was wrong. "Did I hurt you?" he asked, fearing he had been clumsy. He stroked her hair and patted her back as he awaited her reply.

Tory rubbed her aching elbow as she attempted to come

up with a tactful way to explain her true dilemma without insulting him. He already knew why she found his forceful affection objectionable and she did not want to have to remind him. Mayleen and Ivan were seated perhaps ten feet away, and while the curve of the cliff as well as the deepening twilight shielded them from view, she was uncomfortably aware of how close the two were.

"I hit my elbow," she finally explained. "There really isn't enough room here for what you were trying to do."

"For what *I* was trying to do?" Jesse repeated incredulously. "I wasn't alone just now, Tory."

Disappointed to have said the wrong thing despite her best efforts not to, Tory sat huddled against the rocks, rubbing her sore elbow and wishing they were anywhere but where they were. "I told you you were wasting time on me," she blurted out when the lengthy silence between them became unbearably awkward.

"No, I'm not!" Jesse could no longer see her face clearly, but he felt her flinch at the hostility of his tone and regretted hurting her. "Look, I'm sorry. There's a lot you don't know about me, but when I say that I love you, you can be certain I mean it. Please don't tell me not to love you when I already do."

"But how can you?" Tory whispered, the disbelief tainting each word.

Jesse didn't understand her dismay. "You're bright, charming. Even dressed as a boy you're beautiful. How could I not love you?"

"But after Paul . . ." she reminded him hesitantly.

"Oh, hell, I don't blame you for shooting the bastard. If any man ever deserved it, he did. Just forget him. I'm a different man, and I'll never give you reason to wish me dead."

While Tory had long considered him wonderfully generous in his views, that had not been what she had meant. "No, you misunderstood," she explained softly. "How can you want me after what he did to me?"

That question hurt Jesse worse than the knife wound in his

arm. His throat clogged with emotion, he drew her back into a fervent embrace and pressed her close to his heart. "It shouldn't have happened," he finally assured her. "But it doesn't make you any less desirable as a woman, or any less worthy of love. My God, who made you think that—those fools in Cactus Springs?"

The citizens of Cactus Springs had said every hateful thing possible. Several had even spit on her. More than one had suggested that she ought to have shot herself if she could not live with what Paul had done. None of them had understood why Paul had been the one to die. "It doesn't matter now," she murmured against his chest.

Jesse was positive that it did, but he did not want to force her to talk about something that obviously had caused her a great deal of pain. "I'm sorry I didn't get there sooner. You shouldn't have had to spend even one day in jail."

"You shouldn't have been in prison, either."

She had just provided him with the perfect opportunity to admit he was an escaped convict rather than a United States marshal with a criminal past, but Jesse did not want to talk about his own troubles when her mood was so downcast. He wanted to concentrate on *her,* to make her feel loved. The wildness of his kisses had obviously failed to move her. Until she could fully grasp the fact that he loved her, and dearly, he doubted that she would ever feel any love for him.

"I'm sorry," he apologized again. "I shouldn't have jumped on you like that. It's just that our chances to be together are, well . . ." He paused then, not wanting to admit he feared they might all end up dead and that he did not want to die without making love to her. "I just wasn't thinking is all."

"Under the best of circumstances, I don't know how to make love," Tory revealed. "This doesn't seem like a good place to learn."

"Well now, I thought a moonlit cliff was sort of romantic, but if you don't agree, I'll wait until there's a big feather bed available."

Fearing that he was making fun of her, Tory leaned back

slightly. "Are you laughing at me?" she asked shyly.

"No." He pulled her close and kissed her, but this time very gently. The Army chose the next instant to bombard the face of the mountain with random fire. A bullet slammed into the cliff not two feet from Jesse's head and he cradled Tory in his arms protectively as airborne chards of granite went flying all around him. He tried not to cry out as one slashed into his left shoulder, but Tory felt him wince and knew he had been hit.

"It's just a scratch," he assured her, "but I think you're right about this being an inappropriate place to make love. There's no telling where we might get hit if we got lost in each other, and I sure as hell don't want to risk losing anything vital."

Tory was certain he was teasing her now, but she was too badly frightened to appreciate his attempt at humor. She knew there were some scraps from his shirt lying nearby, but it was too dark to see them so she raised her hand to his shoulder and felt the warm stickiness of blood. "Oh, God, you *are* hurt," she cried.

"It's nothing."

"Why are they shooting at us now when they can't possibly tell if they hit anyone or not?"

"Apparently the officer in charge had the same idea we had and thinks the Apaches might get away tonight. He's trying to make them stay put."

"Are you two all right?" Ivan called out.

"We're fine!" Jesse assured him. "Don't tell him any different," he warned Tory in a hoarse whisper. "He's already scared to death."

"Aren't you?"

Jesse responded with a sly chuckle. "I've been scared so long I don't recognize the feeling anymore. Now don't fret. We'll get out of this."

Tory kept her hand clamped over the gash in his shoulder until she was sure it had stopped bleeding, and even then she remained snuggled in his embrace. "What if I hadn't been pretty?" she asked. "Would you have taken me on

204

up to Prescott?"

"No!" Jesse answered truthfully. "You could have been a hundred years old and ugly as sin and I'd not have delivered you to the hangman."

Perhaps it was because she had lost her mother so early and had not been fussed over while growing up, but Tory had never given much thought to her looks. In her teen years she had discovered that men found her attractive, but she had never allowed their compliments to spoil her. If anything, their flattering comments had annoyed her, for she feared they saw only her appearance and were blind to the person within.

Prettiness was such a superficial quality in her view, and she had endeavored to cultivate her mind so that a man drawn to her beauty would find she had meaningful thoughts as well. Some men had clearly been disappointed to find she possessed a keen mind, but she had thought them insufferably arrogant to believe only men's ideas mattered and had not missed their company one bit. She had expected to return to Connecticut when her father had completed his research on xerophytic plants and to one day marry an ambitious young professor who would appreciate her intellect as well as her feminine charms.

To have veered so far from that predictably comfortable path that she now found herself perched on a mountain ledge wrapped in an ex-convict's arms, while hoping to survive a battle between the United States Cavalry and Apache renegades was ludicrous in the extreme. Since arriving in the Arizona Territory, her life had taken so many excruciatingly painful turns that she scarcely dared hope she would ever return to the placid existence she had once enjoyed. She inhaled deeply, and decided she ought not to think too far ahead. Just surviving the night would be a sufficient challenge for the time being.

A long while passed before Tory fell asleep in Jesse's arms. She had failed to admit that she even liked him, he mused, let alone had any feelings approaching love. That was damn disappointing, but the fact she had welcomed his touch provided some encouragement at least. He still longed to make love to her, but knew she deserved a far better setting than this one.

The soldiers fired at irregular intervals all night, but the Apaches did not respond. During the long stretches of quiet on the mountain, Jesse strained to listen for sounds that would prove the renegades were still occupying the ledges below, but the silence was unbroken. Occasionally he overheard bits of Mayleen and Ivan's conversation, but not enough to follow it. They seemed as restless as he, and he began to envy Tory's ability to rest in such an impossible situation.

Gradually the darkness began to lift, and when it grew light enough for him to see the pale sheen of Tory's long curls, he thought it a shame she would again have to cover her pretty hair. A few minutes later the soldiers began to shout to the Apaches to surrender, and when there was no rifle fire in response, Jesse shook Tory to wake her.

"Something's happened," he explained. "Better put on your scarf. We might not be stuck up here as long as we'd feared. Ivan!" he shouted. "You and Mayleen awake?"

The geologist risked crawling around the ledge to greet them. "The Indians are too quiet. Do you think we ought to start yelling so the Army will know there are civilians up here before they start shooting again?"

"No," Jesse argued. "That would also remind Araña that we're up here. We're hostages, remember, not simply citizens who were out for a picnic and happened to get caught in the middle of a war."

"Good point," Ivan agreed, and after negotiating a tight squeeze, managed to turn around on the ledge and return to Mayleen.

Frightened away by the gunfire, there were no birds singing that morning and Tory found the eerie silence unsettling. "Something's wrong," she whispered to Jesse. "Either the Apaches have fled, or too many of them are dead to continue the fight."

Jesse nodded. He ran his hand over his beard and hoped it

would serve to disguise his appearance sufficiently for him to fool the Army even if they had his description. "I think you're right, little brother, but let's just wait for the Army to make the first move. The O'Shaughnessys have never been noted for being impulsive men."

"Do you actually know them?"

"No, but if I say Patrick and Sean are two of the most deliberate individuals ever born, don't contradict me."

"The less we say to the Army the better," Tory assured him. She worked to tuck all of her hair up under her scarf, and then donned her hat. "Do you think they'll give us time to clean up before we have to leave?"

"We'll just take it," Jesse explained. "We don't have to travel with the Army."

"Won't they think it strange if we don't?"

"Probably, but remember, we'll be heading back to New Mexico, and they'll be returning to Arizona."

They heard Ivan cry out then, and Jesse picked up the knife he had been loaned to fight Araña. "Stay behind me," he ordered as he drew himself up into a low crouch. He dared not stand and draw the soldiers' fire, but he had no intention of sitting meekly on the ledge if the Apaches came up after them.

When the Apaches had failed to answer their call to surrender with either insults or gunfire, the soldiers had begun a slow ascent of the mountain. The corporal who reached Mayleen and Ivan's position was so astonished to find the Apaches had white captives that he failed to greet them with the proper enthusiasm. He simply turned and yelled down to the lieutenant that he had found someone alive.

Hearing that exchange, Jesse shouted, "There are a couple more of us over here." He waited for the corporal to round the curve before he rose and offered Tory a hand to help her to her feet. "Glad to see you," he greeted the young soldier. "We haven't been able to see a damn thing from up here. What's happened?"

While Tory was vitally interested in hearing the young

207

man's response, she pulled her hat low to shade her face before turning his way. She was ashamed that both she and Jesse looked so disheveled until she realized it was to their advantage to be completely unrecognizable.

"We've only found nine bodies," the corporal reported. "There's no sign of the rest of the Apaches. Maybe they turned into bats and flew away last night. Come on, let's get you two down to the lieutenant. He'll have plenty of questions."

"I just bet he will," Jesse remarked with a wide grin he hoped would fool anyone who might doubt he was elated to have been rescued. He winked at Tory, and then followed the corporal down to the foot of the mountain. Ivan and Mayleen had already been given cups of coffee, but the lieutenant had waited to gather all four captives together to interrogate them.

Ivan saw Jesse's curious glance and realized the Texan had no idea what names they had just given, so he repeated them. "As I said, we're John and Ethelrose Stone and these are the O'Shaughnessy brothers, Patrick and Sean. I guess you already know how grateful we are that you arrived when you did."

The Army officer reached out to shake hands with Jesse and Tory. "Roger Barlow," he introduced himself. "We've been tracking Araña ever since the day after he left the reservation. He's responsible for nineteen deaths that we know of, but there are probably people missing that we haven't heard about yet. It isn't like the Apaches to take prisoners. What made you four so lucky?"

Jesse shrugged. "Can't say."

When his companions did not provide opinions of their own, Barlow prodded them. "None of you know why your lives were spared?"

"It was God's will," Mayleen interjected when she realized no one else was going to speak.

"Well, yes, of course," the puzzled lieutenant agreed, "but Araña was shooting people right and left. He obviously wasn't out of ammunition, so why didn't he shoot you all as well?"

"We listened to him," Tory responded. "Apparently no one else did."

"Listened to him?" Barlow scoffed. "Just what did he have to say?"

Jesse quickly stepped forward to shift the officer's attention away from Tory. "He had a list of grievances about the way his people have been treated. Maybe if the Apache had received the proper respect from the Indian agents and Army personnel charged with their care, those nineteen people would still be alive."

Lieutenant Barlow stared at Jesse with a peculiar mixture of amazement and disgust, then shook his head as though he considered the newly freed captive plain crazy. "You've got a gash in your head, one on your shoulder, and a bandage on your arm. It sure doesn't look like Araña treated you with a large dose of respect." He then gestured toward Ivan. "Mr. Stone doesn't look much better."

Ivan had hoped the effects of the beating he had taken had begun to fade by then, and he was disappointed to learn his appearance still evoked pity. He knew he had behaved in a cowardly fashion the whole time they had been held captive and he just wanted to be on his way. "We're alive," he reminded the officer. "So we got better treatment than anyone else these Apaches met. I for one am not going to complain about their hospitality."

"Neither are we," Jesse stated, clearly speaking for his kid brother as well. "If you've no more questions, we'd like to clean up and be on our way. We're from Las Cruces, and while we'd intended to live in the Arizona Territory for a while, we've decided we'd rather just go on back home."

"What about you, Mr. Stone?" the lieutenant asked.

Ivan nodded. "My wife and I feel the same way. We don't want any part of Arizona now. We're all going back to Las Cruces."

"So the four of you were traveling across Sonora from the East when you were captured?"

"That's right," Jesse assured him.

209

"Well, we'll be happy to give you an escort out of these mountains," the officer offered. "As far as we know, there were fifteen men with Araña. We can only account for nine of them today. That means seven are still loose. We'll try and find them, of course. Our trackers should pick up their trail today. You want to wait for us, don't you?"

Jesse gazed out over the valley to make it appear he was giving the lieutenant's question serious thought before he replied. "The renegades wouldn't have gone back toward Arizona," he said. "They'll be traveling south, so we won't be in any danger from them."

"No, probably not," Barlow agreed. "But the situation is a lot worse than you realize. General Carr ordered the arrest of Noch-ay-del-klinne, the medicine man who set Araña on the warpath. The Army had meant to take him in peacefully, but the Apaches started shooting and he was killed near his camp on Cibicu Creek. Araña's band left the reservation the day before that fiasco, but there's a score of other firebrands who haven't stopped shooting since The Dreamer died. It's a sure bet that they're all headed this way. I wouldn't risk getting captured twice if I were you."

That was a complication Jesse had not foreseen. "The Dreamer's dead? Are you positive about that?"

"Yes, there's no mistake. He's had his last dream, and I doubt his followers will have any more success raising him from the dead than he had with the chiefs he promised to return to life."

Jesse's heated conversation with Araña over The Dreamer had cost him a painful blow to the head and he felt as though he had actually known the revered medicine man. "Well, that changes things considerably. We'll have to talk this over among ourselves," he informed him.

"Take your time," the lieutenant replied. "The burial detail will have to finish up here before we pursue the missing braves."

Tory's back had been to the men digging graves, and now that the conversation with Barlow had drawn to a close, she turned toward them. Jesse grabbed her arm, but she pulled

210

away. "I want to see who died," she insisted, and rather than argue, he followed, but he was as stunned as she to discover Araña had been among the casualties.

He stepped behind her and leaned down to whisper in her ear. "It's possible the lieutenant didn't realize Araña was killed. You can't let him see that you cared about him."

Tory understood Jesse's point, but her emotions were too near the surface to hide. The nine slain Apaches had been lain in a row. Several of the bodies had been riddled with bullets, but the bloodstain on the front of Araña's shirt made it plain he had died instantly of a single shot to the heart. He looked as though he had simply stretched out to take a nap, and Tory had to fight the impulse to lean down and shake his foot to wake him. Her eyes filled with tears and she made no attempt to wipe them away.

Seeing the O'Shaughnessy brothers studying the bodies, Lieutenant Barlow followed them. "We think this one is Araña," he pointed out accurately. "Do you know the names of any of the others?"

"That's Araña all right," Jesse confirmed. "None of the others ever spoke to us, so we had no cause to learn their names."

Despite Jesse's attempt to block his view, Barlow noticed Tory's tears. "I never thought I'd live to see the day a white man would weep over the death of a murdering renegade," he muttered cynically.

Not about to allow the officer to criticize Tory for any reason, Jesse gripped her shoulders in a brotherly hug. "Sean is a sensitive lad. He's long talked of becoming a priest, and I believe the fact we've escaped death at the Apaches' hands means he has a true calling. You should consider yourself blessed to have met him. He may well be a saint someday. He's not crying for Araña, but, I can assure you, for his victims."

Not a religious man, Roger Barlow was badly embarrassed by that show of brotherly pride and affection, and he excused himself immediately to speak with his scouts. Jesse did not take a breath until the officer was out of earshot.

Four soldiers were digging graves, but they were occupied with that task and unmindful of Tory's grief.

"I want you to find our things and go down to the stream to clean up and change your clothes," Jesse instructed. "Do your laundry while you're there. I'll bring you something to eat and then I want you to lie down and sleep for the rest of the day. I don't mind if you want to shed a few tears over Araña when you came damn close to being his wife, but these soldiers will never understand why you have such strong feelings for the man and we can't afford to arouse their curiosity about you. Now go on, get going."

While Tory knew Araña may well have been the murdering renegade the lieutenant had described, he had treated her with a touching kindness she would never forget. "Do you still have the knife?" she asked.

Jesse had tucked it in his belt. "Yes, why?"

"I'd like to have a lock of his hair."

Jesse started to swear and then caught himself. He watched the gravediggers a moment, and when they were occupied, he quickly bent down beside Araña's body and cut off a hank of hair a good foot long. He stood and shoved it into Tory's hand. "There, now go and wash up while I get us something to eat."

Tory clutched the ebony streamer tightly in her hand. Araña had been so full of life that she did not want to stay and watch him being lowered into the ground, but she did not want to abandon him, either. "Please mark his grave somehow so that I can visit it later."

Unable to think of a polite response to that absurd request, Jesse simply nodded. He was not certain what sort of a tombstone might be appropriate for one of The Dreamer's followers, but he could at least place a rock or two on Araña's grave to identify it. Tory left him then, but he lingered to watch the burial detail work. He knew Araña could have killed him whenever he pleased, but the Apache had repeatedly spared his life, and Jesse was certain he had done it out of consideration for Tory. The handsome brave had chosen the wrong way to fight injustice, but Jesse still had to admire his devotion to his people.

"I'll not forget you, friend," he promised minutes before the Indian was laid to rest, and when he turned away, there were tears in his eyes, too.

The professionalism with which Lieutenant Barlow commanded his troops impressed Ivan and he swiftly came to the conclusion that he was not the type to permit drinking among them. Knowing his men would probably not share the same strict view of Army life, he went straight to a pot-bellied sergeant who looked to him like a drinking man. In less than five minutes he and the sergeant had become fast friends and had toasted each other from a bottle the lieutenant had no idea the sergeant habitually carried.

Buoyed by what he considered a life-saving elixir, Ivan wandered about the Indians' camp gathering up his scattered belongings. He was shocked, but nonetheless delighted, to discover his money was still at the bottom of his saddlebags and that Mayleen's strongbox remained in her satchel. He gazed out over the valley and wondered where the missing seven Apaches had gone. Wherever it was, they had obviously not thought they would need money, or perhaps had simply been unable to get to it before they fled.

The cavalry troops had ridden through the camp, destroying the newly constructed *wickiups* before they had ever been used. The sight of the flattened dwellings made Ivan realize how close they had come to being among the Apaches' victims. Had it not been for Tory's mysterious allure, he knew Araña would have shot them all within minutes of waking them. The surprising discovery that Tory was a woman had removed Ivan's previous sense of discomfort in her presence, but he had not been at all surprised that Araña had found the pretty youth as fascinating as he had.

Ivan knew he had no chance of impressing the lovely woman with Jesse around, but he feared he also had no hope of impressing Mayleen, either. Despite her constant complaints about Jesse's lack of interest, Mayleen had not turned her attentions to him. They might have spent several of the worst days and nights of their lives together, but she had failed to develop any real fondness for him. Perhaps that was his fault, he mused thoughtfully. He had always paid for her affection in the past. Maybe now she felt he was taking advantage of her to expect her to care for him for free. He did like her, though, he really did.

By the time Jesse came looking for Ivan, he had cleaned up, had his injuries looked at by the private who was in charge of medical supplies, and had found a change of clothes. He still felt as though he had been up all night, but he was making the time to speak to the geologist before he joined Tory in the tent the lieutenant had assigned them.

"There's something I want to say to you . . ." Jesse began.

Certain he already knew what it was, Ivan started backing away. "I know, you told me not to bring any liquor with me, but I was hurting so bad I had to have something to ease my pain. Mayleen didn't know I had it, and you didn't, either, or you would have said something long before this. There wasn't enough to get all of Araña's men drunk, so nobody suffered when they got ahold of it." Ivan had begun to sweat the instant Jesse had reached him and he had to pause to push his spectacles back into place.

"My ribs still hurt, but I can stand it now. I can get along without any whiskey from now on," Ivan swore with what he hoped was convincing sincerity.

"I don't want to hear any more of your lies," Jesse scoffed. "I'd break you in half, but you're not worth the trouble. It looks like we'll have to stay with the Army a couple of days, but when Tory and I head east, you and Mayleen can just keep on traveling with the troopers. We don't want you with us."

As Jesse started to turn his back on him, Ivan suddenly found the courage to lash out at him. "Letting us believe Tory was a kid was a bigger lie than hiding a bottle or two of whiskey," he shouted. "I think the less said about lies the better, or I just might be tempted to tell Lieutenant Barlow the truth about your kid brother."

Jesse halted in midstride and turned back to face Ivan. "If you so much as whisper a word about Tory to anyone, I'll slit your lying throat. Now stay away from us, Mr. Stone, or you'll find me a worse enemy than any Apache could ever be."

Ivan was shaking so hard he had to sit down as Jesse left the meadow. Jesse had told them to choose new names because it was possible the Army was looking for him and Tory. My God, the shaken geologist wondered, what horrible thing had the couple done?

Chapter 14

Mayleen's sparkling brown eyes widened in horror as Ivan related Jesse's threat. "You don't mean it!" she squealed.

"Oh, yes, I most certainly do," Ivan vowed. "The man actually threatened to kill me. I don't know what to do now. I don't want to go back to Tucson any more than you do, but—"

"Oh, no," Mayleen appealed. "We can't even consider going back there. I'll talk to Jesse after supper. He's been hurt. None of us got much sleep last night. I'll bet he just wasn't thinking clearly."

Ivan scoffed at her summary of the situation. "He despises us both, Mayleen. Why can't you accept that? It won't matter what you say to him. He won't care."

Mayleen had thoroughly enjoyed the respectful way the soldiers had treated her that day. As the happily married Ethelrose Stone, she had been showered with sympathy rather than being the recipient of the numerous lewd suggestions Mayleen Tyler was used to hearing. She was the same woman. The only difference was that Ivan had introduced her as his wife rather than a whore who just happened to be traveling with him.

She had enjoyed the admiring glances that had come her way, but she had savored the soldiers' courtesy even more. Now Ivan had reminded her she ought not to pretend things were other than what they really were. Jesse barely tolerated her and here she was talking like she could influence his decisions. Crushed, she grew as forlorn as Ivan.

"Maybe I could say something to Tory," she finally offered.

Ivan had already thought of that, but he preferred to save that excuse for a reason to talk to the willowy blonde himself. "No, let me speak to her. You and she haven't been on friendly terms for more than a few hours."

Mayleen watched Ivan polish his glasses on his shirttail. "You don't have any better chance of impressing her than I have with Jesse. You ought to be able to see that even without your spectacles."

Not amused by her insightful comment, Ivan straightened his shoulders proudly. "All I'm trying to do is prevent us from being stranded in the desert. I'm not nearly so taken with Tory as you are with Jesse."

"Just remember you called yourself my husband so don't go making a fool of yourself over her in front of the lieutenant and his men."

"I've never made a fool of myself over any woman," Ivan contradicted sharply. "Now we've been invited to join the lieutenant for supper. Let's try and make him think we're actually who we said we were." He tucked in his shirt, then offered his arm and Mayleen looped hers through it, but her expression was not that of a happy wife as they left their tent.

Try as he might, Roger Barlow could not seem to find a topic his guests wanted to discuss. They had obviously enjoyed his food, but they now sat staring off into space rather than being the entertaining companions he had hoped they would be. Disappointed, he made a final attempt to engage their interest. He fumbled in his coat pocket and withdrew some notes he had made.

"Being from New Mexico, I don't suppose any of you have ever heard of a man by the name of Luke Bernay. He's one of the Territory's best trackers. He's in Bisbee waiting for the Apaches to settle down before he continues his pursuit of a man who escaped from the Yuma prison."

Mayleen glanced over at Jesse. His expression did not reveal even a flicker of interest, but the lieutenant's report had certainly piqued her curiosity. "What's the man's name?" she asked.

The lieutenant consulted his notes. "Jesse Lambert . . . but here's the intriguing part . . ." He paused, hoping they would think his information worthy of that description. The Stones appeared eager to hear more even if the O'Shaughnessy brothers weren't, leading him to embellish his tale in hopes of impressing them. "Lambert was serving twenty years for robbery, but escaped and shot a U.S. marshal. He then posed as the dead lawman and abducted a murderess awaiting execution in the Cactus Springs jail."

Thinking that an audacious move, Roger paused to gauge his listeners' reaction. For the first time, Sean O'Shaughnessy was looking directly at him, and the officer was shocked not only by the boy's finely sculpted features, but by the cool green of his eyes. He bore not the slightest resemblance to his older brother, and Roger found his unexpected prettiness strangely disconcerting. With such an angelic face, he supposed the youth might make a fine priest one day. Fearing that he was staring rudely, he again checked his notes.

"Jesse and his deadly companion then traveled to Tucson to meet with a . . . well, another woman employed in one of the more unsavory establishments. Mr. Bernay thinks she must have been holding part of the money taken in the robbery. He also has reason to believe the three were taken prisoner by Araña. I told him the Apaches only kept prisoners alive long enough to kill them. I certainly never expected to find the four of you in their camp. You didn't catch sight of Lambert and the two women, did you? Perhaps Araña mentioned them?"

"He said only that he'd killed people. He didn't describe them," Tory explained, hoping to bring the evening to a swift close so that she could ask Jesse for his side of the lieutenant's astonishing tale.

Mayleen jabbed Ivan in the ribs to put a stop to his gawking. She had never heard the Silver Spur referred to as "unsavory," and was insulted to learn she was suspected of being in on the robbery that had sent Jesse to prison. Maybe he had escaped rather than been released, but she could not believe that he had killed a marshal.

"That's an amazing story, Lieutenant." Mayleen shook her head as though she was completely befuddled by it. "Were those women pretty?"

"From Mr. Bernay's report, the murderess from Cactus Springs, Victoria Crandell, is a beauty, but I doubt the woman from Tucson is attractive. Her profession extracts a terrible toll."

Certainly working at the Silver Spur had not sullied her looks, Mayleen had to force herself to smile rather than dispute the officer's opinion.

Ivan adjusted his glasses. "A murderess, you say?"

"Yes, but I didn't get any details on her. Sorry. They're a dangerous trio, and if justice caught up with them in the form of Araña and his men, so much the better."

Jesse leaned forward slightly. "Fate has a way of overtaking the wicked, so they're undoubtedly dead. If Araña did not kill them, then one of the other bands of renegades you mentioned probably did. Now we'd like to thank you again for the fine meal, but I hope you'll excuse us. Sean and I are still awfully tired."

"Of course. I didn't mean to keep you," Roger apologized. He smiled at the Stones, hoping they might want to remain with him a bit longer, but they leapt up the instant the O'Shaughnessy brothers did and left with them. "Good night!" he called after his guests, but Mrs. Stone was the only one to turn and wave.

The soldiers had made camp near the stream, but Jesse led his party out into the middle of the meadow where Araña had built his *wickiup* to ensure their privacy before he stopped to explain the problem with the lieutenant's comments. After his last conversation with Ivan, he understood the man's obvious fright. Mayleen appeared merely curious, but Tory was watching him with a glance filled with as much hurt as skepticism, and he was now desperately sorry that he had failed to reveal the truth about himself when he had had the chance.

"You already know I didn't rob the stage," he began, "and I took the first chance I had to escape from prison. As for the marshal, he'd been dead a couple of hours when I happened by. I found his orders and used them to free Tory. Her story is even more pathetic than mine. She didn't deserve a death sentence any more than I deserved to be sent to prison.

"You two can believe whatever you like, but keep your thoughts to yourselves. We can go our separate ways once we leave here and there will be no reason for you to mention that the O'Shaughnessy brothers were anything other than what they seemed."

Mayleen already knew Ivan was terrified of Jesse, but *she* was not. "Look, I don't care how you left prison, since I'm partly responsible for putting you there. As for the marshal, I believe you're innocent of his death, too. It sounds like Tory's in a heap of trouble, but that's none of our business. Nothing the lieutenant said changes my mind. I still want to go to El Paso and tell Gerry what I think of him. There's nothing for me back in Tucson or anywhere else in the Arizona Territory. We've come this far, I say we ought to stick together."

Jesse glanced over at Tory, but she simply walked away, leaving him to deal with Mayleen and Ivan on his own. "I can't trust you, Ivan, and that makes you too dangerous to have around."

Insulted, the geologist gathered courage. He took Mayleen's hand and pulled her close. "You should have told us that you were both wanted for murder before we left Tucson. Whether you're guilty or not doesn't matter. You're both fugitives. I'd say you and Tory were the ones who are dangerous to be around. If I'm willing to risk being caught with you, then you ought to be willing to take a chance on me. What do you say—is it a deal?"

Jesse was far more interested in catching up with Tory than he was in arguing with Ivan. "I'll think about it," he assured him, "but I'm not going to make any promises now." The subject was closed for the time being, and he turned away and hurried after Tory.

"Do you believe that?" Ivan asked Mayleen. "He's got a price on his head and he's worried about traveling with me?"

"We convinced him," Mayleen insisted with a triumphant

smile. "I know that we did. Now come on let's go back to our tent. We don't know where the missing Indians are, and I for one don't want them to find me standing out here defenseless."

Ivan never carried a weapon, so they were defenseless indeed, and thinking her point well taken, he escorted her back to their tent where he hoped they might straighten out their differences now that Mayleen was certain Jesse was going to see things their way.

Jesse soon caught up to Tory. She had not been trying to escape him but merely to avoid Mayleen and Ivan. She sat down in the tall grass and folded her hands in her lap. "I don't understand any of this," she sighed softly.

Jesse sat down opposite her. "I know you must be angry with me, and I can't blame you. I let you believe you were my prisoner long after the time I should have told you the truth. I'm sorry for that. I really am."

"Why did you really come to the jail in Cactus Springs?"

She had apparently believed his claim of innocence in the marshal's death, and Jesse was so grateful for that, he blurted out the truth. "I'd been in prison for four years. I just wanted a woman, any woman."

"I've been a great disappointment to you then, haven't I?"

"No! Not at all," Jesse assured her.

Tory had slept all afternoon, but she still felt only half alive. "Marshal Kessler," she whispered more to herself than to him. "I trusted you and you weren't a marshal and you weren't named Kessler. I don't know what to believe about you now. Is anything you say true?"

"I said I'm sorry," Jesse explained. "I wanted you to stay with me, so I made you believe you were my prisoner. Granted, it was wrong, but hell, I did save your life. That ought to be worth something."

At that moment, Tory doubted her life had any value at all. It was now too dark for them to be observed from the soldiers' camp. She reached for the top button on her shirt and began to undo it. "Of course, you expect to be paid, don't you? You've been remarkably patient."

"What are you doing?"

"Don't you want me to take off my clothes? You were so anxious last night that I thought you'd want me to hurry."

Instantly Jesse realized how badly his lies had hurt her. He had made her believe in a lawman who did not really exist, and now that she knew Marshal Kessler had been no more than a convenient phantom, she had no one to trust. He reached out to catch her hand. "Stop it. I may have ridden into Cactus Springs just to pick up a woman, but when I saw you, well . . . saving your life became a hell of a lot more important. It may have been a real strange twist of fate that brought us together, but I can't help but believe that's what was meant to be."

"Fate has played a great many cruel tricks on me lately," Tory mused thoughtfully. "But to give me a man who would speak of love while failing to reveal the truth about himself is among the worst. I don't know who you really are, Jesse, but I'd rather just pay my debt to you now and get it over with."

She withdrew her hand from his to release the next button on her shirt and this time Jesse lunged for her. He pushed her down into the grass and kept her pinned beneath him as he spoke in an anguished whisper. "You don't owe me a damn thing, lady. Whatever I've done for you has been for love, and there's no debt involved."

As he looked into Tory's eyes he saw neither fear nor revulsion, but sorrow so deep, a torrent of tears would not relieve it. Paul Stafford had destroyed the vibrant young woman he knew she must have been and left only a hauntingly beautiful shell that could neither give nor receive love. In that instant he felt as though he had been pouring all his attention and affection into a sieve, for not a single drop had ever been returned.

"How could you have cried for Araña?" he demanded. "How could you have wept for that murdering snake when you give nothing at all to me?"

Tory turned her head and closed her eyes, but Jesse's defiant snarl remained vividly imprinted in her mind. She had understood Araña's rage as easily as he had felt her pain, but the brief emotional bond that had existed between them was not something she could express in words Jesse would ever understand. One tortured soul had simply called out to another and been heard. It had not been the sweet heights of love but the agonizing depths of despair that they had shared.

Tory's hat had been knocked askew when he had shoved her down on the grass and Jesse now tossed it aside and pulled away her scarf. She had washed her hair in the spring and her glossy curls were scented with sunshine. He had meant only to look at her for a moment, to recall the refined lady she had been when they had met. He had not expected the silken texture of her honey-blond hair to excite him so and, overcome with the desire she continually rebuffed, he leaned down to kiss the elegant curve of her neck. The delicate shape of her ear was incredibly appealing, and he drew her earlobe into his mouth for a teasing nibble before again nuzzling her throat.

Jesse was beyond thinking, beyond analyzing the violence that had sealed Tory's emotions inside the coldest of hearts. Her flawless skin was warm, the soft swells of her body inviting, and he slid his hand inside her open shirt to caress the surprising fullness of her breast. He rolled the pale-pink crest between his thumb and fingers and felt it harden into a delightful bud. Certain she would taste as delicious as she felt, he shifted his position slightly and spread an adoring trail of kisses across her now exposed chest.

Jesse had also lost his hat, and now, when Tory raised her hand to stroke his curls, the move was deliberate. She was uncertain what had inspired the man's latest attempts to seduce her, but she found this sweet affection much more enjoyable than his usual far more spirited approach. His gentle loving created a tender response she made no effort to fight. Instead, she pressed his face close and savored the roughness of his beard as well as the softness of his lips.

Surrounded by fragrant grass, and lying beneath a brilliant canopy of stars, Tory felt enveloped in Jesse's affection rather than crushed under his weight. If for only a few precious moments, she felt blissfully free of the cares that had burdened her soul and she slipped her hand inside Jesse's shirt to caress his chest. She had been embarrassed to take pleasure from touching him when they were hiding on the cliff, but now she combed the crisp curls that covered his broad chest without any shyness.

Her breath caught in her throat as his hand moved to her belt, but she swallowed the protest that leapt to her lips. His touch was still gentle rather than possessive and she closed her mind to the strident cries of alarm that so often filled her thoughts. Again following Araña's advice, she thought only of Jesse. The web of his life was as tangled as hers, but she had always felt safe with him. He could have died fighting Araña, and she now knew she would never have recovered from his loss.

When Jesse again kissed her lips she opened her mouth to welcome him. Her fears were vanquished in his arms, and she curled her tongue over his, luring him past all reason into the pure realm of passion she had never expected to feel. He had made her want him, and she bent her knee, rubbing her leg against his to coax him into taking still more. His fingertips slid over the flat hollow of her stomach then inched lower to begin a slow exploration of the soft folds of her most feminine flesh that immediately brought tremors of ecstasy surging through her whole body.

That he could provide such a delicious sensation with no more than the light, rhythmic motions of his fingertips caught Tory completely by surprise. The resulting aching sweetness created a longing for so much more. When he paused briefly to remove the clothes that hindered them both, she returned to his arms with an eagerness she had no need to disguise. The attraction between them had begun the first time he had smiled and grown steadily until she could not get close enough to feel whole. She hugged him tightly, returned his fevered kisses with wanton abandon, and still did not feel satisfied.

It was not until he spread her legs with his knee and lowered himself over her that she understood what love between a man and woman should be. She held her breath, but now it was in expectation of even greater pleasure rather than fear of pain. He entered her slowly, withdrawing slightly after each forward thrust until he had finally buried himself deep within her. He paused then, and, propped on his elbows, looked down at her with his expression so full of love that she raised her arms to encircle his neck and bring his mouth down to hers.

When he began to move, she mirrored each of his motions, timing the thrusts of her hips to his with a spontaneous delight that encouraged him to hold back his own climax until he was certain she had found hers. He felt it throb within her, beginning with tremors that caressed him with wave after wave of shared rapture until he could stand no more. He had no control over his powerful body then, and shuddered as he collapsed in her arms, sated with the love he had mistakenly believed she could never provide. That was one secret he was glad he had kept to himself, since she had so readily disproved it.

"I really had meant to wait for the feather bed," he whispered when he could at last draw a deep breath.

Stunned by the beauty of what they had shared, Tory had no need for conversation. She smoothed his curls away from his temple and thought it a terrible shame they would not be able to spend the night there in the meadow. She wanted the contentment of the moment to last forever, rather than for mere minutes.

"Tory . . ." Jesse spoke her name in an urgent whisper. He knew he could not demand promises of love from her, but he wanted some sign that she had enjoyed being with him. "Can't you think of anything to say?"

"No, there are no words to describe tonight."

Jesse did not agree, but as her lips sought his for a kiss filled with a lingering promise of passion, he tasted the hope for many more such glorious nights and voiced no further complaint. Knowing their absence from camp might have already caused comment, he helped her dress and sent her back to their tent first. When he returned to it later, she was already asleep, but the sweetness of her smile thrilled him clear through.

Ivan lay on his back staring up at the dark folds of the tent.

Earlier in the evening, Mayleen had been quick to point out he had called her his wife, but she certainly had shown no interest in playing the role now. Restless, he wished he had chosen to chat for a while with the sergeant who had been generous with his whiskey rather than to retire with a woman who intended to keep to her own side of the tent. He knew she was still awake, too, and that made being so close, and yet, at the same time, being ignored, all the more difficult to endure.

"Do you want me to pay you?" he finally blurted out.

Shocked by his question, Mayleen sat up and regarded the amorous scientist with a perplexed frown. She had not really made a conscious decision to leave the Silver Spur. She had simply leapt at the chance to travel to El Paso and see Gerry again. To suddenly be reminded of her former life in such an insensitive way hurt her very badly.

Her shoulders slumped dejectedly as she realized she was again indulging in wishful thinking that had no basis in fact. Gerry would not welcome her to his home after abandoning her so callously. In all probability he would just be embarrassed to see her. She had not thought past the moment of their initial confrontation to what would become of her after that. At least she still had her savings, but not an inkling of what she wished to do with her life.

Tom Pankow and Gerard Chambers were the only men she had ever loved and neither had appreciated the devotion she had lavished upon them so willingly. Love and pain were inseparably entwined in her mind now. She had had more than enough of the pain, however, and not nearly enough love. Ivan's question forced her to realize that affection was not something she was willing to sell anymore, though.

"I thought we were friends," she replied defensively.

"Of course we are," Ivan assured her.

"Then don't offer me money ever again." Mayleen lay back down and pulled the scratchy army blanket up to her chin.

The disappointment had been so plain in her voice that Ivan knew he had said the wrong thing, but he was completely lost as to what the right thing might be. Mayleen had always been able to make him laugh and forget his troubles. He had never stopped to consider that she might have problems of her own until the night Jesse Lambert had strode into her room and demanded information about Gerry.

"I didn't mean to insult you," he apologized, but there was no answer from Mayleen and he gave up trying to make amends. He heard Tory enter the adjacent tent and wondered what had taken her so long to come to bed. He supposed she had been with Jesse. Those two were certainly a secretive pair, but he could not believe she was a murderess. That just made no sense at all to him, but he did not want to insult her as he had Mayleen by referring to her past.

"Damn," he sighed to himself. Women were a complete mystery to him, and he feared that was the way they would remain.

Knowing Luke Bernay was waiting for him in Bisbee made Jesse anxious to be on his way. The missing renegades had to be dealt with first, however. Lieutenant Barlow's two scouts were Apaches who excelled at tracking their own kind, but Jesse could not help but feel they were traitors. He did not ask what had prompted them to side with the Army rather than their own people, but each time they entered the camp he found a reason to leave.

The seven missing braves had apparently scattered in as many directions and when none had been captured after a full day of exhausting search, Jesse drew Tory aside. "I think we ought to move on. I know Barlow thinks there are other Apaches headed this way, but I can't help but feel trapped camped here in this narrow valley, and I don't like it one bit."

Now that they were lovers, Tory found it difficult to keep her affection for Jesse from showing in her glance. The bright blue of his eyes was such an appealing sight that it took real effort to listen to his words rather than simply to stare up at him while her mind filled with the most erotic of images. Forcing herself to concentrate on his comments, she scuffed the toe of her boot in the dirt while she tried to think how to advise him.

"The mountain trails were awfully narrow," she reminded him. "If we met any Apaches coming this way, we'd be unable to avoid them."

"I know that," Jesse agreed, "but if we were to travel at night—"

"Through the mountains?" Tory gasped.

"Yes, I know it will be dangerous, but just sitting here waiting for someone to discover who we are is dangerous, too. I think we ought to leave before that happens."

"Won't that make Barlow suspicious?"

"Probably, but I've heard of Luke Bernay. He's as tenacious as a leech and we'd be far better off staying ahead of him than trying to peel him off once he finds us."

Tory nodded thoughtfully. "Whatever you think is best is all right with me. What do you want to do about Ethelrose and John?"

"I'd like to just go off and leave them, but I honestly don't trust Ivan to keep quiet about who we are. He was quite a loquacious drunk as you'll recall, and if the wrong person heard him refer to us there's no telling how difficult things could get."

"They could scarcely get worse than they are now!"

Jesse arched a brow to prompt her imagination. He could envision disastrous complications even if she could not. "If I'm captured, I'll be sent back to Yuma. If you're captured—"

"That's enough," Tory scolded. "Let's leave tonight."

"Let's make it this afternoon," Jesse replied with a teasing wink. He left her to tell Ivan and Mayleen their plans, and while the couple was as frightened by the prospect of crossing the treacherous mountain trails at night as Tory had been, they did not refuse the invitation to go along.

Jesse then sought out Lieutenant Barlow. "You just can't imagine what being prisoners of the Apache was like, Lieutenant. We're all so edgy that sitting here is pure torture. I know you promised us an escort, but we've decided to go on ahead without one. If you'll sell us a couple of lanterns, we can make it across the mountains tonight and be on our way back to Las Cruces tomorrow."

"Have you taken leave of your senses?" the astonished officer asked. "Perhaps three men might be able to survive such a difficult journey, but what about Mrs. Stone? You can't possibly expect her to cross the winding mountain trails at night. She would undoubtedly be terrified and fall to her death if her mount took a single misstep. No, I'm afraid I simply can not allow it."

"We're civilians, Lieutenant, not soldiers under your command," Jesse reminded him.

Barlow shook his head. "I take my responsibilities very seriously, and whenever the lives of civilians are in jeopardy—and yours certainly are here—then I don't hesitate to exert my authority. Believe me, I am most definitely in charge here, and if you attempt to leave on your own I'll promptly prevent it with whatever force necessary."

Roger Barlow's hair was light brown, but his brows were blond and provided no accent for his pale-blue eyes. He looked fiercely determined, but Jesse returned his menacing stare without flinching. "Araña and I fought with knives, and I'm standing here to talk about it. Do you honestly think if I'd fight an Apache warrior, I'd be afraid to go up against you?"

Jesse was several inches taller than the Army officer, and more ruggedly built, but Barlow had been threatening to use armed soldiers to prevent his departure, not challenging the man to hand-to-hand combat. "There's no reason for us to come to blows," he insisted. "I think after you've had time to consider the dangers inherent in the journey, you'll decide to stay with us."

"Our minds are already made up," Jesse assured him. "We're leaving as soon as we saddle our horses. Now you might be able to shoot the four of us in the backs and say the Apaches did it, but I can guarantee that there's at least one honest man among your troops. He'll tell the truth and see that you hang for it."

"How can you even imagine that I'd fire on you?" Barlow demanded, obviously outraged by Jesse's suggestion.

Jesse simply stared at Barlow until the officer had to look away. "All right, if you're determined to go, then I'll assign several men to escort you in the morning," the disgusted lieutenant offered grudgingly. "Will you agree to that compromise?"

A few soldiers would come in handy should they encounter renegades on the trail, and Jesse knew they would make much better time traveling during the day than at night. He offered his hand. "Excellent suggestion, Lieutenant. I'll tell the others to be ready to leave at first light."

Jesse hid his grin until he turned away, but he was elated to think he would have another opportunity to spend the night with Tory before they had to be on their way.

Chapter 15

While Jesse was conferring with Lieutenant Barlow, Tory walked down to the stream to avoid having to speak with Ivan and Mayleen on her own. She had not actually gotten along well with either of them when they had believed her to be a boy, but now that they knew she was a woman convicted of murder their stares had ranged from openly curious to abject terror.

Knowing it would be impossible to spend much time by herself once they resumed traveling, she savored her last few minutes of privacy. She trailed her fingertips in the cool water, washed her hands and face, and then followed the meandering stream as it flowed away from the mountain.

She was perhaps one hundred yards from camp when a stand of oaks growing close to the water's edge forced her to swerve around them. She then came upon the seven Apaches still at large huddled in the thicket on the opposite side. Rather than turn and run she reached out to steady herself against the gnarled trunk of the closest tree. The weary braves appeared just as startled as she to have been discovered, but they simply stared numbly rather than make any threatening gestures.

Their bloodstained clothes provided clear evidence that they had all suffered minor wounds in the fighting. Under Araña's leadership they had been proud and defiant. Now they were heavily burdened with the heartbreak of despair. They might have escaped the Army's detection by cleverly hiding almost under the troopers' noses, but none looked like he possessed the strength to travel much farther.

"The Dreamer's dead," Tory revealed, but it was impossible to tell if the Army had shouted that information during the fighting or they were simply too exhausted to care. "The scouts circled the mountain and have searched the next valley for you. If you wish to surrender peacefully, come with me now."

The braves exchanged troubled glances, then each shook his head. One struggled to his feet and placed his hand on his knife in an unspoken threat. "You were Araña's woman. Will you betray us?"

Tory knew they had been accused of killing people whose only crime had been the pale color of their skin, but she doubted they would receive anything even remotely approaching justice should she disclose their hiding place to the Army. "If I don't return to camp shortly, the search will focus on the stream and you will be found," she pointed out shrewdly. "You'll have to trust me not to betray you. That's your only choice."

Again the braves engaged in a silent exchange that Tory could not hope to translate into words. She supposed her life was in danger, and yet she felt no fear. She reached into her pocket and withdrew the slender braid she had made of Araña's hair. "I've saved part of Araña to keep with me always," she told them. "You needn't fear that I'll harm his people."

That she had created a talisman from their slain leader's hair impressed the braves favorably and their spokesman dropped his hand to his side. "Go, and do not return," he warned her, "for we will be gone."

Tory attempted to leave them with some expression of hope, but the dread in their dark eyes mirrored their coming doom and she did not insult them by wishing them good luck. They had been willing to follow Araña down a bloody trail to death, and she knew it was only a matter of time before they met his fate. She returned the braid to her pocket, and left them with no more than a wistful smile as a memory.

234

* * *

Jesse saw Tory returning to the camp and quickly reviewed their change in plan. She seemed preoccupied, but he dismissed her mood as a predictable one. They may have become lovers but that newfound joy had not lifted the threat to their lives should their identities be discovered. He longed to reach out and touch her, but he had to jam his hands in his hip pockets and walk beside her as though he were dispensing endless amounts of brotherly advice. That role was becoming increasingly difficult to play and he glanced up at the sky, hoping for the darkness that would conceal his true intent.

Tory paused when they came near the Apaches' graves, and he fully expected her to drop to her knees and weep at Araña's, but her lapse in attention was only momentary. She then looked up at him, apparently eager to plan the rest of their trip, but the sweetness of her expression distracted him completely.

"I can't wait to get out of here," he bent down to whisper. "I feel like we're constantly being watched."

Tory had felt the very same uncomfortable sensation and readily understood his concern. She knew she made a peculiar young man, and despite her efforts to mimic Jesse's forceful stride, she feared she had completely failed to portray an accurate model of masculinity. None of the soldiers had laughed at her within her hearing, but she had seen more than one turn away to hide his smile.

"Do you suppose I'll ever be able to dress like a woman again?" she asked.

"Just as soon as we get home," Jesse promptly assured her. "I'll buy you a mountain of dresses then—silk, satin, lace, whatever you want."

He was obviously sincere, but Tory did not understand how arriving in El Paso was going to improve her situation all that much. Jesse might be certain he could force his stepbrother to tell the truth and clear his name, but there was no way she could ever clear hers. He had not robbed a stage, or murdered a marshal, but there was no way for her to deny

235

that she had shot Paul Stafford. She glanced over his shoulder, back toward the stream where the last of Araña's band had hidden and wondered if she ought not to have stayed with them since her future was as bleak as theirs.

The startling blue of Jesse's eyes drew her into his dreams so easily, but even as she returned his smile, she feared there would never be a place for her in his world. They would share that night, perhaps others, but not a lifetime. He would never be able to introduce her as his wife or to carry their children on his shoulders. The recognition of that loss filled her with nearly unbearable sorrow.

"No matter what happens," she insisted suddenly, "don't you dare let them bury me next to Paul. Will you promise me that?"

"Dear God in heaven, what made you think of such an awful thing?"

Unable to explain, Tory just shook her head. She saw Mayleen and Ivan coming their way and braced herself. They would probably have to join the lieutenant again for supper and she looked down at her shapeless pants and shirt and wished she had never left New Haven. Her life had once been so safe and secure, and now there was only the oppressive need to run as far and as fast as she possibly could.

"Just promise me," she begged.

Jesse longed to crush her in an embrace so tight she would never have any thoughts save those of him. To be forced by the presence of others to simply stand there and act like they were discussing the weather was excruciatingly painful. "I promise," he vowed, but what he truly meant was something far more profound.

Depressed by the confrontation with Patrick O'Shaughnessy, the lieutenant expected supper to be a slow, solemn meal, but John and Ethelrose Stone were still a pleasant pair and he made a point of being especially gracious to them. Knowing his guests were anxious to make an early start in the morning, he offered his best wishes for a safe trip and bid

236

them good night the moment they were finished eating.

He would certainly not miss the O'Shaughnessy brothers, but the vivacious Ethelrose Stone had provided a welcome diversion and he stood in front of his tent and watched with real regret as she walked away. He had met few women as charming as she since being transferred to the Arizona Territory and that he had no hope of ever seeing her again saddened him deeply.

Ivan had noted the frequent glances Roger Barlow had sent Mayleen's way and had had a difficult time keeping his thoughts to himself on the matter. Now that he could express himself without fear of making an unfortunate scene, he went right ahead and did it. "Had the lieutenant been any more impressed with you, his eyes would have popped right out of his head!" he swore suddenly.

Amused by what she considered misplaced jealousy, Mayleen disagreed. "He was a perfect gentleman. Besides, I'm not really your wife so it doesn't matter how he behaved."

"It matters to me!" Ivan continued to fume.

It was too lovely an evening to return to their tent, and the couple strolled out into the meadow. Without thinking, Mayleen looped her arm through Ivan's. "What are you going to do when we get to Texas?" she asked. "There will be no need for us to pretend to be man and wife then. Have you already made some plans?"

Ivan shrugged. He was thirty-one years old and had damn little to show for it. What he needed was a drink, not conversation about his goals in life. "I'll decide when I get there," he answered morosely.

Mayleen had seen Ivan wearing that same sullen frown on numerous occasions, but she had always been able to coax a smile from him and sometimes even laughter. She reached out to tickle his ribs and then withdrew her hand at the last instant. It was not only the sudden recognition of his injuries that had stopped her, but also the fact she was through being a whore, and that made such an intimate gesture completely inappropriate.

"I guess we'll both just have to wait and see what we find," she mused aloud.

Ivan nodded and began a slow curve that would take them back to their tent. He already knew Mayleen would not be eager for his company, but he thought he might be able to play a hand or two of poker with the sergeant he had befriended. Pleased to think the rotund soldier would again share his liquor, Ivan quickened his step, and even without Mayleen's charming attentions, his frown began to lift.

Jesse and Tory also went out for a stroll, but when he started down toward the stream, she suggested they follow Mayleen and Ivan out into the meadow.

"I'd rather not have any company," Jesse explained, but Tory went her way rather than his. Unable to take her arm and force her to go where he wished, he gave an exasperated sigh and followed her lead. She skirted the edge of the meadow, however, taking them a long way from their traveling companions, and that pleased him so much he would have liked to have hugged her and tossed her into the air. Unable to express his pleasure in such exuberant terms, he had to settle for a wide grin.

"You'll like my ranch," he enthused. "It's right on the Río Grande and one of the prettiest places on earth."

"I'm sure that it is," Tory agreed, "but your stepbrother certainly isn't going to welcome you home. And what about your stepmother? She'll side with Gerry, won't she?"

Jesse had wanted to talk abut pleasant things that evening, not enumerate their problems. "Thinking about the ranch kept me sane the last four years. If I'd spent all my time cursing Gerry, the hatred would have eaten me alive. I plan to see he gets what's coming to him, and I'll not waste a minute getting it done, either, but I want you to let me worry about him. All you need to think about is that pretty new wardrobe I promised you."

Insulted by his cavalier dismissal of her concerns, Tory stopped and turned toward him. "I don't know how I could have been so blind, but it didn't occur to me until this very minute that you don't think much of women, do you? That's the real reason you didn't tell me the truth about yourself, isn't it? After all, I'm only an insignificant female, so why would my feelings matter?"

Astonished by what he considered a totally unprovoked accusation, Jesse stared down at Tory's menacing frown for a long moment before attempting to provide a rational reply. "It should be obvious in the way I've treated you that I regard women very highly. That's why I held back things, so you'd not have more to worry about than you already do."

Tory shook her head sadly. "Last night you admitted that you'd lied about yourself to force me to remain with you. What's your excuse going to be tomorrow night?"

In a vain attempt to hold his temper, Jesse raked his fingers through his thick curls. "What in the devil has gotten into you? If you're just spooked by the soldiers, we'll be gone in the morning and be able to bid our escort good-bye by tomorrow night."

The soldiers did present a constant threat, but they did not trouble her half so much as Jesse's failure to see the truth about her. She turned away, and in her anger trampled the tall grass rather than continuing to pass through it with the ease of the gentle evening breeze as she had earlier. When Jesse kept up with her, she attempted to explain her despair.

"You want to clear your name, and I hope to God that you can, but I can't allow you to ignore the fact that I'm not innocent like you. You aren't going to be able to dress me in fine clothes and pass me off as a sweetheart you met on your travels. I'm a murderess, pure and simple, and nothing is ever going to change that. Didn't you notice how Ivan and Mayleen looked at me today? Oh, their stares have always been suspicious, but now they look at me as though I were some type of hideous vermin."

Jesse caught her hand and pulled her to a halt. It was almost dark enough to make love where they stood, but not quite. "I'm sorry. I didn't notice anything unusual about the way Mayleen and Ivan treated you today, but I'll put a stop to it first thing in the morning."

"Don't bother. They can't help the way they feel."

"Perhaps not, but they can help the way they behave, and

I'll not allow either of them to persecute you."

Tory left her hand in his, but looked away, for it was all too easy to imagine a lifetime of being the subject of furtive glances and whispered innuendoes. Jesse was a proud man and would try to protect her, but eventually he would grow resentful. Everything had its price, and hers was far too dear.

"I'm sorry," she murmured. "I got myself into this awful mess. None of it is your fault."

"If you ask me, the Staffords are the ones who are responsible. You mustn't make the mistake of blaming yourself for their treachery."

"What treachery? What are you talking about?"

They had never discussed his suspicions, but Jesse decided it was high time that they did. "Sit down," he suggested first, then when she did, he knelt opposite her. "When you described the incident that took your father's life, I couldn't help but think maybe it wasn't an accident. There must have been a reason why he lost control of the team pulling his buckboard. I think it's more than likely that the horses were deliberately frightened into running wild."

Tory's expression grew even more befuddled. "That doesn't make any sense, Jesse. Everyone liked my father. What possible motive could anyone have had for wanting to harm a man who spent his days cataloging plants?"

"I don't think his death was anything personal." Jesse frowned slightly as he strove to make her understand. "It was just a lot easier for Paul Stafford to get to you once your father was out of the way. I'll wager any sum you name that the Staffords sent your housekeeper to Sonora, too. The timing of Paul's visit was too close for her departure to have been due to a real 'family emergency.'

"When you didn't encourage Paul's attentions, I think he removed the people who would have protected you from him. The crazy bastard must have convinced himself that as an orphan you would feel you had no choice but to marry him after he had forced himself on you. I'll bet it never even occurred to him that you'd choose a different means of settling the score between you."

Tory had been so grief-stricken over the death of her

240

father that she had not once gone out to the site to look for evidence that might have proven Jesse's contention. Could her father have been murdered? Could the dear man who never even raised his voice, let alone his hand, to anyone, have been murdered? And for what? Had Paul Stafford really been so mentally unbalanced that he had thought killing her father would enable him to marry her?

"If what you say is true," she moaned, "then my father is dead because of me."

"No!" Jesse contradicted sharply. "He's dead because Paul Stafford killed him and made it seem to be an accident. It wouldn't surprise me in the least to find out that your housekeeper never made it home. I'll bet she's dead, too."

"Oh, please, I can't take any more of this. That Paul could have killed two innocent people to get to me is too monstrous to believe."

"It's no more monstrous than beating and raping you. The man was violent, Tory, and if you had continued to fight him rather than meekly submitting to his marriage demands, I think he would have killed you too. He would have had to. His pride wouldn't have allowed him to do otherwise."

Tory shook her head as she tried to grasp the enormity of what Jesse had proposed. "How could any man be so unspeakably evil?"

"I met his father," Jesse reminded her. "He was a vicious bully and didn't strike me as completely sane. You said Paul resembled him. Did he share the same hot temper?"

"His was even worse."

Appalled by that thought, Jesse leaned forward to draw her into his arms. "You see, there *is* a way to clear your name. If we can convince the authorities that Paul killed your father and housekeeper, then what you did will be deemed justifiable."

Tory sat back so that she could look up at him. "No, I don't want another trial. The verdict went against me once, and I won't turn myself in and take the risk of it going the same way a second time."

"I'm not asking you to turn yourself in," Jesse quickly assured her. "I'd never do that. All I'm saying is that I'm

241

confident we can prove Paul Stafford was a murdering snake who deserved to die. No one will dare refer to you as a murderess then. The charges will be dropped. There will be no need for a second trial."

When Tory did not instantly grasp the hope he was offering, Jesse provided additional evidence to prove his case. "Marshal Kane's death was no random accident, either. He was shot to prevent him from taking you out of the Cactus Springs jail. You saw how furious Eldrin Stafford was to find out I'd taken Kane's place. I think he meant to deal with you himself and when I happened along, his carefully laid plans went awry. Like father like son. They might not have had the guts to do the actual killings themselves, but truly evil men like the Staffords always employ scoundrels who do."

Jesse's description of the Staffords' arrogant disdain for any law save their own was too accurate a description of their behavior for Tory to argue. She had not understood how her life could have gone so swiftly from idyllic to disastrous, but if she accepted Jesse's theory and blamed the Staffords, then all her questions were answered. Paul had sunk to murderous depths to make her his bride never dreaming that she would go him one better.

She took a deep breath and let it out slowly. "Thank you," she murmured. "You've just solved a great many puzzles that have troubled me, but it's still impossible for me to separate Paul's misguided passion for me from my part in the horrendous consequences. Had I only realized that he would not accept my polite refusals of his attentions, I would have returned to Connecticut. I obviously didn't know the man well enough to understand until it was too late that he always got what he wanted by whatever means it took."

"Tory, none of this is your fault!" Jesse insisted again. "You mustn't blame yourself."

Tory knew that Jesse really believed what he said. He wasn't simply trying to make her feel better, but she could not agree. Had she not accompanied her father to Cactus Springs, she would never have met Paul, and Earl Crandell would still be alive. That was a burden of guilt no amount of loving assurances would ever ease. She simply could not absolve herself of the blame in her father's death. Two men had died because of her, three if she counted the marshal, and possibly her housekeeper, too. That was far too much sorrow for any young woman to bear alone.

When Jesse again pulled her close, she sought to forget that misery in the bliss of being with him, and her kiss was flavored with desperation as well as desire. He pulled her down into the grass, and she pressed against him, as eager to receive his loving as he was to give it. She unbuttoned his shirt and slid her hands over his back. His skin was warm and smooth, the muscles rippling under her fingertips with the lively energy that filled all his motions. Jesse responded by peeling away her shirt, but when his hands strayed from her spine, she felt him flinch and, embarrassed by the scars on her back, she pulled away.

"I'm sorry I'm not as pretty as I was," she sighed unhappily.

Jesse did not respond in words. Instead, he turned her in his arms and spread light kisses along the welts that marred her skin. He traced the crisscross pattern with his lips and tongue, cherishing her even more for what she had suffered. "The scars will fade in time," he promised, "but my love never will."

A tear escaped her lashes as Tory clung to him again. He was so strong and good and she did not understand why his stepbrother had not emulated rather than despised him. Surely Gerry was as dangerous a man as Paul Stafford had been, and for the first time she was truly frightened for Jesse.

"We'll have to be very careful when we get to El Paso," she whispered anxiously. "You can't just ride up to your ranch and accuse your stepbrother of theft and perjury. He might shoot you and make up more lies to explain why later."

Jesse untied her scarf and combed the tangles from her long tresses with his fingers. "I have a good friend, or at least I did, who'll help us. I'd planned to go to him first for news about the ranch. You'll like him. He's not only much better-looking than I am, but far more charming, too."

"I doubt it," Tory argued.

243

Jesse's sly smile widened. "You're real sparing with compliments, lady, but I'll take that as one."

Tory blushed as his fingertips moved slowly down her throat to her breasts. After Paul's assault, she had never expected to be able to relax around a man, and yet here she was lying half clothed in a meadow, and entranced rather than repulsed by the contrast of Jesse's deeply tanned skin against her pale flesh. He had a gentleman's hands, with long, slender fingers, and as he caressed the tips of her breasts, she was captivated by the delicious sensation he was creating.

She reached out to touch his chest, and let her caress linger at his nipple. "Does this feel good to you?" she asked.

Jesse leaned forward to kiss her. "Everything you do feels good to me," he confessed. There was so much he wanted to teach her, and yet he did not want to ever force her to do something she did not find appealing. He didn't want to ask about Paul. He didn't want to know what that maniac had done, but he did not want to inadvertently repeat any of his actions, either.

"If ever you want me to stop," he explained, "don't be afraid to tell me and I will. I don't want to ever frighten you or make you do something you'd rather not do."

Puzzled by the seriousness of his tone, Tory considered his request for a long moment. The well-educated daughter of a brilliant botanist, she would never have met an amorous rancher had her father not had the daring to leave his comfortable post at a prestigious university to explore the wilds of the Arizona Territory. That decision had led to the end of his life and changed hers irrevocably, but Jesse was undeniably the one worthwhile element in a sea of despair.

"We might never have met . . ." she began.

That was not a possibility Jesse could accept. "Hush," he scolded before smothering any further wistful comments with a flurry of teasing kisses. He had never excelled at clever repartee. He stuck to the truth and spoke it plainly, but now he wished he had a gift for poetry in order to impress her. Lacking a talent with words, he strove with actions to make her feel what he did. Gathering her in his arms, he pressed her close. He could recall how violently she had rebelled the first time he had embraced her, and his heart swelled with pride at the way she returned his enthusiastic hug now. He would never tire of holding her and again applied all his imagination in making love to her so that she would never grow bored with him.

The pleasure Jesse gave was so intense, the possibility of ever tiring of him did not occur to Tory. All she knew was that touching him was not nearly enough, and she molded her supple body to his in a silent plea for even greater intimacy. She had had her share of ardent suitors in New Haven, but none of those earnest young men had ever stirred her blood with this glorious excitement she could not even name.

Readily understanding her need because he shared it, Jesse brought their prelude to love to a close. Each helped the other discard the remainder of their apparel. Again striving to be a careful, considerate lover, Jesse tempered his passion with tenderness. He would not risk causing Tory even the slightest twinge of pain. He wanted to fill her heart with the abundant joy she continually gave to him. He longed to shout as the ecstasy of his climax threatened to overtake him, but instead concentrated on slowing the speed of his thrusts to again carry Tory to the heights of rapture with him.

She was the first woman he had ever shown such consideration, and the first he had ever cared enough about to want to please. Her joy increased his immeasurably, however, and when he at last surrendered to his body's need for release, it was indescribably sweet. That he had again made love to the woman he adored in an open field was such a small embarrassment compared to the thrill they had shared that he felt no need to again apologize for the lack of a feather bed. Wherever they chose to make love would be the perfect place as far as he was concerned, but the valley held special dangers that he felt he ought not to ignore.

"We've got to get back to camp," he urged. "I don't trust Araña's men not to come back for you."

While she did not like being jarred out of the peaceful calm their loving had created, Tory chose not to comment on Jesse's assumption until they were both dressed. She then provided a brief summary of her meeting with the renegades.

Jesse made an attempt to hold his temper but failed miserably. He simply could not understand why Tory would not have mentioned such an important encounter immediately. "You mustn't keep secrets from me ever again. Those braves might have fond feelings for you, but they wouldn't think twice about slitting my throat. You should have told me where they were as soon as you'd seen them so that I could have avoided them."

"Please don't yell at me," Tory begged.

"I'm not yelling!"

Tory turned her back on him. She crossed her arms over her chest and clutched her arms as if shutting him out physically could force away the anger in his voice as well. He was frightening her, and she did not know how to make him stop.

Tory's shoulders began to shake, but Jesse knew she was not shivering from the cold, for the evening was still pleasantly warm. He stepped up behind her and wrapped her in his arms. "I'm sorry. I didn't mean to scare you, but you can't expect me to be calm about something as important as this."

"We've been together constantly since I saw them, so you've been in no danger," Tory whispered in her own defense. "Besides, they told me they were about to move on."

Jesse continued to hold her as he repeated his request. "Don't hide anything from me. I don't care whether it's life-threatening or not. Tell me everything from now on."

"My thoughts are my own, Jesse."

The very last thing Jesse wanted was an argument, but this issue was too important to let slide. "We're lying to everyone we meet," he warned. "We can't afford to lie to each other."

Tory was equally firm in her opinion. "You lied about who you were to me, but I'll not use that as an excuse to treat you the same way. All I'm saying is that my thoughts are private and I'll decide which ones I'll share."

"You are one stubborn woman. Do you realize that?"

"Stubborn does not begin to describe me," Tory contradicted. She had killed a man to avenge her honor, and even if Jesse could forget it, she could not. She stepped out of his arms and started back toward the camp. When Jesse did not follow, she understood he was again giving her time to reach their tent first. As brothers, they could not be seen together constantly, but she could not help but wonder if they would live long enough to bring that pretense to an end.

Several hours passed before Ivan reached the tent he shared with Mayleen. He was staggering so badly he had to stop and use what remained of his powers of concentration before stumbling through the entrance. In his efforts to be quiet, he made so much noise he woke Mayleen. She sat up, and after taking one look at his pitiful condition, she leapt up to help him to his bedroll.

"What's the matter with you?" she scolded. "You know better than to do this to yourself."

Ivan covered his mouth in an attempt to stifle his giggles. "I'll be fine by the time we leave in the morning. I was just giving myself a little send-off party is all. Jesse wasn't invited and he'll never know."

"But you and I know!"

"I won't tell if you don't," Ivan promised with a burst of hearty chuckles.

"Damn it, Ivan. Can't you ever be serious?"

"I'm serious about you," Ivan replied as he wrapped his arms around her waist and pulled her down beside him. His eyeglasses were smudged, which prevented him from making out her expression clearly, but it appeared more murderous than pleased. He tried several sloppy kisses in hopes of improving her mood, but that only upset Mayleen all the more.

"You stop that this instant," she demanded in a savage whisper. "If you want me to care about you, then stay sober like you promised instead of sneaking a drink every chance you get." She shoved him away and moved over to her side of the tent where she turned her back and tried to pretend she was alone.

"I don't like being pawed by a drunk," she called over her shoulder. "I never liked it, but, damn it, you were never sober."

She started to cry then, and Ivan was completely dumbfounded as to how to offer comfort when his touch obviously upset her. It was true that he had never visited the Silver Spur sober, but he had never guessed Mayleen did not like him. Chagrined to think all she had liked was his money, he turned his back on her and was sound asleep long before her gentle sobs had ceased.

Chapter 16

Unlike the previous evening, Tory's dreams were anything but blissful that night. She awoke frequently, and unable to find any comfortable pose, was maddeningly alert long before dawn. Jesse lay within arm's reach, but she did not want to disturb his rest when she knew how strenuous the coming day would be.

It was the torment of her recent memories that made sleep so elusive. Since her father's tragic death, no amount of tears had eased the painful tightness in her chest. She had escaped that agonizing heartache while in Jesse's arms. The respite his abundant affection provided had proved distressingly brief, however, discouraging her from turning to him now.

Her mother's untimely death had created a bond between father and daughter that had been much closer than that between most parents and their children. What she knew of the Staffords had convinced her Jesse was correct in believing her father had not perished in a senseless accident. That horrible realization added immeasurably to her anguish, for she blamed herself for not having had his death investigated thoroughly.

Had she suspected foul play, perhaps it would have been Paul Stafford who had faced murder charges instead of her. Dolores, her housekeeper, would not have disappeared, and Marshal Kane would still be alive. So many lives would not have ended tragically had she only had the sense to question Sheriff Ross's version of her father's "accident." She had been raised by her scientist father to question everything, and yet she had failed to examine the circumstance of his death.

Giving up all hope of sleep, Tory left the tent before dawn, and went to Araña's grave, which Jesse had thoughtfully marked with a heap of stones. The proud Apache would have understood her bitterness and pain, for his suffering had been the same. His quest for revenge had mirrored her own, but it was difficult to stand at his grave knowing how badly he had failed to avenge the wrongs done his people. She had also failed just as miserably in her efforts to convince the citizens of Cactus Springs what an evil brute Paul Stafford truly had been.

Jesse sensed Tory's absence even in his sleep and awakened soon after she had left the tent. Knowing exactly where she would go, he gave her a few minutes to be by herself, and then followed. He walked up behind her, and waited quietly until she noticed his presence.

"You couldn't sleep?" he asked, since it was much too early for her to be wandering around the camp.

Tory shook her head. "I've too much on my mind."

Jesse was not about to criticize her affection for a dead man when it would be an utterly pointless waste of breath. He just stood there and waited for her to confide in him as he felt she had with Araña. He could understand why she had admired the renegade, for he had fought being mistreated as bravely as she had, but Jesse did not want her dwelling on violence and death. He was near the end of his patience, however, before Tory turned to him.

"I hope there won't be any trouble getting our weapons from those the lieutenant recovered from the Apaches' bodies. We can't leave here without a means to defend ourselves."

That was scarcely the hope for the future Jesse had wanted to hear, but he understood her concern. The best tracker in the territory was following them and he would not discount the danger Luke Bernay presented. "I've already got the marshal's Colt and rifle, and Ivan has his rifle, too. Talking Barlow out of ammunition won't be easy, but I think we can get enough to see us to the first Mexican town where we can buy more. He's sure to be more generous with food, so we'll have ample supplies."

"Good," Tory said, shoving her hands in her hip pockets. After a moment's thought, she made another suggestion. "Maybe I ought to say I lost a knife at least. Mayleen could say she had one, too. Some women do carry them, you know."

"Yeah, I know, although not from personal experience," Jesse teased. "You're right. I forgot that you would have had a rifle at least. I'll see that you have one before we leave. Now come on, let's go back to the tent. You can at least rest even if you can't sleep and it will be a long day."

Tory walked ahead of him, but she knew her thoughts were still far too troubled to make peaceful rest possible.

"I don't understand it," Lieutenant Barlow complained. "Our trackers haven't found so much as a single footprint that would lead us to the missing renegades. I'll give it one more day and then I'm calling off the search. I'm certain my troops are needed back in the Territory and we're just wasting our time here in the mountains."

Jesse's expression provided no clue to his feelings for the Apaches still at large. He could see where the officer's comments were leading, and spoke his mind before the man finished. "Don't ask us to wait for you. We're leaving today."

"Somehow I knew you'd feel that way," the exasperated lieutenant replied. "Just let me know when you're ready."

While Jesse had already picked out an additional rifle, he knew he was in a poor position to bargain for much more. That did not stop him, though. He asked to buy ammunition and food for the first portion of their trip. "We'll be ready as soon as we can pack up those supplies."

The lieutenant did not even consider refusing Jesse's request. Even if he was not overly concerned about Ethelrose Stone's traveling companions, he did not want the pretty brunette to be hungry or in any danger. "I'll see that you have everything you need," he promised.

Barlow had already chosen an escort, and as soon as the necessary ammunition and provisions had been packed for transport, the six men were mounted and ready to leave. He had hoped for a chance to exchange a few words privately with Ethelrose, but the opportunity did not present itself. Undaunted, Roger made a point of approaching her to wish her good luck.

Mayleen was flattered by the lieutenant's attentiveness, for she knew that if one intelligent man thought her a respectable woman, then she could certainly convince a great many more that she was indeed a lady. First she meant to see that Gerry Chambers got what was coming to him. Then with her savings, she could call herself a widow and live comfortably until she found an ambitious man who needed a wife.

"Your hospitality meant a great deal to us, Lieutenant," she complimented him sincerely. "If you're ever in Las Cruces, perhaps you'll allow us to entertain you."

"Thank you, ma'am, I'll remember that." Roger actually blushed at the prospect of seeing her again even if he did not know when it might be.

Disgusted with the touching scene taking place between Mayleen and the lieutenant, although he knew damn well an Ethelrose Stone would never be found in Las Cruces, Ivan urged his horse up beside Jesse's. Now that his head was pounding with a furious rattle he was sorry that he had sampled the sergeant's liquor so liberally, but he was more concerned about where he would get his next drink than whether or not he could stay in the saddle.

"Can't we get this parade underway?" he complained.

Jesse thought Ivan's eyes looked more bloodshot than usual, but before he could confirm his suspicion, the geologist cocked his head and the sun glanced off his spectacles obscuring his eyes. Disgusted he had so little choice about having Ivan along, Jesse nonetheless urged the corporal in charge of their escort to get started. The young man paused for a final word with the lieutenant to confirm their plans to rendezvous outside Bisbee, and then led the way out of the valley.

The corporal and two troopers were followed by Jesse, Tory, Mayleen, and Ivan. Three additional soldiers brought up the rear. While Jesse would have preferred to take the lead and set the pace, he soon discovered the corporal was equally anxious to cover the mountain trails. They slowed on the sharp curves, steep inclines, and hazardous descents, but whenever the trail was level, they made almost as good time as the Apaches had on their sure-footed ponies.

While the soldiers kept a sharp lookout for Apaches, none were sighted before they reached the foothills and called a halt for the day. The difficult nature of the trails had made for an exhausting ride, and the group shared a quiet supper and turned in early. While the soldiers took turns standing watch, Jesse and his companions slept without stirring until dawn.

Watching the soldiers bury Araña had given Jesse an idea, but he waited to explain it until after they had bidden their military escort good-bye. The soldiers were heading north toward Bisbee, while they would be traveling northeast toward their supposed goal of Las Cruces. They were near the spot where they had camped the first night with Araña, and Jesse considered it the perfect place for what he had in mind.

"We already know Lieutenant Barlow suspects an escaped convict and the two women traveling with him were killed by Araña and his men. I think we ought to provide three graves that he could have missed seeing when he passed by here the first time. Let's make it look like three bodies were found and buried by travelers who then moved on. We can mark the graves in such a way that Barlow will believe they belong to the three people Luke Bernay is tracking. He'll be sure to see that Luke gets that message."

Tory raised her hand to shield her eyes as she studied the hilly terrain. "Perhaps a small fire could sweep away the underbrush that hid the graves?"

Delighted by that suggestion, Jesse gave her a hug. "Perfect, but we'll have to make certain we control it so that the troopers don't come back to find out what's causing all the smoke."

"We can manage that," Ivan volunteered, "if we start the fires near the river and put them out quickly. All we really have to do is blacken the brush so that the lieutenant will notice the scenery has changed and stop to investigate."

Pleased that the geologist actually had a useful idea, Jesse clapped him on the back, nearly sent him sprawling, and had to grab his shoulder to keep him upright. "Sorry. All right, Ivan, let's get some sticks and start digging. We won't have to make holes deep enough to actually hold a body, but they'll have to look as though they do."

"Mayleen and I can gather rocks along the river to fill in these 'graves' so the mounds of earth will look like they're covering something solid," Tory suggested, and without waiting for a second word of praise from Jesse, she started off toward the water.

"Doesn't anybody think it will bring us bad luck to fake our own deaths?" Mayleen asked with a shudder.

"The only bad luck we're going to have is if we're standing here arguing when another Apache war party rides up. I don't intend to allow that to happen." He stalked off then, leaving the superstitious young woman wringing her hands.

"Come on, Mayleen," Ivan urged. "This is no time for your whining."

Offended that neither man was taking her worries seriously, Mayleen followed Tory down to the river, but she was not at all pleased about having to help with such a gruesome task. She carried as many of the smooth stones from the riverbed to the gravesite as Tory, but she shivered in disgust with every trip.

When he was satisfied they had created as realistic a burial ground as possible, Jesse fashioned three crude crosses from the digging sticks he and Ivan had used. He jammed one into the soil at the head of each grave and then stepped back to observe their work. "How can we mark the graves?" he asked. "We can't very well burn our names into the crosses. Anyone finding our bodies wouldn't know who we were."

"That's true," Tory agreed, "but we could at least identify the deceased as being a man and two women. That would be enough to make Lieutenant Barlow jump to the conclusion that it was us."

"Let's put it in Spanish," Jesse said with sudden inspiration. *"Un hombre y dos mujeres.* I'll burn that into a piece of wood and hang it on the center cross. At least one of the troopers with Barlow will be able to translate it for him."

Ivan started a small fire, and sat back to watch as Jesse heated his knife and alternately scorched and carved out the agreed-upon message on a flat branch he had found down by the river. When he affixed it to the center cross with a bit of ribbon Mayleen found among her belongings, it appeared touchingly authentic.

"I've seen prospectors' graves that didn't look any different," the scientist remarked. "That's sure to fool anyone who happens by." He yanked a dried branch from a mesquite bush and lit the end from the remains of the fire. With Jesse, Mayleen, and Tory bringing water from the river in their canteens to snuff out the flames before they did any real damage to the underbrush, Ivan spread a blackened path from near the graves to the beginning of the trail they had followed from the mountains. With an irregular outline of twists and turns, it appeared as though a campfire had gotten out of control but had been contained swiftly.

The mock graveyard complete, Jesse washed his hands in the river and looped his arm around Tory's shoulders as they walked toward their horses. "We've lost a couple of hours staying here, but I'm hoping the additional rest we allowed our mounts will pay off before the end of the day. I'm sorry to have to make you ride so hard, but you can rest all you like once we get to El Paso."

Tory glanced back at the graves. They would certainly fool the unsuspecting troopers, but she doubted the men tracking them would accept their deaths as easily as Barlow and his men should. Just as she had told Jesse, her thoughts were private and she kept her doubts to herself rather than share them.

True to his word, even with frequent stops to rest their horses, Jesse kept them traveling at a speed that by the end of the day carried them well out of the path of any Apaches bound for the Sierra Madre Mountains. The terrain was now level, the ride easy, but Jesse did not for even an instant allow his party to slack off and enjoy the scenery. Just as he had on their way out of the Arizona Territory, he urged them to push themselves, as well as their mounts, to the limits of their endurance.

The sun was low in the west before he called a halt. They made camp on a rise that provided a clear view in all directions, but Jesse still did not feel that their position was secure. "There were other travelers on the roads when we were in the Arizona Territory, so a campfire didn't attract any particular attention there. Way out here, we don't dare light a fire because it would serve as a beacon to anyone following us," he warned.

"In a couple of days, we should start reaching Mexican villages, and having hot meals won't be a problem. Until then, just think about how good that food will taste while you're munching jerky."

Tory had swiftly grown used to the primitive conditions Jesse imposed, but it was plain Mayleen and Ivan weren't pleased. After they finished a cold supper, Ivan grew restless and Tory eyed him with a curious gaze as he strolled around their campsite. His head down, hands jammed deep into his pockets, he appeared to be lost in thought, but when he finally sat down he did not share whatever conclusions he might have reached.

Mayleen was the first to retire, but Tory sat up with the men until they were ready to go to sleep. Jesse had spread out their bedrolls, again leaving little space between them, and she could not help but wonder what he had in mind for when they lay down. She was again physically tired enough to sleep without being plagued by violent dreams or merely troubling thoughts, and she certainly hoped that Jesse was, too. While making love with him was more than merely enjoyable, she felt uneasy about being with him when Mayleen and Ivan were so close.

Jesse had had sufficient opportunities to study Tory's expressions to understand the subtle difference between her preoccupied frowns and those that indicated real worry. He could see something was on her mind, but it did not look like anything major. Hoping he was making an accurate guess, he broke into a wide grin as he lowered himself to his bedroll.

"Relax. I'm planning to wait for that feather bed, or at least a straw mattress, before I make love to you again. I hope you aren't disappointed."

Relieved rather than discouraged by his promise, Tory tried to return his teasing smile. "Disappointments strengthen character, don't they?"

"Oh, yes, definitely," Jesse assured her, but then he couldn't resist pulling her into an affectionate hug he relaxed only slightly so that she would have to sleep in his arms. She had removed her scarf and he patted her curls to keep her head in place. "Just use my shoulder for a pillow like you used to," he encouraged, and when she cuddled against him without complaint, he kissed the top of her head.

He wanted to say that he loved her, but because she had not provided any verbal encouragement for his devotion, he decided not to tell her so again. She had to know that he loved her without his endlessly repeating the words, but he could not help but wish she would speak them to him. He had not missed any of the women he had known in El Paso, but he could not bear the thought that he and Tory might ever part.

He gave her another squeeze, wished her a good night, and fell asleep hoping they would soon be able to share the comforts of a bed.

When his Apache scouts again returned to camp without any clues to the missing renegades' whereabouts, Lieutenant Barlow gave up the search and began the trek out of the mountains the next morning. His only comfort was that he had a string of Indian ponies, so the Apaches who had eluded capture would be stranded on foot wherever they were hiding. Still, he didn't look forward to the prospect of having to report that his mission had only been a partial success. At least Araña had been slain, and he hoped that villain's death would make up for the fact seven renegades were still at large.

A much larger group, the cavalry troops navigated the mountain trails at a slower pace than the previous day's travelers. They had only the last golden rays of sunset to light their way by the time they camped for the night in the foothills. It was too dark for the blackened underbrush to be noticed, but a trooper stumbled over one of the carefully fabricated graves on his way to the river and hurriedly brought Lieutenant Barlow the news.

With lantern in hand, the conscientious officer read the makeshift epitaph and understood the Spanish words without needing a translation. Instantly convinced the graves were genuine, he was elated to think that he would be able to add such an interesting appendix to his report. That two wanted criminals and a female accomplice had met an undoubtedly gruesome end at the Apaches' hands was somehow fitting, and it also added three more deaths to Araña's tally, making the lieutenant's killing of the renegade all the more impressive. Cheered to believe his expedition had been more successful than he had first thought, before retiring he practiced reciting modest speeches he hoped to use while being praised for his daring.

As planned, the troopers who had ridden ahead were camped outside Bisbee, and once the lieutenant had heard the corporal's summary of their uneventful journey, he sent for Luke Bernay. The famed tracker soon appeared with another man he introduced as Tad MacDonald, the leader of a posse pursuing Victoria Crandell.

"Well, gentlemen," Barlow greeted them warmly. "It appears your search is over." Taking credit for the discovery, he glossed over how the graves had truly been found. "Our efforts were focused on a pursuit of the Apache renegades when we entered the Sierra Madre, but we noticed the graves on our return. It was clearly Araña's work, and some Christian soul passing by gave the deceased a decent burial. Not that they deserved such consideration according to what you've told me, Mr. Bernay, but they were buried all the same."

Luke had a great deal more experience with escaped convicts than Roger Barlow could ever hope to have, and he pondered his report with a skeptical frown. "I've had more than one man I've been tracking try to convince me he was dead by putting his name on a fresh grave," he finally commented insightfully. "While there might not have been any names used this time, that you could have come across the graves of Lambert and his two women just seems too good to be true."

Insulted by the insinuation that he might have been duped, the proud lieutenant staunchly defended his version of what he had discovered. "The inscription was in Spanish," he explained this time. "So it was obviously Mexican travelers who buried the slain individuals. There was no attempt made to fool anyone involved."

"Lambert's from Texas," Luke reminded him. "More than likely he speaks enough Spanish to make himself understood, no matter what the occasion."

Disgusted that he was being accused of being gullible rather than praised for his helpfulness, the now-disgruntled officer decided the conversation was becoming tedious and sought to end it. "I'll see you're provided with a map if you'd care to investigate this matter further. Otherwise, I can't offer any more information than I already have. If I were you, I'd consider Lambert, his mistress, and the whore from Tucson all dead and be done with them."

"Well, you aren't me now, are you?" Luke pointed out slyly. "You have any questions?" he asked Tad.

As exasperated as Luke by the lieutenant's failure to have tangible evidence of just who was buried in the graves he had seen, Tad made a single request. "I'll need the map you offered. My men and I will have to identify Victoria Crandell's body before we call off our search."

"You mean to exhume all the bodies?" the lieutenant gasped in horror.

Tad had to smile at the officer's dismay. "If we're lucky and start with the right one, that's all we'll have to dig up."

Clearly repulsed by that gruesome jest, Barlow turned back to Luke. "I suppose you'd also like a map?" he asked.

"Yes, sir, I would." Luke watched with an appreciative eye as the officer consulted the notations on his own maps and then made two rough copies. As he took the one offered him, Luke realized he still had some unanswered questions.

"You didn't see any sign of the Mexicans that supposedly buried these people, did you?" he asked.

"No, we didn't."

Luke nodded. "Did you meet up with anyone at all? Lambert might have been disguised, but he'd still be tall."

Barlow shook his head. "Araña had four white prisoners. One of them, Patrick O'Shaughnessy, was quite tall, but he wasn't your man. He and his brother were from Las Cruces and are on their way back there now."

Intrigued by the direction they were traveling, Luke took out the photograph of Jesse. "I showed you this once before. Did Patrick O'Shaughnessy resemble this man even faintly?"

Barlow took a brief glance at the photograph and handed it back to Luke. "No, Patrick had a beard."

"What kind of beard? One that reached clear to his waist, or just a short one he might have started growing recently?"

Not enjoying having his judgment questioned, the lieutenant shifted his stance nervously. "It was a closely cropped beard, but I've no way of knowing how long he'd worn it."

Luke used the corner of the map he had been given to cover the lower half of Jesse's face. "If you just look at the eyes and curly hair, does Jesse resemble Patrick?"

Barlow hesitated to even bother looking, but when he did, he began to frown. "Well, now that you mention it, yes, he does, but that's probably just coincidence. He was traveling with his kid brother, not two women."

"Who were the other two people you rescued?" Tad asked.

"A Mr. and Mrs. John Stone."

"Where are they now?"

"They're with the O'Shaughnessys on their way back to New Mexico. They left the mountains a day before we did."

"Was Mrs. Stone a tall blonde?" Tad inquired eagerly.

"No, she was petite, and her hair was dark-brown, black actually. She wasn't your murderess." Just the thought that someone might mistake the charming Ethelrose Stone for a criminal made him laugh. "She was a very lovely lady," he added with a fond smile.

Understanding the lieutenant had warm feelings for the woman, Luke refrained from asking any more about her, but he was still full of questions. The officer's halting identification had convinced him that Patrick O'Shaughnessy and Jesse Lambert were one and the same. He supposed it was possible Mrs. Stone was Mayleen Tyler, although he had no idea who Mr. Stone might be if he were not actually Mr. Stone. What about Victoria Crandell? Could she have been the younger O'Shaughnessy? he wondered.

"Tell me about Patrick's kid brother. Was he quite a bit shorter, and thin rather than well built?"

"Well, yes. How did you know?"

"Just a lucky guess" was all Luke would admit. "Did he have the same curly, reddish-brown hair and blue eyes?"

Roger Barlow clasped his hands behind his back and looked down as he struggled to remember just how Sean had looked. "I can't recall ever seeing his hair. He always wore a hat pulled low, even to meals. As for his eyes . . ." Barlow could describe the color with no difficulty. "His eyes were green."

"Green? Are you positive?" Tad challenged.

The lieutenant looked up and nodded. "Yes, I'm certain. His eyes were an unusually clear green. The two brothers were nothing alike. Sean was far more reserved. Apparently he wishes to become a priest."

"A priest?" Luke exchanged a startled glance with Tad, who seemed totally confused by that comment and decided he had heard enough. "Thank you for the map and your time, Lieutenant." He offered his hand and hurried away from the officer's tent. Before he had reached his horse, Tad caught up with him and placed his hand on his shoulder, but Luke shook it off.

"I'm in a hurry, MacDonald. I can be halfway to Las Cruces before you sober up your posse."

"Aren't you going to look at the graves first?"

"Why? They're undoubtedly empty."

261

"Maybe not. I'd rather not ride all the way to Las Cruces if I can avoid it," Tad explained with a derisive snort. "It's true Tory Crandell had green eyes, but I just can't picture a woman that pretty convincing a man she was a boy who wanted to become a priest."

Luke had absolutely no desire to travel with Tad and his men so he cleverly encouraged him to head south toward the Sierra Madre Mountains while he would be going east. He frowned as though he were making a difficult decision. "I know chasing off after three men and a woman when I was looking for a man and two women doesn't make a whole lot of sense, but they're only a day's ride ahead of me. I'd rather catch up with that bunch on the long shot Jesse's one of them."

"And if he isn't?"

Luke tried to look real perplexed. "I don't know what I'll do then. Come back here to Bisbee, I guess. If you recover Miss Crandell's body, you'll tell the newspaper here, won't you?"

Tad chuckled at that possibility and then decided he liked it. "Yes, I sure would. It would make for a real interesting article."

"I'll check with the newspaper then," Luke promised. He touched the brim of his hat in a mock salute, mounted his horse, and, having left behind nothing at his hotel, he was ready to continue his pursuit of Jesse Lambert. With any luck, and he usually had considerable, he would overtake him in less than two days. He certainly did not want to travel all the way to Las Cruces, either. Of course, if he was correct, there weren't any O'Shaughnessy brothers, and they weren't on their way to Las Cruces. Amused by that thought, he rode out of Bisbee wearing the widest grin anyone had seen on him in days.

Chapter 17

At first glance, Tory mistook the glistening image of the wide river for a mirage, but it looked so real she could almost feel its cool essence trickling down her throat. She licked the dust from her lips and reached for her canteen.

"There's fresh water just ahead," Jesse assured her.

"You mean the river is really there?"

"Sure is." There were times, although they were few and far between, when Tory projected an endearing innocence that was far removed from her usual reserved demeanor. She appeared enormously relieved to learn the river was real rather than mere illusion and that tickled him.

"It's the Río Casas Grandes," he explained. "North of here it makes a big loop and nearly reaches the border. We'll pass the lake from which it flows in another day or so."

"You seem to know northern Mexico very well."

"I thought it would be a good experience for Gerry if we traveled this way to Tucson rather than the easier northern route through the New Mexico Territory. I'd studied maps, and had the whole trip well in mind before we left the ranch. Gerry was so lazy he hadn't bothered to learn anything more than to head west." Even after nearly five years, Jesse's expression mirrored his disgust.

"He sounds like a pitiful excuse for a man."

Jesse could not argue with her opinion. "That's being kind."

"I hope you were very hard on him on that trip."

The Texan chuckled. "Very. Although Mayleen and Ivan would probably say I'm being hard on them, which I'm not."

Tory glanced over her shoulder at the bedraggled pair who were trailing by at least a dozen yards. They were riding side by side, but with their heads down, not conversing or taking in the scenery. "Mayleen was so protective of Ivan when he was beaten. Now it doesn't look as though they are even speaking. I wonder what happened?"

The answer to that question was painfully obvious in Jesse's mind, but rather than be flippant, he tried to find a gentlemanly way to express his opinion. "Their friendship had a pretty flimsy base, Tory. Mayleen may have been genuinely fond of Ivan, but her affection had a price. Once she left the Silver Spur, nothing was the same between them."

Tory readily grasped his meaning: Mayleen had been a whore and Ivan had paid for her favors. They had simply been partners in a business transaction, not real lovers. Paul had shown her the worst way a man could treat a woman and Jesse the best, but Tory could not understand how any woman could make love to a man with the complete indifference a whore had to feel.

That was not a question she wanted to pursue, for it made her skin crawl with revulsion. With the river now within easy reach, she called out, "I'll race you!" and urged her gentle bay into a canter.

Jesse immediately took up her challenge and Río sprinted by Tory's mount in a flash of fluid silver. Beating her to the river by several seconds, Jesse dismounted, and then swung Tory down from her horse the instant she reached him. He picked her up and carried her out into the water, where his deep laughter drowned out her protests.

"I won," he exclaimed. "Don't I get some sort of prize?"

"Surely this isn't it!" Tory looped her arms around his neck in a frantic attempt to prevent him from dropping her in the water, but Jesse outsmarted her by walking out a bit farther and then pulling her under with him before releasing her. Drenched, she came up sputtering and laughing, too, for the water felt so good after the day's long and tiring ride that it was impossible to be angry with him. She splashed him and then turned to try to get away before he could dunk her again, but Jesse easily caught her waist and spun her around creating a wild spray of water.

Ivan and Mayleen reached the shore then, but neither had the energy to plunge into the river with the abandon Jesse and Tory were displaying. The pair were cavorting like children, and all Ivan and Mayleen could do was stare sullenly, jealous of the fun they longed to share, and yet unable to join in it. Oblivious to the pair's envy, Jesse and Tory stopped only long enough to pull off their sodden boots and toss them up on dry land before they continued to refresh themselves in a boisterous fashion.

Mayleen found watching Jesse surprisingly painful. She had always admired men who were tall and well built and wished that he had wanted to make love to her, if only once. Watching him play with his mistress as though they were the only two people within miles hurt her badly and she tore her gaze from the distressing scene in the river to tend to her horse. He was a faithful friend, even if Jesse wasn't. She was then overcome with guilt when she recalled that she was the one who had betrayed Jesse, not the other way around. She had gotten exactly what she deserved from the handsome rancher in return, but that did not mean it hurt any less.

When Mayleen dismounted, Ivan's glance was finally distracted from Jesse and Tory, and he also swung down from his saddle. His legs felt so weak that he stumbled and had to grab the saddlehorn to keep from falling. He was exhausted, but that did not keep him from wanting to tease Mayleen. "It looks like they're having fun, doesn't it?" he commented enthusiastically. "Care to join them?"

"No! I most certainly do not," Mayleen shot right back at him. She was now a respectable woman, she reminded herself, and frolicking in a river fully clothed did not appeal to her. It might not matter what a murderess did, but she was different. She had a future, and she intended to see it was not clouded by the kind of gossip that horseplay in a river could bring.

"What's wrong with you?" Ivan complained. "You used to

love to have fun. You were always laughing and singing. Why can't you be the same way now?"

Mayleen struggled to lift her saddle from her horse's back and laid it in the dirt before replying. She couldn't blame Ivan for remembering the good times they had shared. She recalled them fondly, too, but the past held no attraction for her now. "I didn't have much choice about it then, Ivan. Now I do."

"You mean you were only pretending to be enjoying yourself?"

After catching her breath, Mayleen again picked up her saddle and carried it far enough from her horse so that she could use it for a pillow that night without fear of being trampled. When she looked back at Ivan, she found him awaiting her reply with such a pathetic expression that she had to be kind. "How much do you remember? You usually had a great deal to drink before you came to see me. One time you slipped on the stairs and fell on your way up to my room. Did you imagine that I had a good time that night?"

Growing defensive, Ivan squared his shoulders. Falling down a flight of stairs had created memories too painful to forget, and Ivan did indeed recall that particular visit to the Silver Spur. Either Jack or Ross, he couldn't remember which man it had been now, had helped him back up the stairs. His whole body had been sore when he had awakened in Mayleen's bed, but what had happened between the fall and that morning was lost in the dark void that always descended when he had had too much to drink. He was usually too smart to reach that point, but for some reason, he had not shown much intelligence that night.

Not willing to admit he had been as drunk as she claimed, he tried to imagine what had transpired that night and describe it convincingly. "I know what happened," he insisted stubbornly. "You took real good care of me. I remember falling asleep with you stroking my hair. If I didn't say how much I appreciated your kindness, I'm sorry. I always thought of you as a friend, Mayleen. You were my only lady friend in Tucson and I, well . . . I liked you a lot. I still do."

While Ivan could definitely be an awful jackass at times, he was more frequently a gentleman, and Mayleen was ashamed she had been so hard on him. "Thanks, Professor, it's nice of you to say so, but I'd like to forget everything that happened in Tucson. I'm going to make a new life for myself, and this time I'm going to do it right."

"Just tell me what you want me to do," Ivan asked.

"See to the other horses while I set up camp," Mayleen replied, not realizing he had not been asking about chores.

Appalled that she had misunderstood him so badly, Ivan had a difficult time holding his temper. Then he realized she was every bit as tired as he was and he ought to just let it go. It was plain she did not care for him and he would be damned if he would make a bigger fool of himself than he already had by trying to change her mind.

After supper, Jesse and Tory sat snuggled in each other's arms, exchanging hushed whispers and, exasperated by their incessant show of affection, Mayleen took out clean clothing and walked upstream to find a secluded place to bathe. It was nearly dark, and she did not have to go far to be certain she would not be observed. She wished that she could cleanse her soul of desire as easily as she could scrub soil from her body, but unfortunately it didn't happen. As she washed her hair, she still longed for someone like Jesse to love. A man who would be tall, strong, and always treat her like the lady she wished to be.

It was not until she had stepped out of the river that she realized Ivan had followed her. He might think the thick chaparral hid his silhouette in the gathering dusk, but it didn't. "Ivan, you snake!" she shrieked. She hurriedly pulled on her clothes, not caring if they were buttoned properly as long as they covered her still-damp figure.

"Hell, Mayleen," Ivan complained. "I wasn't spying on you, and even if I was, you don't have anything I haven't seen. You've no reason to be angry. I just wanted to make certain you were safe."

"Safe!" the hot-tempered young woman scoffed. "Safe from what? Lecherous turnips like you?"

The word lecherous hurt, but it was being called a turnip

267

that Ivan could not abide. The intent of that bizarre pejorative completely escaped him, but he knew it was meant to be demeaning. When Mayleen attempted to rush by him on her way back to camp, he reached out to stop her. "You owe me an apology," he demanded.

"I catch you being a Peeping Tom and you want an apology? You'll have a very long wait before you hear it!"

"I already told you I wasn't spying, and I'm no damn turnip, either. Take that back," he insisted through clenched teeth.

"Never!"

Ivan already had a firm hold on her arms. As he yanked the defiant brunette against his chest, her damp curls brushed across his hands, instantly causing his anger to erupt into flames of desire. What little control he had over his emotions was gone then, and he ravished her mouth with a bruising kiss that left them both dizzy when he finally came to his senses.

He slackened his hold on her only slightly. "Say you're sorry," he insisted again.

Mayleen could not even think, let alone provide an apology. She had never imagined Ivan was so strong, or that kissing him could be so wildly exciting. That night he seemed far removed from the tipsy professor who had frequently fallen asleep in her arms without asking for more than a sisterly kiss. They had made love a few times. At least she thought that they had, but try as she might, she could not separate Ivan from the scores of other men who had shared her favors.

Rather than arousing her desire, or curiosity, Mayleen suddenly felt ashamed for having slept with so many men she could not remember if there was anything unique about this one. As he had kissed her, he had ground his hips against hers so she could not mistake the level of his need. Despite his show of temper, he wanted her. She knew all she would have to do was apologize and, when he released her, she could let her hand slip down his chest, glance over his belt buckle, and then drop lower for an insistent caress.

She had been very good at her trade, and seducing Ivan

when he was already so eager to have her would have been no challenge at all, but she refused to be a whore again. She wanted to be courted with flowers and poetry by a decent man who would offer marriage before he expected her to give her body as well as her heart.

Ivan was astonished when tears began to roll down Mayleen's cheeks and he released her immediately. "I'm sorry, but you shouldn't have called me a turnip. I'm a man, not some unthinking, uncaring vegetable."

Unable to respond with any coherent comment, Mayleen bolted and ran all the way back to camp. She was relieved to find Jesse and Tory had already fallen asleep and hurriedly lay down so that she could pretend to be sleeping, too, when Ivan arrived. She didn't want to have to face him again that night, but she knew it would be a long time before she forgot his stirring kiss.

Not wanting any company, either, Ivan went for a long swim. The chill of the river swiftly cooled his ardor, but it was no help in clearing his mind. He could readily understand why Mayleen thought so little of him because he had never given her much to admire. She had been happy to pamper him when he had paid her, but now it was obvious she preferred to pretend they had never been intimate. Well, she wasn't the only woman in the world, he reminded himself as he walked back to camp. The problem was, she was the only one he wanted.

Tad MacDonald and his men rode out of Bisbee at first light. The Army patrol's tracks were easy to follow across the Sonora desert, and using Lieutenant Barlow's precisely drawn map they had no difficulty locating the graves when they reached the foothills. Having had the forethought to purchase a couple of shovels, the men debated which grave to excavate first.

"If Lambert is buried here, he would be in the middle," José Gonzales offered persuasively. "There's no point starting there."

A low chorus of muttered assents indicated general

agreement with that opinion, but it also required another decision.

"The right or the left, Boss?" Hank Short asked.

Tad took out a five-dollar gold piece and flipped it. "Heads for right, tails for left," he called while it was still in the air.

It landed in front of George Flood. The southerner bent over to observe the coin closely. "Heads it is," he announced before scooping it up and handing it back to Tad, who quickly pocketed it.

The matter was decided to everyone's satisfaction. Hank removed the cross and began to dig at the head of the grave that had been selected while Juan Lopez took the other shovel and went to the foot. They had worked only a few minutes before they struck a thick layer of stones and drew back. Tad motioned for them to continue, and they did, but it soon became obvious to everyone that the grave consisted of nothing more than a mound of soil and stones.

Tad began to swear and did not stop until he had exhausted every abusive phrase he knew. "Bernay was right. I should have had sense enough to stay with him."

Carl Olsen took the shovel from Hank and moved to the foot of the middle grave. "Just because one grave was empty doesn't mean they all are. Tory might still be buried here."

"You're wasting your time," Tad exclaimed.

As curious as Carl, Manuel Ochoa took Juan's shovel and moved to the last mound. Not bothering to remove the cross, he started digging in the center. Almost simultaneously, he and Carl struck stones with a resounding clang and neither man cared to dig any deeper when it became clear that all three graves were fakes. The two men leaned against their shovels, looked toward Tad, and waited for him to give the orders.

"It's too late in the day to go any further," he complained. "Let's make camp and get another early start tomorrow. From now on we're sticking to Bernay. He's the damn expert at this."

The men with Tad cared little where they spent the night and none offered any objection to his plan. During their pursuit of Tory they had fallen into an easy routine. They took turns with the cooking after they discovered none of them could produce anything truly worth eating. The Mexicans spiced whatever they cooked with more chilies than the Americans liked, while the Mexicans complained that the Americans' efforts at producing meals lacked any flavor at all.

Tad tried to stay out of their petty arguments over food, but he was sorry they had left Bisbee, where each of them had been able to order whatever type of meal he wanted. As long as the coffee was strong and hot, he had no complaints, but he was getting real tired of chasing Tory Crandell. He was not even tempted to return to Cactus Springs without proof she was dead, however. That was something he would not even consider. He wasn't convinced Tory had been masquerading as the younger O'Shaughnessy brother. He simply did not understand how anyone could mistake her for a male, but since Luke had been right about the graves being empty, he was willing to give him the benefit of the doubt again and follow his lead.

Late the afternoon of their third day of travel, Jesse sighted a village in the distance. They would reach it before sundown, but he called a brief halt to make certain they were all in agreement before entering the pueblo. They had been discussing new names all day, and now they would have to make their final choices.

Jesse had shaved off his beard that morning, but had left his mustache. If their ploy with the false graves failed to fool Luke Bernay, then he wanted to make certain every description the man heard of him was more confusing from the next. Like chameleons, he and Tory would continually change colors until they reached the safety of his ranch and could be themselves.

Rather than a brother, Jesse had decided to now describe Tory as a stepson. Because he knew he looked every one of his thirty-one years, and with her hair again covered, Tory could pass for a gangly youth, he was certain they would be believed. This time their names would be Caleb and Zeke Jackson. Their only disagreement had been over who would be whom. That had provided such a silly argument, Jesse gave in with a deep chuckle.

"I'll let you have whichever name you'd like," he offered graciously. "What's your choice?"

Tory was hot and tired and truly no longer cared. "Caleb, I guess, but just call me Cal."

"Fine, Cal it is." Jesse then glanced toward Ivan and Mayleen. He did not think they had exchanged a civil word all day, but he hoped they still had sense enough to choose good names. "What are the Stones calling themselves this time?"

When Mayleen looked away as though the topic were too boring to discuss, Ivan replied, "Being a geologist, I couldn't resist calling myself Mr. Stone, but I think I'll try being a minister now," he announced. "We'll be the Reverend and Mrs. Leopold Martin. What's your first name, my darling wife?"

Rather than being a polite request Ivan's question had dripped with sarcasm and Mayleen replied with equal disdain. "Virginia."

"Wonderful choice!" Ivan exclaimed. "I couldn't have thought of a more virtuous name myself."

Bristling at that taunt, Mayleen was quick to criticize him. "I can call myself whatever I want when you're calling yourself a minister and you don't even have a Bible!"

Ivan frowned pensively. "That is an unfortunate oversight, but it can't be helped. The citizens of whatever town lies ahead are undoubtedly all Catholic so none will seek out a Protestant clergyman anyway."

"They'll certainly be disappointed if they do," Mayleen continued to complain.

Ivan removed his spectacles to polish them. "I doubt it. I never missed church as a child and I'm certain I could recall a prayer or two if the need arose."

"You should have been saying them all along," Tory pointed out with an impatient sigh. She had to cover a wide yawn before urging her mount on toward the town. Jesse immediately drew alongside her, but she could not manage more than a faint smile.

"You had a good point," he agreed. "We can use all the prayers we can get."

Unlike some scientists, Earl Crandell had an abiding faith in God and an appreciation for all His creatures, but he had belonged to no particular religious sect and neither did Tory. Prayer had never been a part of Tory's daily routine, and it struck her as disrespectful to turn to God in bad times when she had not thanked him when her life had been going well.

"I didn't have a chance to get rid of my clothes before Araña discovered I wasn't a boy, and then it no longer mattered. Do you suppose I should dump them out here?"

"No, save them," Jesse insisted. "Your blouse is real pretty. Not that your skirt wasn't, but I especially liked your ruffled blouse. Just keep your things. I should have realized the Apaches would have assumed any women's clothes they found belonged to Mayleen. Don't worry about them being discovered now. I've never stayed in a hotel where the owners searched my luggage."

"Can any town out here possibly have a hotel?"

"No, but they'll have a *cantina* with rooms upstairs we can rent. If this is the place I think it is, then Gerry and I stopped here when we were on our way to Arizona. It was a nice little town as I recall."

Tory had had ample opportunity to learn Jesse always tended to be optimistic, so she wasn't surprised when the town of Santa Maria Del Consuelo proved to have a name longer than its main street. The low adobe buildings reminded her all too vividly of Cactus Springs, but she knew the architecture preferred by the Spanish conquistadores prevailed all across the Southwest. The small town's single unpaved street ended in a wide plaza in front of the city's most impressive structure: its Catholic church.

"What day is this?" Mayleen asked. "I sure hope tomorrow isn't Sunday or you might be asked to preach, Reverend."

"There's not the slightest danger of a Protestant minister being invited to give the sermon at a Catholic Mass," Ivan scoffed. "Now please start calling me Leo. A husband and wife ought to be on a first-name basis."

"Perhaps, but that rule doesn't apply in our case," Mayleen reminded him.

"Will you two at least try to get along?" The pair had spent the day either lost in a hostile silence or heatedly bickering, and Jesse was thoroughly bored with their company. "Just remember that a preacher doesn't drink," he cautioned Ivan. "And even if some do, you don't!"

Ivan merely nodded in reply, but he had no intention of following Jesse's rules any longer. He would not be obnoxious about defying him. He would take the same care he had before to be discreet, but he could not wait to enter the *cantina* and buy a bottle of whatever passed for whiskey in the sleepy little town.

There were only a few elderly women seated around the fountain in the plaza, but there were more than a dozen horses tied to the hitching post out front of the *cantina,* and the volume of music and laughter coming from inside made it appear that the rest of the town had gone there that evening. Uncertain whether or not a crowd would work to their advantage, Jesse again conferred with his companions.

"I'll go in first and ask about rooms. If there aren't any free, then we'll go on and camp farther down the trail."

"Be careful," Tory cautioned.

"I will," Jesse promised with a sly wink, but the only problem he foresaw was a possible shortage of rooms. After he strode through the door, it took a moment for his eyes to adjust to the dimly lit interior and it was then he realized just how much trouble they were truly in. The *cantina* was nearly filled, but the customers who crowded the bar and slouched at the tables did not resemble the peaceful citizens he had met on his previous visit to the tavern with Gerry.

These men were a far tougher breed. Heavily armed, they were well on their way to becoming drunk and, to a man, they eyed Jesse with a malevolent gaze. He turned on his heel and promptly headed right back out the door. It wasn't until then that he noticed the horses were too fine to belong to Mexican peasants. Even if he had failed to take that into consideration at first glance, he did not need another look at their owners. The *cantina* was full of bandits and he did not want any part of them.

Unfortunately, *they* wanted his company and the three seated closest to the door filed out after him. *"Señor!"* one called before Jesse could reach his horse.

Jesse turned slowly. He had learned Spanish as a child and spoke it fluently, but thought he would be better off in this situation if they believed him to be some stupid American who could not understand a word they said. "You talking to me?" he asked impatiently.

The heaviest of the men gestured and waited for Jesse to approach him to speak. "Come back in and bring your friends," he invited in English. "We are all very friendly." His companions laughed as though that were an immensely amusing joke.

"We're tired," Jesse explained. "We just wanted a place to sleep tonight, but I can see the *cantina* is full." He began to turn back toward his horse, but the bandits moved to block his way.

"All the rooms are free," the bandits' spokesman revealed with a broad grin. "Bring your friends inside."

At one time, Jesse had had the speed to outdraw even men who made their living as hired guns, but he would not take that risk after going without practice for four years. Besides, even if he could shoot these three men, he would still have to face the others inside, and he did not see any way he could shoot them all and get the three people traveling with him out of town uninjured. He had been so anxious to make love to Tory in a bed, he had failed to consider how dangerous entering a Mexican town might possibly be.

As he saw it, his only option was to keep the bandits amused. "Well, thank you," he replied, hoping to sound sincere. "Is there somewhere we can take our horses?"

"We will care for them," the grinning bandit promised. "Now come inside."

Jesse smiled as he waved to his companions. Tory looked suspicious of the men welcoming them to town. Ivan appeared dismayed, while Mayleen, having grown up in

Mexico, knew bandits when she saw them. She dismounted with the others, but kept a tight hold on her satchel. She had specific plans for how she intended to spend her savings, and allowing her hard-earned money to fall into bandits' hands was not one of them.

Her curls were tucked up under her hat, and she assumed that spending all her days out of doors since leaving Tucson had darkened her once-fair skin to an unappealing shade of a potato. Setting her features in a petulant frown, she began to berate Ivan in a high-pitched whine.

"Be sure and tell them that I want to bathe first thing. It's bad enough you've brought me along on this wretched trip, but you can at least get me a hot bath. I don't suppose there's any hope of a nice supper, but I want to be clean to eat whatever it is they serve here."

Jesse shrugged as though he were embarrassed by Mayleen's demands. "This is the Reverend and Mrs. Leopold Martin," he announced to the men at the *cantina* door. "My stepson and I are taking them to our church in Las Cruces."

At first glance, the bandit who had invited them inside had thought Mayleen pretty, but once she came close enough for him to see the harshness of her expression and hear the nagging tone of her voice, he swiftly changed his mind. What the *cantina* needed was a *puta*, not a *bruja*, and he was sorry he had not let the tall American and his friends continue on their way.

"A preacher," he bemoaned under his breath. He had shot a great many men, and if the truth were known, a couple of women, too, but he had never shot a man of God, and that was one pattern he hoped he would not be forced to break. "Are you a gambling man?" he asked Jesse before the Texan could step inside.

"Sure am," Jesse responded enthusiastically, although he had little more than spare change in his pockets. He knew he would have no choice but to lose no matter what game was being played, but he intended to take all evening to do it and hoped by that time the bandits would have drunk themselves into a mindless stupor. They would awake in the morning to

276

find him and his friends long gone.

"I'd be right proud if you'd invite me to join one of your games." While that remark obviously pleased the bandit who had inquired, Jesse could see by Tory's expression that she did not approve at all. But that was the least of his problems for the moment, and he clapped her on the back as though she really were his mythical wife's son and propelled her on into the noisy *cantina*.

Chapter 18

As she was pushed into the *cantina,* Tory recoiled at the overpowering stench of stale beer and unwashed bodies. The smoke-filled air stung her eyes. She had not expected deluxe accommodations, but she had certainly never envisioned having to spend the night above a smelly tavern filled with such rowdy and disreputable-looking patrons. She kept her head down and peeked out at them through her lashes so as not to attract attention to herself, but her mind was made up within a few seconds. She turned to tell Jesse that she did not want to stay there, but he shot her such a severe warning glance that she thought better of rendering her opinion aloud.

Jesse was even more appalled than Tory, but he forced himself to smile agreeably as he looked around for the owner of the tavern. He recalled him as being a gregarious sort who had made every effort to make his and Gerry's brief stay enjoyable. He was hoping that after nearly five years, the friendly man would have forgotten his earlier visit, but the sad-eyed fellow who approached them was a stranger.

"Dagoberto Cortez," he introduced himself, and in broken English welcomed them to his establishment.

He was of medium height, but so painfully thin he was a poor advertisement for his tavern's fare. When he smiled, Jesse could not help but be reminded of a grinning skull. He had remembered the tavern in Santa Maria del Consuelo as a pleasant place, but it had become a den of thieves run by a laughing corpse. Things were not going well at all, and he hoped the hours until sunrise would pass quickly.

"Zeke Jackson," he replied as he grasped Dagoberto's bony palm for a handshake he ended as swiftly as politely possible. "The Reverend Martin and his wife want a room and my stepson Cal and I will need another," Jesse explained before adding that they would all like the opportunity to bathe.

"Rooms, *sí,*" Dagoberto offered with a surprisingly courtly bow. *"Agua caliente, no."*

Having already announced her intention to have a hot bath, Mayleen lashed out at the tavern owner in a fiery stream of Spanish that was every bit as abusive as her earlier comments had been in English in a dramatic attempt to force him to provide what she wanted simply to ensure her silence. When she paused for a breath, Dagoberto immediately promised to heat water for her himself.

"Gracias," Mayleen replied with a triumphant smirk.

Jesse knew precisely what Mayleen was doing, but as he and Tory followed Ivan and her up the stairs, he whispered an urgent plea. "I'd shut up now if I were you. Don't carry your act any further."

Dagoberto was a few steps ahead of her, and Mayleen took the risk he could not overhear her response to Jesse. "I can take care of myself without any help from you," she murmured insistently.

Convinced that she probably could, and more than willing to let her try, Jesse did not argue. She and Ivan were given the first room at the top of the stairs, while Dagoberto showed Tory and him to the one next door. The doors of the tavern's four rooms all opened out onto a balcony which overlooked the main floor below. There was no way to go between the rooms without being seen by most of the men seated downstairs at the tables or standing at the bar.

As soon as Dagoberto had left them with a promise to return with hot water and their luggage, Jesse closed their door and raised a finger to his lips. Having requested Tory's silence for the moment, he hurried to the window and flung it open to air out the stuffy room. He rested his hands on the

280

sill and looked out. There was a separate building behind the tavern which housed the kitchen, a shed where their mounts had been taken, and the usual toilet facilities, but none of the structures was attached to the main building so it was impossible to walk across their roofs to reach Mayleen and Ivan's room unseen.

Fortunately the adjacent room was also in need of fresh air, and when Ivan opened the window, Jesse called to him. "Stay in your room," he advised. "I'll see that some supper is sent up to you. We'll clear out at first light."

Ivan had absolutely no desire to socialize with the men downstairs and waved to acknowledge his agreement. Jesse moved away from the window and glanced around the sparsely furnished quarters. On his previous visit, his room had not only been spotless, but brightened with fresh flowers as well. Now there was a thin layer of dust covering the top of the battered dresser and washstand. He checked the bed and was relieved to find that while the linens had a faintly musty odor, they were clean.

"I'm sorry. Another man owned this place the last time I was here, and obviously conditions have deteriorated badly. I meant for us to have a comfortable bed and the privacy to enjoy it, but I doubt you'll be any more interested in making love tonight than I will."

"Then why must we stay?" Tory asked.

"These people aren't the kind you can insult by leaving before they're ready to tell you good-bye." Jesse came back to the distraught young woman and drew her into an affectionate embrace. "I'm sorry this place is so awful, but I'll have us out of here in the morning. Men can't drink the way they are doing downstairs and be up and about at dawn. I want you to stay up here out of sight. The food used to be good here so I hope they still have the same cook."

"I don't think I'll be able to eat a bite," Tory confessed.

Jesse attempted to bestow a comforting kiss, but Tory's lips were trembling so badly, he gave up the effort to lift her spirits with affection. It wasn't difficult to understand why she was so frightened, but it was hard not to be insulted by the fact she had so little faith in his ability to protect her. He

281

took hold of her upper arms and stepped back.

"Those men downstairs think you're a skinny kid, Tory. I can guarantee that not a single one was consumed with lustful thoughts when you walked by. As for Mayleen, she used a sharp tongue to do a damn good job of discouraging any interest in her. Neither of you will be bothered tonight."

Tory was shocked by his praise for Mayleen. "You approve of Mayleen's behaving like a shrew?"

"Of course. I understood what she was doing. Didn't you?"

The weary young woman shook her head. "No, I thought she was just continuing her endless spat with Ivan."

"Well, she wasn't, but don't give her another thought. We'll clean up, have something to eat, and then you can get some sleep while I play whatever game happens to be the current favorite here. It's probably faro and I've played that all my life."

"Faro?"

"It's a card game," Jesse explained, "in which bets are placed on the order cards are dealt from a dealing box."

"That doesn't sound like much of a challenge," Tory responded with a puzzled frown.

Jesse took her hand and led her over to the bed. He sat down and pulled her down beside him. After a brief pause to judge the quality of the mattress and discover it was more comfortable than he had hoped, he continued. "The challenge is that the bets are placed before the cards are drawn. You can bet any card, or make bets on all of them, to win or lose when it's drawn."

"Like cutting for high card?"

"No, this is different. The value of the card doesn't matter. To begin the game, the dealer discards the top card. It's called the *soda* and it's placed away from the box. The rest of the cards are considered two at a time. One card is drawn and placed beside the box. It's the loser. The card left faceup in the box is the winner. Understand? There's a winner and loser for each turn. The loser is outside the box, while the winner is left inside. All the winning cards are stacked on the *soda* so it's possible to tell which cards won and which lost."

Tory nodded thoughtfully. "There's no strategy involved, is there?"

"Not like chess there isn't," Jesse agreed, "but the money involved makes it an exciting game. It's also real easy for the dealer to cheat the players out of their money, which is what I expect to have happen tonight."

"But you'll play anyway?"

"I don't see as how I have much choice. Besides, there's always the slim chance I'll win some money, and it would sure come in handy because we don't have much."

"Ivan and Mayleen seem to have plenty."

"I'd rather not rely on them for anything," Jesse revealed. There was a knock at the door then, and, hoping it was the hot water, he rose to his feet. "Don't worry, we've got enough to get us home." He leaned down to brush her lips with a light kiss and was pleased that their conversation about faro had left her relaxed enough to respond.

When Jesse went to the door, rather than Señor Cortez, he found a young boy with his saddlebags and Tory's satchel. The lad was followed by the plump woman Jesse had recalled as being such an excellent cook. She giggled happily as she handed him the first of two buckets of tepid water. It wasn't what he had had in mind when he had asked to bathe, but his request for a tub met with a puzzled shrug.

He placed both buckets inside the room beside their luggage and then engaged the smiling woman in a brief conversation about the previous owner. Upon learning the fellow had died, he offered his sympathies, but she simply gave another shrug and mumbled a bit of scripture in response.

"*Y* Dagoberto Cortez?" Jesse asked.

The woman glanced over her shoulder and after having made certain no one else was about whispered in an anxious tone, "*¡Ten cuidado! Todos los hombres son malos!*" She hurried away, but not before promising to return with their supper.

Curious, Tory approached Jesse. "What did she say about Cortez?"

"He doesn't pay well," Jesse lied rather than convey the

283

urgent warning he had been given. "She probably just wanted to make certain that we'd leave her a tip." He stole another kiss and then carried the first of the buckets over to the washstand. He removed the pitcher, and then filled the bowl. "I'm afraid this is as close as we'll come to getting a bath tonight. You go first."

Tory surveyed the small, square room and did not see any way to arrange for the privacy she required. "Where are you going to be?"

"I'll just stretch out on the bed and take a nap," Jesse offered agreeably. He sat down to remove his boots, stretched out on his back, propped his head on his hands, and closed his eyes. "Just pretend I'm not here and then you can do the same for me."

"Pretend?"

"Hush, I'm trying to sleep."

Tory did want to bathe, but not in front of Jesse. It was one thing for them to remove each other's clean clothes to make love, quite another for her to cast off soiled garments and scrub clean in his presence. The first activity was wildly romantic, but the second was just the opposite in her view. To add to her discomfort, the noise from downstairs was growing steadily louder.

When Jesse did not hear so much as a handkerchief drop, he turned toward the window and made himself comfortable on his side. "I didn't realize you'd still be so bashful. Is this better?"

His question embarrassed Tory badly. "I didn't think you'd peek."

"No? Are you too shy to undress in front of yourself?"

Disappointed that he was not being more considerate of her feelings, Tory looked down at the water remaining in the battered oaken bucket. She glanced toward Jesse, and then unable to resist the temptation to repay him for drenching her in the river the previous day, she picked up the wooden pail and hurled its contents all over him.

Shocked by her underhanded trick, Jesse rolled off the far side of the bed so quickly that he slipped and fell rather than landing on his feet with the agility he usually displayed.

Infuriated that Tory had gotten him wet, he turned to tell her what he thought of such foolishness, but the impish light dancing in her eyes immediately brought laughter rather than insults to his lips.

"I'm going to get you for that," he threatened calmly as he started around the bed.

Still clutching the bucket, Tory briefly debated throwing it at him, too, but fearing that she might accidentally hurt him, she set it aside. Standing in the corner, she had little chance of escaping him, but looked toward the door as though contemplating a dash outside.

"Don't even try," Jesse warned. He had rounded the foot of the bed now, and in the next instant effectively blocked her way. He thought he had her trapped, but she just laughed at him and sprang over the bed in a bounding leap a cat would have envied. "Am I going to have to spend the entire night chasing you around the bed?" he asked.

"No," Tory responded brightly. "You could give up now and excuse yourself so that I could bathe."

Jesse rested his hands on his hips. "You want me to leave?"

"Yes, if you would, please."

Jesse eyed her for a long moment. Other than their erotic interludes, they had also gone swimming naked together, so he thought her request was absurd. He had turned his back to provide all the privacy a lady should require, and he was exasperated that his generous show of courtesy had not been enough for her. Lovers were supposed to trust each other, and it was excruciatingly plain that Tory did not trust him. That she could feel this way after all they had been through together left him feeling bitterly discouraged. He began to unbutton his shirt.

"You should have said so before you got me all wet," he scolded. "Now I'll have to clean up first and then I'll be happy to give you hours and hours of privacy if that's what you want. Fortunately, I'm not in the least bit shy."

Tory's eyes widened as Jesse peeled off every stitch of his clothes, but despite the attractiveness of his muscular build, she did not want to look at him. Instead, she sat down on the opposite side of the bed, folded her hands in her lap, and stared straight out the window.

"Hey, I won't be embarrassed if you watch me."

"Obviously not."

Jesse could not help but be amused by how swiftly he had turned the game she had begun to his own advantage. He ignored her as he began to wash, but he was determined to teach the high-strung beauty just what love meant, since the trust that was its essence had eluded her so completely.

The sweetness of the chubby maid's expression kept Mayleen from erupting into another show of temper, but she was not at all pleased to be given two leaky buckets of lukewarm water rather than the hot bath she had anticipated. "Apparently we're supposed to share these," she grumbled unhappily.

Presented with a perfect excuse to leave and fetch a bottle of whiskey, Ivan moved toward the door. "I'll go look for a tub. They've got to have one somewhere."

"Perhaps, but don't bother to lug it upstairs if it's full of spiders or has as many holes as these damn buckets."

"I understand," Ivan assured her. He hurried on out the door, but paused outside their room and looked over the railing to make certain Jesse wasn't seated below. Finding only the raucous crowd that had welcomed them, he whipped on down the stairs and hurried over to the bar. He was by no means fluent in Spanish, but he knew enough to make his needs known.

Dagoberto Cortez regarded Ivan with an incredulous stare. "Whiskey, Reverend?" he asked as though he feared he had misunderstood.

In his haste to get a drink, Ivan had completely forgotten about his newly chosen profession. Desperate, he was struck with a sudden inspiration and leaned close to the painfully underweight man. *"Es por mi esposa,"* he confided in a pleading whisper that readily conveyed his true exasperation with Mayleen.

Dagoberto's expression brightened with understanding. He raised his eyes to the heavens in a silent prayer of thanksgiving for having been spared the anguish of a nagging wife, took the money Ivan offered, and handed him a bottle of tequila.

"*Gracias.*" Ivan jammed the bottle in his coat pocket. Eager to sample the forbidden liquor, he failed to notice the dark stares directed his way as he hurried out the rear door. True to his word, he walked along the back wall of the cantina and around the side, thinking that if the establishment owned a tub of any kind it would be hanging up there, but the only hook he came across held part of an old harness.

Remaining in the shadows, he uncorked the tequila and took a drink. The fiery liquid scorched his throat and burned his stomach. He was used to the pain and grimaced only briefly before the predictable numbing warmth he had craved began to seep through him. He took another drink, savored it fully, then replaced the bottle in his inside pocket and hurried back up to the room he was sharing with Mayleen.

"Apparently the spiders are living elsewhere," he joked. "I couldn't find a tub."

He was out of breath and his spectacles were slightly askew, giving Mayleen the mistaken impression that he had been dashing about searching for a tub for her. That had been such a sweet thing to do, she was touched by his thoughtfulness and did not complain that he had failed in his mission. There were soap and fresh towels by the washstand and she busied herself fiddling with them instead.

"Thank you for looking, Ivan. That was very nice of you."

Ivan picked up his saddlebags and carried them to the far side of the room. He bent down and slipped the bottle of tequila between a couple of shirts while Mayleen was still preoccupied. "Leo, remember? I'm your darling husband, Leopold."

"Leo," Mayleen repeated softly. Despite their long acquaintance, she felt quite awkward having to bathe in front of him. Had he not made the effort to find her a tub, she knew she would have berated him for gawking at her like he had at the river, but that would now be a most inconsiderate way to behave and she held her tongue. She poured some water into the bowl in the washstand, then removed her blouse and tossed it on the bed. She glanced over at Ivan, and discovered he was standing at the window studying whatever could be seen in the fading light.

Deciding he was as embarrassed about having to share the room as she was, she hurriedly laid out clean garments, washed the dust of the trail from her body with all possible haste, and yanked on another blouse and skirt. "There, I'm finished. There's plenty of water left for you."

"Thanks," Ivan replied, but he was far more interested in having another sip of tequila than washing up. Because he did not want Mayleen to suspect that, he chucked her soapy water out the window and poured fresh water for himself. He had grown up in a house with a complete staff of servants and he laughed to himself as he thought about how low he had sunk.

"What do you find so amusing?" Mayleen asked. She had taken up his position at the window, but she was still curious about his mood.

"When I was small, the butler used to have to chase me all over the house before he could catch me and make me bathe. I suppose all little boys hate being clean." That was at least part of what Ivan had been thinking, if not all of it.

"Your family employed a butler?"

"My father was a banker," Ivan explained. "He had to look prosperous in order to convince everyone that he was. In other words, it was good for business to have a house full of servants. My mother certainly never discouraged him from spending his money every way he could."

Mayleen had never had the slightest curiosity about Ivan's family, but his mention of servants had certainly piqued her interest now. "Did you say you were from Kansas City?" she asked.

"St. Louis," Ivan replied. He was finished shaving, and rinsed his face. He had to don his glasses to see himself clearly, but when he did, he was surprised by how tanned and fit he looked. He had spent a great deal of his time out of doors in Tucson, so his tan had merely deepened, but he had also spent far too many nights drinking himself into a stupor and that sorry habit had not helped his looks any. He knew he ought to quit drinking once and for all and vowed as he had so many times before to stop just as soon as he had finished the bottle he had hidden in his saddlebags.

He rested his hands on the sides of the washstand and leaned closer to the mirror. He resembled his mother, a fact for which he had always been grateful, since his father had been a large, raw-boned man, but his features were uniquely his own with no feminine cast. Perhaps he was not handsome in any classical sense, but he did think his appearance was pleasant in a scholarly, refined sort of way. He was certainly a damn sight better looking than the cutthroats downstairs. He turned to look at Mayleen.

"Do you suppose I ought to offer to lead the cantina's other patrons in a brief prayer meeting this evening?"

"Have you lost your mind?" Thinking he was serious, Mayleen rushed to his side to dissuade him from such a suicidal undertaking, but when she stepped near he broke into a wide grin that made it plain he was only teasing her. "Aren't we in enough trouble without you playing jokes on me?" she snapped.

With an uncharacteristic burst of confidence, Ivan moved to silence her before she could lash out at him with the full-blown tirade he knew was coming. He slipped one hand around her waist, and wound the other in her curls to draw her close for a kiss he deepened and savored. Mayleen's resistance to his ardor lasted no more than the space of a heartbeat and then she began to cling to him with unabashed desire. He wanted her, and when it was clear she wanted him just as badly, he saw no reason to postpone making love. He took a step to force her back toward the bed, but before they reached it, Jesse knocked on their door.

Shaken, Mayleen pulled free of Ivan's arms and rushed to admit their visitor. "Yes, what is it?" she asked excitedly.

Jesse's glance drifted slowly from Mayleen's flushed face to Ivan's bare chest and back again. "Sorry to interrupt you folks," he offered with a sly grin. "Dagoberto sent one supper up to our room for all of us to share. Now we can eat together, or divide the *pollo con arroz* in half and each stay in our own rooms. We thought we'd be sociable and invite you to join us, but if you'd rather remain here—"

"Why, no," Mayleen assured him. "We want to eat with them, don't we, Ivan?"

"Leo," he reminded her. "Just give me a minute to finish getting dressed."

Mayleen brushed by Jesse. "I'll go help Tory," she said. Completely flustered, not by Jesse's inopportune arrival, but by Ivan's delicious kiss, she failed to realize it had been flavored with tequila rather than love.

While waiting for the men, Mayleen and Tory took the worn quilt off the bed and spread it on the floor near the window. The room had only a single chair, so creating an indoor picnic was an obvious choice. Tory was still dressed in male attire, but her hair was loose, and while Mayleen did not like to admit it, she looked remarkably pretty.

Mayleen had always been jealous of the attention Jesse lavished on the young woman, but the knowledge that Ivan also found her attractive suddenly hurt even worse. When he entered the room with Jesse and smiled first at her rather than Tory, Mayleen had to look away, she was so thrilled. Then she was embarrassed. She had always liked Ivan, but thoughts of him had never filled her with desire as they did now.

Now she found it nearly impossible to glance at him without allowing their newfound passion for each other to show in a silly smile she feared would make both Jesse and Tory laugh at her. She could stand almost anything but being laughed at. The savory chicken-and-rice dish was superb, and she kept herself busy refilling her companions' plates until none of them could hold another bite while she had eaten very little. She just wanted the meal over and done so she could be alone again with Ivan.

While Jesse was amused by the constant surreptitious glances passing between Mayleen and Ivan, he was too preoccupied by the gruesome possibilities for a truly horrible evening to want to tease them. He enjoyed the delicious supper, but excused himself as soon as everyone had finished eating. "Wish me luck," he asked as he rose to his feet. "Of course, I don't dare win much or I'll probably be robbed on the way back up the stairs to bed."

Still seated on the floor, Tory reached out to touch his knee. "Be careful," she implored.

Astonished by the emotions that filled that plea, Jesse could not help but wonder how Tory could appear to love him now when she had found disrobing in front of him so objectionable earlier. He had gone out to the stable to check on the horses while she had bathed and had stayed there until he had seen the cook leave the kitchen with their supper. Tory had not bothered to thank him for that gift of privacy, though, but this was no time to criticize her manners. He just nodded and went on out the door.

"You ought to give him some money, Ivan," Tory pointed out. "He doesn't have much."

Ivan was on his feet in an instant and caught Jesse before he had reached the end of the balcony. "Wait a minute," he called out. He drew Jesse into his room and hurried over to his saddlebags. "Even if Mayleen and Tory don't realize it, I know you're doing your best to keep the brutes downstairs away from our women and I should have offered to help you out before now." He withdrew a handful of gold coins and dropped them into Jesse's palm. "There's a hundred dollars. Let me know if you need more."

Surprised by the geologist's sudden generosity, Jesse slipped the coins into his pocket. "Thanks. Better keep an eye on things up here. If there's any trouble downstairs, get the women out through the windows if you have to. Don't bother to saddle the horses. Just ride bareback and I'll catch up with you later."

Ivan was appalled to think he might be given such a responsibility, but he hastily assured Jesse he would do his best. "Perhaps they only want to gamble with someone new."

Jesse shook his head at the ridiculousness of Ivan's comment, and did not waste his breath explaining that the *cholos* downstairs wanted someone new to torment, not to entertain. He left Ivan's room confident that the Mexican bullies waiting for him were no worse than the obnoxious

291

Texans he had battled all his life. They were men like Gerry, who were always trying to find shortcuts and live off another man's efforts rather than their own. The memory of Gerry's treachery was enough to inspire him to do his best to make these men sincerely sorry they had ever met Zeke Jackson!

Ivan waited at the door until he heard Jesse start down the stairs. Then he went back to his saddlebags and treated himself to another couple of drinks. He wiped his mouth on the back of his hand, rehid the bottle, and returned to the ladies who had now gathered up all the dishes and placed them on the tray the cook had used to carry the food up to their room. Needing some air, Ivan reached for the tray.

"I'll take this down to the kitchen. Why don't you two just have yourselves a nice chat while I'm gone?"

Ivan left before either young woman could object, but neither felt like beginning another conversation, and when Tory turned away in an attempt to hide a yawn, Mayleen grabbed the opportunity to say good night. "Jesse wants to get an early start," she reminded Tory. "I think I'll go to bed. See you in the morning."

As expected, Tory responded with a relieved smile at the suggestion of bringing the evening to a close and Mayleen hurried away. The impatient young woman left the door slightly ajar so that Ivan would see she had returned to their room and not bother Tory. When he appeared, she sent him only a brief, questioning glance before the width of his smile drew her back into his arms.

They giggled like children and got caught up in a tangle of clothes in their haste to discard their garments and get into bed. Men did not usually kiss her, but Ivan was so eager to display his affection that he soon had Mayleen breathless. Rather than simply using her petite body to sate his own desires as so many others had, his lavish kisses and tender caresses made her feel adored.

He was both playful and passionate, and while she could not recall the previous times they had been together, she knew she would never forget tonight. A talented seductress,

292

she made certain the pleasure Ivan experienced was so intense that he would not forget her, either. When she finally fell asleep in his arms, she was convinced she had found the husband of her dreams.

Ivan was just as thoroughly content for perhaps an hour. Then the steady laughter and shouts from the games downstairs made it impossible for him to sleep. He was supposed to be taking care of two women, not losing himself in one, but he would not have passed up the chance to make love to Mayleen again for anything.

Gradually he eased himself out of the bed and went to his saddlebags. All he needed was another sip or two of tequila and then he would check to make certain Tory was sleeping as soundly as Mayleen. He and Jesse might have to stay up all night, but that did not mean their women did, too. Just thinking of Mayleen as his woman brought such a radiant glow of happiness that he toasted his change of luck where she was concerned with another long swallow.

The night was warm, and he sat down and leaned back against the wall while he tried to decide how best to stand guard over his two lovely charges. He was sorry now that he had not told Tory to rap on the wall between their rooms should she need him. He should have at least told her good night. Discouraged that he had made such a stupid oversight, he again raised the tequila to his lips and tipped the bottle high. It was going to be a long night, but he was sure that, with another couple of swigs, he would be able to handle whatever came his way as confidently as Jesse would.

Chapter 19

Dagoberto Cortez was the most talented faro dealer Jesse had ever seen. The man had not simply mastered his craft but elevated it to a fine art. His bony fingers moved with the lightning speed of a concert pianist and Jesse was swiftly convinced the emaciated Mexican could conjure up any card he wished and make it win or lose.

The observant Texan studied the faces of the five other men seated at his table and found their eyes glazed with greed as Dagoberto moved through the deck with a spellbinding rhythm. To a man they were focused on the cards, not Dagoberto's hands, and Jesse came to the brutal realization that as the only player aware that the game was crooked, he was in a precarious position indeed. He had assumed the heavyset bandit seated next to him had invited him to play to separate him from his money in the most humiliating manner possible, but now Jesse understood that it was Dagoberto rather than the bandits who controlled the game.

Jesse wondered why Dagoberto was not plying his wizardry with cards in New Orleans, where faro had first been introduced as a popular game from France. Perhaps he already had, and had become too well known. In the sleepy village of Santa Maria del Consuelo, Dagoberto was calmly cheating bandits out of their spoils and the outlaws were too drunk, stupid, or trusting to notice. But Jesse noticed.

Bets were placed on a layout consisting of a complete suit

of spades. Clearly selecting favorite numbers, the other players appeared oblivious to the fact that whenever the bets were heavy on a card to win, it lost, and vice versa. Dagoberto kept the game exciting by occasionally paying out large sums on single bets, but the house was the steady winner. When he looked up and caught Jesse's eye, his sly smile dared the traveler to catch him manipulating the cards for his own gain.

Jesse knew precisely what would happen if he accused Dagoberto of cheating: the cantina would erupt in the worst brawl imaginable and the odds of his surviving it unscathed were even slimmer than the odds of an honest deal at Dagoberto's table. There was a strange sort of justice in a cardsharp cheating bandit, and he saw no reason to become involved in Dagoberto's scheme. Instead, he sat back, bet small sums on random cards that drew little interest from the other men at the table, and slowly increased his stake.

His outward calm was an act, however, for he had not forgotten for a minute the danger he faced. The bandits reminded him of the worst sort of rabble confined at the prison in Yuma, and he knew precisely how fast those surly inmates' moods could turn mean. Yes, he thought to himself, the thieves who surrounded him were the same kind of brute: strong and stupid. Far too often he had seen those traits become a deadly combination. Just as in Yuma, he kept to himself that night. He spoke only when spoken to, and made no sudden moves which would call attention to himself or cause alarm.

The bandit who had insisted they stay at the cantina was quite drunk now. He dozed off and began snoring. Jesse ignored him, but his *compadre* on the other side gave him a nudge to wake him. Startled, the thief drew himself upright, but his posture soon assumed a comfortable slouch, his chin touched his broad chest and he again fell asleep. The two others at the table were boys barely out of their teens. Enrique, the one at the end, was so hot-tempered that he cursed loudly every time the draw went against him, which was often since he bet all the favorites which were sure to lose with Dagoberto rigging each turn.

Jesse ordered a beer and sipped it slowly rather than gulping it down like his companions. He rocked back in his chair and hoped the remainder of the evening would become progressively duller. To his immense disappointment, when a beautiful young girl, who was still more child than woman, entered the cantina, it did not.

She was tall, with a willowy grace, flowing ebony hair, and dark eyes that were bright with unshed tears. She was clothed in the simple cotton blouse and skirt of a peasant, but there was nothing ordinary about the girl, including the advanced state of her pregnancy. Her unexpected presence caused a hushed silence to fall over the room. She walked slowly from one table to the next, studying each man in turn with a careful stare, but she did not stop until she reached Jesse's table. She regarded him with no more curiosity than she had the other men, but when she reached the foul-mouthed youth at the end, she drew to a halt and laid her hand on his shoulder.

Badly embarrassed, the young man recoiled from her touch and hissed at her to leave him be. He turned his attention back to Dagoberto, but the owner of the cantina had stopped dealing and sat displaying a gentlemanly composure while waiting for him to tend to his guest. Everyone in the room was now straining to see what the young man would do. Even the sleepy bandit beside Jesse had again been jostled awake. When the youth stood and raised his hand clearly meaning to strike his lovely visitor, every man in the room let out an incredulous gasp.

"Enrique!" shouted the heavyset bandit at Jesse's side. He lurched to his feet and waved his pistol in the air, his threatening gesture urging Enrique to back away.

Infuriated by the interference in his domestic troubles, the younger bandit shoved the pregnant woman in front of him to serve as a shield. He then began to refer to her in the coarsest of terms, while at the same time insisting he did not even know her. Devastated by the harshness of her lover's words, the poor girl burst into heart-wrenching sobs.

With the same speed he used dealing faro, Dagoberto raised a Colt .45 from his lap and shot Enrique in the side of the head, killing the abusive bandit instantly. "I despise cowards," he explained in precise English. He repeated the comment in Spanish for the startled bandits, then moved his chair slightly to put more space between himself and the deceased's body, which lay sprawled at his side.

Understandably sickened, the girl swayed slightly. A handsome young man from the next table rushed to her side, eased her into Enrique's vacant chair, and knelt at her side. That prompted three other men to come forward and carry the corpse from the *cantina*. Apparently Enrique had not been well liked, for none of his companions uttered a single word of protest at the way he had met his death.

Jesse sat very still, hoping the pregnant beauty did not have several brothers who were waiting outside because he certainly did not want to find himself caught up in another gun battle, but apparently she had come to the *cantina* alone. Huge tears kept rolling down her cheeks, and Jesse wondered whether she was crying for Enrique, or herself and her unborn babe.

In an attempt to seize control of the situation, the bandits' leader took it upon himself to interview the distraught young woman. After repeated sympathetic reassurances that she had nothing to fear, she finally dried her tears and explained that her name was Rosalba Gutierrez. She had come a long way to find Enrique, who had made extravagant promises and then abandoned her. Now that he was dead, she was at a loss for what to do.

Believing that what Rosalba needed was a husband, the desperado's chief asked for volunteers from among his men. The first to step forward was the fellow who had helped her to a chair. Several others displayed a similarly keen interest in taking her for a wife, and a heated argument quickly ensued between them.

Hoping to avoid another senseless shooting, Jesse offered the quickest solution. "Let Rosalba decide."

The prospective husbands were surprised by his suggestion, but after a moment's debate, agreed to let the girl choose. Having foolishly fallen in love with the wrong man once, she showed a commendable maturity and questioned each man in turn to determine his present assets and plans for the future. None admitted to being a bandit, and each made promises which Jesse thought were probably just as impossible to fulfill as those she had heard from Enrique. She listened thoughtfully, however, and then chose the one who agreed to take her back to her village and build her a house. That he was also the first one who had spoken for her and easily the best-looking individual in the group were apparently secondary considerations.

Thinking this the perfect time to sneak away unnoticed, Jesse left his chair and started for the stairs but he did not reach them before Dagoberto called out his name and asked him to fetch the Reverend Martin. "The reverend?" Jesse repeated numbly.

"¡Sí! The priest is away," he explained. He gestured toward the girl's swollen figure as clear evidence of the need for a prompt wedding.

"You want to have the wedding tonight?"

"¡Sí!" The bandits agreed in loud chorus and they began moving the tables and chairs out of the way to create a space in which to have the ceremony. They then noticed the need to scour the blood from the floor and several went looking for rags to handle that chore.

Jesse turned back toward the stairs. He sure hoped Ivan had learned how to conduct a marriage ceremony in Sunday school. He knocked loudly on his door, and when Ivan did not immediately respond, he pounded even more forcefully. He was about to kick in the blasted door when Ivan opened it slightly and peered out.

Seeing Ivan was clad in his trousers, Jesse pushed by him into the room. "Get dressed," he ordered. "You've a wedding to perform."

Though Ivan had still been up, the sound of gunfire had awakened Mayleen, and she was sitting up in bed clutching the sheet to her breasts. "What's going on down there?" she asked fretfully. "I couldn't bear to send Ivan downstairs to find out."

"Nothing much," Jesse replied nonchalantly before relating the reason for the hasty wedding. "If you don't hurry," he warned, "you'll be able to do the christening, too."

Ivan was not too drunk to understand what was expected of him, but he feared he was too drunk to carry it out. He leaned back against the wall in an attempt to get his balance. "What comes after 'dearly beloved we're gathered together in the presence of God and these witnesses to . . . to—"

"To join this couple in holy matrimony," Jesse prompted. At first he thought Ivan was merely sleepy or nervous, then he got a whiff of tequila on his breath and knew precisely what the problem was. "I should have known better than to bring you here."

Mayleen leaned over to turn up the lamp. She and Ivan had been too frightened to converse, but she took one look at the professor's slouched posture and understood why Jesse was so angry. "Damn it all, Ivan, why did you have to get drunk tonight?" When she had awakened and found him gone from their bed, she had assumed that it was because he was worried about their safety and had gotten up to keep watch. She felt very foolish now, for, in truth, he had left her arms to get drunk. That was just like him, she thought, but it still hurt, and badly.

"Do you think I ought to attend the wedding, too?" she asked Jesse.

"No, just stay put. The less the bandits see of you and Tory the better." He turned back toward Ivan and cursed softly under his breath. "I'll stand right beside you and grab your collar if you look like you're going to collapse, but you're going to have to come up with something that sounds like a wedding ceremony. Fortunately, I don't think many of the men downstairs speak English. The few who do are nearly as drunk as you and that will be a big help, too."

"What comes after matrimony?"

"How should I know!" Jesse complained. "I'm not the one who's supposed to be a minister! I'll go ask Tory. Maybe she knows. You hurry up and get dressed."

Thoroughly disgusted with Ivan, Jesse left his room and entered his own. He glanced toward the bed, expecting to find Tory asleep, or perhaps awake and sitting up as Mayleen had been, but the bed had not been slept in. "Tory?"

he called.

Too frightened to sleep, Tory had paced the room for a long while and then taken refuge in the far corner. She was seated on the floor, hugging her knees. Paralyzed with fear at the sound of gunfire, she did not even notice Jesse had entered the room until he called her name. She struggled to rise to her feet, but still kept to the comforting security of the corner.

That the young woman he loved had been so frightened she had been huddled on the floor like a terrified child cut Jesse to the quick. He knew he ought not to have left her alone, but truly he had had no choice. He did not criticize her for not having more courage. He just went to her and pulled her into his arms. He patted her hair and explained how Ivan had been called upon to perform a wedding ceremony but was in no condition to do it.

"All we can recall is the first line," he said. "Can you remember the rest?"

Tory swallowed hard before whispering the opening phrase of the only wedding ceremony she knew. Then her mind was as blank as his. "I think something about marriage comes next. Why not just have Ivan give a lengthy prayer, then have the exchange of vows and pronounce them man and wife?"

Pleased with Tory's suggestion, Jesse began a sweet trail of kisses at her brow, brushed her cheek with his lips, and then captured her mouth for a passionate kiss he hoped she would find reassuring. The problem was, he wanted far more than a single kiss and there was no time to pursue his desires. Forcing himself to concentrate on the problem at hand, he took a deep breath and stepped back.

"I'm sure that'll be fine. Of course, the couple won't be legally wed, but they'll never know it. I'll come back upstairs just as soon as the ceremony's over. Will you be all right?"

"I shall have to be."

Jesse looked down at her, longing to say something that would lift her mood and light her face with a smile, but he could not bring himself to lie when she knew as well as he did that their situation was every bit as dangerous as it had been all along. His shoulders were stiff from the tension that had filled him all evening. He had been worried about a possible fight with the bandits that might leave him badly hurt or, God forbid, dead, and Tory alone. Now, as he stood with her in the small room, he was again overcome with the uncomfortable sensation that they were being watched.

In an instant he sensed what was wrong: They were being followed. The false graves had not fooled Luke Bernay. The intrepid tracker was still dogging their trail. Jesse did not want to frighten Tory with his premonition, though. "After the wedding there's sure to be more drinking and we won't wait for dawn to leave. We'll get out of here while the *cantina's* patrons are too busy to notice what we're doing."

"Will Ivan be able to ride?"

"No, but it doesn't matter," Jesse reminded her. "He knew what would happen if I caught him drinking, and now he'll have to face the consequences. I'll give Mayleen a choice, but Ivan is on his own."

Tory frowned slightly, but decided not to argue. Ivan had been warned more than once so she had little sympathy for him. Besides, they were not that far from Texas now that he could not find his way there by himself. She walked Jesse to the door, and this time left it slightly open and remained by it so she could overhear what was happening downstairs.

Ivan stepped out of his room as Jesse came to the door. Mayleen had had to help him, but he was as neatly dressed as a minister would be expected to be on a Sunday morning. He had had a great deal of experience at pretending to be sober when he wasn't and thought he could play his part without embarrassing himself too badly. He listened closely as Jesse described Tory's suggestions for the order of the ceremony and then nodded.

"Don't look so stricken, Jesse. I can carry this off without degracing either of us," Ivan claimed, not realizing how badly his words were slurred.

Exasperated, Jesse took a firm grip on the geologist's arm and made sure that he reached the bottom of the stairs without falling on his face. The room had been cleared, and the voluptuous cook, still in her nightgown, obviously had been hastily summoned from her bed. She had provided a white lace *mantilla,* and the bride was using the mirror above the bar in an attempt to drape it attractively over her long hair while her future husband stood beside her drinking toasts to her beauty. She was responding with shy smiles, the recently deceased Enrique all but forgotten.

It was quite the most ludicrous wedding scene Jesse had ever witnessed. He cleared his throat noisily. "Shall we begin?" he asked without releasing Ivan.

After a shout and wave from Dagoberto, the cutthroats who crowded his *cantina* assembled in a semicircle. He then directed the bride and groom to take their places in front of Ivan. Someone remembered a ring then, and there was a five-minute delay as the only man wearing one was reluctantly talked into parting with it for the ceremony. When the bridal party was finally ready, Ivan favored them with a suitably angelic smile and began what little of the ceremony he had recalled and been able to rehearse while dressing.

Standing next to Ivan, Jesse was prepared for the absolute worst, but rather than passing out midway through the wedding, the professor surprised him by conducting a service that came close enough to sounding authentic to satisfy both the bandits and the bride. His benediction was positively inspired, and Jesse could not help but wonder if perhaps the scientist had not missed his true calling.

Just as Jesse had predicted, the celebration began immediately, but he and Ivan offered only verbal congratulations to the newlyweds and stepped aside when the toasts began. Within a few minutes, the party was so boisterous that the Texan and the tipsy "minister" were able to climb the stairs without being seen.

Jesse shut Ivan's door and was relieved to find Mayleen had finally gotten dressed. "Tory and I are leaving now," he announced calmly. "You're welcome to come with us, Mayleen."

Ivan sank down on the edge of the unmade bed. "What about me?"

Jesse ignored him. "If you want to come with us, Mayleen,

we'll toss your bag out the window. I'll rip up the sheets to make a rope and lower you to the ground. I won't risk having you walk through a *cantina* full of Mexico's worst."

"What do you want me to do?" Ivan asked. "Just jump out the window?"

"I don't give a damn what you do," Jesse shot right back at him. "You've been nothing but trouble the whole time I've known you, and as far as I'm concerned this is where we say good-bye."

Mayleen's glance was troubled as she studied the two men. In both appearance and temperament they could scarcely have been more different. She knew she could count on Jesse. He would never let a friend down no matter what the risk was to himself. By siding with Gerry against him, she had certainly let *him* down, though, and she knew he would never truly forgive her for it. She could no longer be so stupid as to fool herself into believing she could ever have a permanent place in either his life or heart. He was merely asking her to go with him because he felt he must, not because he truly wanted her along.

Then there was Ivan Carrows. She recognized the woebegone expression he wore because in Tucson he had always looked just as thoroughly ashamed of himself each time he had had too much to drink. Jesse might never need her, but it was plain to Mayleen that Ivan certainly did. There were worse things than marrying a wealthy drunk. Mayleen could swear to that because she had done each and every one of them.

"I'll stay with Ivan," she said softly. "When we get to El Paso, maybe we'll pay you and Tory a visit."

While Jesse was amazed by her decision, it certainly did not disappoint him to learn he would have Tory all to himself for the rest of their trip. "Are you sure that's what you really want to do?" he felt he had to ask.

Mayleen nodded. "Neither of us can go back to the Arizona Territory, so we might as well keep on traveling together."

Jesse moved toward the door. "Just ask for the directions to the Lambert ranch. Everyone knows where it is."

Ivan struggled to his feet and tried to block the taller man's way. "Come on, Jesse, don't do this," he pleaded. "The four of us have come this far together, and—"

Jesse put his hand on Ivan's chest and gave him a shove that sent him careening back across the bed. "Stay out of my way, Professor, or the next time I won't be so considerate." He dug into his pocket for the coins Ivan had loaned him and tossed them at him. After that show of temper, he went on out the door and displayed an unusual amount of restraint by drawing it closed rather than slamming it loudly.

As soon as Ivan caught his breath, he pushed himself up into a sitting position and gathered up the gold coins. "I'm sorry, Mayleen. I never meant for this to happen."

Mayleen went to the window and looked out toward the small shed that served as the stable. Although the night was dark she hoped for a glimpse of Río's silver hide when Jesse rode away. "What's done is done, Ivan. It's too late to be sorry now," she remarked wistfully.

"No, I really *am* sorry," Ivan insisted. He rolled off the bed, pocketed the coins, and went to her.

"Yes, of course you are," Mayleen agreed sadly. "You're always sorry, but nothing ever changes, does it?"

Insulted by her cool rejection of his apology, Ivan turned away. He intended to go downstairs and join in the wedding celebration, but he tripped over his own feet, twisted his right ankle, and fell to the floor in a clumsy heap. When Mayleen knelt at his side, he was not only in pain but so badly embarrassed that he brushed her hands away with a hostile swipe.

"Leave me alone!" he shouted angrily.

Mayleen rose and stepped back. She watched him attempt to gain the leverage to rise, slip, and fall again. Had she not noticed the trail of tears trickling down his cheeks, she would never have realized he had hurt himself. "Oh, Ivan," she sighed. "You can't spend the night on the floor. You'll have to let me help you." He did not complain this time, but hung on to her waist to hop the short distance to the bed.

He took off his spectacles and jammed them into his coat pocket. "Jesse hasn't had time to leave yet. If you hurry,

305

you'll still be able to catch him."

Mayleen slipped her hand around Ivan's neck and rested her forehead against his. "Hush. Now what's wrong? You haven't broken your ankle, have you?"

"I fell all the way down the stairs at the Silver Spur without injuring myself badly. I couldn't have done much harm in here. Just ease off my boots, and then you go on with Jesse."

Mayleen helped him out of his boots, but made no move toward the door. "I'm not leaving, Ivan. There's no point in my chasing after Jesse, so stop telling me to do it."

She started to help him off with his coat, but he caught her wrists. His ankle was throbbing painfully, but he had to settle things with her before he lay down. The problem was, he was at loss for what to say. It was easy to blame the tequila for muddling his thoughts, but he had no one but himself to blame for drinking it. He brought her hands to his lips and kissed her palms.

"I am sorry," he swore again.

This time Mayleen did not argue with him. She simply helped him off with his clothes so he could get into bed. Then she went through his saddlebags, found the half-empty bottle of tequila and flung it out the window. She knew he might buy another bottle of that poison in the morning, but for tonight it was out of his reach.

Jesse dropped their belongings out the window. Tory was so light it was no strain to lower her by her wrists until she was within a safe distance to drop. He then followed her out the window. As tall as he was, when he dangled from the window sill, he did not have far to go to reach the ground. Still, it was not the way he would have preferred to leave the *cantina*.

They held hands as they dashed across the yard, but there were no sentries to challenge them, and it took only a few minutes to saddle the horses. Then the pair left the deceptively peaceful-appearing town at a gallop. Neither had had a moment's rest and their mounts were far from fresh, but they managed to travel nearly two hours before stopping for what was left of the night. Jesse threw their bedrolls on the ground rather than spreading them out with any care, but he was too tired to take the time to arrange the folded blankets neatly.

"I keep thinking about Mayleen and Ivan," Tory revealed as she lay down beside him. "What's going to happen to them?"

"We're better off without them," Jesse insisted between wide yawns. "They've had trouble keeping up with us the whole way and now that we're getting close to home, I don't want to have to wait for them. It's been nearly five years since I left El Paso. Can't you understand how anxious I am to get home?"

"Yes," Tory replied thoughtfully, although she no longer had that choice. She could easily comprehend his need for haste, but she did not understand how his homecoming could possibly be a happy occasion. "Do you think your ranchhands will still be loyal to you?"

Jesse chuckled to himself and reached for her. "Come here," he said. He wrapped her in an enthusiastic hug. "You let me worry about the ranch. All you need do is cuddle up with me so I can get to sleep. Do you remember the first night we spent together when I had to kiss you to make you be still?"

Tory recalled the incident vividly. She had been terrified of him, of going to Prescott, of Apache renegades, and of Eldrin Stafford's men, who might have been following them. "God, what an awful night that was," she mused aloud.

What Jesse remembered was the stolen kiss. "Awful?" he asked. "Surely kissing me wasn't *that* awful."

Ignoring his blatant request for a compliment, Tory slipped her arms around his waist and held on tight. "They're still coming, aren't they? Bernay, Eldrin's men, they're probably only a day or two behind."

Being followed created the same sensation as standing in a draft and shivering with the chill. Shocked that she could now feel it, too, Jesse drew her closer still. He could not lie to her. "They may be headed this way, but they're never going

307

to catch up to us, Tory. I told you I mean to go to a friend's ranch first. I won't just go riding up to the house and give Gerry the chance to shoot me. I'm a hell of a lot smarter than that."

"Yes, I know you are," Tory assured him. She reached up to kiss him then, and the low moan from the back of his throat let her know a good-night kiss was not going to be enough. She suddenly felt very foolish for having sent him away that afternoon. They should have bathed together and gotten some use out of the bed. The desert sand was not nearly as soft, but when she loved him so desperately, it didn't matter.

Chapter 20

Jesse had never considered fear an aphrodisiac, but he did not really care why Tory's kiss was flavored with desire now. He was thrilled when she showed even the smallest amount of interest in him. When her need was as intense as it was now, he would not waste a second of it questioning what had inspired her ardor. He always wanted her, and if she suddenly wanted him, he certainly wouldn't disappoint her.

Her aloofness in the afternoon had angered him, but no trace of that cool detachment remained in her manner. Now she was all sweetness and warmth and he wanted every morsel of affection she wished to give. He recalled how prim and proper she had looked seated on her bunk in the Cactus Springs jail. From that moment to this he had never doubted that she was a lady, but when she abandoned her usual reserve to crawl all over him as she was now doing, he could not help but wonder which mood was the most natural for her.

He still regarded her spirit as fragile, but her lithe body had a seductive strength and grace, which conformed to the planes of his muscular build with an ease that imparted an effortless magic to each kiss and embrace. Forgetting her scars, he slid his hands under her shirt to savor the silken softness of her skin. When his fingertips brushed over the long ridges left by Paul Stafford's whip, his mind was flooded with the hideous images he feared must linger in her memory.

Rather than that indescribable pain, he longed to fill her heart and soul with the love that overflowed his own. He leaned back slightly and combed her hair away from her temple with a gentle caress. "I'll have to clear my name in order to regain the power and prestige to enable me to clear yours, but you mustn't even imagine that proving your innocence isn't as important to me as declaring my own. I intend to give you a future that will be free of any sadness from your past."

Tory knew Jesse was sincere. She also knew that few people would share the bias he held where she was concerned. "There's only tonight," she whispered. She slid her fingers through his hair to entice him into kissing her again. That was what she truly needed: the joy of his affection rather than the hope for a future she dared not let herself dream could actually come true.

The urgency of her kiss assailed Jesse with a wanton desire that instantly convinced him to abandon fervent promises in favor of a far more passionate display of his devotion. As usual their clothes were a nuisance to be swiftly discarded and, once naked, he traced Tory's lovely figure hungrily with his hands and lips. In return, the exquisite tenderness of her touch lured him past all hope of reason.

The haunting stillness of the starlit desert night held a beauty as lush as any symphony ever written. With a sensuous grace born of strength and pride, Jesse followed that silent accompaniment as he again made love to Tory. He heard her longing in her breathless sighs and felt it as her fingertips dug into his shoulders. Perfectly matched, he did not abandon himself in pleasure until he had brought her the same shattering joy that she gave him. Blinded even in the darkness by ecstasy's searing flames, Jesse was certain paradise could not be half so sweet.

Reluctant to ever let her go, he buried his face in her curls and kept her clasped tightly in his arms. He rolled onto his back to provide her with an adoring bed. Their bodies aligned in the most comfortable of poses, she soon drifted to sleep, but he remained awake, planning the rest of their journey with far more care than he had given the beginning. He was not going to let Luke Bernay, or anyone else, prevent him from keeping his promises to Tory. If he lived to be one hundred, that would still not be nearly enough time to spend loving her.

The small room was filled with bright sunlight when Ivan awoke. The day was already a warm one and he threw off the blanket and started to roll on his side, but immediately gave up the idea when an agonizing pain tore through his right ankle. As if that were not misery enough, his head felt as though it were ready to explode and his eyes burned so badly he wondered if he could have forgotten to close them while he slept.

Thoroughly wretched, he lay back down and stared up at the ceiling trying to recall what he had done to deserve such a heavy dose of pain. Unfortunately, he had only the vaguest memories of riding down the dusty main street of some Mexican town. He had had blackouts before, and as always he was frightened to find a piece of his life missing. Was it only one night, or had he lost several days? he worried.

He tried to call for Mayleen, but his tongue felt like a big piece of cotton and he doubted he could make himself understood. He closed his eyes and sighed unhappily. They should have been on the trail by now. Had Jesse delayed their departure because of him? Gathering his courage, Ivan raised up on his elbows and took a good look at his ankle. Under the best of conditions, he did not think his bony ankles attractive, but now the right one resembled some sort of grotesque melon.

Just the sight of it made his already queasy stomach lurch, and he quickly lay back down. He knew he was really in trouble now. Jesse was sure to leave him stranded in Mexico, and while Ivan was not lost, he did not like the prospect of being on his own. What if Jesse and the women had already left? he tortured himself. Would anyone come to help him, or would he lie there unnoticed until he either died or felt well enough to hop about on his own?

"I've really done it this time," he murmured dejectedly. He had probably broken his blasted ankle, and what kind of medical care had he received? Obviously none. His imagination promptly provided the grim prospect of infection followed by a grisly scene of an amputation performed without anesthetic. He could hear himself shrieking as a dull saw made the first savage cut across his tender skin. Terrified by that ghastly image, he struggled to again sit up. That pose only intensified his pain, but when Mayleen came through the door carrying a bowl of hot soup on a tray he made a heroic attempt to maintain it.

"Oh, good. You're up," she greeted him. "How do you feel?"

Ivan adjusted the pillow at his back. Gazing through a heavy curtain of despair, he thought the bouyancy of her mood in extremely poor taste. "How do I look?" he asked gruffly.

"You've had better days," Mayleen replied honestly. "Are you hungry?"

"I shall never be hungry again."

Mayleen set the tray on the nightstand and remained by the bed. "You'll have to try and eat anyway," she scolded. "It will probably be a couple of days before you can ride, and you don't want to risk becoming so weak, you'll topple right off of your saddle."

Ivan lost all patience with his vivacious companion. "Just look at my ankle!" he shouted. "It's shattered! I'll be lucky not to lose my foot. I'll not be able to ride for weeks, perhaps months!"

Mayleen refrained from touching him, but she leaned down to study his swollen ankle closely. "Can you wiggle your toes?" she inquired.

Ivan groaned as he attempted to comply with her request. "Did they move?"

"Yes, your toes are fine. I'm sure your ankle is fine, too. It's just swollen, is all."

"Because every last bone in it is broken!"

Mayleen reached for the bed's second pillow, laid it at the foot of the bed, and carefully raised Ivan's leg so his ankle would rest on it. "There, doesn't that feel better?"

"No it doesn't, not a bit. Does this town even have a physician?"

"No, I'm afraid not. I asked Dagoberto to send for the doctor this morning, but he said they have to take care of all their medical problems themselves here. He offered to come up and take a look at your ankle himself, but I thought I should ask your permission before inviting him to pay you a visit."

Ivan made another try at wiggling his toes. This time he thought he detected some slight movement and that cheered him a little. "Who's Dagoberto?"

"He's the man who owns this *cantina*. Don't you remember meeting him yesterday?"

"Was it only yesterday?"

Ivan's hair was standing straight up on his head. Without his spectacles he was squinting to see her, and his belligerent expression detracted further from his appearance. Still, Mayleen found him appealingly pitiful rather than pathetic. It must be love, she thought to herself. "Don't you remember?" she probed.

Unable to return her inquisitive glance, Ivan looked down at his hands. His fingers were trembling badly and he laced them together to keep her from noticing. "No. I can't remember a damned thing, but please don't tell Jesse that. He doesn't need another reason to dislike me."

Mayleen reached out to pat Ivan's hair into place. "Jesse and Tory are gone, sweetheart. We're going to have to get to Texas on our own."

Ivan's eyes widened in horror as he looked up at her. "You mean he just left us here, and me with a broken ankle?"

Mayleen dropped her hand to his shoulder. The previous evening he had been such a passionate lover, it was difficult to believe this petulant child was the same man. "You hurt yourself after he'd gone, Ivan. Besides, I really don't see how your ankle can possibly be broken when you just slipped

313

here in this very room. You didn't have a bad fall. I'll bet it will feel much better tomorrow and perhaps we can leave the next day. Thank God those awful men that were here have gone. The *cantina* is positively peaceful without them."

"What awful men?" Ivan rasped.

Knowing her explanation would call for a long story, Mayleen brought the room's single chair to the bedside and sat down. "Come on, you eat some of this soup before it gets cold. I'll tell you everything you've forgotten after you've finished."

"I'm in no mood for food."

"That's too bad, because you're going to eat anyway," Mayleen announced with a playful giggle. "You need to put on a little weight, Ivan. You've always been much too thin."

When Ivan opened his mouth to argue, Mayleen shoved in a spoonful of soup and the disheveled geologist swallowed it rather than spitting it out all over her. He clamped his jaws shut then, but gradually the delicious aroma wafting from the vegetable-laden broth made him more cooperative. "I can feed myself," he offered.

"Fine," Mayleen agreed. She handed him the bowl and spoon. "I'm glad to see you're making an effort to take care of yourself for a change."

Stung by that insult, Ivan ate the rest of his soup in silence. When he had finished the last drop, he replaced the bowl on the tray. Then he took a good look at Mayleen. The split riding skirt and boots were no surprise, but her blouse was buttoned all the way up to her chin and she had knotted her hair atop her head to create a far more severe hairstyle than he had ever seen her wear. Assuming her appearance was some sort of disguise, he did not question her about it.

"Why did you stay?" he asked in a challenging tone.

Mayleen sat back and folded her hands in her lap. She tried out several responses in her mind, but spoke none aloud. "Don't you remember anything at all about last night?"

"Not one blessed thing," Ivan revealed with a helpless shrug. "Did I miss something important?"

314

Tears began to fill Mayleen's eyes as she realized just how important making love with him had been to her! She had thought that he really cared for her until she had awakened to find him clutching a bottle of tequila rather than her. She raised her hand to her lips to stifle a sob, but failed. Unable to describe that he had given her the joy of feeling loved and then the heartbreak of being abandoned all in the space of a few hours, she rose shakily from the chair and fled the room.

Unable to understand why his question had upset Mayleen so badly, Ivan stared after her for a good long while. It was plain he had done something to hurt her feelings, but he did not have an inkling as to what it might have been. Feeling very sorry for himself, he wished he had a drink, then knowing that was the last thing he needed, he promised himself for the hundredth time that he would never take another drink as long as he lived.

The words sounded empty even in his mind until he realized this was the first time his drinking had hurt someone other than himself. He could only guess why Mayleen had chosen to stay with him, but whatever her reason might have been for not abandoning him, he was certain she must regret it now. She possessed admirable loyalty as well as beauty and spirit, and he was ashamed of how he had repaid that gift. He vowed to make it up to her, but he could not do anything until he felt better. He lay back down, closed his eyes, and hoped the next time he woke up, his body would be far more cooperative.

Later that same day, Luke Bernay reached the Río Casas Grandes. Certain Jesse Lambert would have made camp there, he walked along the riverbank seeking clues that would prove his supposition. While care had been taken to erase all trace of a campsite, he found footprints at the water's edge that he was certain had been made by the petite Mayleen Tyler rather than some unknown child.

There was enough light left to keep traveling and he pressed on until the arrival of nightfall had made continuing impossible. He ate a cold supper, slept soundly until dawn, and then rode on toward the rising sun. When he reached Santa Maria del Consuelo, he headed straight for the *cantina* as the most likely place to gather information. He was astonished to find a couple who fit Lieutenant Barlow's description of Ethelrose and John Stone seated inside.

Certain they had to be Mayleen Tyler and the man he had yet to identify, Luke pretended not to have noticed them and strode straight up to the bar. Fluent in Spanish, he ordered a beer and spent several minutes asking casual questions about the town before he inquired if any Americans had stopped by the *cantina* in the last few days.

Overhearing Luke's questions, Dagoberto approached him. He did not encourage curiosity in his establishment as too many of his patrons had something to hide. That evening there were only a few of the local men present, and they were not the ones he had to protect.

"Are you seeking company or information?" he asked with the wicked grin that had sent shivers down Jesse's spine.

"A little of both," Luke assured him. He had kept an eye on Mayleen and her friend in the mirror above the bar. "What about those two over there? They're Americans, aren't they?"

A more innocent couple Dagoberto had yet to meet. "Would you like to be introduced to the reverend and his wife?"

Luke nearly choked on his beer. "Did you say *reverend?*" he asked incredulously.

Dagoberto nodded.

Luke risked glancing over his shoulder at the couple. The woman did look prim enough to be a minister's wife, but she was far too pretty and he could not shake his original impression that she was a popular prostitute from Tucson. He again focused his attention on Dagoberto. There was something predatory about the thin man he found most unattractive, but he had not been hired to go around handing out prizes for good looks.

He took Jesse's photograph from his pocket and laid it on

316

the bar. "Have you seen this man? It's possible he has a beard now. He's traveling with a pretty blond woman who may be dressed as a boy."

Dagoberto picked up the photograph. He had not seen enough of Zeke Jackson's stepson to say whether he might have been a woman masquerading as a boy or not, but he recognized Zeke immediately. His *cantina* was a haven for men who gambled heavily with money whose source he did not question. He would not violate their need for silence concerning their identities, or Zeke's, either.

"No," he replied apologetically. "I do not know this man."

Disappointed, Luke slid the photograph back in his pocket. "Well if you do see him, be careful," he warned. "He's a murderer, and so is his woman."

"Murderers!" Dagoberto gasped, as though he did not already know a great many such men.

This time it was Luke who nodded. He kept a watchful eye on Mayleen and her companion for another few minutes, and then, seeing they were finished eating, he downed the last of his beer and walked over to their table. Without waiting for an invitation, he drew up an extra chair and joined them. "Mayleen, honey, I can't tell you how good it is to see you here," he greeted her.

Understandably shocked to have a complete stranger call her by name, Mayleen took a moment to recover. "You're mistaken," she then replied in a soft, cultured tone. "I'm Virginia Martin, and this is my husband, Reverend Leopold Martin."

Luke did not bother to tip his hat. "I don't give a damn who he is," he informed Mayleen coldly. "The only man who concerns me is Jesse Lambert. We both know you know where he is, so don't waste my time pretending that you don't."

Despite having had two days' rest, Ivan's ankle was still causing him considerable pain. Bored with their small room, he had hopped down the stairs in order to eat supper in a more entertaining place. The effort had cost him, and although this obnoxious stranger was short, he knew he

317

lacked the stamina to fight him. He did not have to admit that aloud, however, and bluffed instead.

"We didn't invite you to join us, sir, and I would appreciate it if you would spare us your ill-mannered company."

Luke was astonished by Ivan's flowery request. "Good Lord, Mayleen, did you actually marry a preacher?" When she didn't reply, he leaned toward Ivan. "This woman's a whore," he confided. "Better divorce her quick."

Ivan struggled to rise, but having only one good leg to stand on made it difficult. "No one calls my wife a whore!" he whispered emphatically so as not to announce the insult to the entire room.

While she was immensely flattered that Ivan would try, Mayleen knew he wasn't strong enough to defend her reputation and leapt to her feet. "You wait here, sweetheart. I'll take this . . . this *gentleman* up to our room and talk with him there."

"No, that's not a good idea," Ivan argued. "We don't even know who he is."

"I'm Luke Bernay," the renowned tracker declared proudly. "Happy to meet you."

Remembering Lieutenant Barlow's praise for the man's skill, Mayleen shot Ivan a warning glance to ensure his silence. "I want to talk with Mr. Bernay in private," she insisted, and when Luke got to his feet, she hurried him over to the stairs.

Unable to match their pace, Ivan was left to watch helplessly as Mayleen and the obnoxious stranger climbed the stairs and disappeared into their room. Feeling like an incompetent fool, he collapsed in his chair, but when the bartender asked if he would like a drink, he shook his head. He might not be able to contribute much if Mayleen needed help, but he could sure as hell stay sober.

Seeing no need for pretenses, Mayleen turned to face Luke the instant they entered her room. "Jesse's innocent," she proclaimed. "There's no reason for you to be tracking him when it was Gerry Chambers who robbed the stage."

Luke remained by the door. He was surprised by her forceful accusation, since Sheriff Toland in Tucson had also mentioned Chambers as a likely suspect. Of course, in his view, a woman in love could not be counted on to speak the truth about her man, nor would her testimony be any more reliable if she and Chambers had parted. She might just be out to get revenge on the man now so he discounted her comment.

"I leave establishing guilt or innocence up to the courts," he replied. "Lambert was convicted, but he escaped from prison, and I'm being paid to bring him back. I suppose there's a slim chance he might be innocent, but it doesn't matter to me."

"How can it not matter?" Mayleen cried.

"Like I said, I don't argue with the courts. I just track escaped convicts."

"Well, that isn't right!" Mayleen insisted. When that appeal was met with an insolent shrug from Luke, she tried again. "I knew Gerry was the one who robbed the stage and I should have said so at the trial. I would have, but Gerry and I were, well . . . we were in love, or at least I was. I had to protect him even if it meant seeing Jesse go to prison, but I hated lying. I just hated it. I want to help Jesse get everything straight now."

Mayleen had not forgotten Rose Flannery's threats, but she was so ashamed of how badly her lies had hurt Jesse that she was willing to take the risk the madam might try to harm her. "I'll go back to Tucson with you," she volunteered. "I'll explain what really happened, and with Jesse's name cleared, you won't need to find him."

Again, Luke was surprised by Mayleen's apparent sincerity, but quickly dismissed it as an act put on by an accomplished actress. "I don't believe a word you're saying."

"But you must," Mayleen implored him. "Jesse's innocent. It was Gerry who robbed the stage and left the money in Jesse's room. Gerry's the one you ought to be tracking, not Jesse."

"I don't choose the men I track, darlin'. I go after the men

I'm hired to find."

His use of the endearment made Mayleen livid, for he was dismissing her as a prostitute whose word could not possibly be worth anything, and that wasn't true. She knew who had robbed the stage, and she intended to help Jesse prove it. Hoping to draw Luke close, she pretended to burst into tears. She let out a loud wail and then rushed to the washstand. She grabbed up a washcloth, wet it, and began to pat her face as she continued to berate Luke about his methods.

"You're no better than Gerry if you keep on trying to take Jesse back to Yuma when he's innocent. We heard you were a fine tracker. It's a pity you're not a fine man as well."

Luke was disgusted that their conversation had not provided any helpful information. However, he did think Mayleen was a pretty little thing so his time was not being completely wasted. He was sorry to have upset her. "Perhaps you'd like to give me some kind of a statement to take back, Miss Tyler," he said as he walked up behind her.

Mayleen gripped the pitcher on the washstand as though she meant to pour some water into the bowl, but that was not really what she had in mind. She gave another heart-rending sob, and when Luke reached out to touch her shoulder with a comforting pat, she spun around and slammed the heavy ceramic pitcher into the side of his head. It broke, drenching them both, but getting wet was the least of her worries.

Standing in the narrow space between the bed and the wall, Luke had had no chance to dodge Mayleen's blow had he seen it coming, which he hadn't. Knocked unconscious, he slid to the floor and lay there, his temple both wet and bloody. She stood over him, still holding the remains of the broken pitcher while she waited for the sound of running feet on the stairs. When she realized no one was coming, she let out a long sigh of relief and placed the broken pitcher in the bowl.

Regarding each minute she had just bought as precious, she stepped over Luke, threw back the blanket, and yanked the top sheet off the bed. She had to use her teeth to begin the long tears in the cotton fabric, but she managed to rip it into a sufficient number of strips to tie the famed tracker so securely that it would be a long while before he took up Jesse's trail. She left him lying on the floor where she hoped he would sleep until morning and hurriedly gathered up their belongings.

She left money to pay for their room and board on the dresser, then dropped their bags out the window. There was still a couple of hours of daylight left and she prayed that Ivan would feel up to using them. A quick glance in the mirror assured her that her appearance was as neat as when she had entered the room. She ran back down the stairs to Ivan.

"Let's go for a walk," she encouraged brightly.

Understandably startled, Ivan stayed seated. "Where's Bernay?"

"He's decided to take a nap, so we're going out for a walk," she explained. She then leaned close to whisper insistently, "We're leaving right now. Don't argue, just do the best you can to reach the stable."

"Oh dear God," Ivan moaned. "Did you kill him?"

Before tying him up, Mayleen had checked the pulse in Luke's throat to make certain that she hadn't. While she was appalled that Ivan could imagine her capable of murder, she laughed as though he had said something hilarious, took his arm, and hauled him to his feet. While he did not display any enthusiasm for her demands, he did not complain further and she was so grateful, she reached up to kiss his cheek. He had been in too much pain to have any interest in making love the previous evening, while she had still been too hurt by his convenient memory lapse to crave his affection. Now all she wanted was to leave Santa Maria del Consuelo with all possible haste.

Ivan knew something was dreadfully wrong even if Mayleen would not say precisely what. "Yes, some fresh air would be nice, Virginia," he said, hoping to sound like a dutiful husband. He could not bear to put more than a little weight on his right ankle, but with her assistance he managed to hobble out the door. They picked up their luggage, and while they saddled their horses, he made repeated attempts to ascertain what had happened to Luke, but it wasn't until they had reached the outskirts of town that Mayleen felt safe enough to explain in detail.

"You knocked him out with the pitcher?" he asked, certain he could not possibly have followed her description accurately.

"Yes, and you needn't look so horrified because it wasn't the first time that I'd done it, either. There were plenty of occasions at the Silver Spur when a girl had to defend herself with whatever means were at hand."

Ivan had been aware that Ross and Jack were kept busy punishing the brothel's abusive clientele, but he had never before stopped to think how dangerous Mayleen's life must have been. He had been so involved in his own troubles that he had given the lovely young woman very little thought from one visit to the next and that embarrassed him now.

"I'm sorry the men weren't nicer to you," he apologized. "You never should have been working in a place like that."

Mayleen agreed, but she did not want to dwell on how she had gotten there. "Well, I've left the Silver Spur, and I'm not going back, so let's just forget that's where we met. Now what shall we do? We've got to warn Jesse that Luke is only a few days behind him, but can you ride well enough to do it?"

Ivan's ankle ached too badly to place his toe in the stirrup, so his right leg was just dangling rather than providing any support. His foot was sure to become even more swollen, but he did not want to bemoan his own miseries when Jesse's freedom was at stake. "I shall have to," he vowed stubbornly. "Come on, let's go."

Mayleen had been impressed that Ivan had stayed sober without any such request from her. That he would attempt to ride at all, much less as hard as they would have to, truly touched her. "Thanks, Ivan," she said rather shyly.

"For what?"

"For everything," Mayleen responded. "Now we better

322

watch closely. It's getting dark and we don't want to lose the trail."

"I can get us to El Paso, Mayleen. I'm a damn good geologist and I can find my way from place to place without getting lost."

"Yes, I'm sure that you can." Mayleen knew she was the one who couldn't travel from one town to the next without tripping over her own heart, but she kept that weakness to herself. She doubted that Ivan could stay sober for long, but she sure hoped the next time he made love to her, he remembered.

Chapter 21

Luke Bernay's skull was considerably thicker than Mayleen had thought, which allowed him to regain consciousness within a half hour of the time she had struck him. Bound and gagged, he was wedged between the wall and the bed, where it was nearly impossible to twitch, let alone free himself, but he kept rocking back and forth until he finally inched close enough to the door to kick it. He kept up a steady beat with his heels, hoping someone would soon grow curious enough about the noise to climb the stairs and investigate.

Dagoberto had seen the little man go upstairs with Mrs. Martin but not return with her, and he was already suspicious before he heard the strange thumping coming from the Martins' room. Because the minister and his wife had left the *cantina,* Dagoberto felt it was his responsibility to ascertain what was happening in their room. He took his extra key, but found the door unlocked. He tried to push it open, but it was blocked slightly, forcing him to peer around it rather than fling it wide.

"Señor!" he shouted when he saw Luke had been tied up and left lying on the floor.

Luke made a series of frantic and totally unintelligible pleas which Dagoberto ignored while he eased through the door, crossed the room, and leaned out the window. He called out to the stable boy and questioned him briefly about the Martins. Upon learning the couple had just departed,

Dagoberto left the window and pocketed the money on the dresser. He then hauled Luke into a sitting position and untied his gag.

"I do not like people frightening away my guests," he remarked accusingly.

"They had a damn good reason to be frightened. Now untie me!" Luke demanded.

Apparently unconcerned about Luke's predicament, Dagoberto straightened up, laced his fingers behind his back, and began pacing up and down in front of him. "I do not think I should untie a man who speaks of a preacher in such a vile tone."

"Martin—if that really is his name, which I doubt—can't possibly be a preacher. His wife, who certainly isn't his wife, is a whore from Tucson. Besides, they aren't the ones I'm after anyway. It's Lambert and his woman that I'm tracking."

"The murderers?"

"Yes! Now hurry up and untie me. I just might be able to catch up with the 'Martins,' if I leave quickly."

"You just said you weren't after them."

"I'm not, but they'll lead me to Lambert."

"Are you a United States marshal?" Dagoberto stopped pacing to inquire.

"No, but this isn't the States, so that doesn't make a bit of difference."

"Perhaps not to you, but it certainly does to me." Dagoberto pursed his lips thoughtfully. Because he had seen Leopold Martin perform a wedding ceremony, he was convinced the minister was precisely who he had said he was. As for his charming wife being a whore rather than a lady, that was a preposterous accusation. If what this man said about the Martins was absurd, then Dagoberto doubted Zeke and his stepson were actually murderers. His mind made up, he walked to the door.

"Your story strikes me as being full of lies. I will release you in the morning. *Buenos noches.*"

"Son of a bitch!" Luke yelled, but Dagoberto ignored his curse and slipped out the door.

Luke Bernay did not have a reputation for being tough without reason. He knew screaming for help would never produce any assistance with the owner of the *cantina* downstairs to discount his noise as the wild ravings of a drunk or lunatic. No, he was on his own. While that was damn inconvenient, he was a loner by nature and was undaunted by it.

His knife was still in his belt and his pistol in his holster, but with his hands bound behind his back, his weapons were useless. Frowning darkly, he surveyed the floor around him. There were tiny fragments of the broken pitcher scattered about, but none large enough to clean his fingernails, let alone saw through the knotted sheets that tied him. Glancing toward the washstand, he spied the edge of the pitcher's handle sticking out of the bowl. Certain it had to be attached to a piece of broken pottery large enough to serve as a knife, he began to struggle against the wall in an effort to push himself up into a standing position.

Mayleen had done an excellent job of tying him so tightly that such a feat was damn near impossible. Each time he thought he had the leverage to rise, he slid back to the floor, but he kept right on striving toward his goal. It took him nearly an hour, and he was drenched with sweat, but finally he made it to his feet and with the tiny steps his securely bound legs allowed him, he crept over to the washstand. He used his teeth to pick up the handle, laid it on the bed, then turned around and grasped it with his hands. He leaned against the wall for support and began to cut through the knotted sheets.

His position was an awkward one, and before he had made even a slight tear in the sturdy fabric ropes, the ceramic handle slipped from his grasp, fell to the floor, and shattered. Had Luke been the kind who gave up easily, he would have quit right there, but he was a persistent cuss. He peered into the washbowl and found another chunk of the broken pitcher he could use. Again he had to pick it up with his teeth, drop it on the bed, then turn and grasp it.

His hands were numb from being tied and he had to concentrate much harder than he had the first time not to drop this ceramic shard, too. A clever man, he began to speculate about what he would do should that disaster occur. There was always the bowl, he thought. The problem would just be to get it out of the circular opening in the top of the washstand so he could push it off onto the floor. Surely it would break into a few pieces large enough to use as knives. Of course he would have to pick them up off the floor, and after all the time he had spent to stand up, that was a heartbreaking possibility.

He grit his teeth and kept sawing away on the strip of sheet wrapped around his wrist. Mayleen had twisted the strips, increasing the difficulty of his task tenfold. Fighting discouragement, Luke started thinking about how much he would like to get even with Mayleen Tyler for making a fool of him. He had actually been trying to cheer her up when she had tried to kill him with the pitcher. Maybe she had not really been thinking about murder, but Luke had seen grown men die from a lighter blow to the head than he had just survived.

"Bitch!" he swore. The longer he thought about Mayleen, the angrier he got and, fired by the desire to seek revenge, he worked with even greater zeal. When he finally managed to cut through the first layer of strips that bound him, the tension went out of the rest. It was then just a matter of jumping up and down to shake his bonds loose. It was now pitch dark, but he was too eager to catch up with Mayleen and her preacher friend to stay the night now that he was free.

He fashioned a knotted ladder out of the striped blanket on the bed and lowered himself out the window. His horse was still tied to the hitching post in front of the *cantina* and he rode away without anyone noticing he was not merely a regular patron who had left for home early. He waited until he was well past the outskirts of town before he urged his mount to a gallop. He could not see the trail, but he could feel the people he was after looking over their shoulders watching for him. By the time dawn arrived, he intended to be close enough to reach out and touch Mayleen Tyler again and this time she would not be able to trick him into being kind.

Ivan had not ridden far before the pain in his ankle became so intense he had to draw his horse to a halt. When Mayleen pulled up beside him, he apologized. "I'm sorry. I'd tell you to go on without me, but I don't want you to risk getting lost out here all alone."

"This has sure been a miserable trip for you, hasn't it? First you were all beat up, then there were the awful days with the Apaches when we didn't know if we'd live or die, and now you're hurt again."

While Mayleen's voice was soft and sympathetic, all she had done was make Ivan believe she considered him an incompetent fool. He could not blame her for forming such a sorry opinion of him, either. He was just grateful she was too polite to refer to him as a cowardly drunk, which was an accurate description.

"Look, I said I was sorry. We'll just have to stop here and hope I'll be stronger tomorrow." It took a bit of doing, but he managed to dismount without putting any weight on his throbbing ankle. Thoroughly disgusted with himself, he struggled to unsaddle his horse without having to ask for Mayleen's help. At least they had had supper so he did not have to bother with building a fire.

Mayleen was confused by Ivan's suddenly hostile tone. "Please don't be mad at me for tying up Bernay. I really didn't have any choice. He doesn't care at all that Jesse's innocent. He's just doing a job. I had to try and stop him."

Ivan eased himself down on his bedroll and began the excruciating task of removing the boot from his injured foot. He did not understand how he had managed to get it on when taking it off was so horribly painful. "I'm not angry with you about Bernay," he denied sullenly.

Mayleen unfurled her bedroll alongside him. "They why are you mad at me?"

The awful chore with his boots finally handled, Ivan

removed his spectacles and laid them under his saddle where they would be safe for the night. He removed the gun belt that still did not feel comfortable around his hips and laid it aside. His eyes felt tired and scratchy and he rubbed them before responding.

"I'm not mad at you, Mayleen. I'm mad at myself for making such a poor showing."

Mayleen started to argue with him and then caught herself. "Did you do the best job you could have done for those miners who came after you?"

Ivan sighed sadly. "Yes. It isn't my fault that geological surveys can't guarantee a bonanza. I sure hope they weren't able to talk some other geologist into helping them sell their mine as a rich one when it isn't."

"Jesse should have helped you that night," Mayleen insisted convincingly. "He shouldn't have let you take a beating when he could have stopped it."

"Oh, yes, Jesse is absolutely invincible, isn't he?" Ivan asked with no attempt to hide his bitterness. "According to you, Jesse can work miracles, while all I do is trip over my own feet."

"I don't recall ever comparing you to Jesse."

"You do it constantly," Ivan exclaimed, "and I'm always on the losing end."

"Not always," Mayleen murmured under her breath, but she knew it was pointless to refer to the night he had forgotten. She had not been tempted to draw any comparisons then, but unfortunately, those marvelous hours were lost to him. He was in a mood to fight and she wasn't so she got up and walked away. He would assume she was seeking the necessary privacy to see to her physical needs, but all she really needed was to get away from him for a while.

She had been trying to point out that it was not his fault that the miners had given him such a savage beating. He certainly could not be blamed for their being captured by Apaches, either. He had played his part to help Jesse and Tory escape the Army. He had been a mighty fine preacher, too, to help them stay on the good side of the bandits. Maybe he did

330

drink more than he should but plenty of men shared that weakness.

She should have known she did not have a chance with Jesse and kept her feelings to herself; then Ivan would not feel as though he was her second choice. She wondered if he had a sweetheart back in St. Louis. It was easy to imagine some mousey little spinster waiting for Ivan to come home from the Arizona Territory and marry her. All that kind of woman would ever give him was a passel of skinny little children who wore eyeglasses.

What did she have to offer? Mayleen asked herself. Nights of endless rapture that Ivan would not recall the next morning? That was nothing at all. She wiped a tear from her cheek and turned back toward their hastily made camp. She soon discovered that she had wandered farther than she had realized and it was much too dark to retrace her steps. She broke into a run, but that only compounded her problem. She spun around, staring into the darkness for some sign of the horses, but the blackness that surrounded her was complete.

"Ivan!" she screamed. "Ivan, where are you?"

Equally lost in disparaging thoughts, Ivan was startled from his reverie by the terror in Mayleen's voice. She sounded a long way off, and he hoped she could hear his reply. When she did not call out again, he did not know if something had happened to her, or if she was on her way back to him. He managed to get to his hands and knees, intending to stand up, but she reached their camp before he could get upright. She slid to a stop at the edge of her bedroll and collapsed on it.

"What happened?" Ivan cried. "I was just about to come looking for you."

He was still on all fours and Mayleen was so thrilled to have found him, she could not help but laugh. "Did you plan to crawl around looking for me?"

"If I had to, yes!" She was making him feel like a fool again and Ivan had had enough of it. He reached out to grab her arm, pulled her over onto his blanket, and then stretched

331

out to pin her beneath him. "You don't think I'm so funny now, do you?"

It had been Ivan's surprising show of strength by the river's edge which had first aroused Mayleen's interest and she did not fight him now. She simply lay on his blanket and waited for him to make the next move. That he was sober, and would remember whatever transpired between them, brought a slow smile to her lips.

The stars provided barely enough illumination for Ivan to see Mayleen's face, and without his eyeglasses her subtle smile was completely lost on him. All he knew was that despite his many mistakes, he was no buffoon. He wanted her to understand that for once and for all. "Why were you yelling for me if you didn't want me to come looking for you?" he challenged.

"I wasn't paying attention when I walked away," she explained. "I wanted to know where you were so I could find my way back."

"Well, here I am."

"Do you have a girlfriend waiting for you in St. Louis? A fiancée, perhaps?"

"No, of course not. What makes you ask such a silly thing?"

"Why, 'of course not,'" Mayleen mimicked. "The girls in St. Louis must regard you as a fine catch."

"If you're trying to distract me so I'll forget I'm mad at you, it won't work."

"No, I'm really curious about who's waiting for you in St. Louis."

Exasperated with her, Ivan briefly rested his forehead against hers. "I disappointed my father badly when I didn't go to work for his bank. I'm sure he hasn't missed me. As for my mother, she's so busy with her friends I doubt she's noticed that I've left town."

"Oh Ivan, that can't possibly be true."

"Yes it is. Believe me, there's no one who cares whether or not I ever return to St. Louis. I wasn't popular."

Mayleen had enjoyed enough popularity at the Silver Spur to last her a lifetime; she was sorry to learn Ivan had not had many friends. "You're popular with me," she purred sweetly.

Instantly suspicious, Ivan started to move away, but hesitated. "What are you up to now, Mayleen?"

"Nothing."

Her voice was soft and husky, inviting the intimacy he had longed for the entire trip—but he could not really believe she wanted it. She had turned her back to him the previous night and lain all huddled in a tight little ball. Not that he had felt up to doing anything about it had she wanted him, but the coldness of her pose had made it plain that she didn't. Now she seemed to be teasing him and he did not know what to make of it. He released her, and gradually eased himself to the side.

"We stopped because my ankle can't take any more. I think we better try and get some sleep so we can be up with the dawn the way Jesse was. We certainly don't want to get out of any of the fine habits he set."

The scorn in his voice was enough to discourage any further playfulness from Mayleen. She moved back onto her own bedroll. "Good night, Ivan."

"'Night." Ivan pulled the blanket up to his chin and closed his eyes, but he sure did not feel like going to sleep.

A rude poke to the ribs awakened Ivan shortly after dawn. Annoyed, he left the comfort of his dreams slowly, but he was instantly alert when he opened his eyes and found the barrel of Luke Bernay's rifle not two inches from his nose. He could easily imagine Jesse leaping up, yanking the weapon from Bernay's hands, and beating the persistent tracker to death with the butt, but he was not Jesse.

Mayleen was still seated on her bedroll, looking as disgusted as Ivan felt, and he gave her a quick smile. He then raised up on his elbows and regarded Luke with what he hoped would pass for a sanctimonious stare.

"Did you wish to join us for morning prayer?" he asked.

Luke spit in the dirt. "Whoever you are, you're no preacher, and I wouldn't pray with you even if I were on my deathbed! Now get yourself up. We're leaving."

"Surely you don't expect my wife and me to travel without having had breakfast."

"She's no more your wife than I am," Luke scoffed. "Now let's go."

Ivan doubted his ankle was strong enough yet for him to fight Luke, but he could sure as hell argue. "No," he stated firmly. "You might have been hired to track Jesse Lambert, but you've got no argument with us and we're under no obligation to do anything you say."

Luke gave Ivan another poke in the ribs with his rifle. "Your sweet little 'wife' damned near killed me yesterday and that's reason enough for an argument in my mind. If you'd like me to blow a hole clean through you and bury you out here in the desert where your scrawny body will never be found, then stay put. Otherwise, get up and we'll be on our way."

Without his spectacles, Ivan couldn't see Luke's face clearly, but he knew the man's expression had to be as mean as his words. Surprisingly, he did not feel scared. He remained where he was, silently daring Luke to carry out his threat.

Mayleen got up and rushed to his side. "Leopold Martin! Don't you dare leave me a widow. Now get up from there."

With Mayleen pulling and pushing on him this way and that, Ivan managed to rise, but he had to balance on one foot. He began to laugh. "I'll just have to sit down again to put on my boots."

"What's wrong with your leg?" Luke asked suspiciously.

"It's not his leg," Mayleen hastened to explain. "It's his foot. It got run over by a freight wagon when he was just a little boy and the bones didn't mend right."

Ivan was astonished by that imaginative tale, but he readily understood Mayleen's purpose, for if Bernay believed him to be lame, the tracker would relax his guard and not keep a close watch over him. Maybe he was incapacitated for the time being, but in a few days, he just might be able to kick Luke Bernay right where it would do him the most good.

334

"Please, honey," he scolded softly. "You know I don't like you telling folks that story. I don't need their pity."

Delighted that he was playing along with her ruse, Mayleen kissed Ivan's cheek. "Do you mind if my husband sits down to put on his boots? He really can't hop around and pull them on the way most men can."

"Oh all right, sit down," Luke said. He had confiscated the couple's weapons before awakening them, but when Ivan reached under his saddle, he reacted quickly. "Bring your hand out real slow and it better be empty," he warned.

Ivan laughed at him. "I'm just taking out my spectacles. I can't see anything without them."

"You just let me get them," Luke insisted. He walked around Ivan, grabbed the saddle by the horn, and swung it aside. When all that lay beneath it was a pair of eyeglasses, he gave a disgusted snort. "Go ahead, put on your eyeglasses, 'Reverend,' then get your horse saddled."

"I'll saddle him," Mayleen quickly volunteered. "There's no point wearing my husband out with chores I can handle when he'll need all his strength to ride."

"Are you telling me he's sickly, too?" Luke asked in dismay.

"Well, I wouldn't call him sickly," Mayleen replied with a sweetness that belied her words.

"But others do?"

Inspired by Mayleen's latest ploy, Ivan began to cough. He didn't just give a slight cough or two, either; he hacked and wheezed as though breathing were nearly impossible for him. When he finally looked up, he could tell by Luke's horrified expression that he had convinced him he might not last the day. "I came to the desert for my health," he whispered.

"Well, it appears you came too late." Not having expected so damn many problems, Luke shook his head in disgust. "Maybe you should have a little something for breakfast, 'Reverend.' I sure as hell don't want to see you die of hunger before noon."

"Please watch your language in front of my wife," Ivan requested politely.

335

"The bitch tried to kill me!"

"With good reason," Ivan insisted. "You're trying to take an innocent man back to prison, and no one of good conscience can allow that."

"Innocent," Luke grumbled. "Lambert's innocent and you're a preacher." He moved out of their way, but allowed Mayleen to gather firewood and cook them all breakfast before they started the day's ride.

Later that day, the bandits who frequented Dagoberto Cortez's *cantina* returned to Santa Maria del Consuelo. As was their custom, they visited the *cantina* to refresh themselves and gamble with the money that now filled their pockets. It would have been a raucous but uneventful evening had not seven strangers also arrived in town.

Tad MacDonald eyed the Mexican cutthroats with no more than a passing glance before walking up to the bar and ordering beers for himself and his men. They were too tired and thirsty to care who else occupied the *cantina*. They just wanted to be left alone to enjoy themselves. Unfortunately, the bandits did not feel the same way.

Dagoberto saw the suspicious glances passing between the bandits, and shook his head to warn their leader to let him handle things. After only a few moments' conversation with the Spanish-speaking members of the group, he was again asked if he had seen a slender blond woman traveling with two other men and a little brunette.

"We see very few blondes here," he replied with an agreeable chuckle, revealing nothing.

"She is a murderess," Juan Lopez explained, "and must be found."

"A murderess!" Dagoberto repeated dramatically before crossing himself to ensure divine protection. "This is a peace-loving town," he assured Juan.

Juan glanced over his shoulder at the men seated at the closest table. They were too heavily armed to look like peace-loving citizens to him. "Anyone can see that," he commented sarcastically.

Dagoberto pretended not to understand that insult. He refilled the men's mugs and again reassured them that no blond women had come through town. The strangers' skeptical expressions made it clear they did not believe him, but he responded with an innocent smile.

José Gonzales first asked Tad for permission to offer a reward for information and then turned to address the room in Spanish. "We're looking for a blonde." He then proceeded to describe Tory in colorful but vulgar terms. "She's with two men and a dark-haired woman. If you bring her to us, or help us find her, we'll give you fifty dollars in gold."

Such a sum would have been attractive to most men, but not to bandits who each had many times more in his pockets. José's offer was met with indifferent shrugs rather than enthusiasm and he quickly relayed a piece of information he had forgotten. "She may be dressed as a boy. Have a man and a boy been through here in the last few days?"

An unnatural stillness settled over the room for a few seconds, and then the bandits' leader left his chair to approach José. "We mind our own business here," he informed him coldly. "You should do the same."

José regarded that advice as an insult and stepped away from the bar. "Finding Tory Crandell is my business," he boasted proudly. He gestured toward his friends, and with a wicked smirk described just what they intended to do to her before putting a bullet through her head.

The bandits had gotten only a brief glimpse of Tory as she had passed through the *cantina* on the way upstairs to her room, but to a man they were certain she was the one who had been traveling with the preacher, his wife, and their tall friend. Memories of the impromptu wedding ceremony still in their minds, they held the warmest of feelings for the four *norteamericanos* and nothing but contempt for the seven men who were pursuing them. When the bandits' leader used a well-placed fist to put a stop to José's foul-mouthed remarks, they rushed the other six strangers at the bar and began the wild brawl Jesse had feared might occur.

Despite his daring when dealing faro, Dagoberto was a cautious man and he ducked down behind the bar to avoid being the inadvertent target of a stray punch. This was most certainly not the first fight to break out in his establishment and he knew it would not be the last. A few chairs might be broken, a table or two smashed, glasses shattered, but the *cantina* contained nothing that could not be easily repaired or replaced. When the seven strangers were so badly outnumbered, he did not hold much hope for them, but when the noise died down and he risked peeking up over the bar, he found two of them lying dead of knife wounds, and heard angry shouts as the five others rode away.

Certain it was now safe to stand, he called to the bandits crowding around the door. "Let them go. You know where I keep the shovel. Bury these two and let us hope no one else comes here asking questions that are better left unanswered."

Considering that sage advice, several of the bandits stepped forward to carry the dead men down the street to the cemetery behind the church. They were buried near Enrique before their bodies had had time to grow cold. Inured to violence and bloodshed, the bandits returned to the *cantina,* and once its furnishings were put right, they continued the evening's revels as though they had never been interrupted.

Tad led his four remaining men away from Santa Maria del Consuelo at the fastest pace their weary mounts could manage. It wasn't until they were a good mile away that he realized they were not being followed and drew to a halt. He had understood only a few words of what José Gonzales had said, but it was plain now it had been the wrong thing.

He had seen José fall, but not Juan who was also missing. "Is everyone all right?" he asked.

George Flood used his teeth to grasp the end of his bandana and tied it around his right forearm. "I've been cut up worse," he explained in his soft southern drawl.

Hank Short kept looking back over his shoulder. "I saw the bastard that stabbed Juan. We could go back and wait for him to leave the *cantina.*"

"No!" Tad refused sharply. "There are too many of them

for us to waylay one. And what about José? All I saw was the knife, I didn't see who was holding it."

"I did," Manuel admitted. "Hank and I could go back and—"

"Get yourselves killed most likely," Tad predicted. "What would that prove? That we're even more stupid than we looked the first time? What did José say to make those men go wild like that?"

Manuel Ochoa was now the only one left who spoke Spanish, and he gave a quick translation of what had turned out to be José's last words. "I think the men saw her and liked her."

Tad considered that opinion briefly and then nodded. "That's a damn good possibility, isn't it?"

"It sure is," Hank agreed.

"Christ almighty," Tad swore. "We didn't have a chance to ask about Luke Bernay."

Carl Olson was as shaken as the others to have lost two friends so unexpectedly. "I think when we catch up to Bernay, we ought not to be nearly as nice as we were back in that gawdawful town. I don't want to see any more of us get killed."

"Neither do I," Tad assured him. "Come on, let's keep riding. Maybe we can catch up with Bernay. His luck might have been a lot better than ours."

"That wouldn't be hard," Carl offered with a rueful laugh.

Determined to put several more miles between them and Santa Maria del Consuelo before they made camp for the night, Tad jabbed his heels into his horse's flanks. Both José and Juan had been not only tough but mean, and he knew they would be missed. As for himself, he was so angry that his pursuit of Tory Crandell had nearly cost him his life that he vowed the torture José had described would be mild compared to what he would inflict on the cursed blonde when he finally caught up with her.

339

Chapter 22

As the Mexican city of Juarez came into view, Tory felt an overpowering sense of apprehension. She swallowed hard in an attempt to force away her fears, but they continued to mount. "Oh, please," she begged Jesse, "let's not go into town. Let's just stay out here on the desert like we did last night."

Jesse needed only a quick glance at her pained expression to know he ought not to argue. It had been five years since he had visited Juarez. In that length of time the lively border town might have changed in a dozen different ways, all of them dangerous. Their last foray into civilization had proven disastrous and he did not want to subject Tory to a repeat of that sorry experience.

He smiled and reached out to give her hand a comforting squeeze. "That's fine with me. If you're not too tired, let's keep on traveling and make camp just north of Juarez across from El Paso. I told you about my friend, Eduardo Ruiz is his name, but everyone calls him Lalo. I want to pay him a visit in the morning, real early before anyone is awake. The Río Grande is so shallow we can cross it before dawn without worrying about being swept away. How does that sound?"

Tory tried to smile. "Fine. I know you must think me impossibly foolish, but—"

"I think you're entitled to your opinions, Tory. Don't apologize for them. I don't care what it is you want, don't

341

ever be afraid to tell me about it. I promise I'll do my best to see you get it."

Again Tory's smile faltered. Jesse was convinced everything would run smoothly once they reached his home, but no matter how hard she tried, all she could foresee were more life-threatening complications. She did not want his mood to become as dark as her own, however. "Thank you," she replied. "Do you think we might have quail again for supper?"

Jesse turned Río off the trail toward Juarez and Tory kept her gentle bay by his side. "I'll try and find something even better tonight."

"What tastes better than quail?"

"You'll see."

"No lizards, please, nor snakes, either," Tory requested with a shudder. "All I want is a nicely roasted quail."

"Yes, ma'am," Jesse agreed, but after they had made camp for the night, he went hunting along the river and came back with a large bird. "This is a *chachalaco,* or Mexican pheasant. They're better than quail," he promised. He sat down and began plucking out the bird's long tail feathers. "Do you want to keep these for a hat?"

Tory removed the battered hat she had worn since Tucson and tried unsuccessfully to push the crown into its original shape. "I don't think anything would help this."

"Not that hat," Jesse exclaimed with a rumbling chuckle. "I meant one of those fancy bonnets you ladies like to wear."

"Did I used to dress like a lady?"

"Oh, yes, you certainly did." Jesse kept teasing her as he prepared the *chachalaco* for roasting. He loved to make her laugh, and was delighted when she began to giggle with him. When she got up to gather firewood, the cares that had furrowed her brow appeared to be forgotten and he was grateful for that. It took a while for the bird to roast and they took turns going down to the river to wash up. By the time they were ready to eat, both were relaxed enough to enjoy the meal.

Tory had always loved pheasant and this bird was as delicious as any she had ever eaten. She wiped the succulent juices from her chin and complimented Jesse on his cooking.

"I have never tasted anything even half this good," she swore between bites.

"I should have shot two," Jesse said regretfully. "But I've never seen you with such a big appetite."

"You've never cooked this . . . what did you call it?"

"Chachalaco."

"Thank you. Well, you've never cooked *chachalaco* for me, either. This is worth eating."

Jesse was about to complain that he did not enjoy a steady diet of beans, either, but Tory looked so wonderfully content he did not want to criticize her in any way. He just kept his thoughts to himself and enjoyed watching her eat. When they had finished, he again described how he wished to pay a surprise call on his friend. "He'll know what Gerry's been up to and that will save me the trouble of having to ask around elsewhere."

Tory clasped her arms around her knees and stared into the glowing embers of their fire for a long moment. "You say Lalo is a close friend," she finally commented. "Did he contact you while you were in prison?"

"No," Jesse admitted reluctantly. "Nobody from El Paso did."

"Doesn't that strike you as strange?"

"Not really. I'm sure Gerry's story about my turning bandit was real convincing."

"Why would your friends have believed him?"

"Because Gerry was here, looking them in the eye, and I wasn't, I suppose."

"If Gerry is the lying snake you say he is, why would anyone have believed him?"

Jesse took a deep breath and let it out slowly. "Don't you think I've asked myself that same question a million times? I had four years to wonder why none of my so-called 'good friends' came to Yuma to visit me or worked to get me my release. My stepmother wrote to me several times, always with the same message: she didn't care what I'd done, she would still welcome me home when I'd served my sentence. That was real sweet of her, but it didn't make up for the fact she believed I was a criminal and deserved to be in prison."

343

"She didn't suspect that Gerry was the scoundrel rather than you?"

Jesse shook his head. "That woman will never see the truth about her precious son. Don't get me wrong. She loved my father with the same blind devotion; only he deserved the faith she placed in him. Gerry doesn't and never will."

The flickering light cast dark shadows across Jesse's features, emphasizing the depth of his frown. Tory knew she ought to leave the matter alone, but she was too curious to keep still. She made an attempt to phrase her question diplomatically. "I can't help but wonder about Lalo. If he was your best friend, he shouldn't have turned his back on you no matter what wild tale Gerry told. Could it have something to do with the fact you're a very attractive man?"

Embarrassed by her compliment, Jesse disagreed. "No, I'm not."

"Don't argue with me," Tory scolded playfully. "You're a handsome man, and while you've never mentioned other women, did you have someone special? Could Lalo have been interested in her, too?"

Astonished by the turn her questions had taken, Jesse kept his gaze firmly fixed on the fire. "I suppose you could say I had a girl. Carmen is one of Lalo's cousins, but I don't believe he ever paid much attention to her. She was only sixteen when I left for Arizona, but everyone was teasing us that I was waiting for her to grow up. She thought she was grown up enough for marriage but I didn't. I said we'd talk about it when I came back."

Anguished by the thought of his being with another woman, Tory inquired in a breathless whisper, "Were you engaged?"

"No," Jesse denied. "I'd never proposed, but she just sort of assumed that I wanted to marry her."

"And did you?"

"I can't even remember what she looks like."

"That's no answer, Jesse. Would you have married her if you'd been able to return home as you'd originally planned?"

Jesse hesitated a tad too long before answering her question. "I didn't marry her, so what's the point of speculating on what I might have done?"

The point had been to reassure Tory that she was the woman he loved, and when he failed to do so, she refused to coax the words out of him. She wondered if Carmen was a vivacious brunette like Mayleen, and decided she must be. She must also have had a great deal of confidence to discuss marriage with a man who had not proposed. She would either be twenty-one now, or close to it. A girl as eager to wed as Jesse had described would probably have married another man by now. But what if she hadn't?

Tory had too many worries to add Carmen's possible claim to Jesse's affections to the list, but she could not deny that more than a twinge of jealousy had filled her when he had mentioned the girl. "We better get to sleep if we have to cross the river before dawn," she suggested rather than continue their conversation.

Jesse nodded thoughtfully. He had hoped to make love to her again, but now it did not seem like such a good idea. She stretched out on her bedroll, but he remained by the fire. He had waited a hell of a long time to ask Lalo Ruiz why he had left him to rot in the Yuma prison. That question was too depressing to allow him to be distracted by the sweetness of Tory's allure.

Friends since childhood, Jesse knew the terrain of Lalo's sprawling ranch as well as his own property, so even in the predawn darkness he and Tory had no difficulty approaching the adobe house unobserved. They left their mounts at the gate to the patio and crossed the spacious flower-filled courtyard with the stealth of sly foxes. Once inside the large tiled-roofed home, Jesse took Tory's hand and led her down the hall to Lalo's room.

Despite the fact Lalo was Jesse's best friend, Tory felt as though they were trespassing. She kept expecting someone to leap out at them and accuse them of that crime, or worst, shoot before making any accusations, but everyone in the household appeared to be asleep and their presence went unchallenged. Horribly uneasy, she held her breath as they entered Lalo's room and moved into the shadows after Jesse lit the lamp on the nightstand. The light fell across the high bed and shone not just on Lalo's thick black hair, but also on the ebony braids of the young beauty lying curled in his arms.

Shocked to find Lalo with a female companion, Jesse hesitated a moment before awakening his friend. Then after giving Tory an apologetic shake of his head, he placed his hand on Lalo's shoulder.

Apparently a sound sleeper, Lalo moaned softly before turning toward the light. He opened his eyes slowly, and then recognizing Jesse rather than one of his servants, he sat up with a start. He slept without nightclothes, but the fine linen sheet covered him from waist down.

"¡Madre de Dios!" he exclaimed. "Have you forgotten how to knock at a door or pay calls at a respectable hour?"

"You forgot your best friend," Jesse reminded him with undisguised contempt. "Why should I be concerned with something so trivial as good manners?"

Lalo used both hands to comb his coal-black hair out of his eyes before he responded. "I did not forget you, *amigo*. Never."

"No?"

"No!" Lalo swore. "When Gerry showed me the newspaper articles about your trial, I felt sick. I offered to go to Yuma immediately, but he swore a visit from me would only increase your shame."

"I had no reason to be ashamed, Lalo. You should have known that."

"What are you saying? That getting caught did not embarrass you?"

The sounds of the men's voices, although hushed, finally disturbed the young woman's rest. She covered a wide yawn, then also sat up. "Jesse, is that you?" she gasped then.

"Good morning, Carmen," Jesse responded with a slight bow. His glance drifted from her face to her bare shoulders. His expression turned insolent as his gaze lingered on the beginning fullness of her breasts exposed above the sheet she was clutching. "You're looking well."

Even in the dim light, Tory could see Carmen's bright blush. She appeared to be tall and slim rather than petite like Mayleen, but she was undeniably attractive. Tory knew how she herself must look in the shapeless garb she had been forced to wear so long. Not eager to be introduced when she must present a pitiful sight, she stood motionless so as not to attract the attention of the occupants of the big bed.

Having greeted the startled Carmen, Jesse resumed his conversation with Lalo as though they had not been interrupted. He needed only a few minutes to describe what had really happened in Tucson and how he had escaped from prison and returned home to clear his name. "I need your help," he concluded simply.

"You have it!" Lalo exclaimed. "Why didn't you write to me? You know I would have done whatever I could long before this."

Jesse regarded Carmen with a significant glance. "I never thought you'd doubt my innocence, but I can see now why you were too busy to be concerned about me."

"Carmen is my wife," Lalo proclaimed proudly. "We have two small sons."

That news surprised Jesse even more than finding the young woman who had once begged to be his bride in Lalo's bed. "Didn't waste much time, did you?"

"We have no need to apologize to you," Carmen declared with an impudent thrust of her chin. "You abandoned us when you went to the Arizona Territory, not the other way around."

A rueful laugh was Jesse's natural response to what he regarded as a ridiculously biased opinion. "I'll not have that argument again. What I need now is information about Gerry. At best, I'm only a couple of days ahead of the man tracking me so there's not a moment to spare. Come here, Tory."

Jesse extended his hand, and although reluctant to be seen, Tory came forward to take it. He introduced her without attempting to describe the relationship between them, or revealing that her plight as a fugitive was as desperate as his. Lalo and Cortez gaped at her with what he

347

considered a far worse showing of poor manners than they had accused him of displaying.

"We'll wait in the parlor while you dress," he offered before escorting Tory toward the door. "Over breakfast you can tell me how Gerry's been getting along without me."

"Yes, of course," Lalo agreed, but both he and his wife were so astonished by their early-morning visitors that they continued to stare as they left the room.

Jesse kept Tory's hand in his as they made their way up to the parlor. He found one lamp, lit it, and then lit the others to illuminate a spacious white room decorated with heavy oak furniture. The dark beams in the ceiling suddenly reminded Tory of bars, and she shivered despite the pleasant warmth of her surroundings.

"Are you cold?" Jesse asked. "I could light a fire."

Tory rubbed her arms to dispel the sensation of gloom. "No, I'm fine," she said, then sat down on the edge of a ladder-backed chair with a taut leather seat. Jesse began to pace in front of her. She had had ample opportunity to observe him in a variety of moods, but what she saw reflected in his eyes now was a blood-chilling rage. If Carmen had meant as little to him as he had described, then why was he so furious to find her in Lalo's bed?

"Do you want me to leave?" she asked.

"Leave? Why? Where would you go?"

Tory had not thought that far and responded with a shrug. "It doesn't matter, but if you intend to have it out with Lalo over Carmen, I don't want to be here."

Jesse came to her, and after a brief hesitation knelt at her side. "I won't pretend that I'm not angry with him, but Carmen isn't the issue and we won't come to blows over her."

"But I thought—"

Jesse leaned close to still her objection with a lingering kiss. "I can see what you thought, but you're wrong. That Lalo married and sired two sons while I languished in prison is enough to drive any man to the limit of his endurance, but that's Gerry's fault rather than his. I need Lalo's help too badly to waste any time berating him over his lack of faith in me. I want you to have faith in me, too, sweetheart. Can

348

you do that?"

Tory could not recall a time when she had not trusted the confident man. "Yes, you know that I do."

Lalo entered the room before Jesse had risen but halted just inside the door. "I hope that I'm not interrupting something."

Jesse gave Tory another kiss before he got to his feet. "No, we're just a naturally affectionate couple. Now what can you tell me about Gerry? How has he done with the ranch?"

Lalo had donned a loose-fitting white muslin shirt and elegantly decorated black pants which flared from the knee to cover the tips of his boots. He strode on into the room, and after gesturing for Jesse to be seated, pulled up a chair for himself. He smiled at Tory, but her hat still shaded her face so completely that he could not see her clearly. Knowing Jesse's tastes, he assumed that she was exceptionally pretty.

"Your stepbrother has shown no more ambition in running your ranch than he displayed when you were here. When your foreman attempted to teach him how to take charge of the ranch, Gerry replaced him with an inept fool."

"Alex Tucker is gone? He was a friend of my father's."

"That meant nothing to Gerry," Lalo said. "I talked to him myself, many times, but he cared so little for the advice I gave that he yawned in my face. For your stepmother's sake, I kept trying, but he would not listen to me, or anyone else. In the last few months, his gambling debts have become such a burden that he has offered to sell off a quarter of the ranch to anyone who makes him a fair offer."

Jesse had never imagined Lalo's news would be so bad. "Gerry has always gambled more than he could afford to lose, but I never thought he'd be so stupid as to start selling off property." Horrified by the problems taking in another partner could easily present, he sat back in his chair and let out an uneasy sigh.

"Do you remember that my father left half the ranch to me and the other half to Gerry and his mother?" he asked Tory.

Tory nodded. "I don't suppose there's any hope that he meant to sell half of his and his mother's portion, is there?"

Lalo shrugged. "I've not seen a map, but knowing Gerry, if

there is a way to sell your land rather than his, he has found it." He waited for Jesse to respond, but when his old friend remained lost in thought, he felt he had to change the topic. "I need to speak with you privately, please."

Jesse looked up. "You can say whatever needs to be said in front of Tory."

Because it was plain Lalo was reluctant to do so, Tory rose to her feet. "Perhaps I could help prepare breakfast?"

"Sit down," Jesse stated firmly. "Lalo has plenty of servants, you needn't work in the kitchen. Now go ahead, Lalo, what is it you want to say?"

Lalo first wanted for Tory to again make herself comfortable in her chair and then he cleared his throat noisily as though what he wished to say was extremely difficult. "It's not what you think . . ." he finally began.

Jesse leaned forward. "What isn't?"

Again there was a long pause before Lalo spoke. "Carmen became hysterical when she learned you had been sent to prison. Had you been killed she could not have grieved more deeply. She refused to eat, she couldn't sleep . . . Her parents begged me to console her and—"

"You obviously succeeded."

Lalo knew he deserved Jesse's scorn and did not try to dodge it. "I won't offer any excuses for either of us, but I do believe Carmen and I have been far happier together than you and she ever could have been." When Jesse's only response was a skeptical glance, Lalo continued. "You did not love her, *amigo*. You never did."

Jesse glanced over at Tory, who was staring down at her tightly clenched hands. She looked so small sitting there, and he knew she would rather not be listening to his conversation with Lalo. He wanted her to hear every word, though.

"You're right," he agreed without the slightest reluctance. "Carmen is very pretty and her interest in me was flattering, but had I not left for Tucson, nothing would have come of it. She and I would have remained friends, nothing more. Tory is the only woman I've ever loved, and if I had to spend four wretched years in prison to find her, it was a small price to pay."

Thrilled beyond measure at the sweetness of his words, Tory found it difficult to meet Jesse's gaze. Then when she did look toward him, she saw Carmen standing at the door. Her hair was now combed into a chignon and she had donned a pale-yellow gown which showed off her slender figure to every advantage. Clearly she had also heard Jesse's remarks, for her dark eyes were filled with tears. Rather than enter the parlor, she turned away abruptly, and only Tory had noticed her brief presence.

Tory straightened her shoulders proudly. "Thank you. That was such a wonderful thing to say," she told Jesse. "But from what Lalo described of Carmen's behavior it's obvious that she did love you and it would be very kind of you to speak to her, privately, of course."

Jesse frowned in confusion. "What could I possibly say?"

Lalo was quick to prompt him. "Tell her that you're pleased she's been so happy with me. Tell her it's what you would have wished for her."

Jesse could see the danger in being alone with Carmen even if his two companions could not, but he also knew he could not refuse their request. He did not have to fulfill it in the next hour, however. "When this is over," he promised. "For the time being I've got to concentrate on Gerry. I want you to go to him this morning, Lalo, and tell him you've met someone who's interested in buying the land he wants to sell. Say it's a couple who have just arrived in El Paso. Arrange an appointment with him and my stepmother for early this afternoon. That will give us time to clean up and find presentable clothes."

"And when we arrive for this appointment, what's going to happen?" Tory asked before Lalo could.

"Gerry is going to be understandably shocked," Jesse predicted. "Then I'm going to get the truth out of him in front of enough witnesses to have my conviction over-turned."

Lalo broke into a wide grin. "I can hardly wait."

Tory was not nearly so optimistic as the men. "It's not always wise to have a roomful of witnesses," she advised from bitter experience.

351

Jesse understood her reasoning even if Lalo didn't, but he stood and gave her a hug. "Gerry won't dare try anything but argue in front of his mother and Lalo, but he's a coward who can be made to speak the truth easily enough. Please don't worry. Would you rather stay here?"

"And miss meeting Gerry?" Tory cried. "No, I want to go with you."

"Good. Now where's that breakfast, Lalo?"

The handsome Mexican rose and gestured toward the door. "It should be ready by now." He was relieved when Jesse again took Tory's hand. He was confident of Carmen's love, but no man welcomed his wife's former suitor to his home without some reservations and he was no exception.

Chapter 23

Tory was too nervous about what the day might bring to have much appetite, but Jesse ate more than his share of the ample breakfast the Ruiz's kitchen staff produced. There were platters of fresh fruit, and a variety of delicate pastries as well as biscuits and tortillas, followed by piping-hot eggs served with ham and bacon. There were just the four of them at the wide dining-room table, with Jesse and Lalo providing most of the conversation when they were not heaping their plates with food or busy enjoying it.

Tory sipped a second cup of tea and divided an orange into segments which she then ate with small, dainty bites. That way she appeared to be eating as much as her companions when, in fact, she was consuming very little. She noticed that Carmen also seemed to be preoccupied. Tory smiled at her, but her hostess quickly looked away. Embarrassed that her attempt at friendliness had been rebuffed, Tory made no further effort to engage Carmen in conversation.

Jesse knew Tory to be a naturally quiet young woman, but he was surprised to find Carmen so reticent to speak. He supposed he was partly at fault for not inquiring about the health of her sons at least, but he could not bring himself to do so. He had written her several letters from Tucson before the trouble had started. They had been friendly in tone rather than passionate, and she had not answered them. It was difficult to believe that she had been heartbroken to learn he had been imprisoned when she had not written to him even once in the six months prior to his arrest.

She had been a frivolous girl in her teens then, he reminded himself. She was now a grown woman and the mother of two. Perhaps she was no longer the talkative person he had known but far more introspective. "This is all delicious, Carmen," he finally managed to say.

"Thank you," she responded demurely. "Excuse me please. I must see to my children."

Jesse waited until she had left the room to continue his conversation with her husband. "I know this is difficult for everyone, but we won't impose on your hospitality. Tory and I will be staying at my ranch tonight."

"While I hope that they do, things may not go as smoothly as you hope," Lalo advised. "You will always be welcome here."

"I don't believe your wife shares that view. She feels as awkward as I do and we'll have to leave. While I'll have to borrow whatever you have that will fit me, Tory has some nice clothes. Do you have a laundress who can wash them for her and have them ready for her to wear by this afternoon?"

"Of course," Lalo assured him.

"My blouse and skirt have been rolled up in the bottom of my satchel so long that there may be nothing left of them," Tory worried aloud. "I no longer have a bonnet, either."

"Perhaps Carmen could loan you one until we can go into town to shop," Jesse suggested.

Tory did not want to have to rely on any favors from Jesse's former girlfriend. "No, that's too much to ask."

Finished eating, Lalo left his chair and walked around the table to stand behind Tory. He leaned over her left shoulder and confided softly. "You and Carmen are close to the same size. Just tell me what you need and I will get it for you." Being an attentive host came naturally to Lalo, and he wrapped his arm around Tory's shoulders to give her an encouraging hug before he stepped away.

When Lalo touched her, Jesse saw Tory's expression change from one of mere concern for her wardrobe to heart-stopping terror. He knew Lalo had meant well, but he had

354

frightened rather than reassured Tory, and Jesse also rose to his feet and drew him aside. "Give Tory a minute to sort her laundry, and then if she needs anything more than a bonnet, I'll give you a list," he stated loudly enough for her to overhear, but then he whispered to Lalo, "She's suffered a great deal. Don't touch her again."

"What?"

Jesse attempted to convey his message with a menacing look this time, but Lalo still did not seem to understand so he changed the subject. "We'd both like to clean up. Which rooms should we use?"

Lalo could see that Jesse was disturbed about his having embraced his woman but mistook his friend's feelings for jealousy and was insulted. "Come, I will show you. We have rearranged things because of the boys."

"Aren't we going to meet them?" Jesse asked.

Lalo flashed a proud grin. "You'll see them at noon."

Jesse returned to the table and helped Tory from her chair. "There will be plenty of time for you to take a nap, and in a real bed," he assured her with a sly wink.

Tory found it impossible to respond to his teasing. When Lalo had embraced her from behind, she had been so startled that for one horrifying second she had thought it was Paul Stafford. It had only been Jesse's presence in the room that had kept her from screaming in fright. Intellectually she knew Paul was dead and could not possibly harm her, but her emotions had betrayed her. She gripped Jesse's hand tightly as they followed Lalo to their rooms.

"Yes, I would like to rest. I'm more tired than I realized. I'm sorry."

When she looked up at him with a questioning glance, as though she feared he might disapprove, Jesse had to fight the impulse to take her in his arms and make love to her until happiness lit her features with joy. That would have to wait until he had seen Gerry, however, so he restrained himself and did no more than brush her cheek with a kiss when they reached the room Lalo wished her to have.

"We will fetch your things and send a maid to you," Lalo promised. "She will heat water for a bath."

"You're very kind, thank you again," Tory whispered.

When she had closed her door, Jesse did no more than glance into the adjacent room which was to be his. "I left our mounts by the patio. Come outside with me."

Lalo stopped first to summon a maid, but then he matched his stride to Jesse's as they crossed the patio. He could hold his temper no longer. "I am not after your woman," he swore emphatically. "How could you even imagine such a ridiculous thing?"

Jesse did not want to lie to his best friend, but he did not want Tory's tragic past to haunt her now that he had brought her home, either. "I wasn't questioning your motives," he responded agreeably. "It's just that she's painfully shy, so your spontaneous show of affection offended her. Pay her compliments with words if you like, but please don't touch her again."

"I didn't manhandle her!"

"I didn't say that you did," Jesse exclaimed. "I'm just asking you to respect her preference for distance. Treat her like the lady she is and we'll have no problems."

"I was not disrespectful," Lalo insisted between clenched teeth. "I merely showed her the warmth I would show any woman you brought to my home."

"She's not just any woman," Jesse explained with a delighted grin that readily conveyed the depth of his feelings for her. "Treat her as you would my wife."

Lalo shook his head. "How long have you known her?"

So much had happened to him since he had escaped from prison, Jesse needed a moment to calculate the time. "Not quite three weeks."

"Yet she is the only woman you have ever loved?"

"Yes," Jesse replied. When they reached the horses, he removed their luggage from behind their saddles and placed it on the ground. "Now what do you think of my horse?"

Although frustrated by it, Lalo respected his friend's abrupt change of subject and had no difficult gathering the enthusiasm to pronounce Río a fine animal. He summoned a stable boy to tend him and Tory's bay before the two men carried Tory's satchel and Jesse's saddlebags back to the house.

"As soon as I have found clothes for you, I'll ride on over to your ranch and speak with Gerry."

"Say whatever you must to get us an invitation to visit with him and Zina this afternoon. I want him to expect a couple who can solve his financial problems. Then watching the shock register on his face when he recognizes me will be all the sweeter."

"I don't think it will be merely shock, *amigo*," Lalo warned. "I think he will be terrified, and rightly so."

Jesse broke into a wide grin. "Yes, I'm going to enjoy seeing that, too."

"I am so sorry," Lalo apologized again. "I should have left for Yuma the very day Gerry told me you'd been sent to prison. That's what I should have done."

"I agree, but rather than regret your mistake, just help me put Gerry behind bars and we'll be even."

"You're being very generous." Lalo was grateful for it, too. "I have never liked Gerry's insipid smirk," he confided. "If he were to lose a tooth or two, perhaps it would no longer be his favorite expression."

"I like the way you think, Lalo."

"I will keep thinking," the ranchero offered, and the two men entered the house laughing.

Luke Bernay had never traveled with two more inept riders than Mayleen and her so-called preacher husband and they had made such little progress by noon that he despaired of ever reaching El Paso. He was anxious to make up for lost time, but dared not suggest the troublesome pair skip a meal when the man was so far from hardy. They camped near a rocky rise and ate jerky along with the biscuits left from breakfast. Luke was finished quickly while, as usual, his two companions dawdled.

Disgusted with them, Luke climbed the rocky point to survey the land ahead. When he turned back toward the

357

west, he was alarmed by the sight of a dust cloud rising in the distance. He had hoped he had seen the last of Tad MacDonald and his boys, but he had a horrible feeling they were about to meet again. He scrambled down the hillside and grabbed the horses' reins.

"Come on, we're getting out of sight," he ordered. "Someone's coming and I'm afraid it's not anyone we want to see. It's a damn good thing we didn't light a fire." Without waiting for Mayleen and the preacher, he led their mounts up and over the shallow shoulder of the rise to hide them.

Alarmed, Mayleen scattered the remaining biscuit crumbs and then pulled Ivan to his feet. When they reached the tracker's hiding place, he had already removed his rifle from its leather scabbard and was hurriedly trying out vantage points from which to shoot.

Frightened by Luke's warning, Mayleen began to pester him. "If you know, please tell us who's coming. If someone's going to be shooting at us, we have a right to know who it is."

Annoyed with her, Luke spit in the dirt. "I'm afraid it's the men looking for Victoria Crandell. If you two weren't so damn slow, we'd be hours ahead of them rather than just sitting here watching their dust."

Ivan had to wipe the grime from his spectacles to get a good look at the approaching riders. "Why are you so worried? Tory isn't with us," he reminded Luke.

"I'm worried because any man with any sense would be worried!" Luke retorted angrily. "Maybe it's MacDonald and his men. Maybe it's not, but I'm stuck out here with two idiots who are going to be no help at all if there's trouble."

"I can shoot," Ivan informed him coolly. "The only problem is, you've taken my rifle."

"I can shoot, too," Mayleen announced proudly. She had taken a couple of shots at a bottle once with a cowboy who had been showing off his accurate aim with firearms. She figured that was experience enough if they were about to be attacked. "Maybe it's Apache renegades," she suggested anxiously, "or Mexican bandits. Better give us back our weapons."

"And risk getting shot in the back? No thanks, little lady."

358

Insulted, Ivan made their request more emphatic. "A man of the cloth does not shoot people in the back. Now return our weapons to us immediately, please."

Luke squinted slightly. He could make out five riders now and that was two fewer than he had expected. He raised his hand. "Wait a minute, it might not be them after all. Let's just be real quiet and see if whoever it is doesn't ride right on by without noticing us."

But it was them, and although keeping a sharp watch on the trail, Tad saw a sudden flash of sunlight reflect off the lenses of Ivan's eyeglasses and veered to the right toward the rocky rise. His men followed his lead, but as they drew near, they fanned out and came to a halt with at least ten feet separating each rider.

Relieved to see they were neither renegades nor bandits, Mayleen crouched down near Luke. "Is it them?"

"Yes, it's most of them all right. Now you two hush and let me handle this."

While Luke's attention was riveted on Tad MacDonald, Ivan slowly inched away. He knew the tracker could not carry on two fights at once and removed his own rifle, holster, and Colt from Luke's horse. He passed the .45 to Mayleen, and then found himself a good place to watch the preceedings.

"Come on out, Bernay," Tad yelled. "We've missed you."

MacDonald's men laughed but Luke saw nothing humorous about Tad's request. "I prefer to work alone," he shouted back.

"Ah, come on, don't be unsociable," Tad coaxed, but when there was no response, he signaled to Manuel Ochoa and Carl Olson who were at his extreme right and left to circle the rocky outcropping and approach Luke from behind.

"Son of a bitch!" Luke swore. "If he means to force me out, he must want a fight!"

Ivan had been studying the five strangers' faces, and what he saw etched on each one was the same cruelty that had filled the expressions of the bullies who had tormented him all his life. That these men were after Tory rather than him

359

did not matter. He intended to stop them.

"Let's give them one then," he said. Before Luke could draw the breath to protest, he fired off a round that tore through Manuel Ochoa's chest catapulting him backward off his horse in a wide arc before his lifeless body slammed into the dirt. Ivan then aimed for Carl Olson and caught him in the shoulder while he was still staring in astonishment at Manuel's body. Carl slumped forward, but managed to stay in his saddle and gallop for cover with what was left of Tad MacDonald's posse.

"Christ Almighty!" Luke screamed. "Are you trying to start a war?"

Ivan fixed him with a defiant stare. "If I have to, but I'll not allow that type of rabble to harm us or Tory."

Luke raised up to make certain Tad and his men were still riding back the way they had come. With cover scarce in the desert, they were using distance as a defense. Relieved they had not returned the preacher's fire, he turned back to the suddenly vigorous young man.

"I suppose Miss Crandell, or Tory, as you call her, is innocent, too," he challenged.

Ivan glanced first toward Mayleen, who was observing him with a stare that was every bit as incredulous as Luke's. He gave her an encouraging smile before answering Luke's question. Jesse had not confided any of the details in Tory's case, but he knew facts without an appropriate explanation could be misleading anyway. "I don't believe it's a question of guilt or innocence in her case, but one of justice."

"Not justice again," Luke groaned.

"I'll not debate the issue here," Ivan replied. With Mayleen again at his side, he made his way back to their horses.

Luke hurriedly followed and, praying the wounded men would slow down Tad MacDonald's pursuit, he tried to keep up with the pair of troublemakers whose riding skills had suddenly improved tenfold.

Tad could not believe how bad their luck had turned in the

last two days. First they had lost José and Juan in a stupid brawl and now Manuel was dead, and unless they could stem the flow of blood gushing from Carl's shoulder, he wasn't going to last much longer, either. They had eased him off his horse and sat him on the ground where George could kneel behind him and keep him propped up. Hank was holding an extra shirt pressed against Carl's wound as a makeshift bandage, but the fabric was turning red awfully fast.

"Don't worry, Carl," Tad bent down to encourage. "Juarez can't be much farther ahead and we can get you to a doctor there. We'll build us a travois like the Indians do and drag you there in no time at all."

Carl's only response to Tad's optimistic plan was a low moan. When Tad looked at Hank, he just shook his head while George turned away. Both men knew Carl wasn't going to make it, but Tad knew better than to abandon him to die alone. No, sir, he thought to himself. No leader worth his salt treated his men like trash that could be thrown away or he would soon find himself with no men to command. He went back to his horse and brought his canteen over to the injured man.

"Like a drink, Carl?"

Again, Carl managed no more than a pathetic moan in reply. His eyes were closed now. His chin was resting on his chest and his breathing was growing increasingly shallow.

Tad helped himself to a drink and waited with Hank and George for Carl to expire. They each knew it would not be long and none complained about the wait, but their thoughts were focused on the odds for their own survival rather than their friend's impending death.

Jesse was a couple of inches taller than Lalo and had once been heavier, but his stint in prison had pared his build down to a lean one. He discovered Lalo's fancy flared trousers provided a good fit after one of the maids had lengthened them. He would have preferred a much plainer suit of clothes, but donned the short Mexican jacket over a freshly laundered white shirt without complaint. His skin was so deeply tanned he easily could have been mistaken for a man of Spanish descent had it not been for the reddish tint to his curly hair and his bright blue eyes.

"How do I look?" he asked Tory.

"Splendid," she assured him. His appreciative glance had already convinced her she looked her best. She had lost weight and the waistband of her skirt was loose, but once laundered and the front seam Jessie had opened to permit her to ride had been resewn, the pale-green garment looked presentable enough. Her blouse had been washed and ironed so beautifully that it looked new, and she was pleased to again be able to dress like the lady she once had been. It was not until they joined Lalo and Carmen for the noon meal that she realized how complete her transformation had been.

Lalo's startled gaze swung from Tory to Jesse and back again. "You must forgive me, but when you were dressed in men's clothing I had no idea you were so very beautiful."

While immensely flattered, Tory thought it was the fact she was again wearing a feminine hair style that was contributing to her improved appearance. Not seeking praise, though, she did not mention it. "Thank you," she murmured instead.

Carmen was not merely staring, her dark gaze was positively venomous as she studied Jesse's devastatingly attractive companion. That Tory was so fair annoyed Carmen terribly. It had been excruciating to lose Jesse to prison. To lose him again to this green-eyed beauty was an additional agony she did not need. She paid Tory no compliments, but instead summoned her sons' nanny to bring in the boys to be introduced. Attractive and lively children, they became the center of attention and, as always, Carmen took great pride in showing them off.

Jesse watched the pair of justifiably proud parents dote on their offspring through a lingering veil of resentment, for he knew he would never be able to regain the years he had wasted in prison. They were lost to him forever. He reached for Tory's hand and drew her close. She represented his hopes for the future, but he could not let go of the past until he had repaid Gerry for every second the lying bastard had forced him to languish behind bars.

After they had shared another sumptuous meal Carmen left them to read to her sons before their naps. Lalo had succeeded in arranging an appointment for the afternoon and while he, Jesse, and Tory waited for it, he tried to cover possible complications. "In the last couple of years, your stepbrother has hired quite a few new hands as many of your *vaqueros* refused to continue working for him after he fired Alex. The majority should still be loyal to you, though."

"Gerry will be the only one involved in this," Jesse promised. "I don't want you to be in any danger, Tory. I think it might be a good idea if we gave you another name."

Rather than a bonnet, Lalo had provided Tory with a white lace *mantilla* to cover her hair. She had draped it over her fair curls, but was fidgeting nervously with the scalloped edge while she waited to leave. Jesse's suggestion struck her as sensible, but she did not know what name to choose.

"A woman's name for a change?" she asked.

"Yes, of course," Jesse replied. "Do you have any favorites?"

"My mother's name was Patricia."

"Yes," Jesse agreed immediately. "You look like a Patricia. Now what about a last name. What was your father's name?"

"Earl."

"What about Patricia Earl then? It has a nice sound to it."

Tory tried the name out a few times and decided she liked it, too. "Yes, that will do fine, and I'm sure I can spell it, too."

"I do not think there is going to be time for polite introductions," Lalo cautioned. He had already asked for his carriage to be brought around to the front of the house and, thinking they ought not to be late, he rose to his feet. "Shall we go?" he asked.

"Yes, let's," Tory was quick to agree. "Is the ranch far?"

"No, we're neighbors," Jesse explained. "That's how Lalo and I got to be such good friends."

As they rode to the Lambert ranch, the men recalled good times they had shared growing up, while Tory studied the craggy peaks of the Franklin Mountains to the north. Their rocky slopes provided the landscape with a forbidding eeriness that wasn't at all encouraging.

"Do you want me to say or do anything in particular?" she suddenly interrupted them to ask.

Jesse shook his head. "Just listen," he replied. "Gerry probably hasn't had to explain what happened in Tucson for years. He may offer an outrageous tale at first. Whatever he says, you know the truth, so just listen and perhaps you'll hear him contradict himself in some way that I miss."

"I'm just supposed to be a witness?"

Jesse brought her palm to his lips before he spoke. "No, you're my devoted fiancée. It's only natural that I'd bring you home to introduce you to my family."

Never having heard a proposal, much less accepted one, Tory's eyes widened slightly, but she knew this was neither the time nor the place to make wedding plans. "This should be a most interesting reunion," she mused thoughtfully.

"Yes, indeed," Jesse agreed. "Look, there's the house just ahead."

Similar in structure to the Ruiz home, the Lambert ranch house was also a one-story adobe structure built around a large, open patio. The windows across the front were set low and framed with green shutters. A magenta bougainvillaea in full bloom grew beside the front door and provided a colorful welcome to the stately dwelling.

"This place looks as charming as your home, Lalo," Tory confided as their carriage rolled to a stop.

"The house is very beautiful," Jesse agreed. "It's a shame one of the residents has not a shred of character or honor."

"Stay behind me," Lalo ordered as they left the carriage. "If I enter the parlor first, it will be too late for Gerry to summon help when he recognizes you."

Jesse tilted to a rakish angle the wide-brimmed hat Lalo had provided. "How's this?" he asked.

"It shades your face perfectly. *Buena suerte.*"

"*Gracias.*"

Lalo's knock was soon answered by an elderly servant who was so fascinated by Tory's fair coloring that he failed to notice her companion was a long-missing member of the household. He shuffled down the wide hall to the parlor, and with a stiff bow, gestured for Lalo and his guests to enter.

Zina Lambert was seated in a large leather wing chair, while her son was standing by the fireplace. Anxious to make whatever sale he could, he hurriedly came forward as Lalo entered the room. "Good afternoon," he greeted them enthusiastically. "Welcome to our home."

Even though she had known they were not blood relatives, Tory was still surprised to find Gerry's appearance such a contrast to Jesse's. Rather than tall and lean, he was of medium height with a solid, muscular build. His eyes were a deep brown and his dark-brown hair lacked even a hint of curl. His nose was rather long, while his lips had a sensual fullness. He was dressed in a well-tailored gray frock coat and matching trousers and looked every inch the gentleman Tory knew he could not possibly be.

His mother was a petite woman who continued being exceptionally pretty into her midforties. Her hair was the same rich brown as her son's, but so curly that several kinky wisps had escaped the bun she wore atop her head, giving her the appearance of having just dashed into the parlor rather than having been prepared to receive guests. Her eyes were a smoky gray, and her features, while far more delicate, were nearly identical to her son's. She was dressed in an elegant dove-gray gown. She was smiling and seemed to be as genuinely delighted to be entertaining company as her son.

Jesse remained behind Tory while Lalo introduced her to his relatives as Patricia Earl. He then stepped forward and with a ready grin savored the horror that filled both Zina and Gerry's expressions. "What's the matter?" he asked. "Aren't you happy to see me?"

Gerry recoiled as though he had been struck and beat a hasty retreat to his mother's side. He gripped the back of her chair and looked ready to crouch down behind it. His lips moved, but no words came forth, only a small rush of air.

Only slightly less flabbergasted than her son, Zina leaned forward and in a long, anguished sweep took in the changes in Jesse's appearance since she had last seen him. "How have you managed to return home so soon?" she gasped.

365

"Let's just say I was able to secure an early release, which was a damn good thing. If I'd come home any later, I might have found our ranch sold and strangers living here. We have another point to settle first, though. Don't we, Gerry?"

Had it been possible to smell cowardice, Gerry's side of the room would have reeked of it. "I don't know what you mean," he argued.

Jesse walked to his stepmother's side and bent down to kiss her cheek. "I appreciated your letters," he told her sincerely. "It was very thoughtful of you to send them."

"It won't work," Gerry cautioned. "Mother knows the truth and she'll not believe anything you say."

"Really?"

"Yes!" Gerry insisted. "I told her everything. The disgrace was difficult for both of us to bear, just as it was for Lalo and your other friends, but you robbed the stage and deserved to go to prison."

Jesse turned and gestured for Lalo and Tory to be seated. "That's the last time you're ever going to repeat that lie, Gerry. You and Conrad Werner robbed the stage, and while he's dead and can't be prosecuted for the crime, I intend to see that you are, and soon."

"Do you see what I mean, Mother?" Gerry sniveled. "I had an alibi, and while I'm not proud to say I was with that type of woman, she testified in court that I *was* with her at the time of the robbery. I can understand why Jesse is ashamed to admit what he did, but—"

Jesse thought that he had shown remarkable restraint up to that point, but he had heard enough. He grabbed for Gerry while his stepbrother's attention was focused on Zina and struck him such a brutal blow to the chin that his head snapped back with a force that nearly broke his neck. Badly hurt, he swayed lightly and then slumped to the floor. Without allowing Gerry a second to recover, Jesse reached down, hauled him to his feet, and hit him again.

Zina began to scream, a loud, piercing wail that brought servants running from every corner of the large home. Lalo leapt to his feet, and with both gestures and shouted commands, kept those who might have interfered out of the way. He waited until it became obvious that Jesse was likely to kill Gerry before he regained control of his temper and then stepped in to protect the smaller man.

"You'll never prove anything if you kill him!" Lalo yelled. He pushed Jesse back and then stood in his way to prevent him from going after his stepbrother again. It took several moments, but Jesse finally had the sense to back away.

Tears streaming down her face, Zina knelt at her son's side. "Boy, boys," she sobbed. "You must put this terrible argument behind you." She looked up at Jesse and beseeched him to agree. "You know your father expected you to set an example for Gerry. Although you've failed miserably, you're home, and that's all that matters now. Please, no more fighting."

With his mother's attention directed toward Jesse, Gerry began to smirk. "You can't prove a thing," he whispered through bloody lips.

Infuriated by that boast, Jesse started for Gerry again, but Lalo shoved him aside. "No!" he ordered. "Your stepmother's right. You're home. For now that's all that matters."

Jesse glanced over at Tory and found her studying Gerry with an open disgust he found most inspiring. It was plain she saw through Gerry's lies, and in time he was convinced Zina would, too. The only problem was that time was a luxury he just didn't have.

Chapter 24

Jesse's brutal fistfight with Gerry had provided vivid evidence of the vengeance that filled his heart, and the household staff regarded him in awestruck silence as Zina and Gerry retired to the young man's room to treat his cuts and bruises. They all knew how smoothly Jesse had run the ranch before his long absence and they understood that he was again taking charge. Many had known him since childhood and were elated to have him home.

After he had dusted off his borrowed clothes, Jesse proudly introduced Tory to the assembled servants as his fiancée, Patricia Earl. He accepted their best wishes with real pleasure and had a personal comment for each one before dismissing them. As soon as they had filed out of the room, he turned to Lalo.

"I appreciate your coming with us, but you needn't stay. I can handle things now."

Lalo studied his old friend with a perplexed frown. "What makes you think you will succeed in making Gerry confess to the robbery before the law catches up with you? Clearly he is afraid of you, but he must find the prospect of going to prison even more terrifying."

"As well he should," Jesse agreed, "but Gerry is my problem, not yours. I'll let you know if I need your help again."

"Can you make him see reason?" Lalo asked Tory.

While Tory shared Lalo's concern, she would not take his

side against Jesse. "I'm confident he'll make the right decisions," she assured him.

Clearly, Lalo was not assured. "If there is even the slightest hint of trouble here, come back to me," he advised. "I'll help you hide out until you can prove your innocence."

"Thank you," Jesse replied. "But I've gotten used to taking care of myself."

Considering that an insult he deserved, Lalo left without further argument, but he did not intend to allow his best friend to fight this battle alone.

Well aware of the shortness of time even without Lalo's warning, Jesse took Tory into the study. Both he and his father had kept it neat, but now it was cluttered. The desk was littered with old newspapers and unanswered correspondence providing ample evidence of the general disorder that marked Gerry's life.

After pulling up a chair for Tory beside his at the messy desk, Jesse studied the careless notations Gerry had made in what had once been a detailed ledger. From the small amount on deposit at the bank, it appeared Gerry had turned a profitable ranch into one that now barely cleared enough to keep operating. They would be selling more beef that autumn, but Jesse had never seen their reserves prior to the fall round-up at such a low ebb. Disgusted to find things even worse than he had anticipated, he slammed the ledger shut.

"There's a great deal of money on deposit in my name in New Haven," Tory reminded him. "There must be a way for me to withdraw it."

Jesse took her hand and brought it to his lips. "Thank you, but that won't be necessary. Gerry may have managed the ranch's income poorly, but he wouldn't have been able to touch my private account. If the ranch runs short, I can fund its operation myself."

"But you shouldn't have to," Tory complained.

"No, but after the mess Gerry's made of everything—"

"That's not what I meant," Tory interrupted. He had again referred to her as his fiancée without ever discussing marriage, and she could no longer wait for him to do so.

"Money to run the ranch isn't really the problem," she reminded him, "but if it were, I'd insist you allow me to invest my money as well as yours since it's a family enterprise. That's neither here nor there, though. The real issue is the fact that we're wanted for murder in the Arizona Territory. We ought not to be sitting here worrying over whether or not the accounts balance."

"No one is going to take us off this ranch, Tory," Jesse swore convincingly. "It doesn't matter how many men may have been tracking us, they won't get any closer than the front gate."

Too nervous to remain seated, Tory pulled her hand from his and left her chair. "What means the most to you, this ranch or our lives?"

Jesse stood and circled the desk to confront her. "Don't you know?"

Tory shook her head, but when he pulled her into his arms she relaxed against him. "Perhaps you feel safe here, but I don't," she explained. "From the way Lieutenant Barlow praised Luke Bernay, I doubt he ever quits without taking his quarry. Eldrin Stafford said he'd hold you responsible if I didn't hang, so as long as he can draw a breath, he'll have men tracking both of us. Any man who comes here asking for work might have been sent from Cactus Springs to kill us."

Sorry her thoughts were so dark, Jesse cupped her face between his palms to be certain he had her full attention. "I'm tired of running," he said. "We shouldn't have to spend the rest of our lives looking back over our shoulders. Now I intend to get the truth out of Gerry by whatever means necessary. Then we'll clear your name just as I promised. That will put a stop to Stafford's pursuit. Just give me a few days, Tory. I know I can straighten out everything."

"I'm not going to watch you die."

"Tory!" Jesse dropped his hands to her shoulders and was about to give her a good shaking when he caught himself. He had encouraged her to speak her mind and would not criticize her for it now. "No one is going to die. Now come back and sit down with me. I'm going to fire the foreman, then seal off the ranch with the men I know I can trust. Lalo thinks Gerry's terrified of going to prison. I think I'll give him a taste of what being confined is really like."

"They're still coming," Tory reminded him softly.

"I know, sweetheart, but we'll be ready for them."

He led her back to her chair and then summoned the foreman, who proved to be an even worse fool than Lalo had described. Believing Gerry deserved the blame for hiring such an incompetent man in the first place, Jesse removed a month's pay from the safe, handed it to him, and promptly dismissed him.

Well aware of the seriousness of his shortcomings, the fellow left without complaint. Jesse then used the current payroll records to learn which *vaqueros* were still employed at the ranch. While the best had left with Alex, those remaining were all capable men. He had never regarded them as his private army, but for the time being that's precisely what they would be.

Now that Ivan had recovered his weapons, he and Luke were on equal footing. When they stopped for supper, the two men eyed each other warily as Mayleen prepared their meal. "I think we should declare a truce," Ivan offered agreeably. "If MacDonald and his men overtake us again, they're going to be shooting at both of us."

"I always work alone," Luke replied. "With damn good reason!"

Ivan wasn't insulted. He just tried a new tack. "Fine. You're working alone, but we sure don't want to see you make a fool of yourself by returning the wrong man to prison."

Luke covered his ears. "Not again," he moaned.

Disgusted with Luke's failure to listen to the truth, Mayleen whacked him with the ladle she had been using to stir the beans. "Without my testimony, Gerry hasn't got an alibi for the time of the robbery."

"Ouch! Stop that!" Luke rubbed his shoulder. "From what you've said, Jesse Lambert didn't have an alibi, either."

Mayleen could not dispute him there but continued to argue anyway. "If the money hadn't been found in Jesse's room, he wouldn't have been asked for one. Haven't you got any sense at all? Gerry robbed the stage and fixed it so Jesse would take the blame. Maybe I'm the one you ought to be taking to prison since I lied in court. I may have done some stupid things in my life, but protecting a guilty man was the absolute worst. There's no way I can make that up to Jesse, but I can sure see that Gerry doesn't get away with it any longer."

Prepared to ward off additional blows, Luke stared up at Mayleen. While she wasn't saying anything new, the vehemence of her tone finally struck him as sincere. "Did Gerry give you part of the missing money?" he asked.

"You think he paid me to lie?"

"No," Luke assured her. "I just wondered if you'd seen the missing ten thousand dollars."

Mayleen shook her head.

"What about a necklace?" Luke probed. "The sheriff in Tucson mentioned something about a fancy necklace being stolen from one of the passengers. Did Gerry give it to you?"

Encouraged by his interest, Mayleen knelt beside him. "I remember hearing about a necklace at the trial. Pearls, wasn't it?"

Luke nodded. "A cameo and pearls as I recall."

"Well, I never saw it. That shows you just how stupid I am. I should have asked for the necklace in exchange for providing an alibi, but it never even occurred to me. I guess I was too much in love to think at all."

"If Gerry didn't give you the necklace," Ivan interjected, "what do you suppose he did with it?"

"It's been four years," Mayleen reminded him. "Gerry's probably had a dozen girls by now. He could have given it to any of them."

"Maybe he hasn't," Ivan persisted. "He might still have it. If you could coax him into giving it to you, it would prove *he'd* robbed the stage rather than Jesse."

Mayleen rose slowly, and turned away to stir the simmering pot of beans. She had been set on telling Gerry exactly what she thought of him. She certainly didn't want to pretend she still cared for him when all she felt for him was disgust. "If he didn't want to give me such an expensive present four years ago, he certainly won't do it now," she called over her shoulder.

Ivan struggled to his feet and limped over to her. "You can charm a man into doing whatever you want, Mayleen. I'll bet Gerry will be so happy to see you he'll want to shower you with presents. All it would take would be a hint or two that you'd like some pearls."

Mayleen shot Ivan a darkly threatening glance. "I'm not a whore anymore. Don't ask me to act like one."

"I'm not!" Ivan exclaimed. When Mayleen's expression didn't soften, he turned to Luke. "I think it's worth a try. If we can prove Gerry had the necklace, even if he's given it away, will you accept that as proof of Jesse's innocence and leave him be?"

Mayleen was as vitally interested in Luke's answer as Ivan and held her breath as she awaited his reply. It was going to be awfully hard seeing Gerry again, and she sincerely doubted that she could weedle so much as a compliment out of him, let alone a stolen string of pearls, but it was certainly worth a try.

Luke stood up. "I'm going for a walk."

"Must you go now?" Mayleen cried. "Can't you answer us first?"

Luke just shook his head. What he needed was some peace and quiet to think without constantly being interrupted and he sauntered off to find it. Sheriff Toland back in Tucson had had his doubts about Jesse's guilt, and each time Luke recalled his conversation with the lawman he had grown more uncomfortable. He had admitted quite frankly to the sheriff that the question of justice did not concern him, but perhaps just this once it should.

There was the slain marshal to consider, though, and the Crandell woman too. "How the hell do they figure in this?" he asked himself. While he was justifiably proud of being adept at tracking down wanted men, he was not used to working on cases this complex. The Crandell woman

374

worried him. He hadn't liked the looks of Eldrin Stafford or the men who worked for him, either. That didn't mean Tory was innocent, though.

"Tory," he mumbled. "Now they've got me calling her Tory." He jammed his hands into his pockets and walked a little farther. He had learned the hard way not to trust Mayleen, and who could tell what her crazy "husband" might do next? Traveling with those two had made everything more difficult, but he wasn't ready to tell them goodbye. There were just too many unanswered questions where Jesse Lambert was concerned and he had always been an extremely curious man.

After completing a wide arc, Luke started back toward camp. When the preacher and Mayleen greeted him, their smiles were so earnest he felt an immediate twinge of guilt, but managed to force it away. "I got a plan," he announced. "You take me with you to the Lambert ranch. Introduce me as Jed Magrew, a man you happened to meet along the trail. Say you needed my help since the preacher is so sickly. Invite me to stay for a couple of days to rest up. I'll keep my eyes open and do what I can to see it's the guilty man who goes back to Arizona with me."

Mayleen pursed her lips thoughtfully. "I don't know," she worried aloud. "Once we're on Jesse's ranch, what's to stop you from taking him into custody?"

Luke thought her daft. "*I'm* the one who'll be in danger there, lady, not *him!* It's Jesse's ranch, and if he figures out who I am before I want him to know, I'll be in a heap of trouble. Now I'm going to have to rely on you two to protect me. If you do, we just might catch us the man who really robbed the stage. What do you say? Do you trust me enough to work together on this?"

When Mayleen looked up at Ivan, he paused a long moment before nodding. Then he held out his hand. "I'm Professor Ivan J. Carrows, a geologist by trade. How do you do?"

"You're a geologist now? That's a good one," Luke replied.

"No, I really am," Ivan insisted.

"Sure you are," Luke snickered. "And I bet your name is really Ivan, too."

For an instant Ivan was insulted, but then he began to laugh, too. "I really don't care whether or not you believe my name. Just don't make the mistake of double-crossing us, Mr. Bernay, because you won't live long enough to regret it."

"I'm doing you a favor!" Luke protested angrily. "Don't you dare threaten me."

Ivan put his arm around Mayleen's shoulder and drew her close. "Are we threatening him, my dear?"

"No, certainly not," she replied. "Supper's ready. Come on, let's eat. We sure don't want any visitors tonight so we've got to put out the fire before it gets dark."

Luke still thought he was owed an apology, but when it wasn't forthcoming, his hunger overruled his pride and he grabbed a plate and ate every bite Mayleen gave him. He was surprised to find her such a good cook and hoped she did not prove disappointing in any other respect now that he had agreed to take her on as a partner. As for the crazy geologist, he still had his doubts about him.

Zina Lambert took her place at the dinner table with her customary poise. While she failed to provide an excuse for Gerry's absence, if the violent scene between her son and Jesse had upset her, she did not allow it to show in her expression. She was surprised to see Patricia had not changed into more elegant attire but referred to it only obliquely.

"Did you find your room comfortable, Miss Earl?" she asked.

"Yes, thank you," Tory replied.

"Don't hesitate to request whatever you desire from our staff. If you have garments which need to be pressed, it will be done first thing in the morning."

Tory looked to Jesse for a reply and he promptly provided one. "Unfortunately Patricia's belongings were lost in the fire that destroyed her home. We've not had time to replace them so she has nothing which needs to be pressed."

"I beg your pardon," Zina murmured. "I had no idea you had arrived without a change of clothes. While my gowns are much too small to fit you, I'll see if something suitable can't be found tomorrow."

Unaccustomed to being treated like an overgrown orphan who could not possibly squeeze herself into a lady's gowns, Tory was about to insist that she would supply her own wardrobe but Jesse's warning frown convinced her to remain silent. They at least had a roof over their heads that night and a flavorful meal, but she feared she was too apprehensive to enjoy either.

Zina had never deigned to discuss anything of serious consequence at the dinner table, but Jesse thought it was high time to break that ridiculous tradition. Rather than scold her for being rude to his fiancée, he focused on his main concern. "Has Gerry ever told you the truth about what happened in Tucson?"

Dinner had begun with a bowl of vegetable soup. Zina laid her spoon aside and blotted her mouth lightly on her napkin before she replied. "I prefer to consider that unfortunate incident closed and would appreciate it if you did not refer to it ever again."

Jesse had always admired his stepmother's grace and charm, but he found her refusal to see Gerry for the conniving coward he was downright annoying. "Gerry robbed the stage," he informed her calmly. "Then saw to it that I'd be sent to prison for his crime. That's not something I can conveniently forget."

Zina's soft southern accent did not make her demand any less harsh. "This is my home as well as yours, Jesse, and I'll not tolerate any mention of what occurred in Tucson within my hearing."

"Then you'll be spending a great deal of time in your room, because I intend to make Gerry not only admit what he did to me, but pay for it. He's a liar and a thief and I won't allow you to pretend otherwise."

Although shocked that her stepson would make such wild accusations, Zina left her chair with deliberate grace. "No purpose can be served by dredging up the past," she warned him. "We must simply begin anew to reestablish ourselves as a family. Your loyalty to your father's memory demands that you give us your best."

Always the gentleman, Jesse had risen from his chair when Zina did, but that show of courtesy was all she was likely to get. "Do you honestly believe that I can simply return home from prison and never mention the fact that Gerry was to blame for my conviction?"

"Yes, you're home," Zina remarked. "That's what's important. Dwelling on the unpleasantness of the past will only spoil the future for us all."

"'Unpleasantness?'" Jesse scoffed. "Four wretched years in prison can't be dismissed as mere unpleasantness!"

"Oh yes it can," Zina argued, "and it will."

Tory watched the delicate little woman leave the dining room with tiny steps which still managed to convey her distress. When Jesse returned to his seat, she reached for his hand. "I think she honestly believes Gerry's version of what happened rather than yours."

Jesse nodded. He had little appetite now, but signaled for the next course to be served. He waited until they were again alone before he continued. "We have a couple of days at least. We weren't seen in town, and anyone who comes here asking for me will be told I'm in Arizona and promptly sent on their way. That will buy us the time to get the truth out of Gerry."

"What do you plan to do then?"

"Hand him over to the sheriff. After he's made a full confession to the authorities here, he can be returned to Tucson for trial."

Not wanting to insult him, Tory chose her words with deliberate care. "If only Ivan hadn't behaved so badly, Mayleen would be with us. Gerry couldn't continue to lie after she's admitted to providing him with a false alibi."

"I'd already thought of that," Jesse said. "I was in such a hurry to leave Ivan that I didn't stop to consider how valuable Mayleen's presence would be. She said she and Ivan would pay us a visit when they got to El Paso. We'll just have to hope that she does."

"Perhaps you could send someone to escort them to the ranch," Tory suggested.

Jesse sat back in his chair. "That's a good idea, but I really don't have the men to spare."

"Does Lalo?"

"Yes, but—"

"Then ask him," Tory replied. "Our lives are at stake. This is no time to make decisions based on pride."

Amused by that show of spirit, a slow smile curved across Jesse's lips. "It takes a lot of courage to boss me around. You're a real feisty woman, aren't you?"

"Feisty is scarcely a strong enough term to describe a murderess."

Jesse sat up with a start. "I can give orders just as easily as you, lady, and that's the last time you'll ever refer to yourself in such an insulting way. Now let's finish eating, then I want to stop by Gerry's room to wish him a good night. After that, you and I are finally going to make good use of a feather bed."

While that prospect had a decided appeal, Tory was still worried. "Is there a chance Gerry might try and slip away during the night?"

"No, he hasn't the courage to run away."

"What about Zina? Is there someone she might call on to take Gerry's side against you?"

Jesse had to ponder that question for a moment. "She has a great many friends, but they all knew my father and would stand with me, not Gerry. Of course, she may have met someone while I was away but don't forget that they believed my story about an early release. That's going to protect me from outside interference."

Tory sighed softly. She wanted to give Jesse all the support she could, but she was still plagued with lingering doubts as to the wisdom of his plan. They had done all they could for that day, however, and she did not want to spoil the evening. She smiled and wondered how she could ever have considered him less than handsome. It must have been the fact that she had met him in the Cactus Springs jail. Her mood had been far too downcast to appreciate his looks then. Now she found him irresistibly appealing.

"Don't spend too much time bidding Gerry good night," she told Jesse as they parted after dinner.

That seductive remark was so unlike the serious young woman he knew that Jesse could not quite believe she had made it, but he was only too happy to grant her request. "Why don't you go out on the patio? I'll join you in just a minute."

She paused to give him a teasing kiss that held a promise for a delicious night and he hurried to Gerry's room bent on making his visit brief and to the point. The lamp was lit by his stepbrother's bed, illuminating his battered face with gruesome clarity. As he approached him, Jesse watched the young man grip his covers like a terrified child.

"I'm not going to lay another hand on you tonight," he promised with a laugh. "For once in your life, I'd like you to try acting like a man and I don't want you to be in too much pain to think clearly. You've had four years to show what you could do given control of this ranch and you've made a sorry mess of it. Why does your mother think you've been forced to try to sell off part of the land? Have you managed to convince her that raising cattle is no longer a profitable enterprise or have you been truthful about your gambling losses?"

"My luck will change," Gerry insisted.

"A man makes his own luck," Jesse contradicted, "so it's no wonder yours is all bad. Zina is a trusting woman and you've taken advantage of her love. It will undoubtedly break her heart to learn what a scoundrel you really are, but you're going to tell her the truth, and soon. If not—"

When Jesse left his threat undescribed, Gerry imagined tortures too hideous to name. With a twenty-year prison sentence, he had been certain Jesse would die there and he would never have to face up to the treachery he had undertaken to send him there. "And after I tell Mother?" he whispered.

Jesse leaned down over him. "You're going to keep telling the truth until my name is cleared and you're the one behind bars. Don't worry, I'll see that you're not forgotten. I'll write to you every month and tell you how well things are going here. You'll learn to look forward to those letters as a link with home. At Christmas, I might even send you some candy. Of course, you'll have to share it with your fellow inmates, but don't worry, you'll get used to sharing every hour of the day and every part of your life with them soon enough."

Gerry was now cringing so badly that Jesse was certain he had heard enough for the time being. "Sweet dreams," he called over his shoulder and strolled out of his room.

Having been raised on a plantation with magnificent gardens, Zina had always lavished a great deal of attention on the flowers in the patio, and the air was filled with their fragrance that night. Jesse paused for a moment to locate Tory, then hurried up behind her. He wrapped his arms around her waist and held her pressed tight against him. He nuzzled her nape and searched his mind for adequate praise for her beauty. When words failed him, he whispered all he really needed to say.

"I love you."

Tory laid her hands over his and said a silent prayer that their time together would not be as brief as she feared. "I love you, too," she answered him softly.

Jesse lifted her clear off her feet. "Say that again," he begged before putting her down.

"I love you," Tory repeated. "But there's something we really ought to discuss."

"No, not tonight."

"Yes, tonight. You've introduced me to everyone as your fiancée, and I really should have been given a say in the matter."

Stunned, Jesse turned her around. "Don't you want to be my wife?"

The anguish in his expression compounded her own, and Tory gave him a reassuring kiss before she replied. "Yes, I do, but we can't make any plans for the future until we overcome the tragic threat of our pasts. I will always be grateful to you for saving my life and for believing the Staffords are the real murderers, but if that can't be proven, if my

381

name can't be cleared, then I'll have to leave you. I can't stay here and endanger your life and it *would* be in danger every time you tried to protect mine."

The possibility of losing her for any reason, even such a noble one as she described, tore Jesse's heart in two and he gathered her into a possessive embrace. "We've changed your name to conceal your identity."

"Yes, but it won't be difficult for the authorities in the Arizona Territory to place me here with you. Even if Eldrin's men never arrive, which is far too much to expect, there will still be a death sentence hanging over my head."

Jesse closed his eyes as he tried to think how best to relieve her of such an awful fear. "You asked which means the most to me, our lives or this ranch. I'll promise you now that if you're ever in danger, we'll leave. We'll go to Mexico, South America if we must. I'll talk with Lalo tomorrow and draw up some kind of a document that will permit him to run the ranch forever if need be. I'd take you and leave tonight if I had any doubts about my ability to protect you, but I know that I can do it. I know that I can. We've come so far, Tory, don't lose heart now."

"*You* are my heart," Tory whispered, "and I don't ever want to lose *you.*"

Jesse sealed her vow with a kiss that held the unmistakable flavor of devotion. He knew it was not merely his pride that made him so determined to set them both free of wrongful convictions. It was a passion for justice as well as love for the lovely young woman in his arms that drove him now. Tory deserved to be free of the dark cloud of hate that had hovered above her since she had avenged the wrong Paul Stafford had done her.

What she deserved, Jesse thought, was the very best life had to offer rather than the needless suffering Paul had inflicted on her. She deserved every happiness, and he intended to see that she had it. It didn't matter at all where they had to live; as long as they were together he would be content. His desire for her was now too strong to delay and he swept her up into his arms and carried her laughing and

382

giggling to her room. Not trusting either Zina or Gerry to allow them the privacy they required, he quickly bolted the door.

"I want to marry you now," he enthused as he fumbled with the buttons on her blouse. "Tomorrow at the latest. Don't argue with me, just say yes."

Tory had already explained why they could not marry and she did not waste her breath in repeating her objections. Instead, she kissed him again and again until he could no longer remember what he had asked. They shrugged off their clothes and flung them aside, then, recalling Tory had nothing else to wear, Jesse gathered up her garments and placed them over a chair.

He felt her hand caressing his back and reveled in the sweetness of her touch. He turned and, taking her hand, led her over to the bed. It had been made up with fresh linens that afternoon and they held the faint scent of the sachet Zina kept in the linen cupboards. He had once considered the flower-scented sheets unmanly and had demanded that his be kept separate, but this was Tory's room rather than his, and the delicately perfumed sheets seemed perfect for her.

As always, Jesse did his best to keep his emotions in check so as not to overwhelm Tory with the depth of his desire, but that night he found any show of restraint nearly impossible. He wanted her too badly, and he wanted more of her than he had ever dared take. There was no shyness in her touch, no hesitancy as she moved against him and wound her legs in his. With that kind of encouragement, Jesse's kisses grew fevered.

When he finally raised his mouth from hers, Tory was gasping for breath, but she pressed his face close as he began to kiss the soft fullness of her breasts. The room was dark and he wished now that he had paused to light the lamp, but there had not been time. When she grasped his curls and arched her back to lean into his kisses, he ceased to care about seeing her when holding her felt so incredibly enjoyable. He traced her ribs with his thumb, then moved his hand over the graceful curve of her hip before parting her legs.

She was already wet, and he caressed her gently, deftly creating a need within her that matched his own. He kept up his seductive massage as he played teasing kisses over the flatness of her stomach. Adjusting his position, he rubbed his cheek against the smooth flesh of her inner thigh and rejoiced silently when she did not bolt from his unconventional embrace.

Circling, delving, adoring, the motions of his lips and fingertips gradually came together in one fervent kiss that sent waves of ecstasy jolting through Tory with an intensity that rocked Jesse as well. The flavor of her surrender was so delicious he drank it in hungrily until his own body's cravings for release became so intense he could no longer ignore them. He moved over her then, drawing her into his arms as he brought their bodies together as one.

It was not until the rapture of their union had washed through him that he realized she had not replied to his insistent suggestion that they marry. It no longer mattered to him, however, for he knew she was already his wife in every way that truly mattered.

Chapter 25

Tory awoke filled with the lingering warmth of the exquisite joy she had found in Jesse's arms, but she panicked when she realized she was alone in her comfortable bed. She sat up and surveyed her room with an anxious glance and was astonished to see half a dozen colorful gowns folded over the back of the chair where the night before Jesse had placed her single outfit.

Thinking that Jesse could not possibly be in any trouble if he had had time to locate such pretty clothes, she threw back the covers and got up to peruse the unexpected additions to her wardrobe. When the door swung open, she had to grab the gown on the top of the heap to cover the blush that extended from her cheeks to her toes. She then recognized Jesse behind a stack of lingerie topped with a beribboned bonnet that resembled the one she had had to throw away, but she was still embarrassed that he had caught her without a stitch on. That did not stop her from returning his kiss with the proper enthusiasm, however.

"Where did you find such beautiful clothes?" she asked excitedly. "They can't possibly belong to Zina."

"No, they belong to you," Jesse assured her. He placed the things he had been carrying on the end of the bed and sat down next to them to gauge her reaction to the sudden improvement in her wardrobe. "Do you like them? It doesn't look like you've had a chance to try on anything yet. Lalo was confident they would all fit you, though."

Tory's heart fell. "Are these Carmen's clothes?"

Her woebegone expression made it plain she would not wear them if they were. "No, of course not. Lalo went into town yesterday and bought everything especially for you. He was also smart enough to say he was shopping for his wife rather than the future Mrs. Jesse Lambert so no one became suspicious about his purchases. The blue dress is my favorite. Will you wear it for me today?"

"I'll be happy to, but Lalo really shouldn't have done this. It must have cost him a great deal of money and—"

"He owes me a lot more than a few dresses, Tory. Don't worry about the expense." Jesse rose to his feet and paused to give her another kiss before he started for the door. "I'll leave so that you can bathe and get dressed."

Tory knew by his playful wink that he was teasing her again, but her mood was too good to care. It took her nearly an hour to get ready, but when she joined Lalo and Jesse in the parlor, their admiring glances provided ample proof that it had been time well spent.

"Thank you, Lalo," Tory greeted him. "The gowns are all so beautiful I would have had a difficult time deciding which to wear had Jesse not made the choice for me."

Lalo was still taken aback by the fact the disheveled waif Jesse had brought to his home was truly a stunningly attractive young woman. "You're welcome," he responded. "I am grateful to learn that my taste pleases you."

"Stop flirting with her, Lalo," Jesse demanded crossly. "You've already got one woman and that ought to be enough for any man."

"Is he always this jealous?" Lalo inquired.

Tory had to smile. "I've really no idea," she said, then amended her opinion. "No, wait, that's not true. He *is* the jealous type and he has the scars to prove it."

"Scars?" Lalo echoed.

The slash in Jesse's arm was nearly healed and he wasn't concerned about the scar. "I had to fight an Apache for her," he explained with a shrug. "Obviously, I won."

"I think there is a great deal you haven't told me," Lalo prompted.

"Probably, but there's no time to sit and chat. Do you know where Alex Tucker has gone?"

"Colorado, I believe."

Jesse swore under his breath. "What about the men who left the ranch when he was fired? Is there any way to let them know I need them without advertising that I'm here?"

"I will see to it," Lalo promised.

As Tory listened to the two men plan how best to secure the borders of the ranch, she did not repeat the misgivings she had shared with Jesse the previous evening. She simply observed the two old friends. They talked easily as though they were discussing some inconsequential element of the cattle business. Jesse had described Lalo as handsome, and she had to agree that he was, but he clearly lacked Jesse's strength and determination.

Had their situations been reversed, and Lalo been sent to prison, Tory was convinced Jesse would have gone to Yuma and done whatever he had to in order to set him free. Lalo had stayed in El Paso, though, and done his best to console poor Carmen. In her view Jesse deserved more loyalty from his friends. She strolled out on the patio rather than remain with the men.

The weather was warm, but the patio was fragrant and cool and she found a shady bench on which to sit and enjoy the beauty of the day. That was a simple pleasure she had been unable to experience for far too long. She took a series of deep breaths and tried to believe that she was really home and would never again have to flee for her life.

After leaving her son's room, Zina passed through the patio. When she saw Tory seated alone, she hurriedly joined her. "Your dress is lovely," she exclaimed. "It was so thoughtful of Lalo to provide it."

"Yes, it was," Tory agreed.

Zina looked toward the house to make certain their privacy was not about to be disturbed before she continued. "I assume that you have known Jesse only briefly, while I have known my son his whole life. Believe me, Miss Earl, I'm well aware of Gerry's faults, and I know he lacks the courage to rob a stage. It's simply ridiculous for Jesse to continue to

387

insist that Gerry is a thief. Won't you please tell Jesse that for all our sakes he ought to stop repeating his preposterous accusations?"

Tory stared at Zina for a long moment, amazed that she could even imagine that her son was innocent; but clearly she did. "All Jesse wants is the truth," she finally reminded her. "That isn't too much to ask."

Disappointed her stepson's fiancée was as obstinate as he was, Zina rose and backed away. "What do your people think of your marrying a man who's served time in prison?" she asked pointedly.

"Unfortunately neither of my parents is living, but if they were, I know they would be as proud of Jesse as I am."

Clearly doubting that optimistic view, Zina turned away, and Tory was relieved to see her go. She remembered the smugly superior smirk Gerry had given Jesse when his mother's back had been turned. Tragically widowed during the Civil War, it was easy to understand why Zina was so fiercely protective of her son. Tory thought it was high time Zina stopped shielding the spoiled young man, however, and allowed him to suffer the consequences of his actions.

Now propelled by fears of another confrontation with Tad MacDonald and his men and drawn by the desire to force Gerry to admit his lies, Luke, Mayleen, and Ivan pushed their horses to the limits of their endurance. The trio rode hard, at times rivaling the Apache's incredible ability to cover vast distances, and by nightfall they arrived at the gate of the Lambert ranch. When they were turned away by the armed guards posted there, Mayleen burst into tears.

"Don't you dare tell us to go away!" she sobbed. "Jesse said we'd always be welcome here. You go and tell him that Mayleen, Ivan, and a friend of theirs is here this very instant!"

The ranchhands standing guard swiftly decided the three weary travelers posed no threat to their employer's safety and one left to take their names to the house. He returned in less than ten minutes and swung open the gate. "The boss says you're welcome all right. I'll take you on up to the house."

Mayleen wiped the damp trails from her cheeks and favored her male companions with a triumphant smile. They knew as well as she did that her tears had been for show, but as long as they had worked to get them into the house she was not ashamed for stooping to such a theatrical ploy. She was sick of riding and sleeping on the ground, but the prospect of seeing Gerry again outweighed any enthusiasm she might have had for the comforts the Lambert ranch would provide.

Jesse had left Gerry completely alone that day, and too nervous to remain in his room, Gerry got dressed and entered the parlor just before dinner was to be served. That he had been on the losing end of a violent argument was obvious in his numerous scrapes and bruises, but he hoped no one would mention that he did not look his best. He went to his mother's side and bent down to kiss her cheek. Both Jesse and his fiancée regarded him with accusing stares, but he simply ignored them and poured himself a stiff drink. He had just raised the whiskey to his lips when the message that they had visitors reached them.

"Mayleen Tyler's here?" Gerry gasped incredulously.

Jesse had never been more delighted to welcome unexpected guests. "Yes, she's here and I think you'll find it impossible to keep pretending you know nothing about the robbery once she's withdrawn your alibi."

"Surely this isn't the young woman you described as a . . . well . . . as a—" Zina was too flustered to find the words to describe Mayleen's former profession.

Gerry replaced his glass beside the crystal decanter. "Let me handle this, Mother," he said. Bent on twisting Mayleen's sudden appearance to his own advantage, he left the parlor and went out the front door to greet her. Mayleen had once loved him more than truth and he vowed that she would again. If she told what she knew she would ruin him, but Gerry was positive a wife could not be made to testify against her husband, and if he had to marry Mayleen to win her silence, he was prepared to do so.

When the travelers reached the house, Gerry rushed forward to help Mayleen down from her horse. He then drew her into an amorous embrace and covered her flushed cheeks with a flurry of kisses. "Oh, God, how I've missed you," he exclaimed. He took her hands and stepped back to get a better look at her. "You're even more beautiful than I remembered," he swore before pulling her back into a possessive hug.

Mayleen had expected Gerry to be an aloof stranger who would greet her coldly. It would have taken all her talents to request a string of pearls from that uncaring man, but instead of disdain, Gerry was displaying the same enthusiastic affection he had always shown her in Tucson. It was such a shock that she simply stood in his arms unable to think at all, let alone revise her strategy.

As soon as he had dismounted, Ivan took a step toward them, but Luke grabbed his arm. "Let 'em be," he ordered softly. "He's playing right into her hands."

Ivan wasn't at all sure that was what was happening. From his vantage point, it sure looked like Mayleen was as thrilled to be reunited with her former lover as he was to be with her. She wasn't making any objection that he could see to Gerry's forceful affection, and that hurt him so badly it was all he could do not to shove Luke aside and have it out with Gerry right then and there.

Luke also found the affection Gerry was lavishing on Mayleen annoying to watch, but he wasn't about to allow Ivan to put a stop to it. "Just give her her head, son. She knows what she's doing," he whispered.

Luke's attention then shifted to the second man to come through the door. He was tall, well built, and looked enough like the worn photograph Luke had been carrying for the tracker to know he had to be Jesse Lambert. He was dressed in a well-tailored dark suit and looked the part of a gentleman rancher rather than a murdering fugitive. Not one to be taken in by appearance, Luke still thought it likely Jesse was guilty of at least one crime, if not several.

"That Lambert?" he asked Ivan.

Ivan nodded, and pushed by Gerry to reach him. He

extended his hand. "I hope you meant what you said when you invited us to come see you. This is Jed Magrew. He's been with us since, well . . . since we got separated in Mexico."

Jesse was too absorbed in the astonishingly romantic scene Mayleen and Gerry were playing out to take much notice of Luke, but he shook hands with him and greeted him with a distracted nod. "Of course," he assured them both. "You're all welcome to stay for as long as you like."

Too curious about what was transpiring outside to remain in the parlor with Zina, Tory followed Jesse outside. She knew Jesse expected Mayleen to establish his innocence, and she was as shocked as he was to see the young woman clinging to Gerry's arms. She paid no more attention than Jesse had to Ivan's introduction of Jed Magrew.

"It's an act," Ivan stepped close to assure Jesse.

"Hell, I already knew that," Jesse exclaimed, not realizing Ivan had been referring to Mayleen's performance rather than Gerry's. He reached out and grabbed his stepbrother's shoulder and turned him toward the house. "I'm sure your mother is anxious to meet Mayleen. Why don't you bring her inside?"

Gerry recoiled from Jesse's touch, but quickly recovered. He slipped his arm around Mayleen's waist and escorted her inside to the parlor. He was ashamed to have to introduce her to his mother, and especially so when her usually glossy curls were covered with trail dust and her clothes were dirty and wrinkled. Swallowing his pride, he attempted to present her proudly, but he could tell by his mother's startled expression that she was not impressed.

Mayleen, however, was absolutely fascinated with Zina Lambert. She was not only a beautiful lady, but was also elegantly dressed in a peach-colored satin gown. To accent its delicate hue, she was wearing an exquisite cameo necklace suspended on a string of perfectly matched pearls. Mayleen was badly embarrassed by the shabbiness of her own attire, but she was so elated to see Zina wearing the stolen necklace that she broke into an enchanting smile.

"I am so pleased to meet you," she enthused. "Gerry

mentioned you often, but I'll bet he never told you a thing about me."

Appalled to be greeted in such an informal manner by a woman of her class, Zina raised her perfumed handkerchief to her lips to cover her distress. "Please excuse me," she replied. "I must inform our cook that there will be guests for dinner." She then hurried from the room.

Mayleen looked up at Gerry. She had refrained from remarking on his battered appearance as she was certain Jesse was the cause of it, but she could not keep quiet about his mother's peculiar behavior, too. "Did I say something wrong?"

"No, of course not," he assured her. "But perhaps you and your friends would like to, well . . . refresh yourselves before we dine?"

Mayleen looked down at the clothes she had slept in. "Yes, I suppose we should. Just tell us where."

"I better ask Mother which rooms you should use," Gerry responded. He paused to give Mayleen another kiss and then also left the parlor.

As soon as he had passed through the doorway, Mayleen turned to the others. "Did you see it?" she asked excitedly. "Zina was wearing the necklace!"

"We weren't introduced," Ivan pointed out. "I didn't really get a good look at her."

"I didn't, either," Luke apologized.

"What are you talking about?" Jesse asked.

Mayleen quickly looked over her shoulder to make certain Gerry had not reentered the room. She then described Zina's necklace and identified it as the one taken at the time of the stage robbery.

"I'm sorry," Tory confessed. "I didn't notice it."

"Neither did I," Jesse admitted. "My stepmother has a great deal of expensive jewelry, but one necklace looks pretty much like another to me."

Mayleen was exasperated with them all. "Well, pay more attention the next time you see her. That has to be the stolen necklace she's wearing. It just has to be." She heard footsteps approaching, but it was Gerry who had returned to the room, not Zina.

"Mother said to give you the room next to Patricia's."

"Who's Patricia?" Mayleen asked with a befuddled frown.

Equally confused, Gerry turned toward Tory. "I thought that you knew Jesse's fiancée, Patricia Earl."

"Oh, Patty!" Mayleen giggled. "How silly of me. Of course we all know her. I guess I'm just more tired than I thought."

Never having considered Mayleen particularly bright, Gerry believed her. "Good. I'll get your things and show you the way. There are places for you two gentlemen in the bunkhouse."

Jesse had no idea who Jed Magrew was, but he was positive Ivan Carrows did not belong with the rowdy young men in the bunkhouse. "They'll stay here in the house," he contradicted. "They can use the two rooms just past the study."

"But those are storerooms," Gerry argued.

"So they're a little cluttered, but they do have beds and they'll be fine for a night or two."

Clearly upset by Jesse's order, Gerry's expression became a childish pout. "You take care of them then. I'll help Mayleen get settled."

"Fine," Jesse agreed. He waited until they had left the room before he turned his attention to Ivan. "Now suppose you tell me just how you happened to meet Mr. Magrew here and what you've told him."

Ivan stammered, then blurted out the story they had agreed upon. "I hurt my ankle real bad after you left us. Jed was passing through that little town, saw how poorly I was getting along, and offered to help us get here. He knows there was some trouble between you and your stepbrother and that Mayleen's come to straighten it out."

That was more than Jesse thought Jed ought to know, and Mayleen's mention of a stolen necklace had just tipped the man off about the robbery. "I hope you're not in any big hurry to leave," he remarked.

"Why's that?" Luke asked.

"Because just as Ivan said, my stepbrother and I have something to iron out, and you won't be leaving here until we do."

The cool detachment Jesse displayed while issuing that order chilled Luke clear through, but he pretended to be amused by it. "I just plain wore myself out trying to strike it rich out in the Arizona Territory and I could sure use a good rest before I leave for home. To tell you the truth, I wouldn't mind staying on for a month or two."

"I assure you, it won't be nearly that long. Just ignore my stepmother. She grew up on a plantation in Virginia and sometimes forgets she's not royalty."

Tory remained in the parlor while Jesse showed the two men to their rooms. When Zina joined her, she could not help but stare, for rather than being adorned by the incriminating necklace Mayleen had described, the southern beauty's slender neck was bare.

Their guests were so ravenously hungry that Jesse thought better of asking Mayleen to confront Gerry with his lies at the dinner table. That Gerry was behaving as her long-lost lover rather than as the man who had abandoned her nauseated him so completely that he found it impossible to eat. There seemed to be no end to his stepbrother's duplicity and it was all he could do to remain seated and wait for the proper time to speak.

He could tell Tory was as upset as he and smiled at her frequently in an attempt to keep her spirits up. Ivan was now immaculately groomed. He had donned a suit, and when he was presented to Zina as a geology professor, she had actually been pleased to meet him. As for Jed Magrew, he had shaved and put on a clean shirt. He spoke only when spoken to so appeared to be minding his own business, but Jesse still did not like the idea of having a stranger in the house at such a critical time.

As for the necklace Mayleen had mentioned, he thought she might have been so tired from her travels that she had just imagined seeing Zina wearing it. Either that or Zina had known Mayleen might recognize it and had removed it. He was annoyed with himself for not having paid closer attention to his stepmother, but why wouldn't she have expected him to notice the stolen necklace and comment on it? Damn! he swore silently. He felt as though he was being squeezed from all directions and he was thoroughly sick of it.

As soon as they had finished dining and returned to the parlor, Jesse pointedly dismissed Jed with a polite request for the privacy necessary to discuss a family matter. Jed shrugged, said he was too tired to stay up anyway, and went to his room. Relieved to be rid of him, Jesse was eager to begin the conversation.

Zina had chosen her favorite chair by the fireplace. Tory was seated nearby with Ivan standing beside her. Gerry and Mayleen had taken places on the settee and Jesse spoke before his stepbrother could again begin pawing her. "Mayleen came here to help me prove my innocence, Gerry. Don't assume that there's any other reason."

Gerry turned toward Mayleen and took her hands in his. "I can imagine what you must think of me, but it's all untrue. Not a day has gone by that I haven't thought of you, I wanted to return to Tucson and make you my wife. It has just been that I was needed here and couldn't leave my mother alone again. Now that you've come to me, let's agree never to spend another day apart. I love you, Mayleen. Please say you'll marry me."

Intent upon hearing Mayleen's response, the others in the room all leaned forward. Zina's disapproval was evident in her narrowed eyes and tightly pursed lips. Tory's expression mirrored her disgust with Gerry's obvious lies. Ivan was frowning darkly, his gaze focused on Mayleen's incredulous smile. Jesse took them all in and then prompted Mayleen for a response.

"I know you don't believe a word he says, Mayleen. Tell him so. Tell him that you're recanting your testimony and that without an alibi he's the one who'll be convicted and sent to prison."

Flustered, Mayleen licked her lips and tried to think how best to stall for time. She knew Gerry was a liar. He was weak

395

and used other people shamelessly, but when he had welcomed her to his home with such exuberant kisses, his faults had been difficult to remember. She heard Jesse's voice, but only dimly. Gerry had convinced her once that withdrawing her alibi would not exonerate Jesse but only land them both in prison. As she saw it, they still needed the necklace for proof. Why hadn't she had sense enough to ask Zina about it the moment she had seen it? she agonized.

"Mayleen . . ." Jesse urged again.

Gerry saw the confusion in her glance and sought to make the most of it. "You know how happy we were together, my sweet. We'll be that happy again. I know that you still love me. You must! I still love you. Please marry me. We'll start planning the wedding tomorrow. We'll have the biggest celebration El Paso has ever seen."

Mayleen searched his face for some sign of the deception she knew his proposal had to be, but he looked heartbreakingly sincere. "I need time to think about it, Gerry," she told him hesitantly. "Right now I'm so tired I can barely think, let alone make such an important decision."

"You don't need to think about it, sweetheart," Gerry scolded. "You love me. That's all that matters."

Mayleen looked up at Jesse and found him staring at her with the same furious gaze he had turned on her that first night in Tucson. "I need time," she repeated.

The choice clear in Jesse's view, he was so disgusted he turned on his heel and walked out. Tory followed him, leaving Ivan leaning against her suddenly vacant chair for support. He had called Mayleen his wife so often that he had begun to believe it, and to listen to another man beg for her hand was excruciatingly painful. He hoped for his sake as well as Jesse's that Mayleen was just stringing Gerry along, but he was sadly aware that there was a good possibility she wasn't.

The depth of sorrow reflected in Ivan's face gave Mayleen sufficient pause to allow her to see the truth of her situation with shocking clarity. She struggled to free herself from Gerry's grasp and rose to her feet. "Seeing you again has completely overwhelmed me," she explained with a nervous giggle. "I'll need time to decide what's best. I've not heard from you in four years. Surely I should be permitted a few days to make up my mind about becoming your wife."

"But that's just the problem," Gerry argued. "We've wasted far too much time as it is."

"A few more days won't matter," Mayleen assured him, and after brushing his lips with a light kiss and wishing Zina and Ivan a good night, she left the room.

Gerry turned to speak to his mother and noticed how closely Ivan was watching him. "What are you staring at?" he asked rudely.

"I'll be damned if I know," Ivan responded. "I don't think the words have even been invented to describe an amoral snake like you." Proud of himself for having the courage to speak his mind without having had a drop to drink, Ivan followed Jesse and Tory out the front door. They were standing not ten feet from the house, and Ivan winced as he heard the anguish in Jesse's voice.

"Wait!" he called to them as he approached. "Don't jump to any conclusions." He urged them to walk a few steps farther from the house, then spoke in a hushed whisper so he would not be overheard. "We convinced Mayleen to pretend an interest in Gerry. I think that's all she's doing. She couldn't possibly be seriously considering marrying that swine. Excuse me, I know he's your stepbrother, but that's all he is."

Jesse had stormed out of the house too angry to consider any action except wringing Mayleen's neck, and Tory's calmly voiced reassurances that they would prevail had barely succeeded in taking the edge off his fury. "Luke Bernay's going to show up in El Paso in a day or two. There's no time for Mayleen to play games with Gerry's affections, which are a fake anyway. All she has to do is tell the truth! Why is that so damn impossible?"

Ivan quickly explained the significance of the necklace. "Catching Gerry with that necklace will be all the proof Bernay will need of Gerry's guilt. Just give Mayleen time to get it."

"Bernay is looking for me, Ivan. Waving some damn

necklace in his face won't do a bit of good. All that will impress him is Gerry's signed confession."

Ivan could see Jesse was too upset to listen to reason, and after taking a fortifying breath, he blurted out the truth. "Bernay has already assured us that he'd accept the necklace as proof of Gerry's guilt."

"You've met him?" Tory gasped.

One step ahead of her, Jesse reached out and grabbed Ivan's lapels. "Did you bring Bernay into my house? Is that who Jed Magrew really is?"

Ivan gripped Jesse's wrists to stay on his feet. His ankle was still bothering him and his balance wasn't all that good. "I know you think Mayleen betrayed you once, but that's not what's happened this time. Bernay believes you're innocent. He really does."

Jesse released Ivan so quickly that the young man nearly landed in the dirt, but he caught himself at the last instant and managed to remain upright. "I should have known better than to trust you," Jesse snarled. "But I'll never trust a man like Bernay." He shoved the geologist aside and headed back toward the house with a long, defiant stride.

"Wait," Ivan cried. "You can't go after him!"

Jesse didn't bother to reply; he just kept right on walking. He'd spent enough time running from Luke Bernay and he was going to deal with him as swiftly as he should have dealt with his traitorous stepbrother.

Chapter 26

Jesse was a big man and Ivan certainly wasn't, but the geologist knew he had to do something to prevent him from making an enemy of Luke Bernay. His ankle wasn't strong enough to permit him to run, but he managed to take a couple of wild, leaping hops and hurled himself after Jesse. He grabbed him around the hips with sufficient force to knock him off balance. They both slammed into the dirt where Ivan continued to cling to Jesse with the full force of his convictions.

Jesse had been felled more by surprise than strength and he struggled to shake Ivan loose, but each time he succeeded in peeling off the smaller man, Ivan just switched his hold on him. Finally Jesse got a good enough grip on Ivan to push him down on the ground and keep him there. He drew back his fist, ready to slam it into Ivan's face, but the brutality of that move brought Tory into the fray. She grabbed Jesse's upraised arm with both hands and held on with the same fiery determination Ivan had shown.

"Let him go!" she shouted. "It's Gerry you're after, not Ivan!"

Jesse couldn't fight them both and, unwilling to risk injuring Tory, he moved off Ivan and stood up. Tory released his arm, but just as quickly as Ivan had shifted his holds, she grasped Jesse's waist. Not about to shove her away, he squeezed her shoulders, brushed the dust off his clothes with his free hand, and then helped Ivan rise.

"All right, you two," he said. "I give up, but if you think I'm going to entertain the man who's been sent to take me back to prison you're crazy."

The frames of Ivan's eyeglasses were again bent, and as soon as he corrected that problem, he leaned over and rested his palms on his knees to catch his breath. "You've got to trust us," he wheezed.

"Trust you?" Jesse scoffed. "I don't trust anyone anymore. Except for Tory," he was quick to add. "I know she won't let me down."

"You're right, I won't," Tory agreed. "But if Bernay has gotten this far, can Eldrin Stafford's men be far behind? I can't stay here, Jesse, not even tonight. I've got to keep ahead of them."

She was shaking as though she was suffering from a severe chill and Jesse hugged her more tightly. "We've got two problems it seems," he related in a soothing tone. "I don't want Luke here, and neither of us wants to present an easy target for Stafford's men—"

"About Stafford's men," Ivan interrupted. "I shot a couple of them outside of Juarez." He hurriedly explained that Luke Bernay had met seven of them near Cactus Springs but that there were probably only three left now. "They might have turned tail and gone home."

Tory found Ivan's calmly worded tale as astonishing as Jesse did. "You survived a shoot-out with Stafford's men?" she asked.

Insulted that she thought so little of his abilities, although he had to admit he had not demonstrated many in her presence, Ivan nodded. "It wasn't what I'd call a shoot-out, since they didn't return my fire. I'm not proud of the fact I killed a man and possibly two, but it was called for in this instance. I sure wasn't going to lead them to you."

"Thank you," Tory sighed gratefully. "You've been a wonderful friend."

Now realizing that he had needlessly jeopardized her life and Jesse's each time he had taken a drink, Ivan found it impossible to respond. He shuffled his feet nervously and attempted to refocus the conversation on Luke. "It took a great deal of talking, and the credit goes to Mayleen, but Bernay does believe in your innocence. He came here to help us prove it."

Jesse was certain that if they failed in that quest Bernay would rethink his position and try to return him to Yuma. And there was no way he would allow that travesty to occur. He had had enough of the Yuma prison to last him a lifetime and he wasn't going back. He had to make some plans, and fast.

"We'll stay here tonight," he told Tory, "but first thing in the morning I'm taking you over to Lalo's. If Stafford's men reach El Paso, they'll come straight here and, you're right, this is the last place you ought to be. You'll be far safer with Lalo for the time being. I know you and Carmen didn't have much in common, but I think you can manage to get along for a few days."

"I'd say we have a great deal in common," Tory contradicted. "You."

Embarrassed that he had failed to see such an obvious connection, Jesse responded with a self-conscious laugh. "You needn't consider her any competition." He paused to give Tory a reassuring kiss, then gestured toward the house. "Come on, it's getting late. I'll let Bernay rest tonight, but tomorrow I'll tell him that I know who he is."

Despite Jesse's reassuring words, Tory searched the yard with an anxious glance. She knew there were men stationed at the gate, and standing guard elsewhere, but even if there were only three men pursuing her, was that enough? She let Jesse coax her back into the house, but she doubted she would be able to sleep that night when Stafford's men might be lurking in every shadow.

Ivan was also preoccupied as they entered the house. He was doing his best to believe in Mayleen, but when he compared what Gerry had offered her with what he could provide as an itinerant geologist, he could not help but grow fearful about her choice. He knew she felt bad about what she had done to Jesse, but was guilt a strong enough emotion to outweigh the love she had once felt for Gerry?

Too nervous to prepare for bed, he crossed the hall to Mayleen's room and rapped lightly on the door. As he waited for her to respond, he prayed Gerry wasn't in her room, or worse yet, her bed. "Mayleen, it's Ivan," he whispered insistently.

Exhausted, but too distraught over Gerry's proposal to have any interest in sleep, Mayleen rushed to admit Ivan. She checked the hall to make certain no one would see him join her and then reached out to draw him inside. "I'm sorry I made such a mess of things tonight," she apologized. "It just didn't occur to me that Zina would hide the necklace before everyone else had seen it."

Mayleen's eyes were bright with unshed tears and Ivan drew her into his arms for a comforting hug. "Don't fret so," he said. "You've got Gerry so flustered that he'll probably say whatever you tell him to in a couple of days. It's plain he's scared to death."

"It is?"

"Yes. Why else would he have been so eager to offer marriage? He hasn't seen you in four years, but he acted as though you'd been together yesterday. I knew you were too smart to be fooled by him."

There had been a time when Mayleen would have done anything to win Gerry's love. While it had hurt her conscience badly to lie for him in court, she had done it with the expectation she would soon be his bride. He had merely been using her, though, promising love for his own selfish aims, not out of any regard for her. Ashamed of herself, she backed out of Ivan's embrace.

"I knew he couldn't possibly be sincere," she assured him flippantly. "He doesn't love anyone but himself."

Afraid that he had inadvertently hurt her, Ivan attempted to rephrase his remarks. "You'd make a fine wife for any man, Mayleen. I didn't mean for it to sound as though Gerry couldn't possibly be proposing out of love. If he were an honest man, I'm sure that he would be."

Wondering what had prompted Ivan to soften his tone,

Mayleen regarded him with a skeptical stare. "You're right," she suddenly agreed. "The last time I looked, there was a long line of honest men waiting to propose to me. Why I could hardly go anywhere without tripping over them." She went to her door and peered out as though she expected to find them out in the hall. "Guess they've all gone to bed," she announced. "You better get on back to your room before they wake up and come back."

Ivan would have liked to have shared her room, but as usual, she was not showing any interest in having his company and he did not argue with her about leaving. "You will make some man a fine wife," he repeated as he moved through the door. "'Night."

"Good night," Mayleen whispered. She closed her door and leaned back against it. Gerry was a liar, and clearly Ivan did not really care about her either or he would have proposed to her himself long before this. During the trip she had let herself believe she and Ivan might have a future together, but it was clear he had watched Gerry kiss her and beg her to marry him without suffering a single twinge of jealousy.

Mayleen went to the dresser and studied her reflection in the mirror hanging above it. She looked not only tired but as desperately sad as she felt. Try as she might, she could not seem to forget the night she and Ivan had made love. That he had yet to recall it was but another reason for sorrow, and she already had too many. She saw too much in her reflection, turned her back to the mirror, and began to remove her clothes. Maybe things would look better in the morning, but right now, she doubted it.

Jesse followed Tory into her room and locked the door. When she hurried to her window to look out, he walked up behind her. "I have enough men guarding the house to keep you safe, sweetheart. You needn't keep watch, too."

Tory put her hands over his and leaned back against him. "Is there ever going to be an end to this horror? Are we ever going to be safe?"

"You're safe now," Jesse assured her before leaning down to kiss her cheek. He wanted to loosen her hair, but she was holding his hands tightly and he thought he ought not to pull free. He liked having her cling to him, but not for this reason. "We're going to have a long and happy life together, Tory. I wish you believed that."

"I do believe it," Tory replied. At least she wanted to, but with Luke Bernay in the house and Eldrin Stafford's men drawing near, it was too soon to abandon herself to such sweet thoughts. "I believe in you," she said with far more conviction, "and I do want what you want."

"All I want is you," Jesse whispered in her ear. "Come away from the window." He finally withdrew his hands from hers, crossed to the dresser, and picked up her hairbrush. He knew he ought to ask if she felt up to making love again, but he was too afraid she might say no. Instead, he sat down on the bed and patted the place by his side.

"Come sit down and I'll brush your hair for you."

Too distracted to argue, Tory did as he asked. She made herself comfortable and removed the combs from her hair, sending a cascade of soft curls spilling down over her shoulders. She braced herself slightly, but Jesse's touch was surprisingly light and gentle. She could not recall the last time someone had brushed her hair and it was a very pleasant sensation. It made her feel both cherished and protected.

"That's nice."

"I'm glad you like it." Jesse was certainly enjoying himself. He brushed the ends of her curls over his palm and could not help but smile. "I'll brush your hair every night. Would you like that?"

Tory bit her lip to force back her tears but she could not help but wonder how many nights they would have together. No matter what the number, she knew it would never be enough. Tears stung her eyes and escaped her lashes to roll down her cheeks. She knew Jesse expected an answer to his question, but, choked on emotion, she could not supply one.

404

When she did not reply, Jesse leaned forward. He had meant to please her rather than make her cry and he was exasperated to have failed. He laid her brush on the nightstand and doused the lamp. "Come here," he whispered invitingly. Unwilling to wait for her to turn, he grasped her shoulders and pulled her into his arms. Seeking the comfort he was so willing to give, she snuggled against him and he decided that perhaps he should simply let her weep rather than constantly trying to make her smile.

The need she aroused within him was almost painfully sweet, but he managed to pat her back and hold her in a loving embrace without demanding more. He had never expected his feelings for any woman to be this strong but the love he shared with Tory would last forever. It had been tempered by the flames of danger and, with their lives at stake at every turn, it had been fueled with the passionate commitment that kept them alive. She was his life now, an inseparable part of him, his very heart and soul.

And without Jesse, Tory knew she would already be dead. If what he had given her proved to be no more than a brief reprieve rather than a lifetime of wedded bliss, she would still die loving him. Sorry not to be better company for him, she raised up slightly to kiss him and then slid off the bed. "I don't want to wrinkle your suit," she warned.

That Gerry had not thrown away all his clothes had been a pleasant surprise, but the state of his wardrobe was of little concern to Jesse at the best of times and of no consequence now. He rose and pulled her back into his arms. "Ivan has already made a mess of it. Besides, do you think I care?"

Tory shook her head and then realized it was too dark for him to see her gesture. "I doubt that you do," she said, "but that doesn't mean I shouldn't be considerate."

"There are better ways to show consideration," Jesse teased, and they began to unbutton each other's clothes between playful tickles. He attempted to remove her new gown with the care it deserved, but she was making it nearly impossible. "Hold still," he scolded.

"Like this," Tory teased as she rubbed against him with a

405

deliberately seductive grace.

"No, not like that!"

Tory dropped her hands to his belt. "Like this perhaps?"

Jesse grabbed her wrist and moved her hand lower. Afraid she would draw away, he held his breath but instead she responded with a knowing caress that sent his emotions reeling. After being brutally forced to satisfy Paul's base desires, he was amazed that she could touch him when he was fully aroused and not be revolted. Apparently she could separate him from Paul in her mind and he was elated that she had that ability. Now if only he could forget the man who had caused her such torment. He longed to be able to make love to her without the constant threat that he would somehow remind her of Paul. Neither of them needed to carry such an awful burden, but he dared not voice his fears aloud.

Completely unaware of Jesse's worries, Tory was concerned only with removing the bothersome hindrance of their clothes. She wanted to be able to feel the warmth of his bare skin against hers and provide him with the same glorious pleasure he lavished on her. She knew he must find her impossible to understand when her moods swung so swiftly between despair and desire, but she had such little control over her emotions that they were equally baffling to her.

Her sorrow forgotten for the moment, she wanted to make good use of the night. Moving to Lalo's ranch might guarantee her safety, but not being with Jesse would be difficult for them both. She licked the hollow of his shoulder. "You taste awfully good."

"Not nearly as delicious as you," Jesse argued before capturing her mouth for a kiss he did not end until after they had returned to the bed. He growled playfully as he nuzzled her throat. When she responded with a throaty giggle and wound her legs in his, he hugged her tightly and rolled over with her still in his arms.

Tory had not realized it was possible to make love seated astride him, but Jesse swiftly convinced her of how easy it was. His hands rested very lightly on her waist, patiently directing her motions until the wave of ecstasy that crested within her spilled over him as well.

Jesse pulled her back into his arms then and sought his own release in the floodtide of hers. Each time they made love the rapture they shared had become more intense, and he wondered how much more he could survive. While it was definitely worth the risk to find out, his passions were spent for the moment and he hastened to spare her his weight, but Tory wrapped her arms around his waist to hold him close.

"No," she murmured. "Stay."

"I'm too heavy for you."

"No, you're not." When he leaned down to again nuzzle her neck she ruffled his curls. "You're perfect for me."

Jesse kissed her brows, then the long sweep of her lashes. "If ever I'm not, please tell me."

"How could you be less than perfect?"

She seemed truly confused by his request, and he tried to make himself understood without upsetting her. "I don't ever want to remind you of things you'd rather forget."

He rested his forehead against hers in a gesture Tory found painfully touching. She raked her fingers through his thick chestnut curls as she tried to decide just what he had meant. She thought she knew, but she was not entirely certain. "Would you ever mistake a slap for a caress?" she asked.

"No, of course not," Jesse leaned back to answer.

"Then you needn't fear that I'll ever confuse your touch with Paul's."

The dead man's name hung on the air with the evil echo that had made Jesse afraid to speak it. That Tory had was both a cause for relief and alarm. "I didn't mean—" he started to apologize.

Tory interrupted him with a demanding kiss that sent all thought of begging her forgiveness from his mind. Lured by her seemingly boundless appetite for affection, Jesse felt himself again growing hard. How her lithe body could provide such a perfect match for his muscular frame he did not understand, but the joy they found together was too

407

complete to need analyzing. All he wanted was more of the loving she inspired, and her seductive encouragement made it plain she would wecome all he could give.

"I love you," he vowed between eager kisses that threatened to suffocate them both, and although his lips muffled her replies, he readily understood that she adored him too.

Gerry waited until the house was quiet to knock at Mayleen's door. "Mayleen, honey, it's me," he called softly.

Mayleen had just turned back the covers on the bed. She had feared that Gerry might come to her room, but until that very instant she had not known what she would do if he did. If she let him in, she felt certain he would offer more excuses for neglecting her and rely on affection to sway her response. She could still recall the thrill of making love with him. It had been both wild and sweet, but now she knew their love had been one-sided.

She put out the lamp and remained by the bed. Gerry called her name more insistently but still she did not respond. She was ashamed of how tempting the thought of being with him was, but she stood in the darkness willing him to go away. When he finally did, she climbed into the bed and pulled the covers up to her chin. Gerry was part of her past, and that's where she intended him to stay. Tomorrow she would again listen to whatever he had to say, but her heart would remain closed. All that mattered was undoing the terrible harm she had done Jesse, and if Gerry suffered in the process, then he would just get what he had deserved all along.

When Gerry reached his room, he found his mother waiting for him. Just as he always did, he hurried to her side and kissed her cheek. "This has been such a difficult day," he complained. "I hope you know that I would never have invited Mayleen Tyler to our home, but under these dreadful circumstances I don't see how I can possibly send her away."

Zina had spent her entire life assiduously avoiding unpleasant situations and it took a valiant force of will to confront her son now. "I want the truth, Gerard, and the *complete* truth for a change."

Gerry swallowed hard. "Why, whatever do you mean, Mother?"

"You know exactly what I mean," Zina snapped. "I am not stupid. It is becoming painfully obvious that you know far more about the robbery in Tucson than you've admitted thus far. I will not tolerate any more lies, Gerard. You are to tell me this instant precisely what happened!"

Gerry turned away. He jammed his tightly clenched fists in his pockets and searched his mind for a way to save himself. He was a clever young man, and when he turned back to face his mother, his expression was serene. "All right," he agreed. "I'll tell you what happened, although I'm certainly not proud of it. You know I like to play cards. I had some unfortunate losses and Jesse refused to loan me the money to cover them. He said if I was so desperate for cash I ought to rob a stage. Naturally I was appalled he would suggest such a dishonest solution to my problem, but he insisted that we could get away with it.

"The more he talked about it, the more enamored of the idea he became. When I refused to be a party to it, he involved a friend of mine, Conrad Werner, in the scheme. They robbed the stage and when Jesse was caught, suspicion naturally fell on me. I'd been asleep in my room that afternoon and had no alibi, but I didn't want to have to turn in Conrad to save myself. I told Mayleen about my dilemma and she offered to say that I'd been with her."

Gerry paused and shook his head sadly. "I suppose that in a way I was involved, but I never really believed that Jesse and Conrad would do it. I thought they were just making fun of me because I was the one who needed the money. I never got a penny of it, though. Jesse's cut was found in his room. Conrad was killed in a mine cave-in and his share was never found.

"I don't know why Jesse would tell such awful lies about me. I suppose he thinks that he wouldn't have been in Tucson had I not wanted to go and perhaps he wouldn't have robbed the stage had I not needed money to repay my gambling debts. That certainly doesn't make my guilt equal to his, however. Do you think I deserve to go to prison for knowing there might be a robbery and not stopping it? I think that's what Jesse's attempting to do. He wants to call me an accessory and see that I serve a prison sentence, too.

"As for Mayleen," he added, "it's clear she made Jesse believe she was on his side, but as soon as she arrived, she threw herself into my arms and said that she still loved me."

Accustomed to hearing honeyed lies from Gerry's lips, Zina did not recognize his tale for the complete fabrication it was. Convinced that he had just made a clean breast of his involvement in Jesse's crime, she nodded thoughtfully. "The Tyler woman must not be allowed to recant her alibi," she warned.

Pleased he had dissolved his mother's doubts so easily, Gerry broke into a relaxed smile. "Why do you think I proposed to her? She can't testify against me if we're married. She's very pretty, and no one will know anything about her past here. It's certainly to her advantage to keep it quiet. I really have no choice but to marry her, but you know I'll never love her, Mother."

"You can look forward to having children whom you'll love, though," Zina reminded him.

"Yes, of course, and it's high time you had some grandchildren, isn't it?"

"Indeed it is." Zina rose and slipped her hand into her pocket to withdraw her pearl-and-cameo necklace. "Why was it so important that I remove this?"

Gerry walked her to his door. "Mayleen saw it soon after I'd bought it as a present for you, and mistakenly assumed that it was to be a gift for her. I was afraid that if she saw it again, she would demand it as an engagement gift. Give it to me and I'll put it away."

Zina shook her head and returned the exquisite necklace

410

to her pocket. "No, I'd rather keep it. I'll make certain she doesn't see it."

Gerry dared not argue for fear he might arouse his mother's suspicions. "Fine. Good night."

Zina kissed him again. "Good night, dear." Then she paused outside his door. "How did you manage to pay off those gambling debts and still find the money to buy me expensive presents?" she asked.

"My luck changed," Gerry assured her. When she accepted that explanation and turned toward her room, he closed his door and let out a lengthy sigh. With his mother and Mayleen on his side, Jesse would never be able to hurt him. Confident he could win Mayleen's consent to their marriage, he removed his tie and began to prepare for bed. As he saw it, Jesse could never prove him guilty of a damn thing and he knew he would have no more trouble sleeping that night than he had on any other.

That same night, Tad MacDonald rode into El Paso with Hank Short and George Flood. They were all dead tired and looked it, but that didn't prevent them from stopping at the first saloon they passed. It took three beers to quench Tad's thirst, but then he began talking to the bartender.

"I have a friend who works out at the Lambert ranch. Can you tell me how to get there?"

The man nodded, but waited until Tad had slid a gold coin over to him before he provided the necessary directions. "It's a big spread," he added. "You can't miss it."

"Thanks." Tad drained his mug. "I'd like to surprise my friend. Is there a way I can get to the bunkhouse without riding through the main gate?"

"Maybe." The bartender frowned, and just kept polishing the bar until Tad supplied another coin. "Go back to the river," he then suggested. "Follow it up a couple of miles. That'll be Lambert land. Ride east and you'll eventually see some buildings. I guess you can figure out which one is the bunkhouse, can't you?"

"Sure can," Tad assured him. "Thanks." He nodded to Hank and George. They finished their beers and headed for the door.

When they reached their horses, George hung back. "I'd like to have a doctor take a look at my arm. It hurts like hell."

"Your cut's probably infected," Tad said. "A doctor will just want to whack off your arm. Just a minute. I'll get something that will take care of it." Tad went back into the saloon and returned in less than a minute with a shot of whiskey.

"How's drinking that going to help?" George asked.

"You're not going to drink it," Tad explained with an exasperated sigh. "Just peel off that bandage and I'll pour this on the cut. The alcohol will fix it up just fine."

"You sure?"

"Of course I'm sure."

George rolled up his shirtsleeve and unwound the blood-stained bandage. Even in the dim light that filtered through the saloon windows, the sight of the festering wound made him gag. "I didn't think I was hurt this bad."

Hank moved closer to take a look. "That's nothing but a scratch."

George held out his arm, but when Tad poured the whiskey over the cut he winced in pain. "Ouch, that stings!" he declared. Unable to stand still, he jumped up and down as though going through the motions of a medicine dance. "Now it hurts even worse than it did."

Tad placed the empty shot glass on the windowsill. "Why don't you go find the doctor if you're in so damn much pain? Not that having your arm sawed off at the elbow wouldn't hurt like hell, but at least Hank and I wouldn't have to listen to you cry and moan."

Truly horrified by that gruesome possibility George took another look at his arm. The cut was neither long nor deep, but it sure did hurt. His whole arm ached, in fact, but he decided againt consulting a doctor if it meant risking his arm. He had been cut up in knife fights before and still had all his limbs. Finally convincing himself that the wound was painful but not serious, he pulled out his handkerchief, looped it over the cut, and used his teeth to help tie the ends in a knot.

"I can make it," he then announced.

"Well, good," Tad replied. "Because come first light we're going to need you. Come on, with any luck we'll find us the perfect place to hide, and Miss Victoria Crandell will never see the bullet coming."

"That will be a damn shame," Hank said. "She ought to know just who's carrying out her death sentence."

"She'll know," Tad vowed. "Believe me, she'll know."

Chapter 27

Jesse awoke to find Tory again peering out her bedroom window. She was dressed not in one of her stylish new gowns, but in the mannish attire she had worn on their journey. Her hair was knotted atop her head, and she was clutching her hat to her side. She obviously expected to leave as soon as he was ready, but all he wanted to do was lure her back to bed. She turned toward him then and caught him staring at her.

"I thought you planned on leaving early," she said.

"We didn't get much sleep," he reminded her.

"We got enough to get to Lalo's."

That pointed comment made any attempt to entice her into loving play ill advised. Jesse threw back the covers and reached for his pants. "Give me a few minutes to clean up and we'll be on our way." He gathered up the rest of his clothes, gave her a hasty kiss, and left. When he returned to her room half an hour later, she was still at the window.

"If you want to wear one of your new gowns, I'll hitch a horse to the buggy," he offered.

"That would be far too dangerous. I don't want to take a chance on anyone recognizing me. I packed one of the dresses so I'll have something to wear for dinner." She grabbed her bag, but Jesse quickly took it from her.

"All right, we'll ride. I'll have our horses saddled while we're eating breakfast."

"I don't want anything to eat."

"Well, I do," Jesse insisted with a good-natured grin. "Come and keep me company." He started through the door without giving her time to argue. They were the first to enter the dining room that morning and had to wait several minutes for the kitchen staff to provide the ample breakfast Jesse craved. Tory fidgeted the whole time he ate, but he pretended not to notice.

Convinced it was far better to be the hunter rather than the prey, as soon as Jesse saw Tory safely to Lalo's ranch, he intended to ride out with some of his ranchhands to search for Eldrin Stafford's men. He considered telling Tory his plans, but not wanting to cause her any additional worry, he wisely chose to keep quiet.

"Are you sure you won't at least have a piece of fruit?"

"No, thank you," Tory responded. She was grateful for his concern but anxious to leave and unable to understand why Jesse had become such a slowpoke. He had kept his mustache and she could not look at him without thinking how handsome he was, but such thoughts did not distract her from her real concern for more than a few seconds at a time. She wanted to ask him how long it might take to extract a confession from Gerry and send Eldrin's men away, but she knew he was no better at foreseeing the future than she.

Jesse watched Tory shift in her chair again and suddenly felt too guilty about keeping her waiting to continue the ploy a moment longer. He promptly rose and escorted her from the room. Their horses were saddled when they reached the barn and they were riding toward Lalo's within minutes of leaving the house.

"Seems like we've been traveling forever, doesn't it?" he teased.

Jesse's high spirits made Tory feel all the more glum. She tried to smile, but doubted that her lips had moved. "No one saw anything out of the ordinary last night, did they?" she asked.

"Apparently not, or I would have been awakened."

416

"But you weren't in your room," Tory reminded him fearfully.

"Will you please stop worrying? Believe me, if any of the hands had caught someone prowling around, they would have come and found me. Now let's just enjoy the ride to Lalo's. It isn't far and we'll cross some of the prettiest land we own. I'm taking you down by the river rather than on the road to town and no one will bother us."

Tory wanted to believe him, but despite the beauty of the morning, she was consumed with dread. She felt the same horrible sense of impending doom that had plagued her when they had been Araña's captives. They had miraculously escaped harm then, but how many times could a person cheat death before their fate finally overtook them? she wondered.

"I love you, Jesse," she blurted out.

They were riding side by side and Jesse leaned over to give her shoulder a squeeze. "Thank you. I love you, too."

"No, I really mean it," Tory rushed to explain. "If something happens, if things don't work out as we hope—"

"That's enough, Tory," Jesse ordered sharply. "I can't tell you how happy I'm going to be when you finally learn to trust me."

"It's not that I don't trust you!"

Exasperated, Jesse looked away. There was a cluster of oak trees ahead, and while he caught no more than a brief glimpse, he thought he saw someone moving behind them. He drew Río to an abrupt halt. "Wait a minute, Tory," he called, but rather than stop, she merely turned in her saddle to look back at him and kept right on riding.

"Tory!" Jesse shouted, but before the sound of her name had died on the morning breeze she was hit by a bullet fired from the oaks. Blood began to stream down her face and had Río not responded to the touch of Jesse's heels with the speed that made him such a fine horse, he would never have caught her before she toppled from her saddle. Rapid gunfire now began to spew forth from the trees, proving that several assailants were hidden there. Fearing they could not

417

escape the area without suffering further harm, Jesse urged Río toward the small outcropping of rocks that offered the only hope of protection on the open range.

With Tory limp in his arms, he leapt from his saddle. A hasty slap to his gray gelding's rump sent Río racing away after Tory's bay while Jesse dragged the unconscious young woman behind the rocks. He then discovered that they provided such scant cover he had to lie flat rather than risk a head injury himself. He knew someone would soon come to investigate the source of the gunfire and prayed they would not waste a second riding to their rescue.

"Tory," he cried. She had lost her hat and her hair was so soaked with blood that he could not tell if her scalp had merely been grazed or if a bullet had pierced her skull. Either way she would soon die from loss of blood and he ripped off the bandana loosely knotted around his neck and pressed it against her head. That she had been unconscious from the moment of the bullet's impact terrified him, and, remembering their last conversation, he wondered if she had had a premonition of death. If so, she had wanted him to know that she loved him, but completely misunderstanding the urgency of her vow, he had accused her of not trusting him. He would never forgive himself for being so stupid.

He felt for the pulse in her throat but was only slightly relieved when he found it was faint but steady. Still keeping the bandana in place, he pulled her against his side and drew his Colt. He dared not waste any ammunition returning the fire that had him pinned to the ground, but if, as Ivan had reported, there were only three men, he knew he had a damn good chance of killing them all if they left the security of the trees. The only problem was, they had showed no sign of coming out into the open as yet.

"Stay with me, sweetheart," Jesse begged. "Help will reach us soon." From where they lay, the continued noise of gunfire was deafening, and Jesse hoped that it could be heard for miles in every direction so help would not be long in coming.

"I love you, Tory," he whispered, but she could not respond.

*　　　*　　　*

"Let's get out of here!" George shouted. "Tory was hit and the longer we hang around the better the odds are that we'll get shot, too."

Tad took careful aim at a narrow crevice between the rocks and fired again. "We have to have proof that the bitch is dead," he reminded him. "Start circling around to the right. Hank, you take the left. Lambert can't shoot us all."

Equally anxious to get away without being killed, Hank looked over Tad's head to George. "Let's make this fast."

George cast a wistful glance toward their horses tethered a few yards away. Spooked by the noise, they were dancing about and trying to pull free. "We better," he agreed, and, dropping into a low crouch, he began to make his way toward the couple they had targeted for death.

Jesse had been waiting for just such a move and shot George before he had gotten six feet from the trees. The wounded man let out a sharp cry, spun to the side, and fell. Jesse turned his pistol on Hank then, but he dove for cover and escaped being hit. With agonizing slowness, George rolled over and dragged himself back toward the oaks that protected his friends. Unwilling to fire on a man who appeared to already be mortally wounded, Jesse let him go.

Preferring the out-of-doors to the confines of the house, Luke Bernay was leaning against the corral talking with one of the Lambert hands when the sound of distant gunfire reached their ears. "What the hell is that?" Bernay asked.

"Oh, Jesus!" the man cried. "Jesse and his woman are on their way to the Ruiz ranch!" He took off running for the barn.

"Saddle our horses, too, I'll get the others," Luke shouted after him. He ran back into the house and nearly collided with Ivan, who was just on his way out. Ivan then heard the echoing of shots, too, and his eyes widened in fear.

"Is that MacDonald and his men?" he asked.

"Hell, I don't know who it is, but it looks like Jesse and

419

Tory are right in the middle of it. Let's go."

The commotion in the yard brought Gerry outside, and while the prospect of participating in a gun battle terrified him, he dared not miss it, either. Then he was seized with a truly exhilarating possibility. What if Jesse were killed? Hoping against hope that Jesse might already be dead, he returned to the house for his pistol and then leapt astride his horse the instant it was saddled. He paid scant attention to the visiting geologist and his little friend as he and the men who had been stationed near the house raced across the open range.

By the time they reached the scene of the fight, the hands who had been posted along the ranch's southern boundary had arrived. With the grouping of oak trees offering the only cover, they were unable to reach Jesse's position and were stymied as to how to proceed. They looked to Gerry for direction, but he was as lost as they. He could see it would be asking the hands to commit suicide to have them rush the men barricaded in the trees, and he refused to even consider risking his life to lead them.

"What should we do?" he asked with a hapless shrug.

Nothing about Gerard Chambers had impressed Luke favorably, and when none of the Lambert hands stepped forward to assume command of the volatile situation from the young man, he did. "Someone needs to go back to the house and hitch up whatever wagons you have. We can overturn them and make barricades of our own. Well, go on, git!"

Luke was a stranger to most of the men, but his suggestion made such good sense that half a dozen left immediately while an equal number followed his second order to search for whatever ditch or boulder they could find for cover and begin protecting Jesse and his fiancée. Luke then rode as close as he dared get to the rocks shielding the embattled pair, dropped to the ground, and crawled toward them. His heart in his throat, Ivan followed him.

Having badly miscalculated the amount of time they would have to get away, Tad and Hank began shifting position constantly in order to provide fire over a full three hundred sixty degrees. They had plenty of ammunition, and were such good shots they posed a real threat despite the smallness of their number. George was hit in the side and lay curled up clutching the wound. He writhed in pain each time one of his companions stepped over him.

"We've got to make a break for it!" Hank shouted.

While they were surrounded, the ranchhands appeared to be too disorganized to do them much harm and Tad kept firing at them. "We will, but let's even the odds first. Then we'll make a break for the river."

Hank glanced over his shoulder at George. "What about him?"

Tad swore as he missed an easy shot. "We'll kiss him good-bye."

Hank did not want to abandon his wounded friend, but when it looked like the choice was going to be between his life and George's, he was prepared to do it.

Gerry stayed back with the horses, content to watch and wait until he became too curious about Jesse to remain where he was. He then moved even further back, circled around, and started inching his way up behind the rocks until he got close enough to see Jesse was talking with his two friends. While his fiancée looked badly hurt, Gerry was disappointed to find his stepbrother still appeared to be in the best of health. "Damn him," he swore under his breath.

He had despised both Jesse and Lamar Lambert since the day his mother had married into their family. He was nearly choking on the bitter taste of that hatred now. In his view, he and his mother would have been much better off on their own, but at only ten years old, he had been unable to convince her of that. She had wanted another husband, but why had she chosen to wed a coward like Lamar Lambert who had refused to fight in the war that had left her a widow? Lamar hadn't deserved a courageous woman like Zina, and Gerry had not shed a single tear when his stepfather had died. He would not weep for Jesse, either.

The wagons would soon arrive, and with Jesse's friends

using them for a barrier, Gerry was certain they would swiftly get him and his fiancée to safety. If he was going to act, it would have to be as the wagons made their approach, when everyone's attention was focused on them and the angle of a stray shot would not be noticed. He took a deep breath and aimed for Jesse. Now all he had to do was stay cool until the ground began to tremble and he felt the wagons getting close.

"I shot one," Jesse told Luke and Ivan. "I think you were right about there just being three of them left. Now there's only two, but I want to take them alive. I've got a lot of questions only they can answer."

Ivan was positive that two men could shoot them just as dead as an entire army, but he thought better of speaking such a dismal thought aloud. He added his handkerchief to Jesse's bandana, but Tory was still bleeding profusely. "Let's get her out of here before we worry about asking questions."

"We've sent for wagons," Luke explained.

Jesse had been able to report on his situation, but he couldn't find the words to describe Tory's condition or his terror over it. With Luke and Ivan there to return Tad's fire, he clung to her and prayed the wagons would get there in time. When he heard a rumbling sound in the distance, he raised up slightly.

"Get down!" Luke scolded. "You don't want to get your head blown off now!"

Ivan didn't, either, but he eased himself over slightly to give Jesse and Tory more room. When a bullet tore through his hat and sent it sailing out over the rocks, it took him a moment to realize the shot had come from behind them rather than the trees. He looked over his shoulder to scan the terrain and caught sight of a man ducking out of view. He was behind a slope that didn't offer much in the way of protection, but Ivan was positive he was the one who had fired at him.

That did not make a bit of sense as Ivan had no enemies on the Lambert ranch, and he came to the swift and sickening conclusion that the bullet had been meant for someone else.

422

Luke was a newcomer, too, so that left Jesse and Tory. Who could be firing at them? Gerry seemed the most likely possibility. Could he have fired at Jesse and missed?

"Luke . . ." Ivan called in a frantic whisper. "Look behind us. Someone's shooting at us."

Luke had to reposition himself carefully, but then he stared out over the range. The wagons were in sight, their wheels bouncing high off the ground as their drivers kept whipping the teams to maintain their reckless pace. They were only fifty feet away when Luke saw a man raise up from the direction Ivan had indicated. He held his breath, expecting the man to stand and fire toward the trees to provide cover for the wagon, but when he recognized Gerry aiming right at the group huddled behind the rocks, he fired first. If he had needed proof of Gerry's guilt, the man's intended treachery had just provided it. When the nefarious young man slumped to the ground, Luke was satisfied that he had put a stop to one menace at least, and he turned his attention to the wagons.

"Over here!" he shouted, but the drivers were already headed their way. The first wagon skidded to a halt in front of the rocks. The driver leapt down, and while Luke and Ivan provided covering fire, unhitched the team. The second wagon reached them then, and the driver helped overturn the first. That barrier in place, he urged his team around behind the rocky redoubt. The final two wagons were overturned on opposite sides of the trees. The ranchhands moved into place behind them and shouted for the men who had ambushed Jesse and Tory to surrender.

Rather than come out with their hands in the air as ordered, Tad and Hank broke for the rear. They ran toward their horses, firing as they went, but neither man reached his mount alive. Struck several times, they fell dead not three apart.

Cautiously waiting to make certain there were not more men lurking in the trees, the hands held their fire. After a few minutes of silence, one brave soul ventured out from behind his wagon and ran in a zigzag pattern toward the oaks. When he reached them unharmed, he discovered the badly wounded George, easily disarmed him, and shouted to his friends that the danger had passed.

Luke breathed a deep sigh of relief and rose to his feet. A quick glance at the men showed none had been hit, and he did not have to tell them to right the wagons. As they began that chore, he offered Jesse a word of encouragement. He then led Ivan to where Gerry lay. He bent down and felt for a pulse in his neck. "He's dead."

"Oh, Jesus," Ivan swore. "How are we ever going to explain this?"

Luke rose and looked back toward the men who were now rehitching the teams to the wagons. "We can tell the truth," he offered, "and break his mother's heart. Or we can just say he died defending his stepbrother and Tory. I've been a stickler for the truth all my life, or at least I thought I was, but tracking Jesse forced me to consider several thorny questions. Maybe the truth isn't always the best choice, just as the justice the courts dispense isn't, either. Well, what shall we say happened?"

Ivan had never been presented with such a difficult question. "Shouldn't we let Jesse decide?"

"He's covered in his woman's blood. Do you really think he's up to making any decisions?"

Ivan glanced back toward Jesse, who was sitting up now and holding Tory cradled across his lap. "You think she'll make it?"

"I sure hope so."

Ivan looked down at Gerry's body. He had seen only a few dead people in his life and he was always struck by how still they were. They didn't look as though they were merely sleeping and might soon awaken. They looked completely and utterly devoid of life. "I sure as hell hate to call this bastard a hero," he said. "Let's at least tell Jesse the truth, even if we don't tell anyone else."

Luke smiled slightly. "Fine, you get the 'hero's' feet and I'll take his shoulders. Let's take his carcass back to the house along with the others."

Ivan quickly complied and they carried Gerry's body to the wagon already holding the slain gunmen. The ranchhands appeared shocked to see Gerry had been killed, but none showed any grief over it. That told Luke a great deal, for he had seen plenty of grown men cry over the death of someone they admired. Clearly, Gerry had not enjoyed much in the way of respect from his men, which did not surprise either Luke or Ivan one bit.

Jesse had been told one of the men who had ambushed them was alive, but he did not want to leave Tory alone for even the few minutes that interrogating him would require. As soon as he lifted her into the back of the wagon that had shielded them, he called down to Luke, "Ask the injured man if he knows who shot Marshal Kane. Try and find out if he knows anything about the accident that killed Tory's father or what happened to her housekeeper. Offer him a doctor's attention, but see if you can get those answers from him first. Then bring him on in. I want him kept alive."

"I'll help, Luke," Ivan volunteered. "But wait, there's something you have to know."

Jesse doubted that. "Later." He sat down to again take his beloved in his arms and called to the driver, "Let's go."

"No, wait!" Ivan ran alongside the wagon yelling that Gerry was dead. Jesse's expression conveyed his disbelief, but Ivan nodded. "It's true. Gerry's dead!" Certain he had gotten his message across, he ceased chasing the wagon, but he knew he and Luke would still have a great deal of explaining to do once they got back to the house. Realizing he might need his hat for evidence, he went back to get it. Sure enough, it was clear that a bullet had passed through it back to front.

"Just look at this," he told Luke.

Luke grabbed the incriminating hat and jammed it down on Ivan's head. "Since Tad MacDonald shot Gerry, you don't need to wave that hat around."

"Oh, that's right," Ivan agreed sheepishly.

"Come on, let's see if we can get the truth out of the wounded man."

Luke and Ivan walked over to where George lay. He had been pulled from the trees, but due to the seriousness of his wound, he had yet to be placed in the last wagon. He was barely conscious when Luke knelt at his side.

"We're going to get you to a doctor, son," Luke promised. "You just hold on a little longer and you'll be fine."

All George heard was the thundering beat of his own pulse in his ears. Recognizing Luke, he reached out a bloody hand and clutched his arm, but his grip was weak. He understood he was supposed to hold on, but he did not believe that he could.

"Son?" Luke tried again, but it was obvious the man couldn't speak. "Come on, boys, let's get him into a wagon and take him up to the house. Jesse wants him alive." He had to pry George's hand from his arm before he could stand, but he then made certain the badly injured man was lifted carefully into the back of the closest wagon. Knowing he would have a rough ride, he climbed in with him.

"You take my horse back for me," Luke called down to Ivan. "I'm going to do what I can to keep this poor fellow breathing."

Ivan waved, and as soon as the wagon had begun to roll, he headed toward the horses. Men were standing around recounting their part in the brief but bloody battle, but he did not feel like swapping tales with anyone. He was too concerned about Tory, and worried that somehow he and Luke were going to be charged with Gerry's murder.

"Mayleen!" he recalled with sudden terror. "Oh, dear God, how will I ever tell Mayleen what happened?" Hoping to reach her before the wagon bearing Gerry's body arrived at the house, he mounted his horse, grabbed the reins of Luke's, and took off at a gallop. He had no idea what he was going to say, but he knew he had to beat that wagon there to say it.

"I simply don't understand," Zina kept repeating. "Why would anyone want to ambush Jesse?" She wrung her hands and walked to and fro in front of the barn. "What's taking them so long?"

Mayleen didn't know how to reply since she knew neither Jesse nor Tory wanted Zina to know they were fugitives who were being pursued. "It hasn't been long," she contradicted unconvincingly. She was as worried as Zina, but went to the corral and hung on tightly to the top rail rather than pace. She admired both Jesse and Tory enormously and feared they might have been murdered. She was frantic that something might have happened to Ivan, too. He had shown a great deal of courage of late, but, still, he was a professor, not a gunman.

The two women waited for what seemed like an hour for the wagons to return. Mayleen wished she had been up and dressed in time to go with them. Being left out of what could be the final chapter in the greatest adventure of her life was horribly disappointing, but she also felt that someone ought to be with Zina. Torn by conflicting emotions, she clung to the top rail and watched for the men's return. When she spotted a lone rider in the distance, she called to Zina.

"Someone's coming!"

At a distance, Ivan recognized the two women and when he drew near, their anxious expressions did not make his task any easier. He was only a minute or two ahead of the wagons and so he knew he couldn't hem and haw about what he had to say. Zina and Mayleen both hurried toward him as he dismounted and dropped the reins of Luke's horse.

He yanked his hat from his head and addressed Zina. "I'm afraid I have bad news for you, Mrs. Lambert."

Zina raised her hand to her throat. "Oh, no, has something happened to Jesse?"

Ivan glanced toward Mayleen, wanting to see her reaction as he described what had happened. "No, ma'am. Some men who'd followed Jesse and Patricia from the Arizona Territory ambushed them. She's badly hurt, but Jesse's fine. I'm afraid it's your son. He was shot and killed as he was defending his stepbrother."

The horror of Ivan's message beyond comprehension,

Zina stared at him for a long moment before she let out an agonized moan that soon became a high-pitched wail. Ivan grabbed the grief-stricken woman around the waist and held on, but his gaze was locked with Mayleen's. Tears welled up in her eyes and spilled over her lashes, but she was obviously taking the news of Gerry's death far more calmly than his mother.

"Has someone sent for a doctor?" he asked.

Mayleen nodded. "When the men came for the wagons." She wiped away her tears and began to pat Zina's back with a soothing rhythm. She opened her mouth to assure the distraught woman that everything would be all right, but realized that for Zina, it never would be again and remained quiet.

Hearing their mistress's cry, the women who worked in the kitchen came running to tend her, and Ivan stepped back to permit them to do so. Nearing collapse, Zina allowed herself to be led into the house by her sympathetic servants, but he could still hear her sorrowful sobs from where he stood. The wagons came into view then, and he took Mayleen's hand to draw her back against the corral where she would not be in any danger of being run over.

"Tell me what really happened," Mayleen demanded.

Ivan looked down at her. Perhaps she deserved the truth, but he was determined not to reveal it. "Gerry was shot and killed," he repeated. "That's all there is to it."

"Ivan Carrows, don't you dare leave me out of this," Mayleen complained. "We've come this far together. Don't leave me out now."

The first wagon carrying Jesse and Tory rolled into the yard then and, grateful they'd been interrupted, Ivan pulled Mayleen along with him as he went toward it. "Tory's going to need help and Zina won't be able to provide it. Stop imagining there's more to Gerry's death. There isn't."

"Promise?"

"I promise," Ivan assured her. That Mayleen was not sobbing uncontrollably made him feel so good he couldn't resist giving her a fast kiss. "Now let's see what we can do for Tory."

428

Mayleen preceded him to the rear of the wagon, but when the driver lowered the tailgate and she got her first glimpse of Tory, all she saw was the bright red blood that covered the unconscious young woman's head and shoulders and she fainted in Ivan's arms.

"Sorry," he murmured to Jesse, but Jesse was far too worried about Tory's survival to give a damn about what had happened to Mayleen.

Chapter 28

While Jesse waited for the doctor to arrive from El Paso, he wouldn't let anyone else touch Tory. He would not even allow anyone to come near her. He had carried her to her room, laid her on the bed, and removed her blood-dampened clothes. He had bathed her face and shoulders so when she awakened she would be as pretty as always. Because Lalo had neglected to buy her a nightgown, he used one of his own shirts for that purpose. He rolled up the sleeves and kissed her hands, but despite his solicitous attentions, she remained as limp as a well-loved rag doll.

Her wound had almost stopped seeping blood, but rather than a hopeful sign, Jesse was afraid she might merely have little blood left to lose. He could not bring himself to examine the gash closely for fear of what he might find. He knew people who had been shot in the head either did not survive, or if they did, they were never the same, and he did not want to see either tragic fate befall the woman he loved. After tucking her in, he sat on the edge of the bed, held her hand, and told her how much he loved her. When the physician knocked on the door, he was reluctant even then to leave her, and bent down to kiss her pale lips before drawing away.

Dr. Haynes had tended Lamar Lambert during the brief illness before his death, and as their eyes met, Jesse could not help but recall that their last association had been at an equally difficult time. He did not want to see it reach the same heartbreaking conclusion, however. Unable to describe what had happened to Tory, he simply swung the door open wide and gestured toward the bed.

An immensely practical man, Lewis Haynes wasted no time in greeting the obviously healthy man and hurried to the bed of Jesse's fiancée, removed her makeshift bandage, and studied her ugly scalp wound for several moments before looking up.

"This is one lucky young woman."

"Yes, she is," Jesse agreed in a shaken whisper.

"The bullet creased her skull, but didn't pierce it. She's likely to be unconscious for several hours, but don't you worry. She'll be fine. I'll sew up the tear in her scalp and leave you some laudanum to ease her pain when she wakes. Lost quite a bit of blood, didn't she?"

Jesse nodded and came to the foot of the bed. He didn't really want to watch the doctor work, but he would have felt as though he was abandoning Tory had he turned away. "I'll take real good care of her," he promised. "I'll see she gets plenty of rest and lots of nourishing food."

Touched by Jesse's devotion, Dr. Haynes could not help but smile. "She's not going to feel like getting up for a while so it won't be any trouble to see she gets her rest. As for the food, she might not be hungry, either, but make sure she eats and has plenty to drink. She likes tea, doesn't she?"

"I think so."

"I thought you were going to marry this woman."

"I am."

"But you don't know if she drinks tea?"

Although that was a ridiculously simple question, Jesse wasn't certain of the answer. Then he remembered Tory had had a cup of tea at Lalo's. "Yes, she drinks tea. It's just that we've been traveling and haven't been able to enjoy the best of meals."

"Nobody expected to see you home so soon, son."

That all of El Paso thought him a thief who'd be confined to prison for decades wasn't something Jesse wanted to discuss. "I should never have been away."

Lewis nodded sympathetically, then gave his full attention

to his patient as he stitched up the slash in her scalp. "Missed her forehead," he remarked as he tied the last knot. "There'll be no visible scar. She's a mighty pretty lady. What's her name?"

Jesse hesitated a moment before again concealing Tory's identity. "Patricia Earl."

The friendly physician wrapped Tory's head in a fresh bandage, packed up his bag, and then washed his hands in the basin. "I'll come back tomorrow. If she feels dizzy, it'll be because of the blood she lost. She'll soon recover. Don't let her fret over it."

"I won't."

Lewis picked up his bag and started for the door. "Now where's my other patient?"

Jesse had no idea. "In the bunkhouse, I suppose." Tory was resting comfortably, but he still hated to leave her. "I'll come with you. I've some questions to ask him. I hope you can keep him alive long enough to answer."

"That's up to God, son, not me."

"Yes, of course," Jesse agreed. As they walked to the bunkhouse, Jesse mentioned that his stepbrother had been killed. Naturally shocked to hear that news, Lewis halted abruptly.

"I imagine I should see Zina before I go. Poor woman. Gerry was always in one kind of trouble or another. She'll miss him terribly, though."

"Yes, I know." While Gerry would certainly not be widely mourned, Jesse knew Zina would keep his memory alive in her heart. "He was an attentive son," he offered as the only honest praise he could.

"Well, God bless him for that then."

Luke had had George Flood laid on the first bunk in the bunkhouse, but he had been unable to give the injured man much in the way of medical care. When Jesse introduced Dr. Haynes, Luke shook his hand and whispered an aside. "He sure looks bad off to me, but maybe you can make him comfortable enough to talk."

There were several ranchhands standing nearby gawking, and the physician shooed them outside before he examined his patient. He cut away his shirt in order to have a clear view of the wound in his side, but as he removed the bloody garment, he noticed the swelling in George's right arm. After Lewis removed the handkerchief from his forearm, he gestured for Jesse to come close.

"The wound in his side will probably kill him in a few hours, but that's not his only problem. He's got blood poisoning, but there's no point in amputating an arm from a dying man. Of course, if by some miracle he survives the gunshot, and I haven't amputated his arm, it will be too late and the blood poisoning will kill him. It's a difficult choice. I'll let you decide."

The prospect of watching Lewis saw off an arm was more than Jesse could bear. Luke looked equally sickened. "Wait a minute," Jesse asked. "You're saying he might survive the gunshot wound, but he'll surely die if he keeps his arm?"

"Yes, you could look at it that way. Without the arm he has a chance, if a slim one, but with it, he's a dead man. Shall I prepare for the amputation?"

"No," Jesse replied firmly. "If he's so badly hurt he'll probably die, then losing an arm to boot will surely kill him. Just help him rest easy. Besides, as you said, the question of whether a man lives or dies is in God's hands. Let's leave it there. If he feels up to talking, call me."

Jesse left the bunkhouse with the warm, wet stench of George's blood still in his nostrils. He entered the barn and found Rob, one of the men who had been guarding the perimeter of the ranch the previous night, giving Río a good brushing. He walked up to him. "How did those men get past you and the others?" he asked.

Rob swallowed hard and started to back away. "Well now, Mr. Lambert, I don't rightly know. All I can say for sure is that they didn't get by me. I can promise you that. We were spread out kinda thin, and they must have snuck through our line down by the river. We tried our best, sir. You know that we did."

Rob was so nervous, it was plain he feared Jesse was going to hit him, but Jesse was too emotionally drained to become violent. "I appreciate what you did. See the others get a chance to catch up on their sleep. There won't be any need to stand guard tonight."

"Yes, sir, thank you, I'll do that," the man replied with a relieved grin. "How is Miss Earl?"

"The doctor says she'll be fine."

"The boys will be glad to hear it. That's real good news."

"It sure is," Jesse agreed. He turned away and reentered the house. As he walked toward Tory's room, he passed Zina's and heard her crying. She had sobbed for days when his father had passed away, so he expected her to cry twice as long for Gerry. Not up to offering his sympathy now, he returned to Tory's room where he found Mayleen and Ivan seated at the foot of her bed. Their hands were folded in their laps and they were observing the unconscious woman sleep with a touching devotion.

At first, Jesse was annoyed to find them there, but realizing he was on edge, he caught himself before he scolded them for entering Tory's bedroom without his permission. "Thank you for keeping an eye on her. I'll take over now."

Ivan leapt to his feet. He and Luke had agreed that Jesse ought to be told the truth about how Gerry had died, but the strain in Jesse's expression convinced him this was not the time for such an unsettling discussion. "We want to be of some real help to you. Just tell us what to do."

After a moment's hesitation, Jesse thought of the perfect task. "Do you think you could go into El Paso and arrange for Gerry's funeral? Eduardo Ruiz owns the closest ranch as you're going toward town. He's a good friend of mine. Tell him what's happened and he'll tell you how to arrange the funeral."

"Consider it done," Ivan assured him. He had not had a drink since Jesse had deserted them at the Mexican *cantina* and it pleased him to realize that he was getting along just fine without relying on alcohol. He reached for Mayleen's hand, but she hung back.

"I'm sorry about fainting earlier, but I can stay if you need help with Tory," she offered.

Jesse shook his head. "I want to take care of her myself." He was relieved when she did not argue. He bid the couple good-bye and resumed his place on the bed beside Tory. "You're going to be just fine, sweetheart. In a few days you ought to feel up to dancing at your own wedding. I can't wait for that!" He doubted many families hosted a wake and a wedding within a week's time, but he knew he would not be able to wait any longer than that to make Tory his wife.

Her bloody clothes were still in a heap in the corner where he had tossed them. Wanting the whole lot burned rather than laundered, he searched the pockets before giving them to a maidservant for disposal. When he found Araña's neatly braided hair coiled within a handkerchief, he was both startled and disgusted that she had had it with her. Her other pockets were empty, but he toyed only briefly with the thought of tossing out the braid with her clothes.

Perhaps she had hoped the strange talisman would bring her good luck. If so, a case could be made that it was totally ineffective. Then again, she had received only a superficial wound rather than a fatal one. That was damn good luck in Jesse's view. Unhappy about sharing Tory with an Apache guardian angel, he twisted the glossy black braid in his hands, but he could not bring himself to rip it apart. Araña was dead, but if there was even the remotest possibility a lock of his hair had saved Tory's life, he was not going to demand that she part with it. Instead, he put it in her hand and closed her fingers over it.

Finally growing weary, he pulled off his boots and stretched out beside her. He slept for nearly an hour before Luke came to get him. George Flood was drifting in and out of consciousness and Dr. Haynes had said he would not last much longer. Jesse glanced up at the sun as he strode toward the bunkhouse. Judging by its position overhead, it was early afternoon, but he felt as though he had lived ten lifetimes since Tory had been shot. She was still resting quietly and he hoped comfortably, but he did not intend to be away from her for more than a few minutes.

George's eyes were open when Jesse reached him, but he gave no indication that he saw him. "Did he tell you his name?" Jesse asked.

"George, something," Dr. Haynes reported. "I couldn't

436

make it out."

"George," Jesse called softly, "we're doing our best to help you. Can you try and help us?"

George turned his head away.

That was scarcely an encouraging sign, but rather than berate the dying man for his rudeness, Jesse walked around the bunk to again face him. "I need to know who shot Marshal Kane, George. Do you know?"

This time George closed his eyes and moaned softly.

Discouraged, Jesse turned to the doctor and Luke. "Is this really what you two call a talkative mood?"

Both men responded with embarrassed shrugs.

"Look at me, George," Jesse ordered sharply, and surprisingly, he did, inspiring Jesse to try a new tack. "Earl Crandell's death was no accident. He was murdered. Were you there?"

George frowned slightly, deepening the glaze of pain reflected in his pale-blue eyes. "Crandell?" he whispered.

"Yes! Tory's father," Jesse prompted. "Tell us how Crandell died."

George tried to lick his lips, and the doctor stepped forward to help him take a sip of water. Refreshed, George looked straight up at Jesse. "Paul said, 'Make it look like an accident.'"

"That's Paul Stafford?"

"Yes."

Jesse turned to his two companions. "Did you hear him?"

They nodded.

"So you stampeded his team?" Jesse offered.

George nodded slightly.

"What about the Crandell's housekeeper, Consuelo? Where's she?"

That question appeared to confuse George completely and he closed his eyes again. Jesse grabbed his shoulder and gave him a slight shake to regain his attention. "Come on, George. The housekeeper was called away. Where did she go?"

"Home," George finally replied.

Because discovering what had become of the housekeeper

437

was insignificant compared to the other answer he needed, Jesse renewed his quest to discover what had happened to Marshal Kane. "Someone shot the marshal who was supposed to take Tory to Prescott. Was it you? Tell us the truth, George. It's too late for lies to save you now."

Again George closed his eyes. He did not need to be told that he was dying. He could feel his life ebbing away with each breath. He was only twenty-six, and that seemed much too young to die, but he lacked the strength to fight for more time. He heard Jesse's question, but it did not concern him. The man kept on badgering him for the truth, though, when all he wanted was the peace in which to die.

"Tad," George finally whispered, hoping to make Jesse go away. "Nathan and Tad."

"They were Eldrin Stafford's men, weren't they?" Jesse pressed him to add.

George nodded, and then with a long, weary sigh, he died.

Dr. Haynes came forward and quickly pronounced the injured man dead. "I'll be your witness should you need one," he volunteered. "From what I understood, someone named Paul Stafford ordered Earl Crandell killed, and Nathan and Tad shot Marshal Kane. Anything else I should have heard in this man's deathbed testimony?"

Jesse glanced toward Luke. "Just because Tad and Nathan worked for Eldrin Stafford doesn't prove he ordered them to shoot Kane, does it?"

Luke frowned thoughtfully. "Well now, I suppose some smooth-talking lawyer might be able to convince a jury that Tad and Nathan went around murdering righteous citizens on their own, but I'll never believe it. I met Eldrin Stafford. It's a sure bet that he's the one who ordered Kane's death."

Jesse had had every intention of telling Luke that he knew who he was, but it was plain the tracker had already dropped all pretense of being Jed Magrew. "But we've no proof," Jesse repeated.

"The statement of a dying man is usually believed," Dr. Haynes reminded them.

"As well it should be," Jesse said, "but I'll not add anything to George's remarks. Lies sent me to prison and I'll

438

not play the same underhanded trick on any man, not even a snake like Eldrin Stafford."

When Jesse got no argument on that point, he left the bunkhouse. He summoned a couple of the men standing near the corral and asked them to take George's body into town. When they mentioned that Ivan and Mayleen had transported Gerry's corpse to the undertakers, it occurred to him that he ought to be expecting a visit from the sheriff and he had yet to secure the proof of his innocence.

"Stay in town for the night if you like," he told the men. "You've a right to some fun after this grim business."

Jesse walked back to the bunkhouse to a chorus of praise from his hands. He leaned in the door, and finding Luke and Lewis still discussing George's last words, he hurried them along. "I'd like for you to see Zina, Doc. Then if you could wait a few minutes while I ask her about a necklace Gerry gave her, I'd appreciate it. You need to be there, too, Luke."

"Wouldn't miss it," Luke exclaimed.

Zina's room was veiled in darkness despite the sunniness of the late-summer afternoon. Still weeping uncontrollably she was seated in the rocking chair where she had once rocked her only child to sleep. Jesse nodded and the two maids who had been attending her hurriedly left the room. He then knelt by her side. He had never called her Mother, and could not bring himself to do so now.

He had meant to explain how he and Tory had come to be ambushed, but realized that would only make Zina despise the woman he loved. While he would not lie to send a man to prison, he saw no reason not to stretch the truth a little now. After all, Zina had never seen her son for the weak-willed man he was and Jesse would not speak ill of him now.

"Patricia and I were followed from Arizona by men who caught up with us this morning . . ." he began. "They probably would have come right on up to the house and knocked on the door had they not seen us on our way to Lalo's. I know for Gerry to save my life at the cost of his own seems like a terrible price."

Zina blotted her eyes with her sodden handkerchief and reached out to touch Jesse's cheek with a fond caress.

439

"Please don't even think that. I love you, too, Jesse. I can't look at you without remembering your dear father. I don't blame you for what happened today. The pattern of my life has been a very sad one, and you're not responsible for this latest tragedy. Saving you was the bravest thing Gerry ever did. I'm trying to think of it that way. He died doing something important, just like his father."

Jesse patted her hand lightly. He had not expected her to compare Gerry's demise with a Confederate officer's death in the war, but if it eased her mind, he was all for it. "Yes, that's a fine thought." After a brief pause to allow Zina to cope with a fresh torrent of tears, Jesse pressed for the evidence he needed. "You were wearing a cameo-and-pearl necklace the other night. Can you tell me where it is?"

Zina looked puzzled for a moment, but then nodded toward her dresser. "It's in a velvet bag in the top drawer. Gerry told me Mayleen had wanted it. I hope you don't plan to give it to her now."

"No, of course not," Jesse assured her. He rose and went to the dresser. Realizing what he would have to say would provide additional anguish for Zina, he hesitated a moment before pulling open the drawer. The velvet bag was nestled in the corner among her lacy lingerie, and he laid it on top of the dresser before loosening the drawstring. As he withdrew the exquisite necklace, he felt both a surge of heartbreak for his stepmother and a wave of elation for what it would prove. He motioned for Luke to come near, and dropped it into his hand.

Now realizing why Mrs. Tribett had been so anxious to have her necklace returned, the tracker held it with a reverent awe. It was the most magnificent piece of jewelry he had ever seen. The pearls glowed with a lovely iridescent sheen and the profile carved in delicate relief on the oval of coral was of a young woman with the beauty of a goddess. There was absolutely no doubt in his mind as to the rightful owner.

"Do you want to tell her," he asked Jesse, "or shall I?"

"I'll do it." Jesse returned to his stepmother's side and with the utmost sensitivity explained that while Gerry had wished her to have it, the necklace had been taken at gunpoint from a passenger while Gerry and Conrad Werner had robbed the stage. It was the evidence he needed to prove his innocence and would have to be returned to its owner in Tucson to clear his name.

Zina's eyes were already filled with tears, but they now took on a bewildered light. Jesse's story had the unmistakable ring of truth, but then, hadn't Gerry's explanation of the crime always sounded equally sincere? Her head ached with confusion until she realized the necklace was the key. Not only did it prove Jesse's innocence, it also sealed Gerry's guilt.

She now had to face another terrible truth: that her son had been a charming liar rather than the honest man he had wished her to believe. She did not know which was worse— that Gerry was no better than a common thief or that he had allowed Jesse to take the blame. Deeply ashamed, she glanced over toward Dr. Haynes and then at the man she knew as Jed Magrew.

"You knew about this?" she asked in a hushed whisper.

"Yes, ma'am, I did," Luke admitted. "I was sent from the authorities at the Yuma prison," he added, without explaining that it was Jesse he had come to get, not the necklace he still held. "Jesse's served four years for a robbery he didn't commit. Time's precious, and there's no way to give those years back to him. If you would help us restore his good name, though, it would undo at least part of the wrong your son did him. I think you owe Jesse that much, don't you?"

"You mean I have a choice?" Zina inquired.

Shocked by her question, Luke rephrased his words. "Well, now that you ask, ma'am, no, you don't. The necklace is stolen property and I have to return it to the rightful owner. I was just hoping that you'd be gracious about it." He picked up the velvet bag, dropped the necklace inside, and tied the drawstring securely.

Devastated anew, Zina wept silently for a long moment before looking up at Jesse. "I should have known," she lamented softly, "but I believed whatever Gerry told me.

441

Everything always seemed so logical coming from him." She paused a moment, and then described Gerry's latest version of the crime. "He lied about the necklace, too, said he bought it with his winnings at cards. Would he have had to go back to Tucson for trial, Mr. Magrew?"

"Yes, ma'am, and without Miss Tyler's alibi, and with this necklace found in your possession, he would have been found guilty for sure."

Zina nodded. "He would never have survived prison," she mused thoughtfully. "He was never tough like you, Jesse. It's a blessing he died today. In a way, risking his life to save yours repaid at least a small part of the debt he owed you. Will it be possible to keep all this quiet for a while at least? I've no reason to stay in El Paso now, and as soon as, well . . . as soon as my son is laid to rest, I'd like to go home to Virginia. We can work out something about the ranch, can't we, Jesse?"

Jesse had feared Zina might become hysterical, and he was greatly relieved that she had the composure to make plans for the future. "You needn't make any decisions now," he assured her. "Wait until you're feeling better."

Surprised by that suggestion, Zina shook her head. "I'll never feel any better than I do this very minute, Jesse. Don't you know that? Now if you gentlemen will forgive me, I'd like to be alone."

Jesse kissed her cheek and followed Luke out of the room while Dr. Haynes remained to tend the grief-stricken woman. When Luke asked to speak with him out on the patio, he balked and complained he had been away from Tory too long, but the tracker insisted he had something important to tell him and finally Jesse gave in and went outside.

"Your stepmother is a fine woman . . ." Luke began, "and I'd never do anything to add to her grief."

Impatient to get back to Tory, Jesse quickly agreed. "No gentleman would."

"Well now, I like to think of myself as a gentleman, but there are times when a man has difficult choices to make."

"If you're trying to say you want me to go back to Arizona

442

with you, the answer is no. I'll send an attorney with a statement, but I won't go."

Luke raised a hand to plead for silence. "Please, this is difficult enough without you interrupting me. It's Gerry I want to talk about, not you. Your stepbrother is no hero, but Ivan and I hope that the three of us can keep the truth of the situation to ourselves."

Still unconvinced their discussion would prove worthwhile, Jesse decided to give Luke another minute to say his piece and no more. "I'm real good at keeping secrets," he promised.

"So am I." Luke hemmed and hawed a bit, but finally managed to explain how he had shot Gerry to keep him from shooting Jesse in the back. "His first shot went clean through Ivan's hat. That got our attention and I took care of the problem."

Even knowing what a scheming weasel Gerry had been, Jesse was stunned by Luke's tale. It was without doubt the most unspeakably evil trick he could imagine. "I was holding Tory. I didn't realize what had happened."

"It's just damn lucky his aim wasn't better or he would have gotten you with his first shot. With Tory injured, too, Ivan and I would have been so busy he would probably have gotten away before we caught sight of him. I don't know when I've come across a sorrier individual than your late stepbrother, but I still believe we ought to allow his mother to believe he died a hero. It won't hurt us any, and it's obviously a comfort to her."

Jesse felt sick to his stomach. "I helped raise that boy," he murmured.

"Don't go blaming yourself," Luke suggested. "In my line of work I've met some fine families who have children you'd swear must have been spawned by the devil himself. It's just the luck of the draw, I guess. Now you go on back to Tory. She's all that need concern you today."

Or ever, Jesse thought to himself as he turned away. Tory had not stirred while he had been away, and as he sat down beside her and took her hand, he wondered if the stream of luck flowing from Araña's braid had saved him, too.

Growing up, Gerry had had little interest in the actual work of the ranch, but he had certainly loved to shoot. Jesse had frequently seen him hit a bull's-eye with six out of six shots. Why had he missed that day?

Deciding perhaps after all the wrongs Gerry had done to him, murder still had not come easily, Jesse again removed his boots and stretched out beside Tory. He hoped that she would soon wake and he did not want to be too sleepy to tend her. He placed his arm around her waist to pull her close and fell asleep praying that their troubles were finally at an end.

Chapter 29

Tory did not regain consciousness until nightfall. She moved slightly, and the excruciating pain that ricocheted through her head and careened down her spine forced her to lie still. As she attempted to catch her breath without causing herself another blinding jolt of agony, she gradually became aware of the sound of male voices. Jesse was standing nearby with someone who possessed a soft Spanish accent. Lalo, she thought, but she lacked the energy to call out. Instead, she opened her eyes and waited for them to notice that she was awake.

"Regard for Zina will assure a respectable number at the funeral," Lalo predicted. "Gerry had friends who liked to play cards with him. They'll be there, too. I told the minister to prepare the eulogy. Everyone will understand why you declined that honor when they learn what really happened in Tucson."

"The damage to my reputation can't be undone until after Zina's left for Virginia, but that's a small concession. I'd like for you to escort her to the funeral. I don't want to leave Tory here all alone."

"But the danger to her is past."

Jesse fixed his boyhood friend with a steady stare. "I'm not going to Gerry's funeral," he stated firmly. "If Tory didn't need me here, then I'd invent an excuse, but I can't attend. I just can't be that much of a hypocrite."

He glanced toward the bed then, and noticing Tory was no

longer asleep, a smile lit his whole face with joy. He rushed to her side. "I've been so worried about you. Why didn't you say something? Lalo's been trying to keep my spirits up, but he's anxious to get on home now, aren't you, Lalo?"

Lalo followed Jesse to the bed. "It appears I am no longer needed here, but before I go, I do want to ask how you are feeling, *querida*."

Tory's head felt as though it would burst with each throb of her pulse and she was sick to her stomach as well. Because that was not the report she assumed Lalo wished to hear, she smiled as best she could. "If I knew what had happened to me, I'd be in a better position to judge."

Lalo's grin was nearly as wide as Jesse's. "At least she's coherent if not particularly informative. I will come for Zina as you asked," he promised his friend before taking Tory's hand. "If there is anything Jesse does not provide, send word to me and you shall have it immediately."

"I've already warned you about flirting with her," Jesse reminded him.

Amused by Jesse's possessiveness, Lalo laughed, but after wishing Tory a restful night, he hurried from the room rather than risk upsetting him any further.

"Now tell me how you really feel," Jesse instructed.

"Like someone split my head open with an axe. Is that what happened?"

Realizing she truly meant she could not recall being shot, Jesse related the incident and told her that Gerry had been slain during their rescue. He then explained that Luke would return the pearl-and-cameo necklace to the authorities in Tucson. "It'll prove my innocence and I'll be given a pardon," he assured her, "and the whole nasty mess will be behind me."

Tory had never felt so horribly ill, but she did not want to frighten Jesse when he was so relieved to see her awake. She understood why he was elated, and was happy for him, but the impossibility of her situation remained unchanged. "Gerry's dead?" she asked weakly.

"Yes," Jesse replied, intent upon never giving her the

accurate details, "but you needn't concern yourself with him. Just concentrate on getting well. The doctor said you ought to eat and drink as much as you can."

The mere mention of food made Tory's stomach lurch and she had to swallow hard. "No, not yet please."

"Dr. Haynes left some laudanum. Would you like it instead?"

"Will it make my headache go away?"

"It should."

Jesse poured a small amount of the opium-laced alcohol mixture into a glass. He slipped his arm under Tory's pillow to raise her head slightly and encouraged her to swallow what he feared had to be a foul-tasting potion in one gulp. She did, but gagged several times before finally getting it down. Relieved it had not made her sick after all, he eased his arm from under her pillow.

He started to tell her how George's last remarks had confirmed his hypothesis of her father's death, but her eyelids fluttered closed and she fell asleep before he finished. Disappointed that she had not been awake longer, Jesse worried that he had said all the wrong things. He should have told her that he loved her instead of providing the details of the ambush that could have taken their lives.

Disgusted with himself, he bent down to kiss her. She was warm, but there was still little color in her cheeks and he was sorry he had not insisted that she try to eat even if she wasn't hungry. "Some nurse you are," he cursed under his breath. Determined not to make the same mistakes the next time she awoke, he pulled a chair up close to the bed and watched her sleep with a loving gaze.

Ivan and Mayleen had spent most of the day together. After her initial fainting spell, the usually lively young woman had shown remarkable calm. She had selected the best suit from Gerry's closet to take to the undertaker's along with every other article of clothing required to dress the corpse for burial. It helped to have something useful to do, but knowing it was Gerry they were burying provided a constant source of pain.

At suppertime, Zina remained in her room and Jesse was with Tory, leaving Mayleen and Ivan to enjoy a meal alone in the spacious dining room. Their voices echoed against the thick, whitewashed walls. "Are you going to stay for the funeral?" she asked shyly.

Ivan was so startled by her question that his fork slipped from his hand and landed on his plate with a loud clatter, embarrassing him badly. He had once possessed the fine manners of a gentleman, and he did not like to think that he had forgotten them entirely. "I . . . well," he mumbled. "That is, what about you? Are you planning to stay?"

"I asked you first."

Ivan took a deep breath and for a brief moment wished he had not refused the offer of wine with his meal. He then silently chastised himself for believing a drink would make a difficult situation any easier to bear when he had learned from bitter experience that it did not. "Gerry meant nothing to me," he finally explained. "But I *am* concerned about Tory. I'd like to stay on a few days to make certain she's all right."

Mayleen chewed the bite she had just taken slowly in an effort to stall for the time to formulate a noncommittal reply. It certainly was not news that Ivan was sweet on Tory, but it hurt to hear him say it all the same. It made Mayleen feel completely out of place in Jesse's home. She knew a cultured southern belle like Zina could not possibly want a former prostitute to remain there. Jesse would not relinquish any of Tory's care to her, so she was no help to him. She was as useless to him as she was to everyone else.

Her appetite was gone and she folded her hands in her lap. "I've been thinking maybe I ought not to stay for the funeral," she announced suddenly. "After all, I didn't come here to visit Gerry but to try and send him to prison. Whatever love I had for the man is long over. I'll just feel out of place at his funeral."

Ivan was surprised by his dark-eyed companion's remarks.

448

"You loved him once, Mayleen. All you wanted was for him to do the honorable thing. Gerry won't know whether or not you attend the funeral, but for your own peace of mind, I think you ought to go. I'll go and sit with you if you like. That way you won't feel like you're the only stranger there."

Attending the funeral would give Mayleen an excuse to remain at the Lambert ranch, but she was uncertain that would be wise. She knew it would hurt to tell Ivan good-bye, and delaying her departure would only postpone that pain, not ease it. He was awaiting her reply with an expectant expression that made her feel all the worse. He looked very handsome that night, and suddenly the chance to share a few more days with him was too attractive a prospect to give up just to soothe her wounded pride.

"Thank you, Ivan. That's very thoughtful of you. I think I will stay for the funeral if you'll go with me."

"I said that I would."

"Thank you."

Tory's headache remained excruciating and she spent the next day and the day of the funeral in a laudanum-induced haze. She learned to recognize Dr. Haynes by his voice. He was the one who spoke in a soothing, persuasive tone. Ivan always sounded anxious, and Mayleen breathless. Lalo's accent gave him away. If Zina came to her room, she did not speak, but Jesse never left her side so half of every conversation she overheard consisted of his replies. They were all worried about her. She understood that, but the pain in her head sapped all her energy and made it impossible for her to enter into the discussions that took place at her bedside.

Remembering George, Jesse feared that Tory's survival might also be in jeopardy from multiple causes and he leaned down to touch her forehead. While her skin felt cool to the touch rather than feverish, he wasn't relieved. "She should be better by now," he complained to the physician.

Dr. Haynes pursed his lips thoughtfully. "From what you've told me about her these last couple of days, it's not surprising she just wants to rest. She's lucid when she's awake, isn't she?"

"Yes, but she never wants more than a sip or two of tea and a spoonful of broth. I'm afraid she'll starve to death if she doesn't start eating more soon."

"That's highly unlikely. Try to wake her."

Tory had been listening to them and opened her eyes before Jesse could call her name. She had imagined the doctor as a portly man, but he was about Ivan's size. He wore spectacles, too, and was peering at her intently.

"How do you do, my dear?"

"Poorly, I fear."

Dr. Haynes laughed. "You must have more patience, Jesse. She's getting along fine. I want you to try doing without the laudanum except at bedtime," he said to Tory. "Your headaches will gradually diminish."

"And if they don't?" she asked.

"They will," he assured her more emphatically.

Tory was not nearly as certain. All she knew was that she could not live the rest of her life in such incredible pain, and tears welled up in her eyes. "Is it bedtime yet?" she asked.

"No, it's the middle of the afternoon," Dr. Haynes replied.

"I think you better leave more laudanum," Jesse said.

Dr. Haynes withdrew an additional bottle from his bag. "Cut the dose each time you give it to her. As she improves, she'll require less so she won't notice the difference."

Jesse could not bear to see Tory in pain, but he nodded rather than argue with the doctor. After Lewis left, he sat down by her side and took her hand. The house was full of family friends who had come to pay their respects after the funeral. He was not sufficiently interested in speaking with any to leave Tory, however.

"I know you're not up to talking, but I hope you'll want to listen to the plans I've made. As soon as you're up and about again, we'll get married. I've got mixed feelings about inviting the people who were so quick to believe Gerry's lies, but maybe that's just human nature and I ought not to hold a grudge. We'll be making our home here in El Paso and I want us to be part of things, not social outcasts."

Jesse apparently had their whole lives planned, but Tory raised a hand to beg him to stop. "I can't marry you," she stated in a hushed whisper.

"What do you mean?" Jesse responded angrily at first, but quickly caught himself and lowered his voice. "Why not? Don't you love me?"

"Yes, I do love you, that's why I've got to go away."

"You're not making any sense. Try taking another nap and we'll talk about this when you're feeling better."

Tory reached out to catch Jesse's sleeve, and although her grasp was feeble, he sat back down. "Gerry died, but it could have been you," she began. "If I stay here, your life will continue to be in danger. When Tad and his men don't return to Cactus Springs, Eldrin Stafford will send more men after me and more after that if they fail. He won't be satisfied until I'm dead. The only way I can escape him and protect you is to leave El Paso and disappear forever."

. Her eyes had filled with tears when she had spoken of the danger to him and Jesse sat back in his chair and tried to think of how best to allay her fears. "The last of Stafford's men to die confirmed my suspicion that Paul planned your father's 'accident.' He also named Stafford men as Marshal Kane's killers. I don't intend to let Eldrin get away with it either. If I have to go back to Cactus Springs to see he's tried for that crime, I will."

"Oh, no! You mustn't!" Too excited to lie still, Tory struggled to sit up, then, blinded by pain, she slumped back against her pillows.

"Tory?"

Her anguish was unbearable and tears rolled down her cheeks. "You mustn't go back to Cactus Springs. Promise me you won't go."

Jessie leaned forward. "Only if you'll agree to marry me."

Tory studied his sly grin with an incredulous gaze. "I love you too much to put your life at risk."

"Damn it all, Tory, my life hasn't been worth two cents since the hour we met and we're getting along just fine."

"Perhaps *you* are," Tory reminded him.

Jesse brought her palm to his lips. "I'm sorry. I haven't forgotten that you're hurt, but I'll not allow a vicious bastard like Eldrin Stafford to ruin our lives." Annoyed to be interrupted by a knock at the door, he excused himself to send their unwanted visitor away and found Luke waiting to speak with him.

"I'm leaving in the morning," the tracker announced, "and I'd like to tell Tory good-bye if I may."

Luke had frequently come to the door to inquire about her, but this was the first time she had been awake. With the question of their marriage still unsettled, Luke could not have arrived at a more inconvenient time, but Jesse ushered him inside.

Tory was not certain how she ought to react. She understood that Luke would stop in Tucson to clear Jesse's name, but she was still a fugitive. It seemed ridiculous to wish him a good trip when he might one day return to arrest her.

Luke had seen the same haunted expression in too many fugitives' eyes not to recognize it now. He patted Tory's shoulder gently. "Don't you worry none, sweetheart. I have a daughter about your age, and if any man ever treats her as badly as Paul Stafford did you, I'll not hesitate to do exactly what you did. That Paul's father sent a band of cutthroats out after you told me all I need to know about that family.

"I've had several days to consider things, and it occurred to me that Eldrin Stafford would have no reason to doubt anything I tell him. If I were to stop by Cactus Springs to deliver the unfortunate news of his men's deaths and happened to mention that you had also been killed, he would be sure to believe me."

Shocked that Luke would make such an offer, Tory looked up at Jesse. "What do you think?"

"I think it's a damn good idea. We can still make certain that there is an investigation into your father's death, and Marshal Kane's as well. We can also request that a search be made for Consuelo. United States marshals will have to handle it since the sheriff in Cactus Springs is nothing more than Eldrin's puppet. With all we know about the Staffords, I'm confident we can eventually clear your name, too, but if Eldrin believes you're dead, he would have no reason to send anyone else to El Paso in the meantime. I think we should take Luke up on his offer to spread the story of your death."

Luke pursed his lips thoughtfully. He could account for the whereabouts of Tad and four of his men, but the fact that two others had disappeared somewhere between Bisbee and Juarez annoyed him. He was about to wonder aloud what had become of them when he realized such a comment would terrify Tory. Perhaps they had just gotten tired and gone home. "I've got Kane's badge," he said instead. "I'll see his family gets it."

"I wondered what had happened to that. I thought maybe Araña had it."

As Luke explained where he had found it, he had an idea. "What I need is some evidence to show Stafford. A lock of your hair would do. Do you mind if I remove your bandage for a minute?" When Tory did not object, Jesse stepped forward to unwind Dr. Haynes's carefully contrived bandage. Understanding what Luke wanted, he separated a lock that was matted with her blood, and Luke quickly severed it with his knife.

"Thank you," he said. "This will do nicely." He waited while Jesse replaced Tory's bandage and then signaled for him to walk with him to the door. When they reached it, he confided, "The sheriff followed us home from the funeral and wants to see you. I told him about the necklace. He has no idea Tory is wanted. I made him believe Tad and his men were after you."

"Thanks." Jesse glanced toward the bed. Tory had closed her eyes, and certain she would sleep for a while, he left her room and went to find the sheriff, who proved to be more curious than suspicious. Luke had insisted that with the evidence he had gathered, Jesse would swiftly be exonerated and, after a few cursory questions about the ambush, the lawman welcomed him back to El Paso with a hearty handshake. While they had never been friends, Jesse was grateful

453

for his trust and promised him there would be no more trouble at the Lambert Ranch, ever.

When Mayleen had returned from town, she had gone out onto the patio to avoid the well-meaning friends who had come to see Zina. When they had begun spilling outside, she had moved on out into the yard. The hands had all attended the funeral and were milling about in front of the barn looking awkward in their Sunday clothes, but not anxious to change out of them and get back to work. She waved to them, but followed a path that led in the opposite direction and strolled alongside the vegetable garden. She had not tended a garden since she had left home, but the warm, sweet smell of the earth reminded her of those nearly forgotten days. When she came to a bench shaded by an ancient oak, it was such an inviting spot that she sat down, closed her eyes, and let her mind drift to the few happy memories of her childhood.

Equally uninterested in listening to Zina's friends conduct their condolence calls, Ivan began searching for Mayleen. It took him half an hour to find her, and then he feared she had fallen asleep. Not wanting to startle her, he sat down beside her and patted her hand lightly.

Daydreaming rather than napping, Mayleen greeted him with a delighted smile. "Hello, Ivan. The house too crowded for you, too?"

Ivan nodded. Now that he had found Mayleen, he realized he had been so eager to see her that he had not prepared anything to say. "This is a pleasant place to sit and rest," he offered with an embarrassed smile.

"Yes, I thought so."

"We certainly haven't had many opportunities to relax since we left Tucson, have we?"

"No, we haven't."

"Of course we did have a couple of nights at the *cantina* but they weren't particularly restful as I recall."

Unwilling to discuss what had transpired there, Mayleen

looked away. "This is really a wonderful garden, isn't it?"

There had been several occasions when Ivan had tried to discover what had happened their first night at the *cantina*. Each time Mayleen had made it plain she would rather not discuss it, heightening his fears that he had been unspeakably rude to her. "Mayleen?"

"Hmm?"

"I know I performed some sort of a wedding ceremony at the *cantina,* or so I've been told, but what else did I do? I'm ashamed to admit I can't remember that night. I've not had a drop to drink since then so it's unlikely I'll ever have another such embarrassing memory lapse. Won't you please clear up that one?"

Mayleen feared she would sound pathetic if she told him the truth. After all, she had believed that he loved her, only to awaken to find him drunk again. It broke her heart anew to remember that night and it was impossible to describe how wretchedly unhappy he had made her feel. She just shook her head.

"There's nothing to tell," she lied.

Ivan was still certain there was. "I'm sure I owe you an apology for whatever happened," he offered. "I *am* sorry. Truly I am."

That was just the point, Mayleen thought to herself. He had been so sorry he had made love to her that he had gotten drunk. "That night doesn't matter," she repeated. "You've been very helpful since then."

"Thank you." Seizing that opening, Ivan pressed for more. "I'd like to be even more helpful if I may."

Mayleen leaned back to make herself more comfortable now that their conversation was not so painfully personal. "I really don't need any help," she denied.

"Perhaps not, but you stayed with me in Mexico and I want you to know how much I appreciate that. You could have gone on with Jesse and Tory, but you chose to stay at the *cantina* with me. Whatever your reason, I'd like to repay your kindness. If you'll tell me where you're going, I'll make the travel arrangements and go along. That way you won't

455

have to travel alone."

Mayleen shrugged helplessly. "I've not really made any plans, Ivan."

"But the other night, you said you might leave before the funeral."

"Well, yes, I did say that, but I didn't really have any destination in mind."

Astonished, Ivan grew more insistent. "Would you have simply gone down to the train station and boarded the first train?"

"Not unless it was heading east."

Not amused by her joke, Ivan grew impatient. "Mayleen, really. You can't just run from town to town willy-nilly. You've got to have a better plan for your life than that."

Ivan was backing her into an extremely uncomfortable corner. "What sort of plans do you have?" she countered. "Do you have the rest of your life neatly organized?"

"No, but—"

Mayleen leapt to her feet. "Then don't think you can tell me what to do, Professor, because I won't be inclined to listen."

Unwilling to let her go, Ivan rose and reached out to catch her elbow. "Please, Mayleen, don't go running off. This is too important."

"I doubt that," she replied, but she folded her arms across her bosom and remained where she was.

"If you've no plans, what about going to St. Louis?"

"Isn't that your home?"

"Yes, but I haven't been there in several years. Every once in a while a letter catches up with me, so I know my parents are well, but they are getting on in years and I should make it a point to visit them now and then."

"I have money," Mayleen boasted proudly. "I've been thinking about starting a business—millinery, perhaps, or lingerie. Would St. Louis be a good town for that?"

"Oh, yes, it's a beautiful city and women wear pretty hats and lingerie there just like they do everywhere else." That had been the wrong thing to say and Ivan immediately took it back. "What I mean is, it's a wonderful city for business because not only would you have customers among the residents, but among the travelers on the Mississippi as well."

"St. Louis is on the Mississippi River?"

"Of course. Where did you think it was?"

Mayleen shrugged. "I didn't really know."

Ivan saw her shoulders slump slightly and knew he had hurt her feelings, again. "I always say the wrong thing, don't I? I'm sorry. I must be the stupidest man alive. If you were to go into business in St. Louis, I'm sure my mother would be your best customer and recommend your shop to all her friends."

Mayleen turned back to face him. "You'd introduce me to your mother?"

"Why not?" Ivan asked without thinking. Then he knew. "Oh, well, you needn't concern yourself about that. I'll simply tell her we met in Tucson. I don't have to say how."

"Someone will tell her how," Mayleen predicted darkly. "That kind of secret is impossible to keep."

"We'll change your name."

Mayleen shook her head. "It won't be my name that they recognize, Ivan. It will be my face, or some other part of my anatomy that they notice as I pass by. Thousands of men came through Tucson looking to get rich. Just like Gerry, most of them failed and went on back home. Someone in St. Louis is sure to remember me and your family doesn't need to be embarrassed like that."

"Thousands? You slept with thousands of men?" Ivan forced himself to ask.

He looked so pained by that prospect Mayleen had to smile. "Well, maybe it wasn't thousands. I didn't keep a running tally, but it was a lot."

"I'm sorry, I shouldn't have asked."

Again, Mayleen just shrugged. "I think I better go somewhere else, New Orleans, maybe. Someone is sure to recognize me there one day, too, but at least you won't have to be shamed by it."

"Do my feelings mean that much to you?" Ivan asked in

surprise. When Mayleen again turned her back on him rather than reply, he had his answer but it wasn't the one he had expected and he was flabbergasted. His ankle still hurt, but it didn't keep him from hurrying to face her. He put his hands on her shoulders. "Is that why you stayed with me in Mexico, because you care for me?"

"Why is that so difficult to believe?" Mayleen responded grudgingly. "Do you think I'm incapable of love?"

"But when? How?" He had always been fond of Mayleen, but she had been so aloof on their travels that he had not dared dream that she would welcome his affections. Or had she? "That's what happened the night I can't remember, isn't it? You said that you loved me." He watched her cheeks fill with a crimson blush and knew he was right. Ecstatic, he drew her into an enthusiastic hug. "That was the wrong night to forget, wasn't it? Can you ever forgive me?"

Actually, as she recalled, neither of them had said anything about love. It had simply been understood. Later she had wondered how she could ever have been so foolish. "No, you didn't say that you loved me. You didn't make any promises at all," she whispered against his cheek.

Ivan took a very small step backward. "Then I'll say it now. I do love you and I want you to be my wife. I'll find work as a professor again so I won't have to travel. I have excellent qualifications and I won't have any difficulty finding a good position now that I'm sober."

Mayleen did love Ivan, she really did. "I can't marry you," she insisted softly. "The first time someone recognized me, you'd be ruined."

"I doubt it," Ivan repeated in the same tone she had used with him earlier. "There's nothing you could do to damage my reputation that I haven't already done myself. If there's ever any gossip, we'll ignore it."

"Do you really mean that?"

Ivan's response was a kiss that didn't end until Mayleen had returned it so eagerly, he knew she understood. "Let's go get married." He took her hand and began to lead her back toward the house.

"But the minister's here because of the funeral!"

"Yes, I know. It would be indelicate to ask him to perform a wedding this afternoon, but that doesn't mean we can't find a justice of the peace in town. I've waited too long to marry you to put it off a day longer. Don't argue with me. Let's just go into El Paso and do it."

"I'm not arguing, Ivan."

Had his ankle been strong enough, Ivan would have picked her up and carried her to the barn, but he had to content himself with walking by her side. He asked the first hand they saw to hitch a horse to the buggy, and in less than ten minutes, they were on their way to become husband and wife.

Chapter 30

The Southern Pacific Railroad had connected El Paso
with the West in May 1881, enabling Luke to ride the train
back to the Arizona Territory. The uneventful journey
provided him with ample opportunity to rehearse his tale
before he reached Cactus Springs. His stop to see Sheriff
Toland in Tucson had necessitated only a retelling of the
truth and required no prior preparation, but the story he told
Eldrin Stafford had been polished to perfection. He even
managed to conjure up a catch in his voice as he described
the horrible sight Tory Crandell had presented with half her
face blown away. It was at that precise instant that he tossed
the bloody curl onto Eldrin's desk. The wild-eyed man
jumped in alarm and Luke had a difficult time not bursting
out in raucous laughter.

"Like I said, your men were killed a few minutes later, but
they sure took care of Miss Crandell. Yes, sir. That was one
dead woman all right."

Eldrin studied the lock of Tory's hair as he posed a
question. "What's become of Lambert?"

"He was able to prove his brother had robbed the stage,
and with the brother dead, the case is closed."

"But he escaped from prison!"

"Well, yes, sir, that's true, but he shouldn't have been there
in the first place so no one is going to prosecute him for
escaping." This time Luke couldn't hold back a chuckle.

Not amused, Eldrin's perpetual frown deepened. "He shot

461

Marshal Kane and broke Tory out of jail. He'll surely have to stand trial on those charges."

Luke nodded thoughtfully. "Lambert claims that when he came across Kane's body, the marshal had been dead a couple of hours. There are no witnesses to the crime, and I doubt a jury would convict Lambert when he's already served four years in prison for a crime he didn't commit. As for helping Miss Crandell escape, she's dead, so his actions didn't change her fate any. Again, he wouldn't be convicted so there's no point in having him stand trial for the crime."

"Are you telling me that he'll get away with murdering a marshal and breaking out of jail?"

Thanks to Luke, marshals would soon be investigating Jonathan Kane's death, but he had no intention of giving Eldrin any warning that his part in the lawman's murder had already been established. Instead, he just shrugged. "Like I said, there's no proof Lambert killed Kane and I'm inclined to believe someone who held a grudge against the late marshal followed him from Prescott and shot him. Now I'm sorry about your men. I hope none had families."

Eldrin shook his head. "Can't Lambert be prosecuted for their murders?"

"They ambushed Lambert and his woman on his ranch. He had no idea they were a posse from Cactus Springs. He was just defending himself. There's no case there, either." When the silence between them grew to an uncomfortably length, Luke sat forward and glanced toward the door. "If you've no more questions, I'm sure you can understand how anxious I am to get home."

Eldrin dismissed Luke with a preoccupied wave, and he left the house with all possible haste. From the brief glimpse Luke had gotten of Mrs. Stafford and her two daughters, they appeared to be excruciatingly shy, and he knew they must be as intimidated by Eldrin as most people were. Luke was so happy he didn't look back, and he hoped the next time he saw Eldrin Stafford the hostile man was on trial for his life.

Seething with a frustrated rage, Eldrin remained seated at his desk for nearly an hour. From what Luke Bernay had told him, the law had no further interest in Jesse Lambert, but he certainly did. He wasn't finished with Victoria Crandell, either. If he could not have her body exhumed and reburied beside Paul's, then he could at least desecrate her grave.

"Rest in peace," he snickered as he tossed her lock of hair into the wastebasket. "I think not." He rose slowly and stretched his angular frame. He had not been to Texas in several years, but he intended to pay a call on Jesse Lambert just as soon as it could be arranged.

Despite Jesse's assurances that the ranch would continue to be her home, Zina had absolutely no desire to remain there, and a week after her son's funeral she left for Virginia in the company of her favorite maidservant. Jesse took them to the depot himself, but the minute their train pulled out of the station he started back home. He knew he ought to reestablish contact with the merchants with whom his family had always done business so they would not gawk when he and Tory came into town, but he missed her too badly to stay away a moment longer than absolutely necessary.

When he reached the ranch, he went straight to Tory's room where he found Mayleen and Ivan convulsed in giggles. Certain they were taxing the strength of the still-recuperating young woman, he would have scolded the hysterical pair had Tory not spoken first.

"They got married last week," she announced with genuine pleasure. "Out of consideration for Zina's sorrow, they kept it a secret. Now that she's gone, I think we should celebrate."

Jesse had no way of knowing whether it was the excitement of sharing in the newlyweds' joy, or simply confiding the reason for their high spirits which had made Tory breathless, but it concerned him. While he was trying his damnedest to be patient, he ached to have her well again, and each day she remained confined to her bed was an eternity for him. He quickly crossed the room and bent down to kiss her before offering Mayleen his best wishes and congratulating Ivan.

"Aren't you surprised?" Mayleen asked.

"That you decided to get married? No, not at all. I think you're very well suited. If you're still speaking to each other after the horrendous trip we had, then having a happy marriage should be no trick at all."

"Well, it's certainly been happy so far," Ivan boasted proudly.

"Ivan, you hush!" Mayleen scolded playfully. "Tory thought maybe we could have a special dinner together. You'll carry her into the dining room, won't you?"

"Tonight?" Jesse asked.

"They've already been married a week," Tory reminded him. "Don't you think it's time?"

"For them maybe, but not for you. Will you excuse us a minute?"

Ivan took Mayleen's hand. "Of course."

Jesse waited until they had closed the door behind them before he sat down on Tory's bed. "How do you feel?"

Tory's smile was wistful. "Tired, but I'm getting better."

"And your headache?"

Tory's head was still swathed in bandages. "It's not as bad today."

Jesse was too considerate to describe how frail she looked, but he was convinced she was not nearly strong enough to leave her bed. "Neither Ivan nor Mayleen has expressed any hurry to leave us. I think they can wait a few more days for a dinner party."

Tory leaned back against her pillows and closed her eyes for a moment. She had always been such an active person, and lying in bed day after day almost too weak to move had been extremely trying for her. Jesse was wonderful company. Mayleen and Ivan were always attentive, too. She had had several nice conversations with Zina when the bereaved woman took time out from her packing. Still, her being confined to bed was a strain on everyone.

"I'm sorry," she said.

"For what?"

"For taking so long to get well that I can't even go into the

464

dining room for dinner."

Her progress was painfully slow, but steady, and Jesse was so grateful that she was alive, he did not want to hear her complain. "Dinner doesn't matter," he assured her. "What does is our wedding. I think we should set a date. You ought to be well enough in three weeks, don't you think?"

They had discussed this subject before, and each time Jesse had brushed aside her objections. Tory could not deny that she loved him, and that was his only concern. She still did not feel completely safe, but feared she had been through too much to ever be as carefree as she had been before her father's death.

Araña's braid was in the top drawer of the nightstand. It would be an odd keepsake to carry on her wedding day, but she was now a firm believer in its value as a good-luck charm. Confident her answer was the correct one, she still took a deep breath and let it out slowly.

"Three weeks is fine," she agreed before her courage deserted her.

Tory's hesitant reply conveyed such little enthusiasm for Jesse's plan that he found it difficult to project any himself. "I wish we could go away for a while, but Gerry's made such a mess of things here that we don't dare leave. I'd like to take you to Europe, or wherever you want to go for an extended honeymoon, but—"

Tory reached out to take his hand. "If the dining room is too far, I think Europe is out of the question. Besides, I've had enough travel to last me for several years. I'll be perfectly content to stay right here on the ranch."

Her words were reassuring even if her manner was subdued, and Jesse let himself hope that it was the lingering discomfort of her injury rather than the prospect of marrying him that had depressed her. He leaned forward and pulled her into a warm embrace. He had spent every night in her bed, just holding her in his arms as he had their first nights on the trail. He did not want her to awaken during the night and have no one to attend to her needs, at least that was the excuse he gave her. The truth was, he could not bear to sleep alone when he loved her so dearly.

As he sat back, his grin was wide. "We've got a lot to do in the next three weeks. You'll need a new dress for one thing."

"But I haven't worn but one of the pretty gowns Lalo bought for me. I can wear one of the others."

"No, you'll need a special dress for your wedding day."

Tory ceased to argue as Jesse continued to enumerate what had to be done to prepare for their wedding. She wanted to feel as happy as he did about it, and vowed to do her best in that regard. After all, it was Luke and the U.S. marshals who would be taking care of Eldrin Stafford now, not Jesse. Jesse wanted to put all their problems behind them to concentrate on re-creating the ranch's former success and building a life together. He was a wonderful man and she did not want him to doubt her love. She smiled and nodded as he described what he hoped would be a perfect wedding day and tried to suppress her fears—but they remained, as dark and ominous as the deep shadows that filled the corners of her room.

With Zina gone and Tory bedridden, Mayleen volunteered to work with the household staff to prepare for the wedding. Because Jesse had had no time to hire another foreman, he was running the ranch. Ivan kept busy catching up with all the bookkeeping Gerry had let slide for four years. Having a scientist's love of detail, he soon returned the ranch's books to their former accuracy and neatness. Ivan had no interest in remaining in El Paso, however, and spent part of each day extolling the beauties of St. Louis to his bride.

Lalo paid the Lambert ranch frequent visits, but Carmen never accompanied him. At first Tory assumed Carmen was busy with her sons, but as the days stretched into weeks it seemed unlikely that she would never have a spare hour. One afternoon while Lalo and Jesse were entertaining her with amusing anecdotes from their childhood, Tory's curiosity finally got the better of her. She waited for the men to bring an especially long and convoluted tale to a close and for their laughter to subside before she mentioned what was troubling her.

"Why doesn't Carmen ever come to see me?"

Startled, Lalo gestured with broad, graceful strokes while he attempted to concoct a reasonable excuse for what was obviously unforgivable rudeness on his wife's part. Seeing his friend's distress, Jesse promptly supplied an answer. "She's avoiding me, Tory, not you."

Finally finding his voice, Lalo disagreed. "It is more complicated than that."

"How so?" Tory asked. "Does she intend to avoid both of us indefinitely? Won't she come to our wedding?"

Badly embarrassed by that question, Lalo shifted nervously in his chair. "Yes, of course she will be here," he replied unconvincingly.

Jesse and Lalo were such close friends that Tory did not want their wives to be estranged, but she felt too much like an outsider to know what to do. "Perhaps if Jesse spoke with her?"

"No!" Lalo refused instantly. "There's no reason for that. Whatever feelings they had for each other are over."

"Obviously not," Tory pointed out.

Unwilling to debate the issue, Lalo rose to his feet. "You must excuse me. I should be on my way."

Jesse showed him out, but when he returned to Tory's room he did not look pleased. "I can understand why you're hurt that Carmen's ignoring you, but promise me that you won't say another word to Lalo about her. That's just the way Carmen is, and she'll never change. She's not merely proud, but incredibly stubborn, and she'll never forgive me for going to Arizona rather than marrying her."

"Is the ability to forgive an important attribute in a woman?"

Jesse broke into a cocky grin. "It certainly is. In case you haven't noticed, men make a great many mistakes."

Tory nodded, and then glanced toward her window as she gathered her thoughts. "If I had forgiven Paul Stafford, he would still be alive, along with Consuelo, Marshal Kane, and the men from the Stafford ranch." Seemingly confused, she turned back to Jesse. "I shouldn't have said anything about Carmen. Compared to me, she's a model of virtue and compassion."

Infuriated by that remark, Jesse clenched his fists at his sides, but he held his tongue until he had his temper under control. "There is absolutely no comparison between what happened with Carmen and me and what took place between Paul and you. Carmen was a spoiled brat who threw tantrums when I refused to offer marriage. She's still pouting over that insult. Paul caused your father's death, got rid of Consuelo, and then made it plain he intended to rape you until you agreed to become his wife. His abuse wouldn't have stopped then, either." Jesse circled the bed and took his usual place at her side.

"When Eldrin goes on trial for ordering Kane's murder, the evidence presented will finally tell the whole story. The jury will understand that you shot Paul in self-defense after he murdered your father and attacked you. No one can be expected to forgive something that monstrous. Our system of justice is designed to punish the guilty, not forgive them. Now I don't want to talk about this ever again because it only upsets you unnecessarily. You'll receive a pardon soon, and then it can all be forgotten. That's precisely what I intend to do about the four wretched years I wasted in prison. If I dwell on them, I'll just spoil what I have now and that would be an even greater waste."

"I know you're right," Tory confided, but she kept still about her own misgivings. Logically, Paul and his father were to blame for the tragic events that had begun in Cactus Springs, but where would the horror end? Jesse was confident Eldrin's trial would conclude it, but nothing about the Staffords followed a logical course and she could not bring herself to hope that it ever would.

Eldrin Stafford arrived in El Paso on a Thursday and registered at the Central Hotel as Edward Sims. As soon as he was settled in his room he inquired as to the location of the newspaper office. Once there, he greeted the clerk politely.

"I understand Jesse Lambert was ambushed at his own ranch a few weeks ago. I wonder if I might see the issue of your newspaper that contained that story."

"Certainly, sir." The clerk left the front counter for several minutes, then returned with the back issue requested. "Here you are. It's right on the front page, and quite a story it was, too."

Eldrin hurriedly glanced through the article searching for the mention of Tory's death. He wanted to savor each delicious word describing her demise, but there was no mention of a Victoria Crandell even being present, let alone killed. "Perhaps I was misinformed, but I understood there was a woman involved."

The clerk glanced over his shoulder to make certain the editor wasn't close enough to accuse him of gossiping before he whispered, "There was, but Lambert asked that her name not appear in the paper."

Intrigued, Eldrin attempted to look relieved. "She must not have been seriously hurt then."

The clerk shrugged. "That I can't say, but I know Doc Haynes has been out to the ranch a lot lately. Of course she must be well enough to get married on Saturday."

That Tory was not only alive but planning to wed astonished Eldrin. "There's to be a wedding?" he gasped.

"She and Jesse are getting married this Saturday. It's a private ceremony, but half the town's been invited to the reception." The clerk looked very pleased with himself. "I'll be there to cover it for the paper."

Eldrin forced himself to smile, and the unfamiliar expression actually made his cheeks ache. "How wonderful. Do you happen to know her name?"

"It's Patricia Earl. Jesse brought her back with him from Arizona. I hope to be able to ask her a few questions about her background on Saturday—for the article, you understand."

"Of course," Eldrin agreed, not fooled by the assumed name.

The clerk rested his elbows on the counter. "I haven't seen her, but knowing Jesse, she's got to be a beauty."

"But Lambert's served time in prison," Eldrin reminded him.

469

"Now that's another story," the clerk revealed with a ready grin before briefly explaining how Jesse had been framed by his stepbrother. He thumped the newspaper he had handed Eldrin. "It's all right here. Gerry's dead, but Jesse's free and about to marry his sweetheart."

"On Saturday, you say?"

"Yes, sir, Saturday afternoon at two."

Eldrin smiled along with him. If half the town had been invited out to the Lambert ranch on Saturday, then surely one extra guest would not be noticed. He laughed to himself as he left the newspaper office. If anyone had the audacity to ask him who he was, he would simply reply that he was a friend of the bride.

After supper on Friday, Jesse kissed Tory good night and abruptly announced that he planned to sleep in his own bed for a change. While Tory was both surprised and disappointed, she offered no objection. He had been so attentive and patient during her convalescence that she did not want to appear difficult now.

As Lewis Haynes predicted, her headaches had gradually diminished. her stitches had been removed, so she could again wash her hair. Outwardly, there was no lingering sign of what she had suffered, but she had yet to regain her former strength and vitality. She was able to leave her bed for several hours each day, and had managed to stand while the lovely ivory lace gown Jesse had bought for the wedding was fitted properly. Her spirits were generally good, and she had laughed easily with her companions the night they had finally celebrated Ivan and Mayleen's marriage.

Now her own marriage was imminent, and while she assumed Jesse had believed she would be able to sleep more soundly alone, she knew the exact opposite would prove true. After preparing for bed, she grew almost unbearably lonely. Because she had no male relatives living, let alone present, Ivan would be giving her away. He and Mayleen would be leaving for St. Louis after the wedding, and Tory knew she would miss them both. Jesse was anxious for her to make friends and she would have ample opportunity at the reception, but right now, the only company she wanted was his.

When she was certain enough time had elaspsed for him to have gotten into bed, she left the room. She paused outside his door for a long moment, and once assured he was alone, she entered without knocking. Jesse was in bed, but reading rather than asleep, and appeared badly startled to see her. He hurriedly set his book aside, but she grabbed the hem of her gown and climbed up over the end of his bed before he could get out of it.

"Stay where you are," she ordered in a seductive whisper.

"No, if you need something, I'll be happy to get it."

"All I need is you."

A month had passed since the last time they had made love, and Jesse had not allowed himself to hope Tory might feel well enough to enjoy their wedding night as he had dreamed they would. He had simply been grateful she was alive and content with that miracle for the present.

"Me?" he asked with an innocent shrug, as though he had no idea what had brought her to his room.

Tory was beside him now, and leaned close to tickle his ear with her tongue. "You," she repeated. "You've spoiled me so terribly that I can't sleep without you."

"You need your sleep, so I guess you'll have to stay."

"That's what I thought."

"This is a very nice feather bed," Jesse pointed out. "It's just like yours."

"Even better."

"Better? How?"

"You're in it." Jesse pulled her across his lap then and she nuzzled the hollow of his bare shoulder with eager kisses.

Her touch was incredibly appealing but very light, and he knew that was because she wasn't completely well rather than from a lack of enthusiasm. "If this is going to be too much for you . . ." he began.

"No, it's not nearly enough."

Tory had never been such a blatant tease and Jesse had to laugh. There had been a time when he had feared she would

471

never want him, but he would not remind her of it now. Instead, he wound a blond curl around his hand and drew her closer still. "I love you," he murmured against her lips, and her response was a nearly endless kiss that spoke of love with a silent eloquence.

Jesse was completely relaxed now. He closed his eyes, and rather than rush Tory, he let her take the lead in their loving play. She moved off his lap, and with affectionate nibbles, licks, and kisses began a teasing trail that crossed his broad chest. His stomach muscles grew taut as her tongue dipped into his navel, and when she pulled away the sheet, he reached over to douse the lamp.

Tory raked her nails lightly up the inside of his thigh. "You didn't have to put out the light," she whispered. "I think you have a magnificent body."

"Magnificent?" Jesse was glad she could not see his blush. "Being tall has definite advantages, but I'm scarcely magnificent."

Unable to agree, Tory again swirled her tongue into his navel, and as the ends of her long curls brushed across his lap she felt him shiver with what she hoped was delight. His skin was smooth and warm, inviting both taste and touch. She wanted him to share in the pleasure she found in his arms. It was so easy to make love to Jesse, she did not want to ever stop.

Jesse stroked Tory's sun-streaked tresses as her kisses grew increasingly bold. While he was truly shocked she wanted to explore his body in such a captivating fashion, he was not even remotely tempted to tell her to stop. Fully aroused, he wanted whatever she would give and his breath caught in the back of his throat as her tongue caressed the satin-smooth tip of his manhood. The warm, sweet wetness of her mouth wrenched an ecstatic cry from his lips and brought an end to his fears that Paul's abuse had scarred her for life. She was his woman alone and he savored her devotion until the desire to possess her compelled him to pull her back into a fervent embrace.

He had bought her silk nightgown as a token of his love, but he removed it with a haste that threatened to leave it in tatters. He was sorry the room was dark now, but his imagination painted the delectable swells of her lithe figure with lush perfection. It was his turn to caress her with lavish kisses now, and he felt her tremble with the same desire that tortured him. As he hugged her close, she clung to him with an ageless grace, and with a single fluid motion he brought their bodies together as one.

Still mindful of her fragile health, he moved slowly, deliberately, until the joyousness of her response became his as well. He was no longer aware of conscious thought, but only the intensity of the need to pierce her very soul with the power of his love. If being with her was all he would ever know of paradise, he would die believing he had had it all. Blinded by an inner light, he felt their bodies fuse in a union blessed by the richness of their love. She was his heart, his soul, his life, and he could not wait for the hour she would finally be his wife in the world's eyes as well as his own.

Exhausted by the rapture Jesse bestowed so generously, Tory fell asleep in Jesse's arms. He combed the soft, silken strands of her hair with his fingertips, and vowed to make every night of their marriage equally glorious. He had waited so long for love and now that he had found it, he wanted to make certain Tory understood how precious she truly was. The fires of hell could be no worse than the trials they had overcome to be together. Before falling asleep he whispered a sweet promise of a future overflowing with the joy his courageous bride so richly deserved.

When friends began to gather at the Lambert ranch, Eldrin Stafford was among them. He had purchased a pair of silver candlesticks, and with that handsomely wrapped wedding gift in hand, he walked through the front door behind the shopkeeper who had sold him the expensive present. They were greeted by a friendly, dark-haired young woman who knew only a few of the guests by name. Eldrin did his best to smile.

"I'm Edward Sims," he announced with a courtly bow and Mayleen set his gift on the table at her side.

473

"I'm sure Patricia and Jesse will be delighted you could be here today to celebrate with them," she said.

"Indeed they will," Eldrin assured her, and he followed the others making their way outside to the patio. A string quartet was playing a spritely tune, and the first guests to arrive had already begun sampling the champagne. While Eldrin intended to greet both the bride and groom, it would be in his own time. Taking care to remain out of the newlyweds' line of sight, he reconnoitered the patio and positioned himself behind the bougainvillea-covered trellis which framed the gate to the yard.

Content to bide his time, he waited patiently for the patio to become sufficiently crowded to make his actions impossible to observe. He had come armed with a knife rather than a pistol. Music and laughter would cover the initial panic when Tory and Jesse fell dead, and the resulting confusion would mask his departure. In his view, it was a perfect plan and he could not wait to put it into action.

Lalo and Carmen had been among the close friends who had attended the private wedding ceremony, but it was not until her husband drew her aside that Carmen realized how transparent her hostility was. Shocked and embarrassed, she looked away as he asked her point-blank if she still preferred Jesse to him, but the response that sprang to her lips was a sincere one.

"No, of course not," Carmen insisted. "You are the man I love and you're the best of husbands."

"Then it is about time you started acting like a contented wife," Lalo demanded in a hoarse whisper. "I don't want to lose Jesse as a friend, and that means you'll have to be much nicer to both him and his wife. Now after they dance the first dance, I'll invite Tory to dance, and you'll dance with Jesse."

"Patricia," Carmen reminded him. "We're supposed to call her Patricia." Why such a ruse should be necessary, Carmen did not understand, but she was willing to go along with it. Finding it difficult to meet her husband's gaze, she scanned the patio hoping to see some friendlier faces. She was greeted with smiles and waves that cheered her, but for one brief instant, she caught a glimpse of a stranger. He ducked out of sight before she had gotten a close look at him, but what she had seen alarmed her. She grabbed hold of her husband's arm.

"Come with me. Let's just stroll across the patio, but when we reach the trellis, look at the man standing in its shadow. Perhaps you'll recognize him, but I don't."

"First you must promise me that you will be civil to Jesse and Patricia."

"I will do better than that. I will be wonderfully gracious. Now come with me," Carmen urged and, again tugging on Lalo's arm, she crossed the patio.

Lalo walked right on by the bourgainvillea-laden trellis and then turned suddenly to get a good look at the man Carmen wished him to see. Their eyes met, the stranger bowed slightly, and Lalo continued walking with his wife. "No, I don't know him," he confided, "but I didn't like his looks." Keeping Carmen by his side, he circled behind Jesse and Tory and whispered the disturbing news to his friend.

Unwilling to take any chances, Jesse reached out to catch Carmen's hand. "Please stay with my bride for a moment." Before either woman could object, he and Lalo walked away and, keeping the crowd of well-wishers between them and the shy stranger, they approached him from the rear. Neither man was armed, and when Jesse recognized Eldrin Stafford, he knew that had been a serious oversight.

"Why, Mr. Stafford, what a pleasant surprise," he greeted him. Certain they would have the worst of confrontations, he opened the gate and backed out into the yard.

Enraged that his plot had been foiled, Eldrin followed Jesse out of the patio, and, screaming obscenities, drew his knife. He lunged for his enemy, but Jesse had successfully defended himself against equally crazed men in prison and possessed both the agility and the skill to avoid his blow. Unharmed by Eldrin's wild, stabbing swing, he grabbed the man's wrist and began to twist the knife from his hand.

Lalo slammed the gate behind him, and the gaiety of the reception continued undisturbed with the guests unaware of the vicious fight. Eldrin was still shrieking filthy names, but rather than react with an outburst of anger and risk growing careless, Jesse kept his head. He was the taller and stronger of the two, but the wildness of Eldrin's fury drove him well beyond his usual limits. He was like a demon, his soul possessed with hatred for the man who had wed his son's killer. With a violent lust for blood he broke free of Jesse's grasp. He threw himself at the younger man, but when Jesse leapt aside to avoid being stabbed, Eldrin lost his balance on the sandy soil, slipped, and with a startled scream, fell on his own knife.

While Jesse stared in awe-struck silence, Lalo came forward. Unwilling to risk being slashed if the man was only feigning an injury, he used the toe of his boot to roll Eldrin over on his back. His eyes were still open, but held no spark of life. "He's dead, but I saw the whole thing and it was clearly an accident. The sheriff's here. Shall we tell him about this now or wait until later?"

While Jesse was certain Tory would be relieved to learn Eldrin was dead, he did not want to share such shocking news with their guests. "I'll tell him everything later, but for now, let's just get the body out of sight. Ask the sheriff to stay when the others leave, but don't tell him why."

When they reached the barn, Jesse explained who Eldrin was, covered him with a blanket, and posted one of the hands to watch the body. He and Lalo then hurried back to the house. They stopped by Jesse's room to clean up, but returned to the reception after an absence too brief to cause comment except from their wives.

"Where have you been?" Tory asked.

"Just tying up a loose thread," Jesse explained, and rather then elaborate, he took her hand and led her out into the center of the patio to begin the dancing. Seeing the bridal pair, the musicians began a waltz. They had never had an opportunity to dance together, but Tory was as graceful a partner as Jesse had expected her to be. He was enormously proud of her, but did not want to tire her and led her away from the patio at the completion of that dance. Thinking the study the perfect place for a quiet talk, he took her there.

After an enthusiastic exchange of passionate kisses, he leaned back against his desk still keeping her in his arms.

"I've just learned that Eldrin Stafford is dead," he informed her.

"Dead? Are you sure?"

"Positive. Paul was his only son, wasn't he?"

Tory nodded as she attempted to grasp the enormity of Jesse's news. "He has—*had* two daughters, but they're timid souls who take after their mother rather than their father as Paul did."

Jesse gave her another lingering kiss. "Then it's over," he promised. "The marshals will still conduct an investigation, and with the testimony Luke gives, the Staffords' guilt in your father's death and Marshal Kane's will be established. I'm certain you'll soon win a pardon, but no one need ever know that Tory Crandell and Mrs. Jesse Lambert are one and the same. You're safe, sweetheart, you're finally safe."

With the terrifying menace of Eldrin Stafford's insatiable lust for revenge now at an end, Tory's eyes filled with a radiant light. She wrapped her arms around Jesse's neck and hugged him tight. "I won't ever get in another bit of trouble, Jesse. I promise I won't."

Jesse's chuckle was rich and deep. "I won't, either, sweetheart. Let's make a pact. We'll be El Paso's most upstanding citizens."

Tory kissed him soundly. "Agreed."

"We ought to get back to the party," Jesse urged reluctantly, "but first, do you have Araña's braid with you?"

Tory shrank back slightly. "Yes, but it's brought me such good luck, please don't ask me to throw it away."

Jesse put his hands around her waist and lifted her clear off her feet. "That's the last thing I'd ask. I want you to give me half of it. I don't want to run out of good luck, either."

He put her down gently, and Tory took his hand as they started for the door. "I'll divide it in half later," she said. "That way you'll be sure of having plenty of good luck tonight."

Jesse caught her eye and winked. He was already assured of having excellent luck that night and so was she.

Note To Readers

While Jesse and Tory's love story is a work of fiction, the Apache Indian uprising taking place in the Arizona Territory in 1881 is factual. The medicine man, Noch-ay-del-klinne, The Dreamer, did indeed inspire his followers to dance in an attempt to raise several chiefs from the dead in hopes they would restore the once proud Apache people to greatness. The treatment the Apaches had received from the United States Government and their representatives on their reservations was despicable. Their grievances were justified even if their methods of redressing them were not.

The character of Araña was inspired by the exploits of Geronimo, a Chiricahua chief, who often fled into the mountains of northern Mexico after attacking white settlements. The Indian wars continued in Arizona until Geronimo's surrender in 1886.

The inspiration for this book began with the first line, and once Jesse had pinned the slain marshal's badge to his own vest, his quest for justice became a much more ambitious pursuit than he ever could have imagined. I hope that you enjoyed reading his and Tory's romantic adventures and that you will send me your comments. Please write to me in care of Zebra Books, 475 Park Avenue South, New York, NY 10016, and enclose a legal-size SASE for a bookmark.

CATCH A RISING STAR!

ROBIN ST. THOMAS

FORTUNE'S SISTERS   (2616, $3.95)
It was Pia's destiny to be a Hollywood star. She had complete
self-confidence, breathtaking beauty, and the help of her domi-
neering mother. But her younger sister Jeanne began to steal the
spotlight meant for Pia, diverting attention away from the ruth-
lessly ambitious star. When her mother Mathilde started to return
the advances of dashing director Wes Guest, Pia's jealousy sur-
faced. Her passion for Guest and desire to be the brightest star in
Hollywood pitted Pia against her own family — sister against sister, mother against daughter. Pia was determined to be the only
survivor in the arenas of love and fame. But neither Mathilde nor
Jeanne would surrender without a fight. . . .

LOVER'S MASQUERADE   (2886, $4.50)
New Orleans. A city of secrets, shrouded in mystery and magic.
A city where dreams become obsessions and memories once again
become reality. A city where even one trip, like a stop on Claudia
Gage's book promotion tour, can lead to a perilous fall. For New
Orleans is also the home of Armand Dantine, who knows the secrets that Claudia would conceal and the past she cannot remember. And he will stop at nothing to make her love him, and will
not let her go again . . .

SENSATION   (3228, $4.95)
They'd dreamed of stardom, and their dreams came true. Now
they had fame and the power that comes with it. In Hollywood,
in New York, and around the world, the names of Aurora Styles,
Rachel Allenby, and Pia Decameron commanded immediate attention — and lust and envy as well. They were stars, idols on ped-
estals. And there was always someone waiting in the wings to
bring them crashing down . . .

*Available wherever paperbacks are sold, or order direct from the
Publisher. Send cover price plus 50¢ per copy for mailing and
handling to Zebra Books, Dept. 3593, 475 Park Avenue South,
New York, N.Y. 10016. Residents of New York and Tennessee
must include sales tax. DO NOT SEND CASH. For a free Zebra/
Pinnacle catalog please write to the above address.*